This is a well written and very fast-paced book. It is not overly long and there is quite a bit of action crammed into the pages. Shepard builds great tension throughout the book through both the plot and the bourgeoning relationship between Charlie and Gail. The two story lines complement one another well and keep you enthralled in compelling action and evocative romance.

If you are looking for a fast read that will keep you on the edge of your seat, then look no further. The adrenaline rush of jumping into the chaos of a prison riot on the moon, where every decision can mean the difference between life and death for everyone in the facility, is intense. Then throw in a fiery attraction between the two strong women that need to save the desperate situation...the result is heart-pounding excitement throughout!

- The Lesbian Review

Bird on a Wire

This is the second novel by Tagan Shepard. I said for her successful debut that it is a sign that many more fine books are yet to come. I am glad that I was right. *Bird on a Wire* is even better than *Visiting Hours*. With all main elements done well, this makes for another very good book by this author. Keep them coming!

- Pin's Review, *goodreads*

This is a book I had no idea how it would end. It looked like one way, then another. Shepard kept me turning the pages since I had no idea. I will say I was very happy with the ending. It was what I was hoping for. This is Shepard's second book and both have been good. She has become an author that I will automatically read now. If you are looking for a good drama book with a little romance, give this a read.

Visiting Hours

...*Visiting Hours* is an emotional tale filled with denial, pain, struggle, commitment, and finally, more than one kind of deep, abiding love.

And Then There Was Her

About the Author

Tagan Shepard is the author of four novels of lesbian fiction, including the 2019 Goldie winner *Bird on a Wire*. When not writing about extraordinary women loving other extraordinary women she can be found playing video games, reading, or sitting in DC Metro traffic.

She lives in Virginia with her wife and two cats.

Other Bella Books by Tagan Shepard

Across the Dark Horizon
Bird on a Wire
Visiting Hours

And Then There Was Her

Tagan Shepard

BELLA
BOOKS
2020

Bella Books, Inc.
P.O. Box 10543
Tallahassee, FL 32302

First Bella Books Edition 2020

Editor: Cath Walker
Cover Designer: Judith Fellows

ISBN: 978-1-64247-106-9

Acknowledgments

One of the many advantages of being a writer is getting to put pen to paper and make your wildest fantasies come to life. I dreamt up Minerva Hills as a winery I wanted to create and run. Short of winning the lottery, the dream seems unlikely to come true in the real world. That's where Jessica and Linda Hill come in. I am amazed and awed every time they accept my manuscripts and my gratitude is boundless.

I used beta readers for the first time on this novel and I learned so much from the process. Thank you to Celeste, Cade, Andy, and Kate for your advice, your support, and your time.

To Cath for reminding me of all the lessons I have forgotten in the years since my last English class. You make my work better with every swipe of your red pen.

To the wonderful staff at Early Mountain Vineyards for letting me pick your brains about the process of making wine while pouring some of the best bottles Virginia has to offer. I received further inspiration (and wine) from Jefferson Vineyards and Pippin Hill Farm & Vineyards. I cannot recommend a trip to Virginia Wine Country highly enough.

Finally, to the woman who makes it all worth it. The only one I ever want to share a bottle and a life with—Cris. Thank you for being my cover girl.

Dedication

To Chrissy and Callie
The most enduring love is
the most unexpected.

CHAPTER ONE

"These are beautiful," Jada said, her long fingers tracing the curve of one of the vases on display. "Some of your best work yet."

Madison smiled, relief working its way into her aching muscles. Jada Welch had enough years under her belt as a gallery owner and art dealer to know good work when she saw it, and she was not the type to sugarcoat a review. Still, Madison wasn't entirely sure how she felt about the pieces she was showing her friend. She wasn't so modest as to ignore that they were good, but she also knew she had the potential to do better. Even when she was throwing these pots, she wondered what her next project would be. It wasn't exactly the mindset one had when making a masterpiece.

Jada moved to another table, this one holding an amphora-shaped vessel with diagonal slashes of color, all different shades of blue. It was larger than the vases she'd remarked on, standing on its own pedestal like it would be if it made its way into the Welch Gallery. Jada leaned over Madison's favorite piece, her razor-sharp eyes examining the handle seam. She gave a quiet grunt and moved on.

"Not bad." Jada stood and turned her focus back to Madison. "Not bad at all. I think I can find a place for them in the gallery. I have a buyer in mind, but he's sticky. He prefers known artists, but he appreciates good work. I think I can work him around the corner."

"Thanks Jada," Madison said, managing one of the smiles that was all-too elusive for her these days.

"Well, I expect a return on the investment. Keep doing work like this and I might be able to set up a solo show for you."

Madison skipped over to Jada, hugging her arm and placing a kiss on her cheek. "You're so good to me. I don't deserve you."

"No one does, dear." Jada pulled her into a one-armed hug, dropping a motherly kiss on the temple before taking a step back. "No offense, but this is Gucci and you're covered in clay."

It was an exaggeration, of course. She hadn't even worked that long this afternoon before Jada arrived. Madison had spent the morning working at the coffee shop, so she hadn't had time to get really dirty. She looked down at her clothes, a worn-out pair of jeans two sizes too big held up with a wide canvas belt, and a short-sleeve pale-yellow T-shirt that hung off one shoulder. They had a liberal streak of dried clay, sure, but nothing like she would have if she'd been working all day. Her feet were shoeless. She felt the pedal on her wheel better in bare feet and it saved her shoe budget. Gray blobs turning white at the edges dotted her feet like chickenpox.

"It's not that bad."

Jada dusted her arm with an exaggerated motion before nodding at the coffeepot in the corner. "Does that thing work or is it full of glaze?"

"Are you kidding?" Madison scooted off to fire the coffeemaker into life. "This machine is sacred. Have a seat and I'll bring you a cup."

Rather than sitting down, Jada wandered around the studio while Madison busied herself making coffee. As the machine started bubbling and burping, Madison looked around her studio. It was a small space—a single room with a high ceiling crisscrossed with exposed pipes and vents—and she knew it as well as she knew her own skin. The floors were concrete that had been stained, sealed, and stained again. The white cinderblock walls were splattered with paint in sharp lines and voids compliments of the previous tenant who fancied himself the new Jackson Pollock until his Pollockesque abuse of alcohol left him without rent money. Slim windows high on the wall were so encrusted with grime they let in very little light. The building was warehouse-chic without the chic.

Seconds before the coffeemaker beeped its readiness, Madison yanked the pot out and poured two cups. Both women took it black, lucky since there was no refrigerator in the studio and barely enough room for a single sugar packet. Luckily, Madison had inherited a relatively clean couch from the evicted splatter painter. She handed Jada her cup before flopping down on one of the plush, salmon-colored cushions.

At first glance, Madison and Jada could not be more different. Where Jada was African-American with skin so deeply brown it could appear almost purple in certain light, Madison was almost luminescent white due to her limited access to sunlight. Jada was on the shorter end of the spectrum and carried slightly more weight than she would like. Both Madison's height and weight were squarely centered on average. Madison's auburn hair would fall below her shoulders if she took the time to straighten it, which she forced herself to do as often as she remembered, whereas Jada's was cut a quarter inch off her perfectly shaped head.

The differences weren't just physical. Their personalities were as different as they could be. Jada enjoyed referring to herself as a "married cougar," embracing her middle age in a way that Madison had never seen—by combining her world experience with perennial sexiness. Madison had turned twenty-eight less than a month ago and lived in mortal dread of her thirtieth birthday when she imagined she would be sent to some sort of retirement home. Jada was ferociously loyal to the sort of clothing labels that cost as much as the average mortgage while Madison shopped exclusively at thrift stores. Jada once wore a pair of four-inch heels on a camping trip. Madison wore shoes as little as possible, and only snowstorms could force her out of her strappy sandals.

Despite all those differences, they had one thing in common, and it was the only thing that mattered: they both lived and breathed art. In the final year of her ceramics degree, Madison had met Jada, visiting the college pottery studio late one night looking for a professor. Everyone else had gone home hours before, but Madison was in her own world in front of her wheel. Jada had watched her throw long enough to determine that she had talent, then introduced herself. Madison had liked her immediately because she was as excited to talk about ceramics as Madison and because she was generous with the contents of the snakeskin-wrapped flask she carried in her two-thousand-dollar purse.

They'd been friends ever since. Jada stood next to Madison's family at her graduation from Rocky Mountain College of Art and Design. She stood alone when Madison graduated with her master's from University of Colorado at Boulder, long after Madison's parents had lost interest in their children. With a level head she had helped Madison move back to Denver and helped her through her grief and shared in her happiness. She was like a second mother and best friend wrapped into one. In fact, Jada had found this studio, which, while small, had a reasonable rent for space in downtown Denver.

Madison pulled her knees up to her chest and cradled the steaming mug between her hands. She breathed in the aroma of good beans, roasted to perfection. Coffee was something of an obsession for Madison. The only reason she could stomach the need for a day job, apart from a pathological fear of facing the same fate as the former tenant, was that she loved good coffee nearly as much as she loved a well-made piece of art.

Jada sniffed her mug dubiously. "This isn't from that god-awful Seattle chain, is it?"

Madison laughed and leaned back into the couch. "No, it's not from Starbucks."

"Just checking."

Jada took a long sip, closing her eyes and groaning at the first taste. Jada was also a java devotee and her taste in coffee was nearly as good as her taste in art. The espresso she served in her gallery was imported from a specialty shop in Milan. This wasn't quite the same standard, but it was a locally roasted coffee, better than the usual swill.

"I'll try not to be offended by the insinuation."

"You are a starving artist, Maddie."

"I'm dating a chef. I may not be able to pay my rent or buy clothes, but the one thing I'm not is starving."

"How is Kacey? I haven't seen as much of her since she got back from her brush with fame."

"She's good," Madison said with a smile. Talking about Kacey always made her smile. Thinking about Kacey made her smile. "Really good."

Madison's girlfriend, Kacey, had been a sous chef at an exclusive French restaurant in the heart of Denver until her "brush with fame" as Jada put it. Madison's encouragement had reached nagging levels and Kacey finally took her advice to apply for *Top Chef.* Kacey pretended to be shocked when she had been accepted for the show, but Madison knew her confidence better than that. Even though being on television had separated them for the first significant time in their three years together, it turned out to be a great decision.

Kacey was a favorite on the show, her runway-model good looks and natural charisma made her a hit with the audience. Her skills made her popular with the judges. Her competitiveness, amplified by the nature of the show, made her less popular with the other contestants. She didn't do anything to sabotage them, but she wasn't the helpful, supportive person Madison was used to seeing. In the end, she didn't win. She didn't even make it halfway through thanks to a poorly executed group challenge where the fault lay equally between Kacey and another chef, Carter. Kacey ended up taking the fall, but she got her name out there in a big way and earned herself a legion of fans. Her career trajectory had never looked better than right now.

"Is she going back to the Palace Arms?"

"No, she had to give up her position for the show and she doesn't want to go backward."

"Can she move forward here in Denver?"

"Maybe, but if not, I'll go anywhere she wants."

"Anywhere?" Jada pronounced the word as though there was danger in it. "Is that a good idea? Following her anywhere?"

"Of course. I love her. I want to be wherever she is."

Madison thought Jada would argue the point. The crease between her brows seemed to say she wanted to, but she changed the subject instead.

"So that's what these…what did you call them? Audition meals? That's what they're all about."

"Yeah." Madison finished her coffee and wanted another, but she was too tired. Work this morning had been busy and it was delivery day. Then she had come here and moved around some of her larger pieces to show Jada. With all that lifting, her shoulders and back ached, so she wasn't ready to give up her comfortable cushion yet. "I don't know if that's what it's called, but it sounds like an audition to me. She has these restaurant owners coming in and she cooks them a meal to convince them to hire her as their executive chef. Like a sample menu, I guess."

"How are they going?"

"Pretty good, I think. She had another one today. She's had five or six this week with owners from around the country, as well as John Snow."

"From *Game of Thrones*?"

"From *Food and Wine* magazine."

"He's the one who judged the challenge she won."

"Yeah." Madison decided she wanted that cup of coffee after all, and when she got up, Jada held out her empty cup. "He was very impressed with her. He's been lining up the auditions."

"Is that the way a chef gets a restaurant?" With a warm grin Jada took her refilled cup and continued, "I don't know anything about restaurants apart from how to flirt with the host for a good table and which ones have the best martinis."

"It isn't the only way, but it's really the only one we can swing at the moment. Kacey would love to open her own place but being owner and executive chef would be such a huge commitment of time and money, we just aren't there yet."

"You're happy to have her back."

It wasn't a question. The knowing smile that came with the statement made Madison blush just a shade.

"She was gone a long time."

Jada sighed and sat back. If anyone knew how hard those days apart were, it was Jada. She'd dried enough of Madison's lonely tears.

"It was good for her."

"Definitely. I've never seen her so happy and so confident."

"I don't recall confidence ever being a problem for Kacey."

"Maybe not, but she's like a new person now. I love seeing that sparkle in her eye."

"I'm glad." Jada put her cup down on the battered coffee table, then turned thoughtfully back to her friend. "How about you? How are you doing?"

Her vision blurred instantly, and Madison stared hard into the cooling dregs of her coffee, trying to will back the tears. It wasn't that she didn't want to cry in front of Jada—she had so many times over the years and she was never judged. In fact, there was no one in her life, not even Kacey, that she would rather talk to about what was going on in her heart. But she was tired of crying. Tired of the pain and the sadness. Tired of the sleepless nights and the emptiness in her chest. She had suffered so much with Kacey gone, now that she was back, Madison just wanted it to go away. She wanted to be happy again. She would be happy again if it was the last thing she did. Grabbing the chain around her neck, she toyed with the necklace until the ring of polished onyx fell out from her shirt collar.

"I'm okay," Madison replied, and when the gumminess in her throat and the tears in her eyes threatened to show the depth of the lie, she added, "I'm finding a way to deal."

CHAPTER TWO

Madison accidentally dropped her keys at the top of the stairs. She cursed quietly and bent at the waist to grab them. Days like this, when she spent the morning at her day job and her afternoon in her studio, were always bag days. Today she carried five—one with her neatly folded work uniform, another held her studio clothes, now covered in more drying clay than when Jada had visited, her purse, a plastic bag of groceries and finally her backpack containing a sketchbook, art magazines, and supply catalogs. Fortunately she hadn't taught any pottery classes that morning or she'd have a sixth bag to contend with.

Things would be much easier if she didn't have so many bags of clothes. She would love to come home in her studio clothes and clean up here, but Kacey didn't like to wait while she washed up for them to spend time together. Madison understood. Even after three years, they had a hard time keeping their hands off one another long enough to even ask about each other's day. Of course, it hadn't been quite so hot since Kacey got back, but then she was frantic about finding a job.

They'd saved some cash before she left, and she did get a paycheck from *Top Chef*, but it wasn't much of one. Kacey needed to get back to work, not just because she thrived in the fast-paced, constant pressure of the kitchen, but also because they had bills not covered by Madison working five mornings a week as a barista. Unfortunately, their shoebox apartment was in a high-rent hipster neighborhood.

Having collected her keys, and accompanied by the deep tremor of bass from the nightclub across the street, Madison started toward her door, the last one in the long hall of the fourth floor. They had practically lived in that club a year ago. Kacey was still at Palace Arms then, so Madison had only worked three days a week. Now Madison came home tired a lot more and she didn't have the stomach for the club. She would much rather sit on the couch with Kacey and the remote control. Hopefully that's exactly what she would be doing in a few minutes.

Madison dropped the keys again trying to fit the right one into the lock. This time she swore a little louder and dropped the two bags of clothes unceremoniously to the floor rather than wrestle with them. An apple fell out of the grocery bag and tried to escape off down the hall. She grabbed it and shoved it into her mouth rather than back into the untrustworthy bag. When the juice trickled around her teeth and into her mouth, she realized she hadn't eaten since noon and she was ravenous. She took a big bite of the apple and chewed while snatching up her keys. She wondered when Kacey would be home and if she had any money to grab takeout.

Fitting the apple back into her teeth to free up a hand, Madison shoved the key into the lock. She nearly tumbled into the apartment and cursed a third time because she had forgotten to leave lights on. The interior was dark and sticky-warm. She kicked the dropped bags through the door and dragged herself after.

It wasn't until she reached for the light switch that she noticed the room wasn't as dark as she thought. The coffee table was dotted with assorted candles from tea lights to tall pillars, all flickering in the draft from the overhead vents. With a loud click Madison closed the door. She dropped her bags and took a hesitant step into the room, removing the apple from her mouth again.

"Kacey?"

There was no answer to her summons, but her girlfriend did love to make a splash. No doubt she was waiting for the perfect moment to appear with her devilish grin and smoky-smooth voice.

Madison kicked off her sandals and padded barefoot into the living room. Since the room accounted for the entirety of their apartment apart from the postage stamp bedroom and surprisingly spacious bathroom, it was also their dining room. Her eyes were drawn to the tiny, two-seat dining table and she gasped. The table held only two candles, long, slim, bright white tapers placed on either side of a vase of blood-red roses. In front of the roses stood a sweating ice bucket, the neck of an open champagne bottle poking over the rim.

Madison snatched the apple from her mouth. Her stomach growled, but there was a pleasant anticipation flowing through her that had nothing to do with hunger. She and Kacey hadn't talked about marriage, but this setup certainly screamed proposal. Closer to the table, Madison could see the two glasses of champagne bubbling away. She was about to reach for one when an arm wrapped around her from behind.

"Welcome home."

The combination of that seductive, lilting voice and the way her breath brushed against Madison's exposed neck sent a shiver through Madison from the very center of her scalp down to the tips of her toes.

"Hey you."

Kacey dropped a wet kiss on her shoulder with a barely audible chuckle. Madison stepped out of her grasp, the better to let her appreciative eyes paint over her girlfriend. Kacey was a year younger than Madison and at least a half-foot taller. She was a study of enigmas, nearly everything about her personality at odds with her looks. She was a butch in a femme's body. She was in control of every room she entered, confident to the point of cockiness, aided by a supermodel's body, which made her the object of interest for everyone with a pulse. Her height was mostly long, shapely legs with delicate feet. She had small, perky breasts that she loved to show off with plunging necklines and skintight shirts.

Her mouth was full and, as Madison knew so well, luscious to a fault. Her only physical imperfection was a weak chin, but she found a way to hide it with choppy, shoulder-length dark hair.

Her eyes and the way she carried herself were what had drawn Madison in, and Kacey knew all too well the power she could wield with a simple heavily lidded glance. She was using it now, and Madison responded as she always did, by flinging herself into Kacey's arms. She wrapped her arms around Kacey's neck, pulling her into a lingering kiss. It took everything in her not to blurt out her acceptance of the proposal that had yet to come.

Kacey's lopsided grin showed one, glistening incisor. That smile left no doubt how the latter half of their evening would go, but for the moment it seemed she had other plans. She gently unwrapped Madison's arms from around her neck, slipping the half-eaten apple from her grasp as she went.

"Is this your dinner?"

"I forgot to eat."

"Then maybe you shouldn't have any champagne. Don't want you too drunk just yet."

Madison put on her best pout, fluttering her eyelashes at Kacey and tugging at the hem of her low-cut T-shirt. The pout was never effective because Kacey had perfected the art of the pout long before she met Madison. It was one of the sharpest weapons in her kit, and she wasn't vulnerable to her own sword. She laughed and tossed the apple over her shoulder as she walked toward the table.

It was meant as a flippant gesture and it was dramatic, but with annoyance Madison watched the apple splat against the floor, little wet, sticky bits flying in all directions. Kacey only kept one room clean, the kitchen, and so Madison would be doomed to clean up after this dramatic gesture. Still, that was a chore for another day, and her heart was racing with the thought of Kacey on one knee. Nervousness weighed on her chest, twining itself around her happiness. She was sure she'd say yes, wasn't she? She'd been expecting this for a long time, but she thought she'd be happier on the day of the proposal. It was too late to worry about that now though, so she followed Kacey to the table, taking the offered champagne flute.

Madison fought to keep her voice even. She couldn't look Kacey in the eye. "So what's the occasion?"

"Don't you want to take a sip first?" Kacey teased.

"No, I don't want to take a sip first." She felt herself blush, and her smile was so wide it hurt her cheeks. "If you don't tell me what's up, I'm going to explode."

"We'll save that for later," Kacey said, her voice dropping an octave and her hand sliding up Madison's side. She dropped it immediately, though, her nerves obviously getting the better of her. "Right now, say hello to America's newest executive chef."

"What?"

"I got a job."

"Baby, that's fantastic!" Madison threw herself at Kacey again, careful not to spill either glass. She held on tight, probably too tight, but the news was so wonderful and unexpected that her chest was about to rip apart with conflicting emotions. Pride and disappointment fought inside her, and pride won out. "I knew you could do it."

Kacey laughed into her ear. "Of course I could do it."

"I'm so proud of you."

They kissed again, this time Madison cradling Kacey's perfect cheek in her hand. After a long moment, Kacey sat, pulling Madison down into her lap. The champagne and candles lay forgotten as Kacey explained.

"I had a few offers, but this one was by far the best."

"What kind of restaurant is it?"

Kacey had been cooking French cuisine at Palace Arms, but her career had taken her all over the culinary spectrum. She had cooked Italian, Korean, and New American just since they'd been together, and she'd already been out of culinary school a while by then.

"It's whatever I want it to be," she replied with a smugness that showed itself more and more often these days. "A new restaurant on a winery. They're doing this whole destination thing. It's a working winery and they've added a hotel and cottages so people can stay and do the whole experience. Up until now, they've just had a simple hotel restaurant, but now they want to do more. A splash restaurant to bring in more business."

"On a winery? That's cool. So Napa Valley?"

Madison had decided as soon as Kacey got home from filming that she would move anywhere. She would let Kacey find a job somewhere, anywhere, and she would follow. Madison expected them to spend their lives together, she didn't care where those lives were spent. Besides, there was nothing, apart from a few friends, keeping her in Denver anymore.

"No, not Napa. That's old hat, no one looks to Napa anymore."

Madison slid off Kacey's lap and reached for the champagne, refilling their glasses.

"Okay, where then?"

"How do you feel about Oregon?"

"I don't feel anything about Oregon. Is there anything there?"

"There is Minerva Hills Winery, with their award-winning pinot noir and their new restaurant run by a fabulously beautiful and talented executive chef, Kacey Willis."

"Wait, you mean *the* Kacey Willis?" Madison's joke spoiled only slightly when she cracked a small smile. "The one from *Top Chef*?"

"That's the one."

"She's hot."

"You better believe it, baby."

Madison set her glass down and slid back onto Kacey's lap, straddling her legs, pressing their bodies close. Kacey's hands went immediately to her butt, pulling their hips together.

Madison rocked forward, dipping her lips to Kacey's throat and kissing her way toward her neck.

"I haven't told you the best part."

Madison's hand found the hem of Kacey's shirt, pulling it up slowly.

"Better than the fact that my girlfriend has her own restaurant?"

Kacey groaned as Madison sunk her teeth into her ear lobe.

"Better than that. Room and board are covered."

Madison's hand faltered in the act of moving up Kacey's bare side.

"What do you mean?"

"I mean," Kacey said, pulling her head back enough so she could look into Madison's eyes. The glint in them told her this was something special she'd been saving. "In addition to a ridiculously high salary, I also negotiated for us to live in one of the cottages on the vineyard. Rent free."

"Rent free?"

"Rent free."

"So…"

"So no more slinging coffee or teaching at the local arts center for you." Kacey's eyes softened, and for a moment Madison saw the woman behind the bravado. "You can focus on your art fulltime. I made sure of it."

The tears flowed down Madison's cheeks before she could stop them. "Oh, baby… Thank you so much."

"You deserve it."

She didn't really. She'd done little to earn it, but there was nothing in the world that she wanted more and she would work to earn it now that she had it. Her excitement surprised her. Even with the prospect of being a fulltime artist, she wanted to be out of Denver. She hadn't realized how much until this moment when it was a reality. She needed to leave. There were too many ghosts here.

"I love you."

Kacey couldn't respond because Madison threw herself so hard into their next kiss that the chair toppled over with both of them in it. They giggled at the ridiculousness of it, but that didn't stop them for long. All the candles had burned themselves out before they stumbled off to bed.

CHAPTER THREE

"This whole thing has been a goddamn nightmare!"

Madison tried not to get annoyed with her girlfriend, but the headache arcing its way across her temples made it difficult. She gritted her teeth and looked out the window of their rented SUV, watching the ethereal green landscape whip by. Except the scenery wasn't exactly whipping by, hence Kacey's annoyance. They were currently creeping along in the wake of a massive piece of farming equipment that spanned the width of both lanes. Oncoming traffic was all but running into the ditch to avoid the enormous tires and deadly looking appendages. Unfortunately, the machine appeared to have a top speed of about ten miles an hour. They'd been stuck behind it, acquiring a growing tail of traffic behind them, for what seemed like hours.

It wasn't just their speed making Kacey scream. She'd been yelling since breakfast, a meal they'd had to grab on the run because the alarm they'd set on Kacey's phone hadn't gone off and they nearly missed their flight. When they'd arrived at the Denver airport, they discovered they needn't have assaulted their taste buds with soggy airport croissants, because their flight was delayed three hours. When they finally arrived at the Portland airport, they discovered their rental car had been given away when they didn't arrive at the scheduled time. Kacey wasn't thrilled when Madison pointed out that she had suggested they call. And to top it all off, their baggage was the last onto the carousel.

All in all, Kacey had been in a rage for so long that Madison wanted nothing more than to be as far away from her as possible. They'd been on the road for over an hour already and they had a ways to go.

The saving grace, at least as far as Madison was concerned, was the shocking beauty of the landscape. It was almost enough to whisk her headache away and block out her girlfriend's constant complaining. Everywhere she looked were rolling green fields and perfect lines of grapes. Madison hadn't realized that there were so many vineyards in this area. She hadn't realized there were so many vineyards in the whole state. They seemed to cover every inch of the landscape. The symmetry of the vines, their perfect spacing and their lushness were hypnotic.

Madison had never been to a winery before and she had no idea what to expect. Wine had never really been her thing. She drank it, of course, but she didn't know good wine from bad. Liquor had always been more up her alley, and even then she went for what she could afford rather than what tasted good. After the first drink, it didn't really matter, and there had always been many more after the first one. At least that was how she used to live her life. If this is what they looked like from afar, Madison knew living on a winery would be like a dream.

"Thank the fucking Lord."

Kacey's shout cut through the pleasant lull into which Madison had fallen. The tractor was pulling off onto a side road, and Kacey swerved around the tail end of it, gunning the engine and causing the SUV to hitch and nearly stall out.

"Kacey, calm down!"

Madison grabbed the handle over the door, her heart pounding. Kacey did not slow down, she took a wide curve far too fast, nearly fading off into the ditch before catching the angle and blasting out onto a straightaway.

"Seriously, please slow down." Still she ignored Madison's pleas. "You're scaring me!"

Perhaps it was the palpable fear in her voice that caught Kacey's attention. She backed off the gas, but only barely. They still rocketed down the scenic mountain road much faster than advisable. Kacey didn't apologize or even look over, but she reached out and put a hand on Madison's knee. The gesture felt more possessive than apologetic.

The robotic, British-accented voice of their GPS announced that their turn was in half a mile. Kacey slowed the car in anticipation. She looked around at the mountains and hills. Far from the awe that Madison felt when looking at them, Kacey sneered in disgust at the green hills and wide, blue sky.

Madison was a city girl, growing up in Denver and only leaving it for graduate school and the occasional weekend in Vegas. Kacey had spent most of her youth in Oakland with her mother, moving to San Diego with her father at the age of fifteen. She constantly criticized Colorado as the backwoods, even when they were in Denver, so this was going to be a massive change for her. When Madison started looking into their new home with some basic Internet research, she was surprised that Kacey had taken the job. Although, when Madison saw the contract and the salary, things came into slightly better focus.

A massive stone-and-brick sign appeared on the left side of the road, announcing the entrance to Minerva Hills Winery. The turnoff was only paved for a few feet, then changed to gravel. When she didn't adjust her speed accordingly, Kacey bounced the car and spun the tires, kicking up stones behind them.

"Damn country bullshit," she barked, finally slowing and scanning the lot. "How are we supposed to get in?"

The gravel road let off immediately into a massive parking lot, full of cars of every make and model. There had to be at least a hundred vehicles lined up here even though the vineyard was nowhere in sight.

"Head toward the gate."

Madison indicated the tall brick pillars with a wrought-iron spiked fence between. They stretched into the trees on one side, and off to a slope in the land to the other, ending only when the precipitous angle of the ground made the barrier unnecessary. Madison studied the structure as they grew closer. It was grand in a breathtaking sense. The brick pillars were capped with creamy beige stone and vessels like the Roman amphorae she adored. They were spaced every five or six feet, gradually increasing in height, with an undulating wave of metal fencing between. Now that they were closer, Madison saw the vineyards beyond and, with an artist's eye, noticed the sloping curve of the fence and the parallel lines of each spike mimicking the rolling hills behind them. The central pillars abandoned the graceful increase in favor of a dramatic explosion of height.

Those pillars were easily twenty feet high and the gate between them was the same fence of wrought iron. Set into the massive gate was a pair of smaller, door-sized gates. Each had a flat metal decoration set in the center, an ancient Greek battle helm with a flat nose piece and oval eye slits inside a flaring, bullet-shaped helmet that, Madison knew from her brief time on the winery's website, was the company's logo.

"How the hell am I supposed to get in?" Kacey barked, throwing the car into park in front of the gates and leaping out. "Who's gonna open the damn gates?"

Madison sighed, unbuckling her seat belt and steeling herself for the inevitable renewed anger. She got out of the car and joined Kacey.

"The gates don't open," Madison said, indicating the two doors in the fence that were the only openings. "The winery doesn't allow cars onto the property."

"What?"

Madison winced at the shrill scream, her headache throbbing. "They don't want car exhaust around the grapes. It's supposed to be this whole clean air thing. The grapes are alive and they don't want to poison the air they breathe."

"How can they possibly run a business like that?"

Madison pointed up the packed dirt path on the other side of the gates. A horse-drawn carriage with polished painted wooden seats and high sides crested the hill and rattled toward them.

"Horses."

"You've got to be fucking kidding me."

Madison turned to her, annoyance beginning to seep into her own voice to match Kacey's. "How could you not know that? Didn't you learn anything about this place? We're going to be living here."

Kacey turned on her, eyes full of withering disapproval. "All I needed to know was that I had free rein with my restaurant, a huge salary, and a free place for you to live and make your pottery."

The rebuke was well-aimed, if ungraciously expressed, and Madison dropped her eyes to the gravel. She looked up when she heard the bell-like chime of the horses' approach. They were beautiful animals, one with a milk-chocolate coat and a bright white slash down its nose and the other pure, unblemished black.

The cart made a wide circle on the other side of the gate, the horses facing back toward the vineyard and coming to a stop after a gentle command from the driver. He jumped down and tied the reins to a hitching post near a small gatehouse, then went to the back of the carriage to help the passengers down.

"I didn't realize it applied to people who live and work here as well as the guests," Madison admitted.

Kacey accepted her admission with less grace than Madison had hoped. "Apparently it applies to everyone."

The carriage driver opened the door in the gates, letting out a flow of happy guests. Madison watched him as he ushered everyone through with a charming smile and an occasional handshake. He was devilishly charming and the female guests, especially the older ones, lingered over their goodbyes. Kacey rolled her eyes and crossed her arms over her chest, but Madison couldn't help but smile as she watched him.

He was younger than them, probably around twenty-five, but he had a jovial, boyish face that made him look like a teenager. He wore a dingy cowboy hat, which, paired with his red-brown skin and short, raven-black hair, made him look like a ranch hand in some cheesy chick flick. It was obvious from the way he applied his charm liberally and indiscriminately that this was an image cultivated purposefully.

When all the departing guests had spread themselves out through the parking lot, he turned to Madison. "You must be our new chef."

"Actually," Kacey said, pushing herself straight and putting on her own thick layer of charm. "That would be me. Kacey Willis."

He shook her proffered hand but turned immediately back to Madison. "So then you're the artist girlfriend?"

"Yeah." She smiled and shrugged, trying not to let Kacey's grumpiness dim the pride she felt in that job title. His hand nearly swallowed hers when she shook it, but was softer than she expected. "Madison Jones."

"CS said you'd be here today. We expected you earlier. Was your flight delayed?"

"We've had every delay there is." Madison laughed. "What's CS?"

"Who's CS is the question," he replied. "She's the owner and winemaker here at Minerva Hills. Sorry, I thought you'd met her."

"I did. Madison didn't get the chance." Kacey growled, forcing herself back into the conversation. "So how do we move in if there's no way to get to our cottage?"

"I'll take you and your things in the carriage. We take all deliveries here at the gate and lug them inside. How do you think I got so strong and manly?"

"Steroids, I expect."

He laughed at Kacey's joke, but Madison cut her an admonishing glance since she suspected it wasn't that much of a joke.

"My name's Javier Escobado. People around here just call me Boots. Pleasure to meet you both and welcome to Minerva Hills."

Kacey did not return his smile as she asked, "Why do they call you Boots?"

With her back turned, Kacey didn't notice the glimmer of mischief in his eye, but Madison did. She hid her smile as he said, "That's pretty obvious, isn't it?"

"No," Kacey snarled.

With that, he disappeared around the back of their car, pulling open the trunk and grabbing a pair of bags in his large hands. Kacey scowled at him, her anger not dissipating.

For Madison's part, she laughed at his odd humor and puckish demeanor. It seemed obvious he was teasing Kacey, and she thought quite well of him for it. Her girlfriend had a habit of bullying people, both in the kitchen and in life, and Madison appreciated anyone who wouldn't let her get away with it. She decided on the spot that she was going to like Boots.

"Hey," he said, ducking back around the side of the SUV, handling his burden as if it weighed nothing. "I tell ya what. When you figure it out I'll give you a nickname too. Anyone ever give you a nickname before, Kacey?"

Kacey yanked a suitcase from the trunk, struggling under its weight. The venom was still present in her voice when she answered, "Not if they intend to live through the conversation."

Boots winked at Madison as he passed. "I'll keep that in mind."

They finished loading the assorted suitcases onto the cart and Boots pointed Kacey in the direction of the gatehouse where someone would call the rental agency to arrange collection of the car. While they waited for Kacey, Boots told her about the pair of vehicles the winery kept at the gate in case the workers needed to go into town.

Boots busied himself with the horses and securing their cargo, so Madison looked around her new home. A sharp incline blocked nearly everything from view, but she did see that grapevines, bright green with new leaves and neatly twisted around wooden trellises, ran all the way up to the gate. There was even a short row running parallel to the fencing. Whoever this CS was, she didn't waste a single inch of space.

Kacey came striding back through the gate, giving the carriage a curled-lipped glare of disapproval. Once she was inside and seated next to Madison, Boots came around and closed the door, latching it on the outside. She'd been right when she noticed the carriages were more than just your standard hayride fare. They sat on polished, cherry-stained seats that could have accommodated twenty people. The sides of the carriage were tall, the smooth top brushing against Madison's shoulder blades, and providing a surprisingly comfortable backrest. Their luggage fit neatly into the open space at their feet, but Madison assumed there must be a more utilitarian cart for deliveries of goods rather than people.

"How the hell am I supposed to get fresh ingredients like this?"

Boots shouted an answer to Kacey's rhetorical question over his shoulder as he drove. "We get deliveries several times a day. Most of our produce comes from local farms and they deliver it right to us. The cottages are supplied with groceries weekly. Just send a list down to the gatehouse and we'll hook you up."

Kacey shrugged, acquiescing without returning his smile. "That's good at least."

They turned off onto a side track on the right. It was narrower than the main road and sloped down, the rising vines blocking the view of the rest of the grounds.

Madison leaned close, speaking low so only Kacey could hear. "Would you relax? We're here now. This is going to be great."

She didn't say anything to agree, but at least she didn't rant and rave, so there was improvement. Instead, Kacey grunted and slipped her hand into Madison's, entwining their fingers as she looked at their new home with an expression somewhere between a scowl and a grin.

CHAPTER FOUR

If someone had asked Madison what her ideal home looked like, she would be hard-pressed to describe anything more perfect than the cottage she stood before now. Cozy and modern blended perfectly. It was full of dramatic touches, from the extreme A-frame angle of the roof to the front wall made entirely of windows stretching from the deck to the highest pitch of the roof. When Boots pulled up to the building and stopped, hopping down to unlatch the carriage's gate and allow them out, Madison couldn't help but wonder if he was just teasing them. Like maybe there were servants quarters around back for them.

"Welcome home, ladies," Boots said, grabbing three of their bags and marching off with them toward the door. "Cottage One is all yours."

Kacey looked over the house and gave an impressed nod before jumping down and following him with the smallest of their suitcases. Madison stayed in her seat, wanting to take in her fill of the place before going in. Something told her the interior would be even more breathtaking.

Coming up the drive, the road had swung around subtly to the front of the cottage, which faced away from the vineyard's main gate. The view was down a rolling hill of grapes, with only one building visible at the bottom of the hill. From the stacks of hay outside and the barn doors visible against the gray stone, she assumed it was the stables. Even that utilitarian structure was beautiful, tall and wide with graceful lines like a Swiss chateau.

Jumping down from the carriage at last, Madison turned her attention back to the house, noticing more gems. To the far left of the wall of windows was an outdoor fireplace, sharing the chimney with the matching fireplace inside. The deck was massive, stained a deep, rich redwood with a waist-high railing and dotted here and there with chaise longues covered in thick cushions.

Madison trailed her fingertips along the railing until it stopped abruptly at pillars holding up the roof. It sloped down to cover the entrance, a wonderfully carved mahogany door that looked like it might have been snatched from some ancient, torch-lit monastery. She grabbed the last suitcase and hurried to the door. Boots offered to take it from her, but she refused.

"In that case, I'll let you two settle in." Kacey came out and joined her on the porch, a lazy smile replacing the scowl she'd worn all day. "CS wants you to join the gang for dinner up at the main house."

Before he could elaborate, Madison piped up, "Of course, Kacey will be there. I'll get us settled in."

"I meant that for both of you actually."

"Of course you'll come," Kacey said, wrapping an arm around Madison's waist but keeping a wary eye on Boots.

Boots grinned and pushed his hat far enough back for a shock of dark hair and a razor sharp tan line to show on his forehead. "CS specifically included you in the invitation."

Madison blushed and looked away. "In that case..."

"Dinner's at five. Nothing fancy, just everyone getting off work. You can call the gatehouse for a ride or walk if you want." Boots turned and indicated the main road. "It isn't far. Just go back to the main road and turn right, away from the gate. You can't miss the main building. It's the winery, hotel, and restaurant so it's kinda big. Right at the top of the hill."

He gave a flippant sort of wave that was also a tip of his hat and rode off, the jangle of harness and cart wheels filling the afternoon air.

"What an ass."

Madison rubbed her girlfriend's arm in what she hoped felt calming rather condescending and said, "I kinda like him."

"That's 'cause he was flirting with you."

"He was not flirting with me. You're just mad 'cause he didn't flirt with you."

Kacey crossed her arms and stuck out her bottom lip in an exaggerated pout. "Why didn't he? I'm super hot."

"You are super hot." Madison stood on tiptoe to kiss her cheek. "But you're taken, so who cares?"

"Come on inside," she replied, taking the suitcase from Madison's hands. "It's fucking unreal."

Unreal was an understatement, even with the qualifier. Madison fell in love with the place before she even closed the door behind her.

"Oh my god. Kacey…"

"I know right? You should see upstairs. The whole thing is our bedroom and this massive loft. The bedroom alone's bigger than our place in Denver."

Madison took slow, searching steps across the honey-blond hardwood, as though the house were a skittish cat she might scare away if she moved too quickly. Her eyes traveled first to the wall of windows, even more impressive on this side. Exposed beams stained the same color as the deck lined the vaulted ceiling. The interior fireplace had a floating shelf of weathered wood as a mantel and stone facing on the chimney extending to the roof.

She slid into the living room, which took up the majority of the first floor. In front of the fireplace was a small dining area with a simple, round table with seating for four. Beyond that was the kitchen with a full, L-shaped counter and a raised snack bar and high barstools that wrapped around kitchen.

The kitchen was spacious, with a white subway-tile floor and a massive window over the sink. The view was dominated by towering boxwoods marking the property line.

"I've cooked in restaurants with smaller kitchens than this," Kacey said, running her hand over the speckled quartz of the countertop. "That's a commercial-grade stove."

Though she had no idea what that meant, Madison knew that smile on her girlfriend's face, and she was thrilled to see it for the first time today. The move had been stressful for them both, but Kacey tended to bottle her frustrations up, letting them boil over into an explosion before sharing them.

She turned to Madison now, scratching at the back of her neck and staring at the floor. "I guess I've been kind of a bitch today. I'm sorry."

When she finally looked up, the gleam in her eye was almost, but not quite, enough to melt Madison completely.

"Thanks for saying that," Madison replied, her voice calm but firm. "Your yelling has made it a really tough morning."

"Yeah. I know."

Kacey's pout was perfectly calculated to draw Madison across the room. She heeded the call, walking over and wrapping her arms around Kacey's neck. "Everything's better when we work together, Kacey."

"I know," she replied, brushing her lips against Madison's. "Forgive me?"

Madison couldn't help but give in. Kacey liked to roar, but she felt bad about her outbursts later. One gentle, feather-light brush of their lips and she answered, "Always."

"Good, 'cause this place is great," Kacey said, bounding back into the kitchen. "I can practice some of my dishes here."

"I'd like that," Madison said, following her as she explored. "We can both play hooky and just hang out together."

Kacey rifled through the nearest drawer of utensils. "I think I could get used to having you here, waiting for me to get home every night."

"I think I'd like that too," Madison said, slipping away and heading for the stairs. "Hope you like clay in your spaghetti."

She touched the glossy surface of the paired wooden columns in the living room before looking up. She felt greedy for wishing it, but she hoped their bed was king-sized.

"Try not to poison me, babe. If I die you can't stay in these sweet digs."

"I'll keep that in mind," Madison replied, thoughts of what lay upstairs distracting her. If this was what the main floor had to offer, how opulent must the master suite be? She looked back at Kacey, now completely engrossed in the copper pots and pans. When she found a ceramic Dutch oven tucked into the back corner of the countertop, she whistled and stroked its handle in a decidedly unwholesome way.

While she'd hoped to explore their new house together, Madison knew there'd be no dragging Kacey away from a well-stocked kitchen. "Have fun with your pans. I'm gonna go start unpacking, okay?"

"I'll be up later to help break in our new king-size bed."

CHAPTER FIVE

The afternoon melted away in a flurry of unpacking. Madison barely saw Kacey, much less a clock as she floated through her new home, collating what they had and what they would need. Flying in rather than driving meant that they were only able to bring a portion of their belongings with them. The remainder was on a moving truck making its way slowly across the western half of the country.

Unfortunately, as they discovered after opening one bag after another, their perceived priorities when packing did not match the reality of their needs now they'd arrived. They had filled an entire suitcase with sheets for the wrong size bed, only to find that linens had been provided. When they left Denver, the city was experiencing one of the warmest springs on record, and they packed the clothes they'd been wearing. On top of a mountain in Oregon the temperatures were much milder and the breezes significantly colder. Dressing for dinner, including a long walk home after sunset, was a challenge. Madison ended up turning a large scarf into a makeshift shawl over her short sundress.

The day got away from them so completely that they only realized it was time to get ready when they should have been on their way. Now they'd be late and their fragile truce was shattered, leaving them sniping at each other all over again.

Kacey was well ahead of Madison as they hustled along the packed dirt lane leading back to the main drive. Her ballet flats weren't made for traipsing through a vineyard, whereas Kacey's khaki slacks and loafers fit the bill perfectly. Madison was just annoyed enough with her to take savage pleasure in the fine layer of reddish dust clinging to her meticulous girlfriend's loafers. She nearly cried out in relief when she saw a carriage coming up from the main gate, Boots, with a friendly grin, sitting behind the reins.

There were three other passengers—a middle-aged couple with orange tans that had nothing to do with the sun and a smiling young man Boots introduced as José, The Gatekeeper.

"Boots likes nicknames," José explained as the cart lurched into motion again. "No one else calls me The Gatekeeper."

Kacey ignored the young man completely, and Madison was in no mood to carry the entire conversation with a trio of strangers. Luck was with her, though, because the couple, Camden and Holly Caster from San Clemente, proved themselves to be conversationalists who preferred an audience to another participant.

The ride up to the main building was only about ten minutes, sufficient time to learn that the Casters were here because Minerva Hills was the pinnacle of American-made wine. They were staying for the weekend to ensure the new accommodations were adequate to their needs. Their daughter was getting married in the fall and wanted a winery wedding. They didn't like Napa.

"They're all too gauche by half and so proud of their little pedestrian wines," Holly said with a sneer that made her look like a growling Yorkshire terrier. "Those dreadful little merlots."

José laughed along with them. Kacey pretended to understand, but Madison knew only too well how little wine she drank. Vodka was more Kacey's style, and not even good vodka. Cheap and usually by the gallon.

The cart pulled to a stop and Boots hopped down, handing the reins to a young woman in a flannel shirt before helping his passengers. Waiting for Kacey to get out of the cart and join her, Madison scanned the horizon. The fading sunset did not give her much more than sharp shadows and a rich orange, evening hue, but it was enough to highlight the sloping hills and distant view of other mountains. She stood at the highest point of the vineyard, and the valley lay at her feet, preparing to sleep.

"My god, it's incredible," Madison said to the footsteps that approached her from behind. "I had no idea it would be so... green."

"I take it you're a city girl."

Madison spun, nearly losing her balance. The voice was low, a timbre so deep and rich it reminded her of a loamy soil and thick oak trees with roots that plunged miles deep into the earth. It was too masculine to be feminine and too feminine to be masculine and it stirred something deep in her soul. The voice certainly did not belong to her girlfriend.

"I'm sorry! I thought you were..."

Her words stuck in her throat and turned to molasses, coating her vocal cords and paralyzing them. The woman standing in front of her was the perfect embodiment of that fascinating voice. She was tall and powerfully built, but with long, graceful limbs wrapped in the sort of muscle acquired through years of hard work. Her shoulders were square, the shape enhanced by her pale blue button-up shirt tucked inside well-worn but clean slim-waisted blue jeans. The denim stretched tightly across her thighs and fell past the heel of her dusty riding boots.

As Madison steadied herself and pulled her flimsy shawl back into place, she finally looked into the woman's face. Her white skin was richly tanned, weathered enough to lend character rather than age. Her cheekbones were high and prominent, with slightly sunken cheeks and a firmly set jaw. She had a straight nose and a small mouth with full lips, the shape incongruent with her unsmiling expression. Her eyes were cold and uninviting, but they were also a luxuriant shade of robin's-egg blue that drew Madison in and held her in place.

"CS," Kacey said, shocking Madison out of her reverie by walking up and slapping the stranger hard on the shoulder in a fraternity brother sort of way. "Good to see you again."

Kacey held out her hand at waist level. CS gave it a long look before wrapping her own, broader hand around it and giving it a shake. She didn't return Kacey's smile, but her eyes did soften to something between quartz and granite.

"How was the move?"

"It was fine. Just happy to get settled." Kacey strutted over to drape her arm around Madison's shoulder. "I see you've met my girl."

It took a monumental effort for Madison not to roll her eyes. Kacey was something of a social chameleon, adapting her personality to the occasion and the company. It was an excellent trait for a chef who had to schmooze with rich clientele but also befriend dishwashers and busboys. For a girlfriend, it was aggravating at best and infuriating at worst. Madison's least favorite performances were the ones Kacey delivered around butch women.

Perhaps it was frustration because her body didn't match her personality, but Kacey adopted a hyper-butch persona around other butches. The worst possible caricature of masculinity. She slapped backs, made lewd jokes, objectified every woman in sight, especially Madison, and made a complete fool of herself. Any moment now she'd stick her thumbs in her belt and spit.

"We haven't been introduced," she said, holding out her hand to Madison. "CS Freeburn, owner and head winemaker here at Minerva Hills."

"Pleasure to meet you."

Madison wasn't sure if those words were strictly accurate. She shook the woman's hand and looked into her eyes again. They were still as cold as ice, and Madison noted the conspicuous absence of "Welcome" from her few words. She was gorgeous, to be sure, with that strong, graceful body, liquid voice and captivating eyes, but she was intimidating as hell and had all the warmth of a Rocky Mountain snowstorm. Madison released her hand quickly and stepped back as soon as she could without appearing rude herself.

"Nice place you've got here," Kacey said with a smirk, purposefully brushing her dangling fingertips across Madison's breast.

When they all started toward the front door Madison extricated herself from Kacey's clutch. "Thank you for having us to dinner. I'm not sure we could find so much as a fork in the house right now."

"We have family dinner every night."

The deadpan response to her attempt at humor confirmed Madison's suspicions that CS didn't care much for her. "I hope we aren't intruding on your family. If it's an imposition…"

"That's not the type of family she means." Kacey gave her new boss a pitying look. Turning back to Madison, she explained in a way that could not have been more condescending if it came with a pat on the top of her head. "Family meal is served to the staff before a restaurant opens."

CS held the front door open for Madison. Except for the barrels, bottles, and wine-themed art, the room could have been the lobby for any upscale hotel in the world. Sconces lined the walls, lighting the room with a warm, candle-like glow. A grand fireplace sat in the center of the room, wrapped in the same stone that faced the chimney in their cottage. It was more a fire pit with a hood than a traditional fireplace, and guests dotted the circular bench surrounding it, the firelight sparkling off their wineglasses.

"It's more than that for us," CS said, circling the fireplace while avoiding both the front desk and the door to the wine shop. "Most of the winery employees live on the property. We serve three staff meals a day."

"Your employees live here?"

CS stopped and turned to Madison, her eyes darkening at the question. "Does that surprise you? You live here."

Madison's throat was as dry as sand. "I'm not an employee."

CS's gaze flicked momentarily to Kacey before settling back on her. "You're family."

Madison couldn't think of a response but fortunately she didn't have to. They continued through the lobby, dotted with guests, each dressed more fashionably than the last. The more she scanned the crowd, the more self-conscious Madison became. Their clothing would put even Jada to shame, and here Madison was in a department store sundress and ten-dollar shoes. She felt like she was attending a gallery opening, but dressed to work in her studio.

"You won't be in charge of family meal," CS said to Kacey. "Your specialty restaurant is separate from the one that serves the hotel and grounds."

Madison noticed how many eyes in the room followed them, lingering on CS. The women, even some clinging to their husbands' arms, watched her like lionesses eying a wounded antelope. The men seemed oblivious to the lustful energy that had filled the room with CS's entrance.

"Good. Family meal is a great tradition, but I need to focus on my menu."

CS pointed out the glass doors of the tasting room, which was packed with a press of bodies and noise. The number of guests was surprising, given that José told them tours ended at five. After barely more than a glance to see the crowd was similar in makeup to the one in the lobby, older and wealthier than Madison was used to, they moved on. Madison heard snippets of conversation between the other two women, but it was about the restaurant and didn't concern her. She knew she was being a bad guest when she should be charming and interesting for Kacey's new coworkers. Madison had recently found herself more comfortable in the quiet, away from crowds and social situations. Especially when booze was involved.

Madison's life had once centered around going out and having a good time. So much of it a blur of loud, thumping music and lukewarm liquor. Casual flings until her last fling had turned into something substantial. That person, the one she had been for so long, didn't feel like her anymore. More like an old school friend with whom you lose touch for years until you run into them at the grocery store and can't quite remember. Madison what's-her-name from homeroom.

She swallowed hard, trying to shake herself out of the spiral into which she was descending. She had to be social tonight. Kacey needed her to be charming and chat with everyone. She took a deep breath and cleared her throat quietly, testing her vocal chords. CS snagged a ring of keys from her pocket, unlocking a frosted-glass door bearing a closed sign. She held it open for Madison, giving her the chance to test her smile. CS did not return it. Maybe it looked as forced as it felt.

"The hotel and cottages are open year round," CS was saying as she led Kacey through the room. "Though we're certainly busiest during the warmer months of the growing season. The hotel restaurant is nothing too fancy, just meant to serve the overnight guests but open to the public. It's open every day, three meals a day. Tasting room, winery tours, and gift shop are closed on Mondays. Kacey's specialty restaurant will be more exclusive."

Family dinner was a boisterous affair, and Madison was thrilled that those around the table showed a genuine interest in making her feel welcome. They were down-to-earth and friendly, just like family. Even with all the inside jokes and teasing banter, Madison felt comfortable from the outset.

When they walked in, they were met with a roar of applause from the gathered crew. Clearly they'd been expected and the staff was eager to meet the new chef. After a subdued introduction from CS, the ranks broke and they all descended on Kacey, the new employee and celebrity. Apparently the restaurant staff had watched every new episode of *Top Chef* in the dining room after dinner service, so when CS announced she'd hired Kacey, she became the big news on the estate. They'd brought the vineyard staff up to date by rewatching the whole season on Sunday nights.

"It should have been Carter who went home instead of you," a young Latinx woman with a prominent undercut in her raven hair said to Kacey. "That was totally unfair."

"Thanks," Kacey replied, beaming. "He's a great chef, though, and I was just happy to have a chance to show my food to the world."

That was her standard answer and she got to give it several times more during the evening. Everyone who met Kacey these days told her the same thing. It wasn't precisely a compliment, but, when it became clear how many fans she had out there, Kacey had embraced the role of victim-of-circumstance. She hoped it would lead to another call when they decided to do an all-star season.

Madison was left to the side and that suited her just fine. She hung back, sipping her glass of water and listening to the praise Kacey was receiving.

"Okay everyone, let's sit down to eat."

CS had a way of talking in clipped, declarative sentences like she was barking rather than speaking. She was clearly the matriarch of this manufactured family. They followed her direction, seating themselves neatly around the table, but not with the urgency Madison expected. They didn't see the directive as an order, despite CS's brusqueness. Few people spoke to CS as she passed through the crowd toward the head of the table, but they didn't avoid her, just gave her space. Madison found it charming, the way they all understood each other.

The meal was served buffet-style, with platters of pasta, salad, vegetables, and chicken lined up on the bar, a stack of plates at one end and rolled silverware at the other. Boots went through first, dragging Madison and Kacey behind him. Everyone else meandered through in their own time, CS taking her plate last after a heavyset man wearing a chef's coat and, incredibly, an eye patch. Boots directed them to sit at one end of the long dining table. He took the seat opposite Madison, the Latinx woman slid in across from Kacey and started quizzing her on *Top Chef*'s intimidating judge, Tom Colicchio.

Boots immediately started eating, his plate piled high with fettuccine Alfredo and grilled chicken. Watching Kacey interact comfortably with most of the table, Madison picked at her food.

"The food's not up to your standard," CS said, dropping into the chair at the head of the table on Madison's other side. "Roger cooks family meal, but he's just a hotel chef, nothing of your caliber."

The words were clearly meant for Kacey, but she looked at Madison as she spoke.

"Oh no. It's very good." Madison said, trying to eat more enthusiastically. "We don't do anything fancy at home."

"I save all my creativity for work," Kacey said with a wink before turning back to explain that yes, Tom really was that roguishly handsome, but he was married and not exactly her type.

"Jolly Roger makes a mean lemon-caper sauce," Boots said, pointing his fork toward the far end of the table where the man with the eye patch was just sitting down.

"Call me that again and I'll get you a matching patch, Boots."

Boots flashed his childlike smile down the table at him before shoving approximately an entire head of lettuce into his mouth.

Kacey leaned closer to CS, asking in a low voice, "He won't be a problem will he?"

"In what way?"

"You know, some guys don't like to be passed over for executive chef. I just want to make sure there won't be any wounded egos to deal with."

"There won't be."

Without further explanation, CS went back to her food, slicing grilled squash into neat chunks and eating with her fork in her left hand in the European style.

"Jolly Roger likes it where he's at," Boots explained between bites. "He didn't want the job of running this new place."

Noticing that Boots indicated the room with a wave of his fork, Madison asked, "Oh, is this it? This is the new restaurant?"

"Yep," he said, diving back into his salad and sending a ranch dressing-coated pea rolling across the white tablecloth. "Thought we'd give the new chef her first look at the place, right Boss?"

"Don't call me Boss," CS barked without looking up.

"Sure thing, Boss."

"Boots," she growled and he held up his hands in submission. She turned her attention back to Kacey, reluctantly explaining,

"Chef Roger will be relieved to have some of the pressure off his shoulders. They serve breakfast, lunch, and dinner for both guests and staff in the main dining room. He'd rather the crowd was thinner at dinner service. Some of our wealthier guests will choose to dine in Kacey's restaurant."

After dinner, the restaurant staff cleared the plates and brought out big dishes of apple crumble and carafes of coffee before heading off to open the main restaurant. CS disappeared to her office shortly after, evaporating without saying goodbye, which was fine by Madison. She had a hard time determining what she thought of the quiet winemaker. They hadn't exchanged another word during dinner, and Madison wasn't sure she'd played the part of charming girlfriend well.

"Can you believe this place?" Kacey asked, beaming from ear to ear, her cheeks rosy pink and a glass of something alcoholic in her hand. "This is my restaurant. Mine."

"It's beautiful. I'm so proud of you, baby."

"Here, have this."

She tried to shove the drink into Madison's hand. A powerful blast of what smelled like rubbing alcohol and licorice wafted up from the glass. The smell alone made her head swim. She pushed the glass away, hoping the odor would go with it.

"No, god, what is that?"

"Sambuca. It's good stuff. Try it."

"No, thanks."

She grabbed a coffee from the bar beside her and used the slightly more pleasant smell of burnt coffee to clear her sinuses.

"Suit yourself," Kacey said, tossing the drink back and banging the empty glass down. She'd had at least two glasses of wine at dinner and Madison was sure she'd had something else from behind the bar. At least CS was gone. Kacey was more confident in her ability to hold her liquor than she had any right to be. "This place is incredible. Did you see the view?"

"I saw the patio, but it was too dark to see anything else."

"The view from the tasting room patio is better," she pouted, looking around the room with the glassy-eyed appreciation of a mildly drunk lover. "She really should swap the two. The restaurant should have a better view."

"Well, it is a winery, you know."

"A winery that's about to have a new Michelin-star restaurant." She leaned over the bar, grabbing the tall, clear bottle of that wretched liquor and splashed another generous serving into her glass. "Whatever. This place is going to be the best restaurant in Oregon by the end of the year."

"Of course it will."

Madison stretched up on her toes, puckering her lips for a kiss, but Kacey was looking around the emptying restaurant.

"This space has so much potential. Who gives a shit about the view? People will be coming here for my food."

Madison dropped back to her heels. "It'll be booked solid in no time."

Kacey's eyes finally made their way to Madison's. They were glassy with booze, but there was an appreciation in them that was unmistakable. She smiled down at Madison, whose heart melted. That smile had a power over Madison like nothing else. It always had. That was the smile that made a city girl move to a vineyard in the mountains of Oregon.

"What would I do without you, Maddie?"

She shrugged, letting Kacey pull their bodies close with an arm around her waist. She leaned her head back, watching Kacey's full lips descend toward her own with agonizing slowness. They brushed together for a heartbeat, making Madison's pulse race and her eyelids flutter closed.

All too soon, Kacey pulled away just far enough to whisper against her cheek, "Let's head back home."

CHAPTER SIX

Madison woke twisted in yards of fabric. She had no idea where she was, but she heard Kacey's gentle, rhythmic snoring nearby. She pushed and spun, swimming across the massive expanse of mattress until her groping hands found flesh. She pulled herself into Kacey, fitting their bodies together and wrapping an arm around Kacey's waist. Her girlfriend's snoring hitched and then resumed.

She dozed for a few minutes, then spent a few more enjoying the feel of Kacey's body against hers. Sleep, however, would not return. There were parts of this house she had not explored and parts she could barely remember for all their frantic unpacking. Her mind refused to rest until she knew her surroundings. She slipped out of bed and padded downstairs on bare feet.

Madison knew there was a second bedroom in the cottage, but she hadn't found it yet. She also hadn't found a suitable location for her studio, so she assumed the two would have to be one and the same. Hopefully it didn't have the same plush carpet of the master bedroom. Carpet did not get along well with either clay or the superheated oven of her kiln.

Before exploring, she grabbed the jar of coffee beans and buzzed a generous handful to medium-fine grounds. While the pot bubbled and hissed, she continued her mission. A door led off the far side of the kitchen, and Madison left the coffeemaker to work its magic. The second bedroom. It was nice enough, but not suitable for a studio. As she feared, lush carpet covered the room, cradling her bare feet.

Another door led to a mudroom, floored in darker, rougher tile. A washer and dryer took up much of the room, with a sink between and a bench near the door leading out to a small, deck enclosed by the rooms on either side.

The moment she peered into the final room, the rest of the house slipped away. Stepping into it was stepping into a dream. Two walls were floor-to-ceiling windows like the front of the house, but this room had a different aspect, nearly full east, and was surrounded by vines coming almost up to the house. The floor in here was also tile, but dotted with potted plants and wicker furniture. It was set up like a sunroom, but Madison knew what it was immediately: her studio.

Despite the windows and the steadily rising sun, the room was the perfect temperature. Not too hot, but not so cool as to need one of the blankets draped across the chairs. The windows must be UV-coated, which would be perfect for pottery drying slowly. The tile floor was ideal for a quick cleanup, and the many shelves in the mudroom behind her would be ideal for storing her completed pots. It might take her a few experiments to determine how much curing they would need before going into the kiln, but that was standard with any new space. It had taken her ages to figure out the timing in her old studio in Denver.

The real sell came when a gust of wind blew a wisp of cloud across the sun. The room around her sparkled. It glowed, went dark for a heartbeat, then glowed again all the brighter for the light's momentary absence. Madison couldn't stifle her gasp.

Light had always been a muse for Madison. Her earliest memory was sitting in her mother's lap, crying over some childhood hurt long since evaporated in time, and opening her puffy eyes to see a beam of sunlight captured in the tears on her eyelashes. She was so dazzled, she blinked and it was gone. A flash of pure, essential beauty that disappeared the moment you spotted it. Like a snowflake melting in her palm before she had a chance to count the tines.

Whenever she closed her eyes, Madison could see that image with perfect clarity. Sun trapped in a tear. Light made solid. It stopped her tears that day and it was the reason she became a ceramicist. She'd tried every medium she could imagine to re-create that sight, but nothing was right. The closest she ever came was the first time she glazed a pot and took it to the window to search for imperfections. The kiln had fired the glaze hard as glass and it shone like a diamond.

It wasn't right. Wasn't perfect. It was, however, beautiful. She fell in love with ceramics and she knew that someday, somehow, she would make that perfect piece to capture light in solid form. That was her dream and she sought it every day. A day away from the wheel was a day without the chance to find perfection.

Arms wrapped around her from behind. Familiar, sinewy arms with long, thin hands that pulled her close. Madison fell back into the embrace, sharing the euphoria of finding her new studio.

"I like this room," Kacey whispered into her ear, the breeze of her words tickling through Madison's hair. "We can have coffee together out here every morning."

Any hope they were on the same mental wavelength broke. "Actually, I was thinking this would be the perfect studio."

"Here?" Kacey's voice had the barest hint of a sour note. "I thought you'd set up in the bedroom behind the kitchen."

"Then we wouldn't have a guest room."

"We wouldn't have guests."

"The tile in here would be much easier to clean. Plus the light…"

Kacey cut her off abruptly. "I just think it would be a shame to waste this room."

Madison stepped out of her arms, turning to look at her. She was tousled and bleary-eyed from sleep, a look Madison usually appreciated—disheveled and sexy—but not after a comment like that.

She tried not to let the hurt show, but she was sure Kacey would detect it in her voice. "I don't think my studio is a waste."

"That's not what I meant."

"That's what you said."

"I just meant that we can't both appreciate it if you have all your stuff in here."

"My stuff?"

"I meant your wheel and kiln, not your pottery. Don't make me the bad guy here, I got us this place rent free."

"I appreciate that, Kacey, I do." Madison took a deep breath, searching for a way to explain how important this was. "I'm going to be spending most of my day in this house working. The only reason I get to do that is because of you and it means the world to me."

She hated herself for her imminent tears. She tried to stop them. It wasn't fair to cry. She took a deep breath and continued.

"I just really love this space. I think it'll be perfect for me and I really, really want it. What can I do? How can I convince you?"

Madison could see the annoyance melt out of Kacey's body. She took a step forward and pulled Madison to her, pressing her tear-streaked face into her chest.

"Of course you can have it, baby. We can have our coffee on the deck." She kissed the top of Madison's head. "I'm sorry."

Madison burrowed her face into Kacey, breathing in the scent of her and reveling in the softness.

"No, I'm sorry. I don't even know why I'm crying."

"We've had a lot going on. It's been stressful."

Madison nodded, wrinkling the cotton of Kacey's shirt. She wrapped her arms around her girlfriend's waist, holding her tight when she felt they might slip apart.

"I could use some coffee."

Kacey tried again to slip out of her grasp, and this time Madison let her, though it cost her a sharp pang in her chest.

* * *

It took a week for her kiln to be delivered. If only Madison could have waited on the porch so she couldn't see what was happening, she wouldn't have been in such a state. Her body practically shook with nerves, but she had to direct the overburdened vineyard employees so she needed to be there. What if they hadn't understood her directions and she ended up with a fifteen hundred-pound kiln in the wrong place? What if they broke it or busted out half the windows sliding it into place? What if it fell on someone and they had to go to the hospital?

She shoved her hands deep into the pockets of her baggy jeans so the crew wouldn't see the way she gripped so hard her fingernails cut little half-moons into both palms.

"Okay everyone," Boots said, the strain as evident in his voice as the laughter. "Let's get this beast into place. Gatekeeper, pivot your side my way."

Madison was about to yell that he was moving it the wrong way, but the group moved too quickly. Before she could even open her mouth, the massive oven was in the exact place she indicated. It was even spaced exactly in the center of the short wall. Far enough from the walls to prevent a fire, close enough to the windows for good ventilation. Boots went about reattaching the control box to the exterior with quick, sure movements. If she didn't know better, she'd assume he'd installed pottery kilns in a thousand buildings.

"That's…that's perfect. Thanks, Boots."

He stood and tossed his screwdriver into the air, watching it flip end-over-end a few times before snatching it and stuffing it into his back pocket.

"Any time. Just…one thing?"

"What?"

"Don't ever make me move that thing again? It's heavier than my dear old *abuela*, and I didn't think that was possible."

Madison laughed in relief and moved out of the way while the others brought in boxes of her tools.

"It fits!" Kacey strutted into the room, not seeing that she stepped carelessly in front of Gatekeeper and the girl with the undercut, working together to bring in a set of clay-stained shelves. "Good work guys."

"I notice you missed helping with the install."

She winked at Boots. "Had to get ready for work."

"Actually, that shelf goes here in the mudroom." Madison directed them next to the washer. "It'll probably get too warm in there to cure the pots."

She scooted around Kacey, who stopped buttoning her new chef's coat long enough to grab Madison's butt as she passed. Kacey wandered into the room, getting in the way and touching everything. Madison didn't miss the wistful scowl she gave to the view from back here, but it was too late to change the setup now. They'd had the same fight twice more in the week they had waited for the moving van from Denver, and they weren't going to have it again.

"The new coat looks good."

Madison ran her hands over her girlfriend's shoulders, squeezing lightly at the tensed muscles. The fabric was crisp and clean, neatly pressed the night before. The logo sewn into the left side was the Greek helmet of Minerva Hills with a simple, lowercase script: "*ambrosia* at Minerva Hills."

It was a good name, one Madison helped her come up with while Kacey was planning both menu and restaurant décor back in Denver. The food of the gods in Greek mythology. Only divine beings were allowed to eat it. Delivered to Mount Olympus by doves, it brought immortality. Kacey had no idea what she was talking about when she first suggested it, thinking of the fruit salad instead. Once Madison explained, she jumped onboard enthusiastically.

The name was great, but Madison hated the font. The name was majestic and ancient. The font was one of those ridiculous hipster types that looked like it came off a typewriter. The whole thing being in lowercase also bothered her, but it wasn't her restaurant and it fit Kacey's aesthetic well enough.

"Your shoulders are tense," Madison said, massaging a little harder. "Are you nervous?"

"No. Just excited."

The way the words squeaked out, like a mouse being stepped on, made the lie evident. Madison pulled her into a hug.

"You're going to be amazing."

"You know it."

Tonight was the soft opening of the restaurant. It was quick, only a week after they arrived, but Kacey had spent the three-month layover before moving working on every aspect of the restaurant. Apart from the name, she'd picked the furniture, art, linens, dishware, and even the cutlery from a massive online catalog. She'd spent an entire weekend agonizing over salad forks.

Once she got all that out of the way, she went to work on the menu. If she was meticulous with her restaurant's décor, she was ten times so with the design of each dish. From what Madison could tell, the contents were secondary to presentation. She would spend hours on the couch with a sketchpad, drawing her dishes down to the slightest detail. Madison spied one sketch that actually labeled the grains of finishing salt, but the arrow pointing to the rectangle at the base of dish just read "protein."

Kacey had spent a month on her menu, then sent it to CS for review. The email she got back listed the local farms and included a strongly written encouragement to utilize some of their choice products. None of those elements were in any of her dishes. After spewing a litany of vitriol about her boss's interference and poor understanding of the culinary world, she decided to tweak her menu. She added a single first-course option using pork belly from a farm in Corvallis.

"You're coming up for dinner, right?"

Kacey strapped her bag of knives across her back as she posed the question, so she didn't see Madison's forced smile.

"Of course. What time?"

"It's a little informal, since it's just the soft opening. Come whenever you're hungry and I'll get you the best seat in the house."

"Every seat's the best," Madison replied, pecking her girlfriend on the lips as way of goodbye. "Because they're all in your restaurant."

"Damn straight. See ya, baby."

On her way out Kacey slid past Boots. He set down the box he'd carried in and checked his watch.

"It's early isn't it? Dinner service doesn't start for hours."

"The cooks start working hours before a restaurant opens," Madison said, picking the box back up and moving it into the corner out of the way. "Chopping vegetables and braising things that take a long time. She uses some French word for it, but I can't…"

"*Mise en place*," Gatekeeper said as he passed. "She's meticulous about it. Everything where it needs to be, then you don't waste any time."

"How do you…Oh. *Top Chef.*"

"I was one of the few who watched it live with the kitchen staff. Love that show."

Boots must have caught Madison's look before she turned away to sort the contents of the box, because he said, "Don't you have some work to do, Gatekeeper?"

"The cart's empty. We're all done."

"Good. Then you can head back to the gate."

"What about the cart?"

"I'll take it back to the stable. Go earn your paycheck."

The sounds of the crew grew more and more distant as Madison shuffled her tools from one side of the box to the other. She didn't really have the energy to unpack. Maybe if she made a pot of coffee and relaxed for a bit, she'd feel up to it.

"Need help unpacking before I go?"

"No, thanks, Boots. I think I'm gonna make some coffee."

"It's the middle of the day."

"So?"

She waved him into the kitchen and he followed, saying, "Coffee's a morning thing."

"Okay, man," she said, pointing to a barstool and giving him her best angry-mom look. "I like you. We could be friends, but I can't have you talking about coffee like that."

"It's just that…"

"Stop!" She pointed at him angrily, but his exaggerated look of fear made her attempt at a straight face break into a grin. "A morning thing? I don't need that sort of negativity in my life."

"Yes, ma'am!"

He gave her a little salute, and she switched on the pot. "You want something else instead? I've got…water. From the tap."

"Coffee's great in the afternoon."

"I knew you'd see it my way."

"You don't like her food, do you?"

It was the first time Madison heard anything like a serious note in his voice, but it wasn't quite enough to earn a confession that easily. She set the mug on the counter in front of him and cradled hers in her hands.

"Of course I like her food. She's incredibly talented."

"Then why do I get the feeling you'd rather not go up there for dinner tonight?"

Madison sighed, her shoulders not just slumping, but dragging down nearly to the countertop with the weight of her worries. "Am I that easy to read?"

He waved a hand dismissively. "She was too stressed and distracted to notice."

"That's good at least."

She sipped her coffee. It was a good roast.

"It's just…" She stared into her cup, hoping the words she was trying to find would materialize. The words didn't appear, only steam. "You know how there's, like, a great taco from a hole-in-the-wall place or just really good spaghetti at a friend's house and you eat it and it's amazing. I mean, no one would write an article in *Food and Wine* about it, but it's just really good. Then there are those restaurants where every mouthful is delicious, but you're exhausted by the end of it."

"You have to think about Kacey's food too much."

"Exactly." She shrugged and turned away to lean against the counter. "Most of the time, I don't want to have to think about my food. I just want to eat it. Even if it's fine dining."

"I know exactly what you mean. Yesterday at family dinner, my fish had parsley foam on it. I mean, I'm not a big parsley guy anyway, but I am definitely not a parsley-foam guy."

Madison laughed. Then she pictured the look on his face when he saw parsley foam, and she laughed even harder. She had to set her mug down and bend over with it. He was laughing with her and it felt good, so good, to laugh. She hadn't laughed like this in a long time. After a moment, she sobered, wiping a tear off her pink cheek and picking up her coffee cup again.

"Please don't tell her we talked like this."

"Of course not."

"I'm so proud of her and she's so talented."

"I understand." He stood up, pushing his untouched mug toward her on the counter. "You can be too exhausted for someone's art and still love it and them at the same time."

"Yeah. Thanks."

She walked him to the door.

"You know, Boots, you're a lot smarter than people give you credit for."

"No I'm not. I'm just intuitive." He gave her a wink and stepped out the front door. "I'm also gorgeous, so if you have any single, straight, female friends who come to visit, send 'em my way."

"I'll keep it in mind," she said as she closed the door and went back to her studio to unpack.

CHAPTER SEVEN

Madison now had her full wardrobe, all tucked neatly away into the left side of the walk-in closet so large it could be rented out as a studio apartment. She wore her favorite dress, a shade of ghost-pale gray that made her skin look darker and her hair brighter red. It also made her legs look longer and her butt pop like a firecracker, which was why she'd bought it in the first place. It still didn't make her feel beautiful in this crowd, not with the scent of Chanel and money so thick in the air she could barely breathe.

A new hostess, young and perky in a starched white shirt and a black skirt short enough to leave very little to the imagination, met her at the door and asked for her invitation.

"She doesn't need one."

CS approached from the crowd, sending the hostess skittering off.

"Hi." Madison held out her hand to shake, but CS was already turning to usher her into the crowded restaurant. She skipped to catch up. "Thanks for that. I just assumed I'd be expected."

CS didn't say anything, just led her to the bar.

"What would you like?"

"Nothing. Thanks. I'm not in the mood for wine tonight."

The moment the words were out of her mouth, Madison cringed. She'd just told the owner of a winery that she wasn't in the mood for wine. Not her smoothest moment, but one CS seemed willing to overlook. She nodded and the bartender deposited a glass of water in front of Madison, who sipped it more for something to fill the silence than anything else. She looked around the room, trying to spot Kacey, but the first seating had begun and she was busy in the kitchen.

When they were here for family meal that first night on the vineyard, the restaurant had only been partially decorated, but now the full bloom of Kacey's vision was on display. The restaurant was set up on multiple levels, each terrace a few steps below the one above. Lining the walls were simple abstract paintings that Madison loved because they evoked emotion rather than told a story. At the far end of the lowest level was a wall of windows looking out onto a large stone patio dotted with tables and covered by a high awning dripping with string lights. Most of the tables afforded a breathtaking view, even if it was second to the view from the tasting room next door.

"You look nice."

Silence had stretched so long between them, Madison had nearly forgotten CS was there. She turned quickly, sloshing a little of her water on the bar.

"Thank you." She took a moment to look at the woman standing next to her stool. She wore neatly pressed khakis and a flowing, thin white shirt, half-buttoned and showing a black tank top beneath. "So do you."

She smelled good too. Not the heavy perfumes of the other diners but a simple, clean scent like fresh cotton dried in the sunshine. Her hair fell in feathery waves softening the lines of her face and shoulders.

"I hate how pretentious all of this is," CS said, indicating the room with a dismissive wave of her wineglass.

Just then, a woman so thin she must pay people to deprive her of food laughed so loudly half the room turned to look.

Her head tilted back ridiculously as she continued the show, wrapping her fingers around Kacey's forearm. It was standard chef schmoozing, but it made Madison's skin crawl to see Kacey smile back at her indulgently, like she enjoyed being treated as the prize pony on show for all to see. She caught Madison's eye and winked through her toothy grin. Madison forced herself to remember that Kacey had worked hard. She deserved a little attention.

"It's a bit over the top, but then restaurant openings always are," Madison said, forcing her gaze away from Kacey.

"I've never been to one."

"No? I thought you'd be invited to all the big events around here. Being so close to Portland and having a thriving winery."

"I'm invited. I just don't go." CS turned away again, scanning the crowd and sipping her wine.

"Oh. I suppose you couldn't skip this one. As the owner?"

"No."

This conversation was going well. Madison got the impression CS would rather just leave. Perhaps she disliked Madison's company. She hadn't exactly had the impression CS liked her, though she couldn't imagine why.

Maybe she didn't like the idea of Madison living on the estate, free of charge without contributing to the business. It was perfectly reasonable to dislike someone taking advantage of your hospitality, but she had written up Kacey's contract. She could have refused the living arrangement. Of course, that might cost her the celebrity chef she wanted. Then again, there wasn't anything Madison could do about it now, especially since the arrangement was essentially her life's dream coming true. She wasn't about to give it up because some stranger was grumpy.

While they both stewed in their resentful silences, an older man with a broad chest and silver hair strutted up to them. He looked vaguely familiar, but Madison couldn't place him. The radioactive orange of his fake tan amplified the artificial white of his prominent teeth. He held his chin so high it was in danger of scraping against the ceiling and his suit fit so well it may have been painted on, which did him no favors as it highlighted the odd arrangement of his extra pounds.

"CS Freeburn," he said, his hand held out palm down as though he was expecting it to be kissed rather than shaken. "This is a masterpiece. A work of art. Absolutely exquisite."

The avalanche of adjectives finally clued Madison in on the mystery man's identity. John Snow of *Food and Wine* magazine. He had gushed over Kacey on *Top Chef*, though she'd never met him in person. He fancied himself a kingmaker, and that was fine by Madison. She was a full-time artist now because of him.

"Hello, John. Glad you could make it."

"I wouldn't miss it for the world. Not for the world." CS did not kiss his hand, but shook it at an awkward angle. "Any small assistance I might give to improve the culinary map of these lovely United States is the very least I might do."

"John Snow," CS said, stepping aside to indicate Madison. "Madison Jones."

Snow stepped forward, crowding into Madison's space alarmingly. He took her proffered hand in both of his. They were cold and soft, and it felt like sticking her hand in a bowl of chilled pudding.

"Ah, Madison, Madison, Madison. All that I've heard of you and to think this is our first meeting. Hello. Welcome. You are most welcome."

"Um…thanks?" Not the most impressive greeting for a man to whom she owed so much, but she was shocked that CS remembered her last name and was left thrown. She would surely make a better impression if only she could survive this part of the evening, fade into the background and eat a quiet dinner.

He ignored both her confusion and her discomfort, moving closer to her still and adjusting the grip on her hand to cradle it between his own, pressed against his chest.

"I cannot tell you how I have thought of you in these months since filming ended. That terrible, bleak day when Kacey received your phone call."

Every muscle in Madison's body stiffened. She fought the urge to shout at him to shut up and go away. Perhaps the only thing that kept her rooted in place was the look on CS's face just over his shoulder. It was somewhere between confusion and annoyance, but, then again, that was the only expression Madison had seen there.

"The pain in her voice. The love. The despair for your pain when she was separated by time and space that felt no less than infinite. It was that moment, when everything was so dark and she felt at the bottom of anguish, that Kacey shined like a supernova."

He sighed and closed his eyes, holding the pose just long enough to enhance the dramatic effect. CS turned on her heel and walked away to the hostess station, abandoning Madison to his mercy. "I determined, the moment I tasted her food and she explained her tears at the judges' table, that I would do everything in my considerable power to support her. To support you."

He stopped abruptly, smiling down at her like a grandfather. She painted a smile on her face and gently extracted her hand from his grip.

"You're too kind."

"It's the least I could do."

He wore his condescension like a cloak, and she really thought he might bow.

"Our table is ready, John."

"Oh yes, of course." He patted CS's hand where it rested on his arm. "Will you be joining us, Miss Jones?"

"Thank you, no. I'll eat here at the bar."

CS turned her cold stare on Madison. "There's a seat for you."

"I appreciate it, but…"

Kacey charged up into the group like a bowling ball, her grin rooted in place and her shoulders high. "All my favorite people in one place!"

She shook Snow's hand enthusiastically, CS's a little less so and then made for Madison like a bullet out of a gun. She slipped off her barstool just in time to be swooped up into Kacey's arms.

"Congratulations, sweetheart," Madison said, Kacey's collarbone pressing into her windpipe in the crushing hug. "This is amazing."

"Wait'll you taste the food."

Kacey turned back to the group. Madison pulled tightly against her side with her arm hanging low on Madison's hip. In any other setting, she'd appreciate the possessiveness of the gesture, but it seemed a bit too provocative for the night and the audience. Maybe she only thought that way because of how CS averted her eyes. Snow reached out for Kacey's free hand again, gripping it as he'd gripped Madison's—too tight and too close. Kacey didn't seem to mind in the slightest.

"A smashing success. Just glorious."

"Well, this is just the soft opening," Kacey said with practiced modesty. "We can't expect every night to be like this."

"Oh, I have no doubt that we can, with you at the helm, am I right CS?"

She didn't respond, just offered a half-hearted laugh and shrugged before stuffing her hands into her pockets and standing off to the side like a coatrack. Snow and Kacey chatted merrily about their brief time together during filming and the tribulations of finding Kacey the perfect restaurant. Madison and CS stood in their respective corners, waiting to be included in the discussion.

Snow admitted, with much the same pretense of modesty that Kacey had shown, that the whole setup here at Minerva Hills was his idea. He turned to CS for support, and she acknowledged the truth of it with a shrug before he launched into the story of coming here to try the wine and falling in love with both the bottles and the land. The winery was in a smaller building then, with only a simple, always-crowded tasting room.

He had planted the bug in CS's ear about the idea of a resort winery that day and nagged her about it for over a year. He even went so far as to hire an architect. It was the drawings that finally won her over, and she agreed to look into it.

"When CS decides to do a thing, she does it right. This is even more extravagant than my initial plan. The cottages, for instance, were all her brainchild. I will admit that I see myself retiring to one of them when that sweet day of rest comes, but the one I had my eye on was heartlessly given to another."

"You mean our cottage?"

"Of course. By far the best. You've done well to secure it."

"Oh, I had no idea we…"

"Don't listen to him," CS said, cutting into Madison's regrets. "It was never his cottage."

"It may have been," he replied with a cheeky grin. "I am quite persuasive."

"Not as persuasive as me," Kacey said, releasing Madison at last. "This has been fun, but I have to get back to the kitchen."

She scampered off with one last peck on Madison's stunned cheek. Snow held out his elbow to her.

"Now you must join us. I absolutely insist."

Madison held her head low, taking his arm and allowing herself to be led off. CS did not even turn to see if she was coming.

CHAPTER EIGHT

Mist hung heavily on the landscape, pooling in the valleys like bedsheets draped over a sleeping body. Its tendrils reached for the mountaintops, straining to reach the summits, but only managing a wispy caress of the slopes. Madison could see it receding as she walked through the vines, making her way slowly toward the high point of the hill where the rows suddenly changed direction and tumbled down into the fog. By the time she crested the hill, the mist was out of sight, perhaps still lingering in the shadowy places below, but its battle was lost for today.

With the mist like this and the silence of the valley, she may have been living a hundred years ago. A thousand years. The mist could have been the smoke of campfires from the ancient, quiet people who inhabited the valley while she sat here, on top of a hill that she hesitated to call a mountain. It was nothing like the Rockies, but she could scan the countryside for miles around.

Between the farms lay miles of trees, their foliage a thick blanket. From this height, they looked moss-like, growing so thick and close the canopy appeared solid. Even the trunks looked small and inconsequential from here.

At the edge of the winery's rows, marked by a track too narrow for the carts but just wide enough for a single horse or walker, a few hand-painted signs were tacked to the frames. Those in front of her were chardonnay. In the adjacent rows she turned to see similar signs reading pinot noir. Madison knew so little about wine, but she knew at least that these were the two varietals for which this area of Oregon was famous. She made a mental note to research them when she got back to the cottage.

The rows of chardonnay ranged down the slope, radiating stripes of green. She selected a gap in the rows at random and slipped between them, heading downhill. The rows were spaced so that she fit perfectly between them. The leaves on either side of her were just inches from brushing against her shoulders. Maybe in the late summer, when they were fully developed, she would be enveloped by them.

They looked so vibrant, so alive she could almost see them growing. It wasn't hard to imagine that the leaves would close in on both sides, wrap around her and make her a part of the vineyard. She would walk by and a tendril would tickle her ankle or wrist. She would stop and welcome the embrace, feel it reach out and coil itself around her. Its roots would work their way in through her skin, make her a part of their growth; a vine-covered statue watching over the countryside.

Given the peaceful lull of the growing things around her, the image did not frighten Madison. She found the image strangely appealing. Maybe not so strange, to crave this peace and quiet after the turmoil of her life. The chaos of her mind. Because it was peaceful here, and utterly quiet. Stillness that Madison had never felt before.

She came to a stop, the last of her footsteps echoing in the emptiness. She looked around her, but the vines were too high to see the rest of the vineyard. It was a Monday, the one day there were no tours and the tasting room was closed, so the staff had the day off too. No one moved around her. No carts groaned along the main track that split the vineyard almost perfectly in two. The highway was far away. The rumbling, honking, screeching sound of traffic, so ubiquitous in the rest of the world, hadn't reached her ears once in the two weeks she'd been here.

Some people were disturbed by quiet. Kacey had to have noise at all times, even playing music while she read or planned dishes. Madison had thought she was the same. Loud coffee shops or roaring nightclubs were where she'd once felt at home. She'd grown up in the heart of the city and had rarely left. She thought she loved that noise, but maybe she was just used to it. Maybe she only loved it because she didn't know peace like this.

A wind kicked up, driving stinging bits of dirt against her bare calves. It brought the dry, dusty smell of the plains and the rocky, irresolute scent of mountains. Another fragrance swirled in the air too. Lavender. Her grandmother had kept little sachets of dried lavender in each drawer of her dresser. The smell of it always clung to her, mixed with the fresh scent of baby powder and those little strawberry candies that lived exclusively in grandmothers' purses.

The wind died down, taking with it the smell and the memory. Madison looked around for the source, spinning in place in the middle of a deserted vineyard. Finally, she looked down and spotted a flash of purple. She dropped to her knees and found the source of her memory. She hadn't noticed it before. Spreading out at her feet, along all the rows as far as she could see to the horizon, lavender and mint grew at the base of the vines.

The vines themselves had very little footprint in the rocky soil. At the root, they were little more than a bare vine, not much thicker than a broomstick shoved into the dirt. Weaving in and around the vines were other plants, growing with much less order. Thick bunches of mint leaves, and clumps of lavender, their stalks taller than the mint and heavy with delicate purple blossoms reaching for the sunlight. It was so fragrant at ground level that it was now impossible to miss the lovely, bunched smells.

Impulsively, she reached out and broke off some mint and lavender. Madison twirled the stems between her fingers, pressing the bunch to her nose and inhaling deeply as she retraced her steps along the row. The lavender was so strong, it made the mint fade into the background, but smelling them together was incredible.

The soft snort of a horse brought Madison back to reality. She opened her eyes and skidded to a halt. The horse stood a few feet away with CS on top, her stone face locked in neutral. Her shoulders were even more square than usual, and her hands, wrapped in yellow leather gloves, gripped tight at the reins in her lap.

"Oh. Hi." Madison said, dropping the herbs from her face to swing casually at her side. Was she allowed to pick them? They were growing like weeds, but maybe they were part of the crop. "I didn't see you."

CS didn't say a word, just looked down on her while the horse shifted its weight from one foot to another.

"I hope it's okay that I'm here. I just wanted to get some fresh air."

No response from the woman in the saddle, just the impatient fidgeting of her horse.

"It's beautiful here." Madison gestured behind her, turning to hide the lavender and mint by her hip. "So peaceful. And quiet…Solitary."

She turned back, her eyes begged for a response. Anything would do. A lecture about not being allowed in the vines. The story of this place and how she came to be here. Even a simple good morning would do at this point.

"I like the quiet too."

Madison breathed a sigh of relief to know at least that this woman could still speak. It was somewhat premature. No sooner had the words left her lips than CS nodded, flicked a finger on the brim of her dusty, stained cowboy hat and kicked the horse's sides, sending it into motion again. Madison backed up a few steps, retreating into the row of chardonnay as the massive horse passed down the track. She kept her eyes fixed low on CS's well-worn riding boots, rather than her face as she passed.

She stayed there, eyes locked on the herbs, until the sound of metal-shod hooves on soil faded into the distance. She looked up to find herself alone again, but somehow the solitude now felt uncomfortable. It was more like trespassing, and she had never, even in her wilder days, been a rule breaker. She hurried across the track and through the rows on the other side.

It wasn't until she could see the cottage again that she realized she still clutched her odd little bouquet. The mint was bruised beyond saving, but the lavender was unfazed, only wilting slightly in the warm afternoon. She needed to get it into a glass of water. Or maybe she would tie it into a bundle and hang it from the ceiling to dry it the way her grandmother had. She laughed to herself to think of Kacey's reaction if she were to stuff little packs of potpourri into their dresser.

Turning to toss the herbs away, Madison caught, just at the edge of her vision, a ray of sunlight slashing through the last of the mountain fog. It caught in the mist for a heartbeat, making it glow from the inside and sparking a thought that maybe, just maybe, Madison could turn into the first vase she threw in her new studio.

She dropped the mint into the grass but held tight to the lavender. She wouldn't dry it, but maybe she could find another use for it.

One thing was certain, she would not let CS scare her into tossing it out.

CHAPTER NINE

With a satisfied smile Madison wiped the last of the clay off her wheel, taking the rag to rinse in the mudroom sink. Everything she had thrown since she first sat at the wheel in this room was good. Not perfect, not any of them yet, but she hadn't scrapped a single piece since she arrived in Oregon and that was a first.

It was the room, of course. Her studio, though it was hard for her to think of it that way yet. She walked in every morning, awed by the wall of windows that this was hers. It was like no studio she'd ever worked in, though this was what every studio should be. Too much art was forged in dark, dank places. Beautiful things were meant to be made in beautiful places. Every artist should work robed in natural light.

Sure, she needed to cure her pots in a different room, but the plastic-draped shelving in the mudroom was the perfect spot for that too. There was even a nice, dark corner for her to keep her clay and access to a deep sink originally meant for the laundry.

She gave her studio one last, loving glance before stepping away. A smile so wide it burned her cheeks and stayed with her all the way into the kitchen.

"Done for the day?"

Kacey sat at the raised counter, her hair tousled and her pajama shirt hanging loosely from her shoulders. Madison topped off Kacey's coffee before pouring herself a cup from the half-full carafe.

"Yeah. My back's starting to ache." She blew across the surface of her coffee, steam billowing out, and hopped up to sit on the counter.

Kacey nodded, flipping a page of her magazine. She wasn't listening, but she wasn't reading either. Her eyes didn't move across the page, an advertisement for erectile dysfunction medication. Her lids drooped dangerously close to shut.

"You're about to drown in your coffee, babe." Madison reached out and ruffled her hair. "Did you sleep at all last night?"

Kacey pushed the magazine away and looked up. "Not sure. What day is it?"

Madison laughed and leaned over to lay a kiss on her pouting bottom lip. She could still taste the barest hint of tequila there.

"As long as you're sober this morning." She studied Kacey thoughtfully. "You are sober, aren't you?"

"Yeah," Kacey took a long sip from her cup. When she set it down, she used both hands to scrub at her face. "I shouldn't have stayed so late, but everyone needed a little party."

"When did you get home? I don't remember you coming in."

"I'm not sure, but it was late. We needed to blow off steam."

"Service's been rough?"

"No, the restaurant is great. The diners love the menu. It's just… Everyone's stir crazy."

There was a desperation in her voice that Madison, had she been paying more attention over the last couple of weeks, should have noticed.

"We're all feeling a little closed in. It's so far from town here and it's tough to get the cars for a day out. I guess it's fine for the folks who don't live on property, but the rest of us are having a hard time adjusting."

"You don't like it here?"

"You do?" Kacey's eyes were wide now, and full of confusion. "I hate it here. I mean, I guess I'll get used to it, but this isn't exactly what I had in mind."

"What did you have in mind?"

"I don't know." She looked around with a wild glint in her eyes. "I thought we'd be close to Portland. Or Eugene even. This place is close to nothing and it's driving me crazy."

"It's a little secluded, sure, but I like the quiet."

Kacey laughed, shaking her head with a good-natured grin. "When have you ever liked it quiet?"

Madison felt the tears forming behind her eyes, but willed them away. They fell back inside her, leaving a cold sadness that ate at her until she felt hollow. She refused to allow the picture of Robert to form in her mind. If he took shape, if his blue eyes turned to her the way they had ever since she could remember, she wouldn't be able to breathe. She slipped down off the counter, letting her feet hit hard to jolt her mind out of focus. It worked well enough that her hand didn't shake when she picked up the coffeepot.

"I don't know."

Kacey wasn't listening. Madison didn't have to turn around to know. She didn't hear the pain in Madison's voice or detect the lie. She'd already forgotten that she'd asked the question.

"You know what I hate even more than this place?" Kacey stood, her chair scraping along the tile floor. "CS. I can't stand her. She just wanders around the place like a ghost. She never says anything. She's just...I don't know."

Madison shrugged as she turned around. "She's not very warm, is she?"

"She's about as warm as the walk-in and we keep that thing cold enough to freeze my tits off."

"I saw her in the field the other day." Madison set her cup down and looked out the window over the sink, still not sure whether her eyes would give her away. "She wasn't super friendly."

"She spends too much time alone in the grapes. I see her out there all the time. It's like she doesn't sleep. She just walks in the fields and grumbles."

"Do you think…" Madison gave voice to her worry that had been bouncing around since her walk. "Do you think I wasn't supposed to be there? Should I stay out of the vineyard?"

"I see tourists out there all the time."

"Yeah, but they pay to be here."

"So what? We live here. If she didn't want us out there, she should have said something." Kacey dropped her empty cup into the sink. "What're you up to today?"

She hesitated, fiddling with the handle of her coffee cup. "I thought I might take a walk. Stretch my back."

Kacey came around the counter, wrapping her into a tight hug. Madison burrowed her cheek into Kacey's neck, trying to ignore the reek of alcohol.

"Go anywhere you want, babe. She said we should treat this place like home."

Madison nodded into her neck. With the warmth of her girlfriend pressed against her, she felt more confident in the decision. The confidence only partly evaporated when Kacey kissed her on the top of her head and hurried off to the shower.

She forced herself to leave the house, only pausing to shout a goodbye up the stairs before charging out the door, around the house and then beyond to the main gate before she could change her mind. Kacey was right—CS said they should feel at home, and Madison felt like a walk. Her determination almost felt like confidence, and she didn't allow her doubts to creep in until the cottage was out of sight.

She decided to avoid the main path. If CS didn't see her, she couldn't get into trouble. She skirted the edge of the property, sticking to the perimeter of the vines instead of walking along their length.

Unfortunately, that didn't offer the most stimulating walk. She knew she was heading in the general direction of the stables, but the building was too far off for her to see the roof over the grape trellises. A seven-foot tall privacy fence marked the property line, an unbroken row of thin boxwoods in front. There was no path here, only untidy grass brushing her ankles.

In front of her, a stand of trees she hadn't noticed before bulged out from the property line. A breeze kicked up, ruffling the leaves on the tops of the trees, blowing them toward her as though they were reaching out their hands, beckoning her to come in.

The day was hot, summer having arrived in full force in the past week. Here on the mountain there was little cover from the punishing sun. A patch of sweaty T-shirt stuck to her lower back unpleasantly, so she sought the shade of the trees ahead. She bent and picked a stalk of lavender that had made its way out of the rows and into the narrow strip of grass.

The shadows swallowed her up and carried her into another world. Dead leaves clung to the underbrush. Struggling, anemic saplings and low, thorny bushes covered the ground. The canopy was high, blocking out most of the light, and all the branches were out of reach. The wind whistled through the trunks as it did through tall city buildings.

Ahead of her the trees were thinning. Madison could see brighter light cutting through the trunks. The ground was getting softer too, the grass returning to take over from the detritus of dead leaves. A clearing was visible through the breaks. It wasn't large, just a few square feet of grass tucked into the center of a forest.

When she saw the person in the clearing, Madison stopped abruptly. She knew it was CS. Though her back was to Madison, the way she held herself made it obvious that this could only be the stone-faced winemaker. Without thinking, Madison ducked behind the tree in front of her. She did not want to be seen, but turning to leave now might give her away as much as walking forward.

It wasn't until she stopped moving that Madison heard the low rumble of CS's voice. She was too far away to distinguish words, but Madison liked the sound. It reminded her of warm, comforting things with its steadiness and timbre. Pitched low in that butch way that stirred something deep in Madison. In the way that Kacey desperately wished she spoke, but couldn't. CS spoke so rarely it humanized her in some way that made the recollection of her cold stare bearable.

CS moved to the side revealing a gravestone, a simple thing of carved gray marble, with text unreadable at this distance. CS crouched next to it, bouncing slightly on her wide-stretched knees and talking to the headstone. When she reached out and laid a hand on top, Madison felt her cheeks burn. This was a private moment and she should leave. Even if she was seen now, better to be seen walking away than staring.

As she turned to go, a light sparkled in the clearing and caught her eye. A flash of yellow and brightest white just as she blinked reminded Madison so forcibly of the moment she had seen liquid light, the moment she had chased since she was a child. She stopped and turned back. CS had set two small glasses on top of the stone. They scraped along the marble, and it was the curve of the glass that caught the sun, reflecting it into her eyes.

CS held an unlabeled wine bottle, a strange yellow-green so pale it was almost clear. It was a quarter-full and had a cork roughly jammed halfway into the neck. CS brought the bottle to her lips, yanking the cork out with her teeth and holding it in the corner of her mouth like a mobster with the stub of a cigar. She poured two measures of wine, one much larger than the other, into the glasses before jamming the cork back in with the heel of her hand.

Madison told herself to go, but her legs wouldn't move. She was fixated on the figure in the clearing, now wiping a few leaves from the base of the gravestone. CS rocked back on her heels, lowering herself to sit in the grass. She held the fuller glass, touching it to that on top of the stone. A musical tinkle traveled across the empty space into the trees. It sounded like fairy laughter to Madison.

After a long moment, Madison realized this was the longest she'd ever heard CS speak. Apart from the occasional break to sip her wine, she spoke nonstop. Madison craved to know whose grave this was, but knew she had no right to the answer.

Loose strands of hair fluttered to a rest on her forehead as the breeze died down. Heat poured over Madison, bringing new rivulets of sweat. Fatigue stole over her, the tension in her body had returned while she fought to remain a motionless observer. In the stillness, an odd fragrance stole over her, pushing away the scent of the forest and her own overheated skin. It was musty and reminded her of oranges, sweet black cherries, and old books. The combination was confusing but not unpleasant.

CS finished her wine. After a moment of staring into the empty glass, she pulled the cork and poured herself another, setting the now-empty bottle at the base of the stone. She leaned back on one outstretched arm, her long legs crossed in front of her, and held her glass up to the light. The wine was red, rich, and so dark the sunlight could not penetrate it. She swirled it, watching the wave chase itself across the inner surface of the globe. Her words ended in a chuckle and she shook her head, her close-cropped hair twisting with the movement except at the base of her neck where the damp strands stuck to the sweat.

Madison finally pulled herself back into the moment. Her thighs ached from standing still and her arms were too warm. The sun was lowering in the sky and she suddenly remembered her pots drying on the shelf. She'd lost track of time out here and they were waiting for her. She turned slowly, careful not to make too much noise, and retraced her steps out of the woods.

She turned back once. CS hadn't moved. She still reclined against her arm in the sunlight, but the forest swallowed her words.

CHAPTER TEN

Madison slapped the mound of clay between her open palms, shifting it from one hand to the other as she found its center of balance. It wasn't too large, just about seven pounds, enough to make a nice-sized vase. That's what the clay felt like anyway. It was dry, maybe a little too dry. Maybe she wasn't sealing the footlocker of her unused clay tightly enough against the heavy air. She'd have a better idea after this throw.

Once the clay was balanced, she pressed it down onto the wheel, using the rings carved in the metal to help her center it. Definitely a vase. Something tall. She'd start by throwing a cylinder and see where it went from there. Sitting on her stool, she started the wheel spinning with gentle pressure on the pedal and dipped her hands into the water bucket to her right. She put her wet hands on the mound of clay, holding them steady.

This clay took a surprisingly long time to center. It was complicated, this piece, and that didn't bode well for the vase. The simplest part of pottery, and also the hardest, was keeping the hands quiet and still, letting the rotation of the wheel shape the piece. If the clay was even a millimeter off-center, the whole thing would fall apart.

After what felt like hours, the mound of clay, now slick with the moisture she added and much more pliable, found the center of the wheel and she pressed it down into the surface. She looked at it again, holding her wet gray hands in her lap as the wheel spun. It was a beautiful sight, the clay at its rawest state. Full of potential. Full of beauty waiting to be discovered.

Madison dipped her hands into the bucket again before laying them on the clay. She wrapped her palm and fingers around it, applying the lightest pressure just to clean the surface of any ridges. She pressed down with both thumbs into the center of the mound. The clay jumped away from her encroaching touch, pressing against her palms and, when it couldn't escape that way, sliding up, giving the vase the first of its height.

Moments later she had the depth she wanted and she withdrew, careful not to mar the surface inside or out with her trailing fingers. She dipped her sponge into the bucket and squeezed a little water over the clay, keeping it moist enough to work with. This stage always reminded her of children's science projects. A little volcano of clay just waiting to be filled with baking soda and vinegar.

She rinsed her hands in the bucket, the water growing murkier by the minute. Now was the fun part. The part where the clay became what it wanted to become, using Madison's hands to shape itself. She hooked her thumbs together and curled her fingertips, making a crude heart shape, and gently wrapped them around her clay volcano, one hand inside, one outside. Pressing her fingertips with equal pressure on either side, she drew her hands up, pulling the wall of the pot with her. Once she was at the top, she cleaned the rim with her thumb, flattening the surface and discarding the extra clay into her water bucket.

Time and again she repeated the process, moving slowly lest her eagerness stretch the clay too thinly and create a weakness. Patience was key. She had to work the material gently, if she tried to coerce it at this point, the pot would rebel. Run away like a skittish lover. The walls grew higher and the bottom of her water bucket filled with discarded slip clay. The process was mechanical, repetitive, and she'd learned long ago to let her mind wander while she did it, letting the clay speak to her and keeping herself out of the way.

Her mind slid over images and thoughts with the same alacrity her fingers slipped over the wet clay. The feel of Kacey's arm around her while she slept, pulling her close and making her feel safe. The feel of her grandmother's hand wrapped around hers, the skin paper thin but gentle. The sound of wind whistling through the trees as she approached the little glade with the gravestone.

The clearing stuck in her mind. She rinsed her hands and surveyed her work. It was getting there, the clay finally felt right in her hands, but it needed more height. She had to stand now to get her hand inside without her forearm hitting the top. The moment her fingertips touched clay again, her mind was back in the woods.

There was something magical about that scene she'd intruded upon. Something unbelievable in the fact that CS had not seen her. That she'd remained a silent observer. The whole thing could've been a dream. Right down to the way the light caught at her eye. The way it danced around the glass in CS's hand and found her hiding spot. Out of all the billions of directions that beam of light could have gone, it had caught Madison and held her in place. As though the moment were an important one to see. A moment that required a witness.

It felt somehow wrong to spoil it by trying to determine the identity of the grave. What she saw with CS wasn't exactly grief. There were no tears. Even the low rumble of her voice was untroubled. No, it wasn't grief. Madison knew what that looked like all too well. It was more like a visit. Like CS had gone to a friend's house to share gossip over a glass of wine.

Madison stopped the wheel, pulling her hands away to see they were trembling. She couldn't imagine why, unless the thought of death and grief was taking its toll. She didn't feel sad, though. She didn't feel much of anything she could define.

She stepped on the pedal. Her trembling hands would sort themselves out. The clay was forgiving enough for that.

She'd lost her train of thought and had to stare for a long time at the spinning cylinder. It was the right height now, but still too thick. More importantly, her mind was back in its drift, letting her work.

She went back to the glade as she worked, trying to re-create the scene piece-by-piece. The whistle of the wind. The plush grass and brittle leaves underfoot. The green and brown of the earth and the vivid blue of the sky in the break of the canopy. She squeezed clay from her fingers into the bucket. Now she just needed that light to come back. The flash that was like liquid but not quite. That was the image she needed in her mind to make this pot live.

Her fingertips slipped across the surface and she was in the woods again. CS stood next to the stone, her hips cocked just off-center and her thumbs hooked in the wide belt around her waist. Madison hadn't noticed before how strong those arms were. Her shirt sleeves were rolled up to her elbow and her forearms looked like they were chiseled out of granite. In someone else, in someone kinder or someone who smiled occasionally, Madison would have found them distracting.

CS's shoulders twitched. She was turning. She would see Madison in her hiding place and she would be angry. Those cold eyes would light up, but not with warmth. With angry fire. In that moment, Madison realized the blue eyes were already on her. Swallowing her. Taking every inch of her awareness until all she saw was twin pools of robin's-egg blue ringed by shimmering, unblemished white. Those eyes drew her in inexorably.

A bang from the kitchen ripped Madison from her daydream with a gasp. She lurched, the collar of the pot buckled and the whole, beautiful mess crumpled, dropping onto the wheel. As the metal surface slowed to a stop, the deflated remnants gave one final, desolate flop, landing in a heap. Even in this ruined state, it was beautiful. It would have been a gorgeous vase.

"Madison!"

Kacey's shout had set her teeth on edge. If it weren't for the clatter of the empty coffeepot slamming into the maker, the vase would've sung. Madison sighed, dropping her forehead into the heel of her hand. She felt the watery clay soaking into her skin and the hair that fell across her face.

"Was that sigh for me?"

She knew it wasn't Kacey's fault, but the loss of the vase was still too new for her to respond well. The stink of stale booze didn't help either. It was the smell that told her Kacey was coming closer, but Madison didn't have anywhere to run.

"Wanna play out the scene from *Ghost*?"

It was an old joke between them, one that rarely offended Madison. Kacey's hand would snake over her shoulder, heading for her breast, and that would be something Madison didn't want at the moment. She stood abruptly, reaching for the wire to cut her destroyed pot from the wheel.

"That one didn't work out, huh?"

"No. It didn't."

They both had an edge to their voice now. Sure, it was cute, the way Kacey flirted using that ridiculous movie love scene as a line, but it was also belittling and obnoxious. Probably every potter since that movie had had someone come on to them that way. She could shrug it off as Kacey's sense of humor, but with the broken pot on her wheel she wasn't in the mood for teasing. She made her living and found her purpose in this clay. Kacey's patronizing attitude felt like a smack in the face.

"You didn't make coffee?"

"I wanted to get straight to work."

"I'm going to make some."

"Okay." When Madison realized how childish she was being, she added, "I'll be right there."

Madison started working the clay back into a block. Maybe she needed a break. A chance to clear her head. She focused on her breathing as she wiped the wheel clean. When she made her way into the kitchen after washing her hands in the mudroom sink, her smile was genuine.

The toaster popped a slightly scorched bagel and Madison snagged it on her way to the counter. Her stomach rumbled as she smeared cream cheese liberally on both sides. She hadn't eaten when she'd got up, and now she was starving. Just smelling the melting cream cheese made her limbs droop with weakness. Maybe that was the real reason she toppled the vase.

Madison made her way to the dining table with her plate and a coffee. She swallowed just in time to drop a kiss on Kacey's head as she passed. Kacey was eating a bagel too, but she had a neon blue Gatorade next to her coffee along with half the contents of their medicine cabinet.

"Long night?" Madison asked, dropping into a chair.

"Not too bad. I'm just getting old. I feel it after three drinks these days." She gave Madison a wink. "So the moody artist emerges, huh?"

To avoid an unnecessary argument, Madison shrugged and sipped her coffee. It was just easier to give in. Kacey would forget all about it if she did, and she just wanted to eat and get back to work.

"You should come one night. It's pretty low-key. Just the restaurant staff grabbing drinks while we clean up, but it's fun."

"I'll pass. It's too late for me to walk up there."

"So get the jerk with the cart to give you a ride. I miss hanging out with you. It's been a long time."

"I know. I just don't feel much like partying."

"It's not a party, just friends hanging out."

Madison was still trying to avoid a fight. If the reek surrounding Kacey when she came home was any indication, they did more than just have a quiet drink while washing their knives. Last night she woke up at two and Kacey still wasn't home. She just didn't party like that anymore. Not that Kacey had seemed to notice.

It wasn't like they'd talked about it when she got back from doing *Top Chef*. Now it felt like too late to have the conversation. Still, she would expect Kacey to notice something. It had been months and she hadn't gone out once, even to quiet after-service drinks at the restaurant. At first she thought Kacey was giving her time to deal with everything. Now it felt like she either didn't notice or didn't care. Or maybe both.

They finished their breakfast in silence and, just as she'd predicted, Kacey hadn't noticed the uneasy atmosphere. She sat back, washing a handful of aspirin down her throat and looked at Madison with a smile.

"You're gorgeous when you're covered in clay."

"Am I?" Madison reached up and felt her bangs, caked in gray and drying to a firm crust. "I guess I am. Maybe I should shower."

"Me first. I have to get to work."

"Come home tonight?" Madison asked, all too aware of the distance between them and blaming herself. "I miss you."

Kacey hesitated for a long moment, but finally nodded. "Sure, babe. We can hang out before bed."

"I'd like that a lot."

"Why don't you come up for dinner? We can have a secret date. You sit at the chef's table and I'll cook for you."

The chef's table in most restaurants was tucked away into the kitchen. A private place to be served personally by the executive chef. That's not how it was at *ambrosia*. Kacey had a taste for cooking to an audience now, so she made the kitchen, and thus the chef's table, visible from all corners of the restaurant.

As a concept, it worked wonderfully. Diners paid astronomical prices to sit there. They were the second lead in Kacey's little nightly drama.

The concept was great, but Madison felt her blood turn to ice at the thought of having so many strangers' eyes on her. Strangers that were, thanks to Kacey putting their phone calls on television for the world to see, deluded into thinking they knew something of Madison and their relationship. Her mind flashed back to a run-in they had back in Denver when a couple of tourists stopped them and talked to them like they'd known each other for years. Kacey ate it up, but Madison was frightened by how much they knew, not just about Kacey, but about her.

"Not tonight. Jada's visiting in a couple of weeks. I'll bring her up and you can show off both of us."

"Mmmm. Two hot women on my arm. Sounds like fun."

Kacey kissed her hard before heading off to the shower. Madison cleaned up, wondering if she'd only managed to delay the fight. Chances were good that Kacey would try to get them to stay for drinks when Jada visited, and she wasn't likely to respond well when Madison flatly refused.

CHAPTER ELEVEN

The second attempt at the vase wasn't perfect, but at least it was whole. If she allowed herself an impartial eye on her own work, Madison might even call it pretty, but she had always been her own toughest critic. Maybe she'd like it better once she trimmed it. The bottom was chunky and it was too tall. Once she began the catalogue of faults, she knew she was spiraling and had to stop working for the day. Some days just weren't the days to create.

After a shower, she headed out for a walk. She loved walking out the front door of the cottage. It made her feel like she was on vacation. The outdoor fireplace, the comfortable furniture and the wide, blue sky seemed full of dreams. Normally that was a good thing, but sometimes it felt selfish to be here throwing while Kacey was working so hard.

Madison started up the path to the main gate to the left and the main building to the right. She hadn't been this way in a while. Despite the fact that they'd lived on the vineyard for six weeks, Madison hadn't explored the whole property. She wanted to see how far the grapes stretched, and the best view was from the top of the hill.

Before she even made it to the main path, she ran into Boots, leading an enormous horse in her direction. He smiled and waved a gloved hand, stopping when they met on the dusty road.

"The artist emerges," he said with a toothy grin she couldn't help but return. "Haven't seen you in a while. How've you been?"

She hadn't realized how little time she'd spent socializing.

"Just working hard." The horse snorted. She eyed it warily and asked, "Is something wrong with your horse? Why aren't you riding?"

"Violet threw a shoe."

"Um…That sounds…bad?"

"Nothing serious, but it can mess with her gait if I don't fix it."

"Sure."

"You don't have the slightest idea what I'm talking about, do you?"

"Not at all."

She turned to walk beside him back the way she'd come, making sure to put him between her and the massive animal. Boots walked slowly, but she couldn't tell whether that was for the horse's benefit or for hers.

Boots grabbed a horseshoe from his back pocket, holding it out in front of them as they walked. "We were inspecting the chardonnay on the other side of the hill when she hit a rock wrong. The thing just fell right off."

She looked past him to the big, soft eyes of the horse. She had a shimmering chestnut coat thick as a carpet and beautifully long, curling eyelashes. "So how long will she be out of commission?"

"She'll get a nice little manicure first before we replace the shoe. Won't take long, but she'll get the rest of the day off anyway. Too late to drag her back out to work."

"And you get the rest of the day off if she does, too, don't you?"

"You're quick."

They arrived at the stable and Madison got her first up-close look at the building visible from her front porch. It was impressive, with wide barn doors hanging open on one side and beautiful dark siding wrapping around the whole structure. There was an addition sitting off to one side that did its best to match the work building's façade but had the air of something else about it. Whatever it was, that section clearly had two floors whereas the barn was a single story with a deceptively high ceiling.

The temperature and light in the stable dropped markedly. After her eyes adjusted, Madison could make out a row of neat stalls with curving half doors of the same dark wood of the exterior and wrought iron hinges redolent of the expert work on the winery gate. Each stall door had the Minerva Hills logo burned into it like a brand on cattle. The floors were worn hardwood, which surprised Madison in its extravagance, and the whole place smelled like clean hay and some sort of malty grain that she assumed was feed for the tenants.

Only one stall was occupied. A petite horse with a platinum mane watched the three newcomers with a lazy, disinterested stare under drooping eyelids. Boots led his horse to the far end of the room and clipped her into a lead hanging from the ceiling. He stripped saddle and blanket from Violet. Both horses seemed docile as old cats, which set Madison at ease. She sat on an upturned crate at the end of the stalls and watched Boots collect tools.

"Who puts the shoes back on? A blacksmith?"

Boots tapped his own chest with a pair of pliers that would have looked at home in a torture museum. "That's me, but it's farrier, not blacksmith."

"You? Really?"

"Why do you think they call me Boots?"

"Because you told them to."

"Okay, yeah, that's true." He leaned against the horse and lifted her foreleg up, setting it on his thigh and clipping the edges of her hoof with the massive pliers. "But it's also because I shoe the horses."

"I thought you worked with the grapes, not the horses."

"I do both." He went to work on the hoof with a file, smoothing it out with the skill of an expert pedicurist. "CS brought me on as her assistant and I liked the horses, so I learned how to take care of them too. She needed the help anyway. It's a big stable for her to manage alone."

"I didn't know she took care of the horses."

"The grapes, the horses, the wine, and runs the business. She doesn't sleep much."

The blond horse whinnied and Madison jumped, nearly falling off the crate.

"That's Buttercup. She's a bit of a drama queen."

"Oh." She relaxed, looking around the room, noting the exposed beams in the ceiling and the meticulous cleanliness of the whole place. She'd always thought stables would be dirty and smelly, but she'd been in messier living rooms than this place. "This is a nice barn."

"It's nicer than most." He placed the horse's foot back down, patting her back as he went back to the table to exchange tools. "Do you like horses?"

"I don't know anything about them."

"I picked up on that."

"They're beautiful and I'm sure they're wonderful animals. They're just...really big."

"Did you hear that Violet? She called you fat."

"Not fat! Tall."

He picked up her foot again and Madison was amazed to see how easy the horse was for him to handle. She seemed to trust Boots, despite the hammer in his hand and the wickedly curved nails bristling between his teeth.

"They're sweet when you get to know 'em, but they can be a little intimidating. A place like this must be hell for a city girl like you."

That was the second time she'd been called a city girl and she was starting to resent the implication. She could handle country life and was even starting to enjoy it. Still, it was hard to be angry at Boots. With his impish grin and big brother teasing, his statement felt more like an observation than a criticism.

"I thought it would be for a while, but I love the quiet here. And the light."

"I don't find it quiet exactly," he said, banging the last nail into place. "But then you do very different work than I do."

"I guess so."

"How are the pots coming along?"

She thought about the one this morning. The flopping mess that could have been beautiful and the cheap imitation she made after she screwed up the first one.

"Okay."

"Where do you sell them? Or are they just for museums or whatever?"

"Mostly whatever right now. I'm working on getting a solo show together, or I was before I moved. The gallery I was working with is in Denver, so I don't know if I can make it work now that I'm here."

"Tough way to make a living."

"Tell me about it. I used to sell some of my pots in this little boutique place in Denver. Tourists mostly. The cost to ship them back from here would mean I'd lose money though."

"What about here?" He unhooked Violet from the wall and walked her around on the lead, his eyes on her new shoe. "There's the shop up at the main building."

"I thought it just sold your wine."

"You really haven't gotten out much have you? They sell all sorts of local stuff up there. Soap, jewelry, some sort of essential oil perfume. CS lets them all sell in there."

Madison tried not to get too excited—after all, Boots wasn't in charge and CS didn't seem to like her much. "You sure there's space? I mean, it would be nice, but I wouldn't want to impose."

"Trust me, there's plenty of space." He led Violet to her stall, slipping her bridle off once she was secure inside. "Hell, you could probably sell them for double because they're made here on the estate. These rich Minerva Hills devotees would eat that up."

"You really think so?"

"Sure thing. You'll sell out in no time. Wanna come up and take a look?"

Before her nerves got the better of her, Madison agreed and they walked up together, leaving Violet and Buttercup alone in the sleepy cool of the barn. The sun hung low, Boots chattering away and Madison only half-listening.

The sun's departure did nothing to dispel the heat of the day, but it did cover the world in a blanket of orange light. The colors of the sunset were rich and thick, almost tangible in the vast openness. She wanted to study those colors. Memorize them in what she knew would be a vain attempt to mimic them with her glaze. Minerva Hills Sunset. She would try, next time she mixed glaze, to find the right mix of chemicals to capture this exact tone.

Just when she turned her full attention to Boots' conversation she was distracted again, this time by an increasing rumble. By the time they finally arrived at the entrance to the winery, it was a deafening roar.

As the summer progressed, more people descended upon Minerva Hills. Madison saw them from the windows of her studio, but it was something else entirely to be among them. The lobby teemed with people spilling out of the tasting room and both restaurants, their conversation filling every corner of the massive lobby. Madison winced at the crowd, but Boots strolled casually through them, heading for the one place that appeared to hold little interest for the hungry, thirsty crowd. Madison followed at a trot, slipping into the shop as a trio of women, each carrying a bulging shopping bag, emerged into the crush.

She saw that the shop wasn't quite as small as she thought. There was wine for sale, and a lot of it, but the rest of the store, hidden from view from the outside by the rack of bottles, held all manner of goods. It felt like a mix between an art museum gift shop and a farmers' market. Along the back wall was a display of hand-blown wineglasses and necklaces that impressed Madison with their delicate craftsmanship. Soaps wrapped in brown paper on the next shelf made the whole room smell like a rose garden in the spring. Local honey, artisan chocolates and hand-dyed scarves dotted tables and display racks crammed so tightly into the limited space that the few shoppers in the room had to squeeze between them.

Picking up a small, dark brown bottle with a hand-printed label, Madison found the perfumes Boots had mentioned. She unscrewed the top and the concentrated scent of lavender filled the room. According to the label, the oil came from the lavender growing in the Minerva Hills vineyard. Apparently it was a companion crop, grown in between the vines to help condition the soil and enhance the terroir, whatever that was. Even as Madison stood there, another shopper walked up, read the placard on the table mentioning the origin of the perfume and immediately snatched up the only other bottle. Her friend, standing just behind her, eyed the bottle Madison held with a sort of visceral longing. The moment she set the bottle back down, the other woman snatched it up and hurried to the register.

"I told you, didn't I?" Boots murmured into her ear. "Just mention that something's made here in the vineyard and people will buy it. They didn't even smell the stuff. Didn't look at the price. They're practically begging to buy your pottery."

"Oh, I see, you think I need a gimmick to sell my work?" She teased, watching the women hand over credit cards so shiny they may have been chrome plated.

"No harm in having a gimmick. Just think how many zeroes you can slap on the end of those price tags. You might even consider throwing a little commission my way. You know, since I lugged that big oven into your house for you."

"It's a kiln, and you didn't lift a finger."

"I supervised. It's a very important job."

"Oh yeah. Essential."

It was amazing how a few words with a new friend could dramatically alter Madison's mood. Her anxiety in the lobby had disappeared, replaced by the teasing banter. Boots had all the potential to turn into a real friend for Madison, something she hadn't expected to find after leaving Jada behind.

"I think you may be right, though. This looks like the perfect place to start."

"The perfect place to start what?"

Just like that, the confidence fled from her and she was back in the noisy, crowded place that felt like it would suffocate her.

"Hey, CS." Boots turned, but Madison held perfectly still, waiting for the chill of the winemaker's presence to sweep over her. "We were just talking about Artist selling her pottery here in the shop."

"Cut the nicknames, Boots."

He chuckled, cutting it off abruptly when she glared at him. "It's funny. See, because you told me to stop using nicknames while using my nickname."

She didn't respond, and the silence made Madison turn around. She gave Boots a half-hearted smile. "It's fine. He can call me whatever."

"It's a stupid nickname. It isn't even clever."

Boots crossed his arms, smiling at CS and challenging, "What would you call her?"

"Denver," CS responded without missing a beat.

He opened his mouth and closed it again. "Okay. You're right. That's better."

"I know."

Madison caught the flash of a smile, just the barest twitch of CS's lips, but it lit up her blue eyes and, for a heartbeat, Madison was captivated by the glow. As quickly as it appeared, the smile melted again into a frown and the glow faded from her eyes.

"No need to rub it in."

"You were saying?"

"I was saying that Denver and I were talking about selling her pottery here in the store. At this table. It would be perfect, you see, perfume from the winery and pottery from the winery all in the same place."

Boots was talking fast and fidgeting, shifting his weight from one foot to the other, obviously nervous. He thought CS would turn them down. Why had he even suggested the scheme if he knew it wouldn't work? Now she would have to stand here and watch CS say no. It would have been better not to ask at all.

Madison looked up at CS and found the expected annoyance in her stern expression. Why shouldn't she be annoyed? Madison was living rent free in her best cottage, the one meant for her old friend, and not contributing in any way to the success of her business. If their positions were reversed, Madison would resent this woman taking advantage of her. Now she asks for a favor?

"Of course," CS finally said.

"What?" Madison heard her own voice as a squeak and clicked her teeth back together to hold in any more words.

"Of course you can sell your artwork here." She gave Madison a long, level look. "You should have asked earlier."

"I'm...sorry?"

"Thanks, CS," Boots cut in, his voice light and peppy. "This is gonna be great."

"Sure."

It was odd, but CS still watched Madison with that disapproving glare. Madison did her best to match it, to hold her chin high and look back.

"Okay, I'm off to drive these drunks back to the gate." He slapped Madison on the back harder than she expected, pushing her forward a step, closer to CS than she'd like. "See ya round, Denver."

"Don't let anyone drive if they're drunk, Boots," CS said in her usual, level voice.

He gave her a thumbs up and hurried off, disappearing through the door and leaving Madison alone with CS. Quite alone, she realized, as she looked around the store. The shoppers had all gone to catch a ride back to civilization, and the older woman behind the cash register was nowhere to be seen. Madison turned back to CS just in time to see her realize the situation as well. She looked just as uncomfortable as Madison.

"I...um." Madison had to stop when those blue eyes turned back to her, but then caught her breath and hurried on. "Thanks for letting me sell my work here."

"You're welcome."

That seemed to cover all they had to say to each other. They stood there for a long time, close to one another but neither one wanting to point it out by moving. CS looked away again, searching the empty store uncomfortably. After a long moment she shoved her hands into the pockets of her jeans.

"I have to go."

"Okay," Madison replied. She certainly didn't want to prolong the encounter, but there was an awkwardness to the abrupt announcement.

"It's quarterly budget time. I have…bills."

"Okay."

"Good night."

"Good night."

She wrenched the door open and marched through with swift, sure movements. Madison waited before pulling the door gently closed behind her and making her way across the now much less crowded lobby to the exit.

CHAPTER TWELVE

On the far side of the vineyard, sitting alone on a little hillock dotted in the center of a vast field of chardonnay vines, sat a single windswept tree. It was grizzled, with gnarled branches hanging out at odd angles. The land around it was sparse and cracked.

Madison had noticed the tree many times. It was hard to miss any odd marker in such ordered terrain. She'd never visited the tree. It seemed so bleak. Even in the height of summer, when the vines were lush and overflowing their trellises, laden with ripening fruit, the tree looked as though it were breathing its last. Like one strong gust of wind or one hard winter would send it crashing down onto the ocean of vines surrounding its island.

That dilapidation was what drew her there now. It seemed apt to sit here in the shadow of a dying tree and cry for all she had lost. She found a tolerably soft patch of dirt among the roots and settled herself down just as the tears completely obscured her vision. They'd been threatening for the entire walk, but she'd held them in until she'd arrived. Then she let the full torrent go, allowing her body to shake with grief. Robert had always said she was overly dramatic and he had been right. Robert had always known Madison better than anyone else.

She thought saying his name, even inside her own head, would make the crying worse, but she found her sobs waning the moment she thought of him. Perhaps that wasn't so surprising really. Robert had always made her happy. Even when they were little, he was as much her best friend as he was her big brother. Their parents often told the story of when she came home from the hospital. She had been a perfect baby while the nurses and doctors were around, but the minute they hit the parking lot she started screaming. It was a long ride and everyone was very tense when they arrived home to seven-year-old Robert. She'd opened her eyes, took one look at him and stopped crying for good. She was quiet whenever he was around, and he loved her so much that he was always around.

The tears eventually slowed and then stopped. Eventually she was able to take a quiet, deep breath, though it made her lungs shudder in pain, like the days when she smoked endless cigarettes while she drank the night away. Her eyes cleared enough to take in her surroundings. Autumn had begun and the greens that had been so bright were darkening, deepening the vineyard's charm with their maturity.

The tree was in better shape than it had appeared from a distance. She traced the lines of trunk and branch with her eyes and saw that, while it was gnarled by weather and what must have been a tough life on the mountain, it had deep roots and strong branches. It was a tree that had fought for a life in barren soil, and it was stronger than it looked for the struggle. Madison rubbed the pad of her thumb over the polished-circle necklace in her hand and thought she might take a lesson from this tree. If only she could learn to live like that, to take a few knocks, she wouldn't be crying in its shadow now.

Dry-packed dirt crunched nearby, startling Madison. She looked around, trying to blink her eyes clear and dry.

"I'm sorry." CS's voice was like a cooling salve on her shattered nerves. "I didn't mean to scare you."

Madison pressed the handkerchief to her eyes, feeling CS's approach more than seeing it. She looked up at CS who appeared uncharacteristically hesitant and unsure. She and the horse she led by the reins hovered at a distance from Madison.

"It's okay. I just didn't hear you come up."

"I can go if you want."

"No." Madison rubbed the necklace again, trying to control her tears. "I'm sorry. I should have stayed home."

CS walked forward a few steps, and squatted, bouncing a little on the balls of her feet and leaning her elbows heavily on her knees. She was quiet until Madison looked up at her, then she spoke in a soft voice. "What's wrong?"

Madison held out the necklace and dropped it into CS's extended palm. She studied the necklace for a long moment, flipping it over to look at the other side before saying, "I remember these from my days in California. They were very popular once."

"My brother got it for me when I was thirteen." Madison smiled bitterly at the thought of him in those days. "He took a trip to Tijuana his sophomore year of college—the summer before I started high school."

CS held it back out to her, nodding at it with her chin, perhaps noting how worn the stone was. "It's obviously special to you. To keep it this long."

Madison wrapped the cord around her neck and hooked it without difficulty. "He had a matching one." She waited for CS to respond, and when she didn't, she said in a watery voice, "He died a year ago today."

The horse—Madison recognized her as the preening Violet—nuzzled up to CS's ear, snorting loudly and nudging her with her nose. CS wrapped Violet's reins around a low branch before fishing something out of her pocket and feeding it to her.

The horse munched happily on her treat and CS leaned back against the tree trunk next to Madison and looked off into the field. Madison followed her gaze, happy to not have to look at someone else. CS didn't speak, just stood with her hands in her pockets, letting the silence stretch. It gave Madison space. Space to decide if she wanted to talk about it. Eventually, she decided she did.

"He was my hero. My big brother who did all the clichéd big brother things. He stood up for me when people picked on me and danced with me at weddings. It was just the two of us against Mom and Dad all the time. We were troublemakers, but he always took the blame."

CS nodded, Madison could see it out of the corner of her eye, but she didn't speak, just listened.

"He was seven years older, but he always lived in town, even when he was out on his own. We stayed close. Our parents liked the idea of having kids, but I don't think they actually liked us very much. Our grandmother was warm and loving, but she died when I was very young. It felt like all I ever had was Robert."

Violet tried to wander off, pulling on her lead and making the tree creak. CS reached for the lead, putting just the slightest pressure on it and Violet settled immediately.

Madison dabbed at her eyes with her moist handkerchief. A light blue bandana appeared in front of her.

"Take mine."

Madison held it to her cheeks. Pressed against her face, it smelled like clean cotton and the slightest hint of fresh mint. She held it back out to CS. "Thank you."

"Keep it."

Madison was dabbing at the wetness around her nose when she was nearly pushed over. Violet had wandered around the tree and nudged her face hard against Madison's shoulder. The unexpected movement sent Madison sprawling at CS's feet, as she collapsed into a storm of giggles. Violet nudged at her again while she tried to stand up and CS hurried around the tree to get hold of her bridle.

"Violet!"

"It's okay." Madison stumbled to her feet and walked over to the horse to pet Violet's nose. She turned her liquid black eyes on Madison and they were the eyes of a playful dog. "Her nose is so soft."

"She's just trying to find food."

CS pulled a sugar cube from her pocket and dropped it into Madison's hand. Violet's nostrils fluttered around happily and she gobbled it up, her lips curling around it and tickling her palm.

"She's sweet."

"She's a pig." CS patted the horse's shoulder lovingly. "She'd be too fat to walk if she had her way."

"I always thought horses were scary. They're so big." She looked sheepishly at CS. "I have to confess I'd never met a horse before I came here."

Madison gave Violet one last pat on the nose and settled back into her spot between the roots.

"Oh no. On your feet."

"What?"

CS held out her hand. It was large and calloused in a few places, but looked soft up close. "I'm teaching you to ride."

Madison was all set to refuse. She had the "no" on her tongue all ready to go. Somehow, though, she found herself smiling. She slid her hand into CS's and found that she'd been right, it was soft, but it was also strong as it wrapped carefully around hers. She nodded and CS pulled her to her feet.

Violet was a mass of muscle, but surprisingly gentle. She fidgeted impatiently while CS described the proper way to get into the saddle, but she held still as a statue once Madison slid her foot into the stirrup. CS talked her through every step and never let go of Violet's reins. It wasn't nearly as frightening as Madison thought it would be with CS there to guide her. Before she had a chance to think about Robert again, they were riding down the hill toward the rows of pinot noir, Madison wobbly in the stiff leather of the saddle.

CS led Violet in silence, but that silence was clearly an invitation. Words spilled from Madison. She stroked the necklace at her throat.

"High school was the highlight of Robert's life," Madison began. CS slowed her pace, moving alongside Violet so she could look up at Madison occasionally. "He was popular in that way pretty boys are to young women. He wore those oversized flannel shirts and long bangs like Kurt Cobain. It totally worked for him."

"I miss late-nineties grunge culture," CS replied with a laugh. "It worked just as well for us dykes as it did pretty boys."

Madison had a sudden, vivid mental image of a young CS in baggy clothes and scuffed Doc Martens. She guessed that CS pulled it off as well as Robert had.

"In college he was even more popular. He grew into his lanky body and developed a genuine intellect to go with it. He went to Mexico over spring break and brought me back a woven poncho and this necklace." She ran trembling fingers along the waxed, black cord looped around the flat, open-centered circle of onyx tied on both fraying ends to a cheap metal clasp. "I wear the necklace all the time, but the poncho's long gone."

"You can borrow mine. Most of us nineties kids never grew out of that stuff."

She was trying to make Madison laugh, but it wasn't working. The tears were back, hot on her cheeks. "The last time I saw Robert, we were both wearing our necklaces, drinking heavily, dancing in a downtown club, harmlessly checking out the same women and laughing about how Robert's ex-wife and my soon-to-be television star girlfriend would roll their eyes at our antics."

For a moment Madison thought CS was going to reach out, her hand seemed to hover as if to offer solace. She didn't reach out, though she did move closer. Each time Violet stepped on her left side, Madison slid a little in the saddle and sometimes her knee brushed against the denim of CS's shirt. She never touched anything solid, but the heat of her body was close and somehow comforting.

"He overdosed. Probably heroin, but he had a lot of drugs in his system. His roommate found him in bed. Thought he'd overslept for work but couldn't wake him up." Madison heard in her own voice the child Robert always allowed her to be. "I didn't even know he used."

The more she spoke, the farther away the tears felt. She felt lighter than she had in months. Twelve months to be exact. She'd talked to people about Robert, of course. Kacey, Jada, his ex-wife who wept about how she still loved him and always thought they'd work it out one day. No one had just listened like this. No one had let her tell the story without question or surprise. She probably should've gone to a therapist. That's what this felt like, telling her deepest secrets to a nonjudgmental stranger.

"I feel like I lost the person I knew best in the world and found out I didn't know him at all. I hate him for that and I hate myself for hating him."

Still CS didn't say anything, but she didn't need to. Madison could never have told anyone close how angry she was with Robert. She needed the anonymity of this superficial relationship to allow that honesty. That she mourned him and felt betrayed by him too. That she felt guilty for every night they went out partying together, and there were a lot of those nights. She'd never used drugs and never seen him use, but they drank hard enough and did things neither of them was proud of. Madison couldn't count the number of times she woke up in some stranger's bed after a night out with Robert. Hell, that's how she ended up in Kacey's bed. When had he taken it farther than that? When he divorced? When he went to Tijuana at twenty years old? Could she have pulled him back from that brink if she'd known?

She probably should have known. After he died, she could see the warning signs. That meant she should have seen them when he was alive, but of course she was so wasted she wouldn't have. One of the more frightening aspects of it all was how close she had come to the same fate. It hadn't scared her totally sober, but it was enough to make her careful. A turn of events that Kacey didn't like at all. They'd partied hard together the first two years. Kacey wasn't ready to give the lifestyle up yet, but then she'd never gotten a phone call from the police like Madison had.

They'd arrived at the stables without Madison realizing they were heading there. She'd been quiet for a long time, but this silence with CS felt comfortable. If it weren't for the ache in her back and thighs, she might've thought they'd just met under the tree a moment ago.

"Thanks for the lift, Violet," Madison said. She turned to CS, something like concern in her gaze. "Thanks for the lesson."

"Any time."

"And for listening."

This time she said it more slowly and more earnestly, "Any time."

CHAPTER THIRTEEN

The heat was finally dying off, making Madison's walk through the vines much more comfortable than even just a week ago. September was about to give way to October, and Madison was thinking she could make a walk part of her daily routine. If the breeze blew gently like this and the air stayed this thin, she could enjoy the view without sweating through her clothes.

The landscape was becoming more beautiful every day. The grapes seemed to have swollen overnight, and harvest had to be soon. Reaching out to touch the fruit, she was surprised how heavy they were. The skins felt like leather, firm and unyielding.

The sun on this side of the mountain was unencumbered. When she crested the hill, leaving the main building behind, all she could see were grapes and more grapes. At the very limit of her vision was a small building that looked like her cottage, only slightly less grand, but it was the only man-made structure in sight.

The sign at the end of the row labeled this patch as chardonnay, and the fruit was a vibrant yellow-green. As she watched, a cloud crossed quickly across the sun and then moved on.

Madison saw the usual lavender and mint, though the mint was thinner here. Purple flowers swayed in the breeze, the lightest stalks anchoring them to the rocky earth. She reached out and grabbed a fistful, ripping at the greenery. She held the fistful of flowers to her nose and breathed deeply. A contented sigh escaped her lips before she could stop it. She kept her eyes closed and her senses open.

"Feel free to take all you like." The familiar, husky voice made her eyes shoot open, but Madison didn't have to look up to know it was CS. "The mint too. They grow like weeds."

"Th…thank you."

Madison scrambled to stand, but her movements were lumbering and awkward. When she did reach vertical, she couldn't move as pins and needles burst across her foot and calf. She had to do a funny little hop to readjust her weight so she wouldn't fall before her leg returned to normal.

She knew she looked foolish, hopping around on one foot, but CS wasn't looking. Her focus was locked on a bunch of grapes hanging on the opposite row, giving Madison time to look at her. She wore the same work clothes as always, worn jeans, scuffed boots, and a thin, short-sleeve Henley shirt the color of Arizona limestone. Still, there was something different about the set of her shoulders and the muscles of her jaw. Usually she looked like she was chewing on rocks—today she just looked more disinterested than surly. Madison wondered if CS had warmed to her after the riding lesson last week. She had been unquestionably kind to listen to Madison's story, but then she seemed prone to silence.

After inspecting the cluster of grapes minutely, testing their weight and squeezing them gently, CS plucked one and held it to her nose. She squeezed until a bead of juice formed at the stem, spilling over the side of the skin and down to CS's dry fingertips.

She stood abruptly, ignoring Madison. She held the grape up to the sunlight, then bit into it, spat the contents on the ground and tossed the remaining grape half with it. She rubbed her hands together, smearing the stickiness over her palms where it stuck to the loose dirt, leaving little reddish-brown smears.

"Not yet."

Madison couldn't help herself. "What are you doing?"

CS turned her bright blue eyes to Madison, who found her instinct to wither under that glare trumped by her curiosity.

"Checking the grapes."

"Are they still grapes?"

The quip was out of her mouth before Madison could stop and think. CS just stared at her silently for a moment while Madison held her breath, waiting for a rebuke. One corner of CS's mouth went up in a smirk. The smile showed a single, sharp white tooth and made her look like a grinning cat.

"Still grapes."

Madison swallowed hard. "That's lucky."

CS took a few steps forward, slapping her sticky hand on her jeans. A little puff of dust came off them. She marched right at Madison, who stood perfectly still. The image of CS as a grinning tiger was harder to shake now that she was stalking toward Madison. When she was only a few steps away, she veered off sharply, heading toward the vines at Madison's back.

"I'm checking the sugar content."

CS passed over the obvious bunch, the one that Madison had held, and instead reached for one tucked away inside the leaves. It looked smaller, but the berries were plumper. Madison turned to watch her, bending close to the grapes like CS did.

"Why is that important?"

"They'll tell me when to harvest." She dropped the bunch without removing a grape and moved on down the row, her eyes on the fruit, and Madison hurried to follow as she continued, "The sugar is what turns into alcohol when they ferment."

"So the more sugar, the stronger the wine?"

"The more sugar, the more concentrated the flavor. If it rains too much and the grapes swell with water, it dilutes the sugar and the flavor. If it doesn't rain enough, the wine ends up too sweet with the same alcohol content."

"So you taste the grapes to see if they're sweet?"

"Most winemakers use a handheld monitor when they know harvest time is close. It gives the exact composition of the grapes."

"Not you?"

CS shook her head, stopping to inspect another bunch. "I'm old-school."

"What do you use to test?"

She dropped the grapes, letting them swing freely in the cooling air of late afternoon, and stuck out her tongue. She pointed to it and smirked before explaining, "Machines don't drink wine—people do. I need to know what the grapes taste like, not their chemical composition."

"But won't the science help with your wine?"

"You can use math and science to make wine, and it'll be drinkable. Or you can use your heart to make it and it will be divine."

The poetry of her words surprised Madison, not least of which because CS had barely spoken a full sentence to her before this. Madison found herself relaxing in CS's presence after the explanation.

"It's like your pottery," CS said, shooting Madison a quick glance and then heading off up the row again. "There's math and science involved in what you do. Angles and composition of clay. Things you have to know to do what you do, but there's more to it than that."

They crossed a path deeply grooved with the marks of horseshoes and heavily laden cartwheels.

"I guess you're right. I had to learn all those basics in school."

"I can tell by looking at your work that the science is subservient to the art."

They started uphill, moving through the vines back toward the center of the estate.

"You've seen my work?"

"You sell it in my store."

"Oh, right."

For some reason, Madison felt self-conscious with the thought that CS had seen her work without her there to describe the pieces. She liked to see a person's reaction when they first looked at her pots. Especially someone she knew.

"When there's anything left, of course." CS stopped at a new row, checking the setting sun over her shoulder before turning her attention back to the grapes. "It's selling well."

They walked for a long time without speaking. Madison was surprised how much she enjoyed the silence. She didn't have much quiet in her life. Kacey never remained silent for long. The same was true of Jada and even of her budding friendship with Boots. None of them were the type to enjoy quiet.

When they passed out of their row, Madison assumed CS would use the road as an excuse to part company if she wanted to. She didn't seem to, only pausing briefly to pull a small, spiral-bound notebook from her back pocket and jot down a quick note before moving into the new area. The grapes here were different. Darker and larger with a different shade of leaf.

"It's beautiful here," Madison said when CS stopped to taste another grape. "The light is incredible. The red grapes have this way of sucking up all the light around them, they're so dark."

"You should see them when they're ripe." CS stood and came over to her, standing close enough that Madison could smell her sweat mixed with the herbal haze of the air. "These are pinot noir. By the time we harvest, the skins will be the darkest purple you've ever seen. Almost black."

There was a far-off misty look in CS's eyes. Like she was talking about a lover she would never stop aching for. The person Madison found intimidating, cold and unfriendly was nowhere to be seen today. Not on a day when harvest was so near and she could talk about her grapes. It was charming in a misanthropic kind of way. Madison smiled despite herself.

CS snapped out of her reverie quickly, moving past Madison down the row. She slowed, turning her head to allow Madison to catch up. They walked side by side, not looking at each other but wrapped again in companionable silence. Madison's fingers itched to move her hands, so she snatched a sprig of lavender from her back pocket and spun it between her fingers. When she looked up she realized they'd arrived at the main building and CS turned to her, hands deep in her pockets and avoiding Madison's gaze.

"Have you taken a winery tour yet?"

The truth seemed like an insult, but she had no choice but to tell it. "No, I haven't."

"Seriously? People pay a lot of money to stay here and do tours. You've lived here two months now and you haven't?"

"Seven weeks."

"Too long."

Madison shrugged, but she took a step forward. "I don't want to bother anyone."

CS gestured with a jerk of her head down a path leading behind the building and started to walk that way herself.

"I'll give you a special tour. Even include a barrel tasting."

Madison held her place for exactly three seconds before hurrying to catch up with CS.

CHAPTER FOURTEEN

Madison had no idea until today that the entirety of the winery was located down below the hotel and restaurants. Under a small, unobtrusive shelter beside the loading bay was a massive machine that was the first stop for newly harvested grapes. CS glossed over the process of turning the crushed grapes into wine without getting too technical. She took Madison past the fermentation tanks with only the briefest explanation of yeast propagation and sugars converting to alcohol. The tanks were huge, shining aluminum and currently empty, awaiting this year's harvest.

The bottling room had boxes of empty bottles stacked in one corner, much smaller boxes full of corks in the other. CS went off on a brief tangent about how she only used natural cork, eschewing the modern trend of plastic corks or, shuddering as she said it, screw tops. Madison chose not to reveal that she preferred the ease of the latter, but something in the glint of CS's eye said she already knew yet did not judge.

It was cramped, and Madison's arm inadvertently brushed against CS's as they headed for the door. She tried not to linger on the moment, but Madison had not felt so warm all day as she did when CS's skin brushed against hers. She didn't seem to be alone. They both froze awkwardly and tried to get the other to pass. CS eventually rushed out the door first, explaining hurriedly that bottling was done off site.

Madison took a deep breath, forcing herself to listen to the words rather than the hum of her skin. After passing through a room full of empty barrels and an intricate pulley system for lowering them down into the barrel room, they started down the winding stairs.

The temperature in the barrel room was surprisingly mild. They entered from a spiral staircase set into one corner. It was a long way down—at least two or three flights—and Madison took them slowly.

"It's like the warehouse at the end of Indiana Jones," Madison said as she wandered into the room, waiting for CS to take the lead. "All I can see is racks of barrels to the ceiling."

"You won't find the Ark down here."

CS stepped ahead of her at a brisk pace along an obviously well-worn path. Madison had the sense that CS traveled these halls every day. This was her place in every way, and she was quietly proud of it. She didn't brag about her success, didn't regale Madison with the winery's accolades, just explained its workings and the process of making wine.

"It's actually kind of warm in here," Madison said, taking the shawl off her shoulders and folding it over her arm as they turned a corner and went down a new row flanked by barrels on either side. "I thought it would be colder."

"We take advantage of geothermal regulation. If you go deep enough underground, there's a constant temperature year round."

Madison looked up as they walked. The barrels were on their side in nothing more than a giant wine rack like the one on her counter at home. They were stacked well over her head, at least six high, with the ceiling a few feet above that. She wondered how deep underground they were.

CS turned another corner and stopped in a small open space. "The wine needs a consistent temperature as it ages.

Most wineries use cellar storage—we just took the concept a little deeper."

They stood in a nook flanked on all sides by tall racks of barrels. A single pendulum light lit the bedroom-sized space with a warm, orange glow.

"May I?"

CS held out her hand, and Madison wasn't sure what she wanted. She blinked a couple of times as CS reached for the shawl she had tossed over her arm.

"Oh. Sure."

CS spread the shawl over the top of one of the upright barrels. She patted the top and then turned, busying herself with another barrel. Madison hopped up onto her barrel, the shawl providing a splinter-free seat, and let her legs swing.

"The barrels here look different."

"They are different," CS said, rummaging in a box of glasses. "This is a special wine I'm making. A winemaker's blend."

CS set a pair of balloon wineglasses on the barrel beside Madison and held up an odd glass instrument. There was a long tube on one end, about the width of a broom handle, that bent and expanded at the other end into a cylindrical bubble. CS set it down next to the glasses and then picked up a rubber mallet.

"I can only assume you intend to kill me down here, but I don't think those are the most efficient tools for the job," Madison teased.

CS shook her head and gave a wooden plug set in the top of the barrel a sharp upward smack and wiggled the plug out. She gave the plug a sniff and placed it, red-stained side up, on the end of the barrel.

Picking up the glass instrument, CS tested the weight in her hands. "Definitely not. Besides this was expensive."

"What is it?"

"A barrel thief." She held her thumb over a small hole on the bulb end and inserted the long straw into the barrel. "It pulls a sample of wine out of the barrel for a tasting."

Madison didn't really hear the explanation. The moment the plug came off the barrel, a familiar smell filled the room. She felt the heat of the summer sun filtering through leaves of thin trees first, then she smelled that heavenly scent. Old books, oranges and sweet black cherries. There was a depth to it that she hadn't smelled that day, and whether it was the distance the wind carried it or the extra weeks in the barrel, Madison wasn't sure. There was something new, almost like a fine cigar. Her mouth watered at the combination.

She craved a taste of that wine. She'd thought about it more than once since that day in the clearing. She leaned precariously forward on the barrel in anticipation.

CS didn't notice her excitement. Once she released her thumb, a gush of deep red wine sprang into the bulb and began to slowly fill it. It bubbled thickly in the clear glass. CS didn't wait for the bulb to fill, but slid her thumb back over the hole and withdrew the straw from the barrel. She pressed the plug back into place before she filled their glasses with a few quick movements.

"The wine's not done, you understand. It needs more time to age, but it's getting close."

"How long?"

CS handed Madison one of the glasses and held the other up to the light, tilting it slightly and swirling it to check the color. She brought it to her nose and breathed deeply, her eyes unfocused.

"It's been in the barrel for a year now. I've done one mix, but it might require another. Hard to say. It may be another year before it's ready to bottle."

Madison held the glass to her nose—a perfect perfume. She forced herself to wait, not taste it until CS did.

"That's a long time."

"It'll be worth the wait," CS said, her voice silk, her eyes liquid with longing as she stared at her wine.

"You're remarkably patient. To have this incredible wine at your fingertips and not drink it too soon. What if something happens and you lose it? That would haunt me. I would definitely not be patient enough."

"It's in my nature to be patient."

CS tipped back the glass, sipping delicately. Madison's anticipation got the better of her and her taste was far less delicate. It felt like heavy cream on her tongue, rolling over her teeth and making her jaw ache pleasantly.

"My god, it's even better than I thought it would be."

Maybe it was something in the way she said the words that made CS look at her twice. "You knew about my blend?"

Madison couldn't look at CS. "In the summer I went for a walk and I saw…I'm sorry, I wasn't trying to pry. I saw you at a grave in the woods and you were drinking this. I could smell it all the way into the woods. I'm so sorry I intruded."

CS was quiet for a long time, holding the glass close to her lips and looking hard at Madison, who failed to avoid her eye. After what felt like hours, she asked, "You could smell the wine that far away?"

Madison nodded. Another age of silence passed. CS's eyes burned through her.

"It's my father's grave. He died here on the vineyard because he didn't want to waste away from cancer in Beverly Hills. He wanted to spend the end of his life here with his daughter and her wine. That's what he said." She swirled her glass again, watching the wine spin and dance. "His daughter and her wine."

Madison didn't know what to say. CS took another sip of her wine, and Madison jumped at both the distraction and the opportunity to taste it again. The second taste was even better than the first. Like well-seasoned food, each taste brought a new depth of flavor.

"This really is amazing, CS. It's the best wine I've ever had. By far."

CS tipped her glass back, letting the wine flow past her lips. After a long moment, she looked directly at Madison and said, in a low, even voice, "Almost."

A warmth flowed through Madison all the way to the tips of her toes that she told herself firmly was a result of the wine. She sipped, but didn't look away. The longer she spent with CS, the more compelling Madison found her. Her quiet consistency, the smoky tone of her voice and most of all her eyes. Those eyes that seemed to glow with something Madison couldn't quite name.

She forced herself to look away. She pushed her mind out of the dark, recessed corner of the barrel room and up through several floors to the restaurant where her girlfriend was working right now. The girlfriend she loved and had a future with.

With a lazy smile, CS drained her glass. "Almost ready. Another six months maybe and I'll do a final mix before bottling."

"Do you decide all on your own or is there someone who helps with the blend?"

"Just my dad. I talk everything over with him. He doesn't talk back much these days though." CS stopped to smile again in that crooked way she had. "It's why I'm such a good conversationalist."

Madison slipped down off the barrel. "I shouldn't have watched that day. Sorry I butted in."

"I butted in when you were spending time with your brother."

"I'm glad you did. I thought that day would be unbearable, but it wasn't."

"It gets easier." CS stared at the barrel plug, scratching her chin. She came to a decision and turned back to Madison. "Want another glass?"

Madison fully intended to decline, but when she opened her mouth, the word that came out was, "Sure."

CS drew another glass for each of them from the barrel. She held hers out and Madison clinked her glass against it. The gentle ping of their meeting echoed to the high ceiling.

"What are we drinking to?"

"I don't know," CS said, leaning back against a barrel with a sigh. "I guess to the important men in our lives. The ones we've lost."

Madison's smile was bittersweet, but it was genuine. "I wonder when losing them will stop hurting."

"If you find out, let me know."

"Here I thought you'd have all the answers."

"I am older, I should be wiser. Sorry to disappoint."

"You aren't that much older."

"Definitely not that much wiser."

Their laughter was soft when it echoed in their glasses. CS started cleaning up. "I'm sorry to keep you from your work. It isn't very often I have time to give a tour."

"I enjoyed it," Madison said, retrieving her shawl from the barrel. "But I probably should be getting home."

CS walked her as far as the exit of the barrel room, but didn't go back outside. She was quiet again, but Madison was starting to recognize the silence wasn't because she was unkind. What it was, she couldn't quite name, since CS seemed to have few problems chatting with the staff. Madison wondered about it all the way home, forcing herself not to think of the brush of CS's arm against hers in the bottling room.

CHAPTER FIFTEEN

Two months to the day after moving across the country, Madison and Kacey had their first lazy morning together in their new home. Kacey had been so focused on establishing the restaurant she rarely stayed home this late into the day. They'd woken up late together and lain in bed for almost an hour, sharing their impressions of their new location and making plans for their next day off. Madison wanted to make a special dinner but Kacey wanted to go out—drive into Portland and get away from the winery.

"I think I'm getting stir crazy," she said, drawing circles around her bare navel and staring at the ceiling. "I might've made a mistake bringing us here."

"Not at all," Madison said, rolling over to pull Kacey close. "This place is wonderful and you finally have the restaurant you deserve."

"We don't have to live here to run the restaurant. Anna lives in Dundee. It's not that much of a town, but at least it's a town."

"Who's Anna?"

"My sous chef."

"Right. I forgot." How could she have forgotten Anna? A lanky brunette Amazon with a killer smile and the knife skills of a Russian assassin. Not exactly a woman one would want working so closely with their girlfriend.

"There's a bunch of the staff living in town." She sounded sheepish rather than her usual cockiness. "We could swing it."

They could, of course. They could get a little place with the money Kacey made. Her salary was still good, even without living rent-free. It would be just that, though—little. Supplemented with the modest income from Madison's pottery sales, their options were limited. Limited to a choice between this beautiful place with room for her studio or a place where she'd have to get a job and a car and wouldn't have anywhere for her wheel and kiln.

"We couldn't really, could we?" Kacey asked.

Thank god she'd said it, because Madison already felt guilty enough. "But we can make this place work. It's great and you don't have to worry about traffic or a long commute. Besides, it's so beautiful here."

Kacey finally tore her eyes off the ceiling, propping herself up on an elbow. "I miss takeout and bars and sexy strangers on the bus." Her voice had a visceral ache to it that surprised Madison. It had only been two months. "Aren't you tired of seeing the same people every day?"

Madison tried to laugh it off, putting on a flirty demeanor and tapping her fingernail against Kacey's chin. "I can be a sexy stranger for you."

A predatory gleam brightened Kacey's eye and she pounced, covering Madison with kisses and making her giggle. It didn't last, though. Kacey hopped out of bed, leaving Madison with her lips still puckered and the laughter trickling out of her.

Heading into the bathroom, Kacey said over her shoulder, "Did I tell you we're booked solid for a month? We're starting a wait list for reservations."

"That's great."

Kacey continued as though Madison hadn't said a word. "We were letting the hotel and cottage guests book for the evening they checked in, but we've stopped that now. Let them eat at the hotel restaurant. *ambrosia's* too good to be a given part of their vacation if they haven't booked a long time ahead."

While Kacey showered, Madison escaped downstairs to cook for them. Apparently she had even less time than she'd thought, because Kacey took her panini to go, having rushed out to work with a joke about leaving before she was roped into doing the dishes.

Madison considered whether she did miss those things Kacey valued so highly. She had no interest in sexy strangers, on buses or otherwise. Madison liked to cook too much to miss takeout and she had no interest in bars. No, there was nothing about city life that she couldn't do without if it meant more time with her ceramics and Kacey. That revelation was surprising, given her familiarity with city life. But then, people change and Madison had done her fair share of changing.

Grabbing a fresh cup of coffee, she headed for the living room, some vague notion of spending time on that glorious deck directing her steps. Her deck, however, was under invasion. Boots smiled at her as he climbed the stairs, giving her a friendly wave. Madison motioned for him to come inside, but he was already opening the front door.

He poked his head in and called, "Can I come in?"

"Since you already have, I suppose I'll grant permission," Madison answered, the sight of him filling her with his infectious energy. "Coffee?"

"I guess it's early enough," he answered, pulling the door shut behind him and wiping his boots on the mat. "Cream and sugar?"

"Coming right up."

Boots carried a pair of bulging canvas shopping bags which he unloaded into the fridge and pantry. Madison watched him curiously.

"Am I putting things in the wrong place?"

"That depends. You know you're not in your own house, right?"

"Yep." He tossed a box of sugar-laden cereal at her and swapped the nearly empty milk bottle for a fresh one.

Madison looked at the cereal. It was the sort of thing with fruity flakes and marshmallows that she hadn't eaten since grade school. It was also Kacey's favorite.

After he unloaded a few more staples, Madison finally asked, "Why are you putting away my groceries?"

"I have a load of clay that was just delivered for you, I figured you'd feel obligated to help unload it if I put away your girlfriend's cereal."

"Boots!"

She didn't mean to stomp her foot, but he was just so aggravating.

"Okay. Okay. Calm down, Denver." He grinned at her, pleased with his teasing. "I guess I can handle it myself."

"You don't have to put them away. I can do that. You did the shopping, that's the least I can do."

She traded his coffee for the remaining grocery bag and he made himself comfortable while she unpacked it.

Madison laughed, shoving the cereal box into a cabinet with crackers and cans of tuna. "I can't believe she still eats this stuff. I've been trying for years to get her to grow up. Hasn't worked yet."

"How many years?"

"Three."

"I'd say you're stuck with her the way she is then."

Madison turned, tossing the empty bag back to Boots. "Fine by me."

"How'd you kids end up together?"

That was a story she was not going to tell. It took her years to confess the sordid details to Jada, and Madison still didn't know if she'd been disgusted or impressed. Boots would get the edited version.

"In college." It was true in a manner of speaking. Madison had been in college. Kacey had been in culinary school. They just hadn't exactly met in a lecture hall. "How about you? Got anyone special hidden in your apartment?"

"Just a nice pair of Lucchese crocodile skins." He winked at her and waggled his dusty work boot. "There's a reason they call me Boots."

His charm reminded her so much of Robert that a sharp sting went straight through her chest. She forced herself to ignore it. "Nothing between you and the cute girl with the undercut?"

"MMA?" He laughed into his coffee cup. "She'd kick my ass. So would The Gatekeeper."

"Oh. It's like that."

"Yep. This place has love pouring out of the earth just as much as wine. Lucky me, I haven't been infected yet." He stood, sliding his empty cup across the counter to her. "Thanks for the coffee. Let me know by next Friday if you want different cereal in your next grocery delivery."

"There's no way I'll change her mind. Can I get my clay? I've been dying to work."

"Only if you help me unload it."

"Fine, but next time you put all the groceries away."

CHAPTER SIXTEEN

The clay took so long to unload that it was the next day before Madison had a chance to get back to work. It was a larger delivery than before and Boots certainly let her know how much he disapproved. She needed every scrap of it though. Her work was selling faster than she could make it. She'd seriously underestimated the interest of the winery guests and sold out her inventory within a week. Considering that it took close to that long to go from raw clay to finished product, she struggled to restock. Any time she walked the grounds near the main building, Madison would see the shopkeeper looking pleadingly at her. The look wouldn't disappear until she delivered another crate of merchandise.

That look was what kept her wheel spinning all afternoon today, making the same small pot over and over again. It was the best seller and she enjoyed the shape, a cylinder that she expanded to a round, squat belly and a scalloped lip. It was a simple piece, but the proportions were pleasant and, once glazed and fired, it fit perfectly in cupped hands.

The mudroom shelf was loaded down with pieces in various stages of drying. The only empty shelf was the lowest one meant for her larger gallery pieces. All she'd made for two weeks were things for the shop.

Seeing the empty shelf took the energy right out of her. Her working hours were done for today. She needed some time away to remind herself that the more she sold, the more proof of her status as a working artist. She just wished it left her more time to do what she loved.

Dumping her bucket carefully into the mudroom sink, exhaustion washed over Madison. The sun was high overhead and she had been in her studio since dawn. With all the noise outside sleep was harder to come by these days, so she was getting up early to start work.

Madison gravitated back to her studio. It wasn't the wheel that called her, but the light. Normally bright and clear, her studio today was suffused with an otherworldly glow. A fine film of reddish dust covered the windows, tinting the sunlight. Everything glowed faintly red. It was like standing on Mars.

Madison moved over to the windows, leaning against the frame to look out. The harvest was in full swing. There had been no advance warning. No signs or announcement. She just woke up this morning to a small army of young men and women with baskets on their backs and curved little knives in hand descending on the rows. They moved across the fields in a tight pack all day, moving as a swarm through the vineyard, accompanied by a line of horse-drawn carts that were much cruder than those that ferried visitors around.

Now the swarm was right outside the cottage, working their way through the pinot noir vines. The purple grapes that Madison watched grow and ripen all summer disappeared. The pickers were in constant motion as they harvested, slicing off the bunches with their sickled knives and tossing them over their shoulders into the waiting baskets worn like open backpacks. It was mesmerizing to watch. Their movements were like a perfectly choreographed dance. A tango so precise the movements seemed automatic.

The serenity of the scene was broken by a horse trotting swiftly up the lane from the main gate. CS sat stiff-backed in Violet's saddle, her legs wrapped firmly around the horse's sweating flanks. She rode up to the cart just as a worker came over, swung the large basket off his back and emptied it into a wooden crate.

CS swung down off the horse to speak to the man. He mopped his brow with a dingy blue bandana while they spoke. His T-shirt was soaked through and his shoulders drooped. CS gestured off to the shadow of the cart and took the basket from him with her free hand. He dropped gratefully to the ground in the shade of the cart and draped the bandana over his face.

Madison could feel the heat of the sun through the studio's tinted windows. All the workers were shimmering with perspiration. The intermittent breeze picked up little swirling dust devils of bone-dry earth. It was early October, but still uncomfortably hot for manual labor.

Boots, always bright and cheerful no matter how tired or hot, came jogging down a row, dodging workers as he went. He moved with more alacrity than anyone else, but Madison noticed that he was the only one in the field not wearing a basket. He ran straight up to CS, who handed over Violet's reins before his feet even stopped moving. She spoke a few quick words to him, slipping the basket over her shoulders. The man on the ground held out his curved knife, but she already had her own out of the sheath attached to her belt. Just like that she was walking toward the vines, taking her place among the harvesters.

When Boots passed close to the studio, he waved at Madison and mouthed a hello. She waved back absently, choosing instead to watch CS move into the swarm of workers. She fell in perfectly with them, her movements just as precise as those around her. Her wrist snapped and a bunch fell into her waiting hand. She tossed it in a perfect arc over her shoulder, not even bothering to see that it fell in place. She was already on to the next clump before Madison saw the basket settle under the weight of the first.

It seemed CS was full of surprises. Madison hadn't expected to see her out there laboring. She'd already seen enough to suggest CS was obsessed with her vineyard. Madison had sought out CS every day since the wine tour. She'd had such a good time, and she wanted to express her gratitude, but was never able to pin CS down. The few times she did catch sight of CS, it was from afar. She was always working, either in her office or in the stable at the bottom of the hill. The more she saw CS's determination, the more she was impressed with her drive.

Madison walked the fields every day. Part of her hoped that she would run into CS, though she wasn't quite ready to admit that was the reason. She couldn't work out in her heart whether she was drawn to the vineyard or to the winemaker, but she couldn't seem to get either out of her head. Even as the days with Kacey improved, more relaxed now that she'd worked into a successful routine, Madison thought about how she was captured by CS's eyes. It was the magic of the barrel room, of course, the new sights and the enchanting wine, but it had stuck with her.

More fascinating was the beauty of the vineyard. The sloping hills and plump grapes. The way the trellises ran in perfect rows along the landscape, accentuating its features. The smell of growing things and the sound of horses hooves clopping along in the distance. The clarity of the air. If there was any woman who would turn Madison's eye from Kacey, it was Minerva.

A thump and groan from behind made Madison jump in surprise. She'd been so mesmerized watching CS work her way through the vines, she hadn't heard Kacey get up. She turned now to see her girlfriend, tousle-haired and bleary eyed, standing in the doorway in a threadbare white undershirt and plaid boxers.

"Hey."

The gravelly, sleepy voice made Madison's heart beat a little faster and her fingertips tingle. "Hey yourself."

"What time is it?"

"Eleven."

"Shit. I'm gonna be late as hell."

Madison walked across the room, wrapping her arms around Kacey's neck and kissing her gently on the lips. "Didn't sleep well?"

"Not with this going on," she said, waving her hand at the window. The closer Madison pressed her body to Kacey, the more clarity she saw in her girlfriend's eyes. "You got up early."

"Couldn't sleep."

"It's so loud. The dust is killing my sinuses."

"I don't know," Madison smiled and pressed their foreheads together, "it's nice to have a little activity. It's so quiet here normally. I bet the guests are loving it."

Kacey slipped out of her arms, dropping a kiss on her forehead as she passed, and went to scowl at the windows. "They won't like it when they notice the entire patio is covered in red dirt. It'll take hours to clean up enough for me to serve a decent meal."

"I'm sure it'll be fine."

"Yeah." Kacey stormed back through the kitchen and headed for the stairs. Madison followed her as far as the coffeepot. "I need to get up there or tonight'll be a disaster."

"Don't forget Jada's coming for the day. She should be here any minute."

"I've already got a table booked for you two," she shouted down from the top of the loft. "I can send someone over to clean the windows in the studio if you want."

"No, definitely not," Madison called back, noticing the same red sheen on the kitchen window. "I like the light."

The only response she got was the pound of water against the glass shower door.

CHAPTER SEVENTEEN

Jada arrived not long after Kacey had scurried out, her hair still wet. Boots delivered her, helping her down from the carriage like a princess arriving for a ball. Jada had the confidence to command any space she walked into and, if the dazzled smile in Boots' eyes was any judge, any person in said space. He hurried back to the harvest but looked over his shoulder more than once at the pair of them hugging their hellos on the deck. The dust cloud had moved off with the workers as they'd made their way down the hill, but Madison took Jada inside in deference to her expensive outfit.

Jada's eyebrows arched as they scanned the massive stone fireplace and highly polished bamboo floor. The perfect bow of her mouth twitched up noticeably as she took in the exposed beams of the ceiling and the mismatched pillars, one supporting the corner of the loft, the other stretching up to the central ceiling beam.

Her real reaction was reserved for the wall of windows looking out onto the sun, over the bare grapevines and the hint of brightly colored roof tiles of the stable. Jana gave a low, long whistle as she scanned the horizon. The view still brought Madison up short, even after all these months—the grandeur of the mountains and the almost limitless sky above them.

"If I were you, I could get used to this," Jada said as she turned from the windows and hooked an arm through Madison's. "But there'll be time for this later. Let's see them."

Madison hopped and pulled her up the stairs. Madison had set up the loft as a mini-showroom since her studio was too small to display her work.

"I take back everything I said over Skype. These aren't really good. They're breathtaking."

Jada had always been prone to exaggeration, but this time, Madison agreed with her, so she accepted the compliment. "I really like them."

Jada knelt, quite a feat in her skintight leather miniskirt, to study one of the taller vases. She touched the piece delicately, almost hesitantly, after which her hands roamed freely over the vase, one that Madison had only finished glazing yesterday and her favorite.

"This relief work is new. I haven't seen anything like it from you before."

"I've been trying to stretch since I've been here."

"It's working," Jada said, carefully turning the piece.

The vase was nearly three feet tall and two feet at its widest. She'd had to fire it all by itself and even then it barely fit in the kiln. The relief work had taken two full workdays. Days when she did not leave her studio except to eat and sleep. Days when Kacey scowled almost as hard at the pottery as she did the potter when the coffeepot was empty and her bowl of cereal her only company.

"I started on it just after the restaurant opened. It was the first gallery piece I finished in my new studio."

"If this is just the start, I'm excited to see the future." Jada struggled to stand, her knees groaning at the effort, and looked around the loft. "These are the best work you've ever done."

Despite the compliment, her friend didn't shift her focus to Madison. She wandered around the bright space, going from one piece to another, examining them with a mercantile eye.

There were about a dozen pots, ranging in size from a delicate, ornate bowl that fit into her cupped hands like a baby bird to the vase Jada just finished admiring.

"You know, Maddie," Jada turned to her with a smile bursting with pride, "it feels like you've turned a corner."

"You think so?"

"Absolutely. Your work..." She turned a loving eye back to the first vase. "It's shifted to another level. I've never seen anything like this from you."

Madison smiled so hard she felt tears form in her eyes. "It feels better too, you know? I feel like something woke up inside me when I came here."

They left the makeshift gallery and headed to the kitchen for coffee—Jada had brought three bags of beans from her old coffee shop in Denver—and Madison explained Minerva Hills. The way there were no cars allowed, though she had been careful to warn Jada of this before she came to visit for the day. The way there was so little sound this far from the main building. The lavender and the mint. The horses. The trees in the distance and the smell of boxwoods lining the perimeter.

She stopped short of telling Jada about the spot on the vineyard that truly spoke to her. The little copse of trees and the clearing inside it. The way the light filtered through the leaves and sometimes, if she stood in just the right spot, came alive the way it had when she was a child. Madison hadn't found that spot again, not since watching CS at her father's grave, but she'd gone back often to try. She left each time with a deeper love of the trees and the solitude.

They took their coffee into the living room to talk. Jada slipped onto the chaise, holding her steaming mug high in the air as, with a long sigh of relief, she kicked off her shoes and wriggled her stocking-clad toes. Madison curled onto the cushion beside her, tucking her bare feet underneath her and resting her cheek on the heel of her hand. She watched Jada take in the magnificent view.

"No wonder you're making your best work," Jada said with a quiet reverence. "This place would inspire anyone. So peaceful. So beautiful."

Madison hated to tear her eyes away from the windows, but she could see this view any time and Jada would only be here for a few hours. When she finally looked over, Jada was watching her.

"I love it here. There's something in the energy of this place." She turned back to the windows, as much to avoid the questions in Jada's eyes as to take in the landscape she'd grown to love so much. "I've never felt like this before."

Jada gave her a long, quiet moment before asking, in the calm, motherly tone she sometimes used, "Do you think you two'll be settling down here?"

"Oh yes." She sipped her coffee before admitting, "Kacey isn't as thrilled as I am, but she'll get used to it."

"Will she? I've never known Kacey to accept something she doesn't like. She usually tries to change it instead."

"Then it's a good thing she gets to build the restaurant herself. She can change that if it doesn't feel right."

"I wasn't talking about the restaurant." Jada reached out a gentle finger and turned Madison's chin to face her. "It sounds like you don't get to see each other much. Are you okay with that?"

Madison forced herself not to turn away, but she used her coffee cup to cover Jada's knowing eyes from seeing too much. What was she supposed to do? Force Kacey to stay away from her life's dream because Madison wanted more time with her? That wouldn't be fair, but it also wasn't exactly what Madison wanted. She sipped her coffee and tried to decide how much to tell Jada.

"I don't mind the time alone," she said when she couldn't delay any longer. "I've been exploring the vineyard and working. It's been nice."

She didn't mention the growing friendship with Boots or the growing fascination with CS. Sticking to the lure of the winery was honest enough for now. The rest she had to figure out on her own.

"Sure, time alone is good." The purr in Jada's voice showed how little Madison had done to convince her. "As long as you also enjoy the person you come home to."

"I do."

Even to her own ears, the words sounded hollow. Just a simple fact without any real joy. It was still true, wasn't it? Madison sighed and let her shoulders fall. Why had they gone down this road? A moment ago she had been studying the landscape, letting the beauty of it carry her, floating in the direction she had wanted her life to go. Now she was confused again. Adrift.

"I couldn't help but notice." Jada's voice softened again, taking on the soothing tones that sounded more like a mother than a best friend. "It's just over a year since Robert... How are you doing?"

She reached out, slipping her hand into Madison's and entwining their fingers. Madison's tears didn't come this time. There was a lightness to her grief since she'd spoken to CS. An unburdening that did not fully remove her grief, but at least made it bearable.

"I miss my brother," she whispered into the dying light of the day.

"Are you okay?"

"Yeah. I think I am. It hurts less now."

"I'm so happy to hear it. Did you get to spend the day with Kacey?"

"She was busy. I didn't want to bother her with it."

"Maddie..."

She didn't want Jada to ask more. Didn't want to admit that a stranger helped her through that day rather than her girlfriend. It would be too much to explain. Too much that she didn't want to explain just yet. She cut Jada off firmly. "It was fine, Jada. Really. I talked to someone else and it helped."

She hoped Jada would assume that meant she'd spoken to a therapist, and perhaps she did because she didn't pry further. Jada had a knack for letting people find their own strength.

Her grief was profound. She could ignore it for a time. She'd managed that almost perfectly since arriving in Oregon, but that didn't mean it was gone. It was more than just the choice to drink less and stay home. Something had shifted in her that day a year ago. Something inside had changed seismically and now the pieces of her life fit together awkwardly.

Her discomfort must have shown in her tone, or perhaps her abruptness was enough to warn Jada off. They sat in silence a long time, sipping their coffee and watching long shadows creep into the world as the sun set. When they spoke again it was about mundane matters—shared acquaintances, gossip and the movements of their small world of art. Gradually the pressure on Madison's chest lifted and she was able to smile again. To laugh at Jada's jokes and cutting remarks about people and things she found tedious. They caught up on each other's lives until the sun slipped away and their appetites sent them to change for dinner.

CHAPTER EIGHTEEN

Kacey had reserved the chef's table for them and personally seated them. She pulled out Madison's chair and kissed her on the cheek before heading over to help Jada. She wouldn't let her sit without a long, tight hug that Jada obviously enjoyed for the first half.

"I can't tell you how happy I am you made the trip, Jada," Kacey said, gently sliding the chair into place behind her. "Isn't the cottage amazing?"

"Gorgeous. I can't imagine how you two lucked out like this."

The way Kacey threw her shoulders back and widened her smile, she obviously took it as a compliment. Her eyes darted around the room to see how many people were watching them. "Did Madison show you her pottery?"

"She did. It's some of the best she's ever done."

"The best, for sure." Kacey smiled over at Madison, who felt warmth on her cheeks and fiddled with her napkin.

"And you!" Jada chirped, taking in the bustling restaurant. Every table was full, and several people milled about impatiently near the door. "What an achievement."

"I couldn't have done it without Madison." She came around the table and put a soft hand on Madison's shoulder. "She's my inspiration and my rock."

"You did all of this by yourself, darling."

Kacey leaned over and kissed Madison on the lips. The soft press and moisture were only there for a second, but it was enough to make Madison's heart race. Kacey's lips always had that effect, even with the trace of uncharacteristically sweet lip gloss she left behind.

After that, Kacey had to dash back to the kitchen. She detoured through the dining room first, checking on special guests and allowing a few group pictures. A waitress with a high ponytail, slightly vacant eyes, and a perfume that made Madison cough, brought them each a dirty martini. Madison sipped hers once when Kacey was looking and then set it down, knowing she wouldn't pick it up again.

Sipping her martini much more enthusiastically, Jada scanned the room. There was a glint of the mercenary in her eye, and Madison knew she was guessing at net worth and disposable income of every guest. They were the sort of people Jada was used to being around. Not only did she own the most high-end gallery in art-mad Denver, she came from money.

Since they were at the chef's table, Kacey brought each course herself, explaining the food and ending with a little bow before heading back to the kitchen. She was the consummate actor, and this stage suited her better than any other. The first course was flash-seared Hamachi loin with a dry-spice rub. It was a dish she'd been tinkering with for years, and this was the best version Madison had tried. The presentation was exquisite and the curry powder made a nice and unexpected foil for the chipotle in the rub, but there were sharp bitter notes where the spices had scorched. The aioli was silky smooth and aromatic. Jada devoured it, and the accompanying glass of white wine, happily.

"What's next for you," Jada asked. "More of these texturized vases or do you have something else in mind?"

Madison rarely planned her projects until she sat at the wheel, but Jada had been trying to steer her to a more focused schedule. It didn't take long for Madison to think over her artistic vision. "I've been inspired by the lavender they grow between the vines here. In the summer it smelled divine. I'm thinking of incorporating it into my work."

"How so?"

"I'm not quite sure yet. Maybe the shape or the color. I'm researching if I can make a glaze using the flowers themselves."

"How intriguing," Jada murmured, her eyes scanning the room. She sat up with a start. "My god, that one is hot as hell. Is that your host, Maddie?"

Madison snapped out of her reverie to follow the line of Jada's appreciative gaze. CS had just walked in, cleaned up for the occasion with light, well-fitted khakis and a white button-up shirt with a mandarin collar open at the throat. It was open considerably lower than the throat, actually, showing a peek of navy blue from a tank top beneath and a large swath of tanned shoulders and chest.

"Yeah," Madison said, looking hard herself. The memory she'd suppressed all week, of CS's arm brushing against hers, floated to the surface. "That's CS. You can meet her if you like."

"Oh, I like," Jada purred, reaching across the table and appropriating Madison's discarded martini. "Give me a little time to enjoy the show first, though."

Madison covered her laughter with the back of her hand. She'd forgotten how much fun it was to be with Jada. "I hate to be the one to break this to you, Jada, but you're straight."

"I may be straight, but you know there's nothing on me that's narrow," she said, patting her wider than average hips with one hand and holding her martini close to her lips with the other. "Besides, there are exceptions to every rule and she's got exceptional written all over her. If I were ten years younger, I'd be all over her."

"That would be a waste of a perfectly good evening." Kacey slid a plate of plump, bright white fish resting on a bed of shimmering greens in front of each of them as she spoke. The aroma was mouthwatering, full of rich, earthy mushrooms and a sharp citrus tang.

Madison definitely didn't like Jada's implication. She picked up her fork and spun it between her fingertips. "She isn't that much older than we are."

"She's forty-two," Kacey said to her before turning her attention back to Jada. "Really though, she's a cold fish, Jada. You don't want to waste your time with CS."

"Really?" Madison asked, surreptitiously following CS's progress to the bar. That made her fourteen years older than Madison. The gap in ages was significant, but what did it matter really? "She doesn't look that old."

"Must be all that sunshine and physical labor," Jada purred.

"Must be all that frowning and silence," Kacey replied, a bite to her words. The blond waitress was back with a pair of wineglasses, these filled a little higher than the last. "Heads up, here she comes."

"Not the Ice Queen?" the waitress said, squeezing Kacey's arm as she left. "Brace yourself."

"She's not cold." Madison ignored Kacey's eye roll and focused on Jada. "Really, she isn't."

CS stepped up to the table, her neat, brown loafers sliding silently across the floor. Madison refolded the napkin in her lap, using the adjustment as an excuse to check the way the shawl lay across her shoulders and smooth out the creases of her dress. CS smiled awkwardly at all of them, but directed her quiet speech to Madison.

"Nice to see you all. Won't you introduce me to your friend?"

Madison tried not to sneer at the way Jada smiled up at CS, all of her perfectly straight, square teeth on display. "CS Freeburn, this is my friend Jada Welch. She runs an art gallery in Denver."

"Pleasure to meet you, Ms. Welch."

"It's Mrs. Welch, actually, so you should just call me Jada. I'm just in love with your winery. It's like a little slice of heaven."

"As long as you don't mind walking a good deal." CS smiled down at the tall heel poking out from under the tablecloth where Jada had her legs crossed. "Will you be here with us long?"

"Unfortunately not. I have some meetings in Seattle tomorrow, so I have to leave tonight."

"That's a shame."

"We tried to talk her into staying," Kacey said with an unpleasantly suggestive purr. "But she's very stubborn."

"Perhaps next time," CS said. She nodded to Jada, smiled at Madison and left just as abruptly as she arrived, without acknowledging Kacey's presence with as much as a glance.

Just before she was out of earshot, Kacey scoffed, "Like I said, she's a cold old hag."

Madison swatted Kacey's arm, watching CS's retreating form for any sign she'd heard. She turned back to her fish when she felt Jada's eyes on her, watching her watch CS leave.

"I should play the crowd," Kacey said, leaning down and kissing Madison's forehead. "You'll at least stay for a drink before you head into town?"

Jada wasn't driving all the way to Seattle tonight, but she did need to stay in Portland if she had any hope of meeting her client for lunch the next day. Madison could see her doing the math in her head, two martinis, a few glasses of wine, but there would be a cup of coffee at the end of it and the carriage ride back to the gate.

"Not this time. Maybe next visit."

"Oh come on," Kacey pressed. When she leaned over again, Madison could smell the lip gloss again, too sweet and too strong, like it had smeared over her chin during their kiss. "One drink won't kill you."

"But my client will if I'm late. Next time."

Kacey sighed with resignation. Waving, she headed off into the dining room. While they ate their rich and buttery but over-seasoned fish, they watched Kacey and CS make their ways separately among the guests. CS seemed ill at ease and headed for the door just as a burst of Kacey's too-loud laughter drew everyone's attention to her.

"Do be careful, Maddie."

Madison sipped her wine absently as the door shut behind CS's retreating form. Through the glass, Madison could see her heading toward the stairs that led upstairs to her office and, presumably, her apartment. She focused back on Kacey, whose laughter quieted slowly as she soaked in the indulgent smiles of her admirers.

"Kacey's always been a flirt. It keeps the diners happy. It's harmless."

Jada laughed softly. "Oh yes, Kacey. You should be careful of her too."

The rest of dinner passed in a blur and long before Madison was ready to let Jada go, their time was up. Walking Jada to the gate was an unexpected delight. Minerva had been quiet for her—solitude interrupted only briefly by visits from Boots. She didn't have genuine quality time with someone who truly knew her—just late afternoon chats with Kacey through a steamy shower door. All day with Jada she'd had that.

"You know dear," Jada said, her voice rich as the earth beneath their feet. "I think what you've got in the loft is enough for a solo show, and those vases you left with me—the amphora especially—would round it out nicely."

Madison's heart sank. "The amphora?"

"I know you love it, dear, and I know you didn't leave it with me to sell, but you really must consider it. It's a sure sell if ever there was one."

Madison had never had a solo show before, especially not one at such a highly rated and richly attended gallery as the Welch. The opportunity was exactly what professional artists strive for yet so many never achieve. If she lost that now over her attachment to a single amphora, it would be a blow from which Madison's career may never recover.

"Of course," she said, injecting as much cheer as she could into her words. "As long as it goes to someone who loves it as much as I do."

"I'll be sure it does. You can trust me, darling."

When they arrived at Jada's rented Mercedes, she let go of Madison's arm and turned to look back at the shadowy, moonlit hills through the wrought-iron fence. The bare vines glowed gray-black in the pale light of the moon.

"You're right, Maddie." She put her long-fingered hand gently on Madison's shoulder. "This place is perfect for you."

Her smile was genuine and proud and Madison pulled her into a hug, laying her cheek against Jada's collarbone like a child.

"Thank you, Jada."

"Unexpected I think, but the unexpected things in life are the sweetest."

Madison watched until her taillights were out of sight before heading back through the gate. Instead of brooding over the loss of her amphora or the excitement of a potential show, Madison took in the night vista as Jada had, with new eyes as her feet beat the familiar path home.

The feeling of the place was mystical, like an abandoned fairytale she'd wandered into alone. She didn't go inside the cottage. She kept walking, traveling to the edge of their little front yard, outside the glow from the house. A breath of wind stirred the loose folds of her dress, the skirt snapping gently like the banner flag on parapet at Camelot.

She stopped at the nearest trellis to touch the withering leaves of the vine. She looked down the hill, where the first tendrils of mist were starting to coalesce. It was far too dark for her to see anything properly at the bottom of the hill except the faint glow of the light outside the stable.

Her eye caught a flash of movement. A sweep of white and light brown. The clothes, square shoulders, and powerful frame made the figure easy to identify even from this distance. CS slipped inside, closing the door behind her. A second later, the light over the stable door flickered out.

CHAPTER NINETEEN

All interest in work had drained out of Madison after Jada left. For a week she woke up early and sat at her wheel, and for a week no inspiration came. Clouds gathered every day, threatening undelivered rain. Madison's world existed in a perpetual twilight and the gloom seeped into her soul. On the eighth day she had barely sat down at her wheel before the emptiness blossomed into frustration and she launched herself off her stool to pace the cottage. She cursed her energy that had morphed from productive to restless and irritating.

She had even gone so far as trying to convince Kacey to skip work one night. Madison begged her to call in sick, let them play hooky together just this once. Kacey couldn't do it, of course. They were kicking off the new menu that night and she had to be there to make adjustments on the fly. Madison agreed it was the right thing to do, but it didn't keep her from pouting as she watched Kacey hurry off earlier than usual, still buttoning her chef coat as she rushed up to the main building.

Madison was lonely. She realized in the shower that she'd actually been lonely for a while. She had enjoyed the solitude, but she'd had too much of it. There was an emptiness in her that couldn't be filled with work. It was nice to chat with Boots and walk with CS, but that wasn't the solution. The need to connect with someone on a deeper level. It was a need Kacey generally filled, but she was so busy. Madison made a mental note to talk to her about it when she came home from work. The conversation would require tact so it didn't sound like blame, but it was a talk they needed to have.

Solving the dilemma was helpful, but it didn't change the way her skin itched right now. It didn't make the hours pass. It didn't fill the echoing, cavernous rooms that trapped her tonight. She squeezed herself tight around the chest as she paced, for the thousandth time, past the couch toward the darkening windows.

She snatched her phone off the coffee table and punched in a familiar number. The speaker rang hollowly in her ear. She counted the rings, praying they would stop. They did after the fourth, but it was Jada's voice mail that picked up.

"It's Madison. I was just calling to talk. Kacey's at work. I guess you are too."

She checked her watch, pausing to do the mental calculation of time zones, shocked to find it so early. Dinner service had barely started so it would be ages before Kacey came home. The prospect of those blank hours felt like a physical weight.

"Everyone's working except me. Isn't that funny? Back in Denver I ran between the coffee shop and my studio so much it felt like I had a dozen jobs. Now I don't even have one. Maybe I should find something to do part time. Of course the whole point of this was coming here to be a full-time artist. It would sort of be a slap in the face to Kacey if I got a job, wouldn't it?"

She was losing her grip and it was evident in her voice. She sounded frantic and a little crazy even to herself. She needed to slow down. Take a breath.

"Sorry. I don't know what's wrong with me today. Just a little cabin fever probably. I should get out of the house more. Anyway, sorry about the rambling mess—"

The voice mail beeped, cutting off her apology. The automated system asked if she was satisfied with her message, and she nearly deleted it. Jada already knew her—no need to hide anything from her now. Continuing her pacing she tossed the phone onto the couch. It bounced onto the floor and she didn't bother picking it up. She didn't have anyone else to call.

Madison swung herself around the column in the center of the room, retracing her steps across the living room. She avoided looking toward the stable. She'd pointedly avoided it all day. Every time CS came to mind, which was far too often this past week, she'd thought of their tour through the winery. The brush of their skin touching, the easy conversation, the shared wine. She thought of Jada's warning at dinner and the new knowledge that CS lived so close. She knew she shouldn't be thinking of her this much, but she couldn't help her mind wandering.

Madison let her body fall back with a dull thud against the thick, cold glass windows, staring at the wide ceiling beam. CS had been attentive during their tour. She had shared her wine and the story of her father's death. Something had changed between them, hadn't it? It almost felt like CS had been flirting with her and, if she were honest with herself, she wasn't upset about it. Madison knew she hadn't misinterpreted the long looks and the husky musicality of CS's voice.

Madison pushed off the wall with a frustrated growl. It didn't matter. She didn't want CS to flirt with her. Hadn't wanted it then and didn't want it now. She wanted Kacey. She wanted Kacey to flirt with her. To be with her. To marry her and maybe start a family one day. She didn't need CS's deep blue eyes and honeyed-whiskey voice messing that up. She didn't need anything but Kacey. But there was a distance between them that was feeling dangerous. There'd been so little affection since they'd come to Oregon. Had it been before that? Kacey had always had her full focus, but now she was never around. Madison couldn't worry about CS now. She had to worry about what was going on in her relationship, but she couldn't fix it on her own. Another conversation to have with Kacey.

Maybe it wasn't CS at all. Maybe it was the barrel room itself that had compelled her, clouded her judgment. It was an incredible space. She'd dreamt of it often since her time down there. The towering ceilings and row upon teetering row of barrels. The musty, woody scents. The crisp air. The light down there was wonderfully cave-like. She normally liked bright, open spaces, like this living room or her studio drenched in natural light. Somehow the hulking shadows of the barrel room weren't menacing, though. The dark was mysterious. Magical.

Madison had to go back there, find her way down into the dark recesses of the winery right now. She grabbed her wool shawl and disappeared into the night.

CHAPTER TWENTY

Madison had to be right about the magic down here because the minute she slipped into the deserted cavern, she could hear ghosts. Whispers and laughter and just a breath of a voice that almost sounded like Kacey. It was exactly the place she remembered. The ethereal quality of the light. The life humming off the barrels. She slid her fingers down a row, feeling the rough surface as she passed. The soles of her shoes barely whispering in the dark.

Cold air brushed against her skin in that same pleasant way. She pulled the shawl tighter around her shoulders, remembering how CS held her hand out for it. The way she spoke to Madison with only her eyes. Taking another step, she forced CS out of her mind. Reminded herself she was down here for the room, not because of the woman who introduced her to it.

She came to realize how different the magic of this place was today, when she was alone. There was a warning in it. A chill ran through her and she shivered. With each step, the room seemed to be telling her something was wrong. She couldn't halt her footsteps. The cold wasn't outside her anymore. It was in her blood. Seeping into her bones.

Her next breath shook in her throat like a death rattle. Her last thought before she stepped out of the darkness into the pool of light over the private corner was that she wished CS was here right now. It would take a strength like hers to overcome these ghosts.

There was a certain inevitability in the scene. As though Madison knew on the day they'd met that this was how things would end with Kacey. That she would turn a corner and see the woman she loved with her mouth on another's. See her body pressed against a topless stranger. See Kacey's hand buried under that woman's skirt and see the stranger's head tipped back in unmistakable ecstasy. Inevitable as the rising sun.

That inevitability did not make it cut any less deep. Didn't dull the pain of betrayal. It was like a physical blow, catching Madison in the gut and causing her to lurch forward. Even that movement didn't stop the scene playing out before her. Madison watched for a moment, the picture becoming more and more clear as her heartbeat thundered in her ears, ticking away the moments that she could never get back.

The girl was blond, thin, and barely more than a teenager. A waitress in Kacey's restaurant. The one with whom Kacey had been joking while she served Jada wine. Not joking—flirting. The one who'd called CS "The Ice Queen." A private joke with Kacey. How many other private things did they share? How long had they shared them?

Madison entered the ring of light. Moved into the corner holding that enchanted wine. She'd sat on the same barrel the waitress was on now. The waitress's discarded shirt was their bedsheet. Madison stopped right next to the couple. Close enough that she could reach out and touch them.

The girl's head rolled and her eyes opened and fell on Madison. They stared at each other, growing comprehension lighting the blonde's sex-dulled eyes. Madison tried to remember the girl's name. She'd been told more than once, but it hadn't stuck. For whatever reason, it seemed essential she remember that name now. She'd become rather more important in Madison's life in the last few minutes, after all.

Time slowed as the girl began to move. It seemed to take an age of silence before she jerked her body up and away from Kacey, who barked in protest. She skittered backward, nearly tumbling off the wine barrel, her eyes locked in horror on Madison. Kacey turned to see what had disturbed her. The movement was perfunctory. Almost lazy. Their eyes met and held in silence that lasted another lifetime in the magic darkness of the cellar.

"What the fuck?" Kacey's eyes flashed with an anger Madison had never seen. Never suspected in a million years could exist inside the woman she thought she knew better than she knew herself. "What the fuck are you doing here, Madison?"

Perhaps it was the fact that Kacey hadn't bothered to take her hand out from under the girl's skirt before speaking Madison's name that set her off. Perhaps it was because rather than shame, anger had been Kacey's first response. Perhaps it was just a delayed reaction to her heartbreak. Whatever caused it, rage poured out of Madison before she could stop it.

"Don't you dare say my name!" she screamed, her voice echoing off the distant rafters and causing the girl to jump again, this time in unmistakable fear. "Don't you say a word to me! How could you? How dare you? I hate you! I hate everything about you."

The shouting didn't seem to affect Kacey at all. She very calmly pulled her pants back up, buttoning them with slow, languid movements that showed no hint of remorse.

"It's not like you didn't know this was coming. Christ, get a grip on yourself."

"Get a grip on myself? I knew this was coming? Is that really all you have to say?"

"What else is there to say?"

"How about saying you're sorry? How about an explanation? I think you owe me something more than this."

"I don't owe you shit." Kacey buttoned her chef's coat. "I've given you everything you've ever wanted and all I ask for is a little head at the breakfast table once in a while. But that's too much to ask apparently. So, I say again, it's not like you didn't know this was coming."

Kacey's words cut sharper and deeper than her actions. She was acutely aware of the blonde's eyes on her. The fathoms-deep anger bled out of her.

"How could you say that?"

"Well, now you know how to prevent this in the future, don't you?"

Surely Madison had heard her wrong. "What are you talking about?"

Kacey huffed in that exhausted way she did when she had to explain a simple concept. She finished buttoning her coat. "Give it up every now and then and we won't have this problem again."

"You think I'm going to stay with you after this?"

"Of course you will."

"No."

Smugness turned to cold threat as Kacey said, "What other choice do you have?"

Kacey's shout echoed hollowly the massive room, the threatening insult bouncing around the room.

"You are not the woman I fell in love with."

Kacey smiled. It was a villainous smile, dripping with venom. "Same here."

Madison's arm shot out of its own accord. Her open palm landed on Kacey's shoulder and she knew at the moment of impact that the blow stung Kacey far less than it stung her. She thought of the diamond ring she'd been expecting in Denver and slapped Kacey's shoulder again. She thought of all the late nights and the loneliness and she aimed for Kacey's face.

Kacey caught her by the wrist in a painfully tight grip. Madison yelped and raised her other hand, not to hit Kacey again but to pry her hand free. Kacey snatched it out of midair and clamped her fingers around it, her knuckles whitening with the force. She shook Madison's arms, making her whole body jerk.

"If you think you can just walk away, you've got another think coming, baby."

Kacey shook her again, words hissing through her tightly clenched teeth.

"You're mine and you know it. You're going to go back home and sit there, waiting for me or I swear I will…"

Madison found her voice. "I will not."

Kacey shook her again, this time forcefully enough to snap her head back. A popping sound came from her neck and little lights exploded in front of her eyes. Vaguely she knew Kacey was still shaking her, but her body was limp now, riding the waves like a ship in a storm. Kacey's shouts were distant, but they were no less intimidating.

A new voice cut into the scene. "Let her go right now."

CS's calm, rumbling tone brought Madison rushing back into herself. Her eyes cleared, but the pain redoubled. The first thing she saw was the angry red skin of her wrists under Kacey's grip. Even through her haze, Madison could feel CS's presence. Feel her warmth and solidity.

Kacey let her go and took a step back. CS caught her with an arm around her waist. Madison tried to look into her eyes, but CS was focused on Kacey. She removed her arm once Madison was able to stand and took a step forward, putting herself between them.

Like any bully met with an equal adversary, Kacey turned her attention back to the weakest party. Her eyes stayed locked on Madison while she stalked back to the barrel, moving behind the waitress and letting her hand dangle suggestively over her shoulder in front of her naked chest.

"What's the matter, babe? This is awfully close to how you and I got together, after all." Madison looked away, feeling the eyes of the room on her and hating the way her cheeks blazed hot. "Does your white knight know how easily you give it up to a stranger, you slut? She does, doesn't she? That's why you won't give me a piece?"

The insinuation stung all the stronger for Madison's recently wandering mind. She may have thought about CS, but she wasn't a cheater. "I would never do that to you."

Madison's voice was small, but the words traveled across the room. Kacey laughed at them. Laughed while tears began to leak out of the waitress's eyes. She wrapped her arms around her chest, opting for modesty a little late in the game, and tried to shrug out from underneath Kacey's arm.

"Neither would I." The anger was gone from CS's voice. It was back to the cold neutral she used with everyone except Boots and, recently, Madison. "I don't like your implication, Kacey."

"Relax. I didn't mean anything against you."

"I know. That's what I don't like. Ironic that you're calling Madison a slut when she finds you cheating."

"She is a…"

"Don't." The single word brought Kacey's teeth together in silence, and CS let the silence linger for a single, threatening moment before going on. "Pack up and get out. Right now."

"What?"

"I believe you brought your own knives. Collect them on your way out."

"I'm not leaving. We're in the middle of dinner service!"

"Obviously your presence in the kitchen isn't required." CS made a flippant gesture to the now silently weeping waitress. "I said get out. You're fired."

CS had been quiet, calculating as ever. Kacey stormed out from behind the barrel screaming, her eyes wild. "You can't fire me! I have a contract!"

"You probably should've read the sexual harassment and appropriate conduct during working hours sections of that contract."

"This is my restaurant. I made it. I'm the reason this place is making money!"

"I can hire another chef."

"We all talk, you know. I'll blackball this place. I'll tear it apart. By the time I'm done you'll be begging for quarters at stoplights!"

She'd grown hysterical, spit flying from her teeth as she ranted. CS slowly crossed her arms, a joyless smile sweeping across her face.

"Is that so?"

"Yeah! That's so!"

"In that case, you're *fucking* fired." CS dropped her arms and started a slow march forward. "You're a cocky, pretentious ass. The only people who think you're wonderful are you and this waitress you are constantly fucking all over my goddamn vineyard."

Kacey's back was against a row of barrels now. She looked like she wanted to hide behind them. Madison watched the scene with a detached numbness creeping like frostbite over her limbs.

"Get out. Don't do anything else. Go to your place, pack a bag and leave right now. If you don't, it will be a very poor decision."

Kacey wavered for a moment. There was a ghost of something familiar on her face. She looked the way she did the night Madison had met her. Like a woman wearing a mask of confidence, but with a world of softness beneath. Madison had always loved the woman behind that mask. The one who was vulnerable and brave at the same time. At some point in the last three years, Madison had stopped seeing the softness. Now it was back and a pulse of sadness shot through her. She should have been the one to show Kacey she didn't need the mask. That the woman she was had always been enough. It was Madison's job as her partner to show her that, but Madison had failed. This was the result. She felt responsible for this night.

Then, in a heartbeat, Kacey was gone. She stormed out without once looking at Madison. Without once looking at the blonde, now shivering in the cold air, mascara running in gray rivers down her cheeks. She was there one moment, and then she was gone. Perhaps she had never been there at all. It was easy to believe that after the waitress slid off the barrel and melted into the shadows herself.

Madison felt alone. Standing on the far rim of the light, her wrists throbbing and her neck aching. Silence filled the space again. The magic had dissolved.

CS stood like a statue, staring at the place Kacey had been. Her shoulders and back heaved with each breath like she'd been running. Her T-shirt was tight, the fibers stretched with each breath. She watched CS, standing solidly but not looking at her.

Madison knew, in a distant place in her mind, that she was in shock. Thoughts finally bubbled to the surface. Everyone's words starting to make sense.

"You knew?" She wasn't sure she could survive the answer.

"I suspected." CS didn't turn. Her back didn't stop heaving. "If I had known for sure, I'd have gotten rid of her on the spot."

"Can't have your employees running off to fuck during work hours."

"That isn't why."

Madison's tears came now, thick and fast. She was tired of crying. Maybe she was just tired. Bone-deep weariness settled into her.

"Were there others?"

"I don't like to make it my business what other people…"

"Were there others?"

CS was quiet for a long time. Her back finally stilled. She looked at her boots. "There are always others."

There were always others. There probably always had been. Something in Madison knew that. The way she had been before Robert, the way she'd partied and talked Kacey into public sex all over town, the way she let her animal instincts take over. There was so much they didn't know about each other, now that Madison thought about it.

She sat down on the concrete floor in the dark cellar and put her head in her hands. She didn't just cry, she sobbed. She broke down. She fell apart. She let the realization that she had nothing left in this world wash over her and she cried even harder. She'd heard Kacey call her a slut and she knew it was true. She felt Kacey's hatred in the way she had shaken her and she wrapped it around herself. She wallowed in all that she had lost and let it spill out of her.

Madison felt a hand on her shoulder. She tried to lift her face. Warm fabric pressed against her hand and she grabbed it. The smell of clean cotton and a hint of mint overwhelmed her senses as she pressed CS's bandana into her face. The hand was gone almost instantly, but she still felt CS's presence.

A long time later, when Madison could control herself enough to breathe, she forced the tears away. A lifetime later, her sadness came to a shuddering stop. She looked up, wiping the last of the tears from her cheeks with the thoroughly sodden bandana, to thank CS. She was gone. Madison looked all around, but the winemaker was nowhere in sight. She was alone in a cold basement.

CHAPTER TWENTY-ONE

Much to Madison's surprise, the sun rose the next morning. She was awake to see it, curled into the fetal position on a lounger on her deck. Everything had crumbled and burned around her in the last twenty-four hours, but the sun still rose. She didn't have the energy to respond physically. She felt it for all of a second or two before she went back to feeling nothing at all.

Yesterday's warmth didn't come back with the sun. Madison was cold. Freezing cold. Hollow inside. Emptied out from the tears that wouldn't stop. Hollow from her loneliness and her shame. The whole night had passed with her here on the lounger until she watched the stars fade in the dawn light and the sun replaced the moon.

The crunch of gravel underfoot caught her attention. She would have moved her head to see who was passing, but she didn't have the strength. When he came into view, Boots waved at her, offering a friendly smile, but didn't come over. He kept his boots pointed to the stables and didn't alter his course. That was for the best. From his distance, he wouldn't see how swollen and puffy her face, how red her burning eyes. She wondered if he knew what had happened the night before. If everyone knew.

Minerva Hills was, after all, a small, closed community. Everyone talked. There were no places for secrets to hide. A wave of nausea rippled through Madison and she squeezed her eyes shut against it. She knew the whole world would know all the sordid details of her humiliation soon enough. At the very least, people would wonder where Kacey had gone. The waitress wasn't likely to return either. Like most of the restaurant staff, she probably lived off property, so she had no incentive to return. It lessened the chances of scandal if they both left, but it also doubled the suspicion. Besides, as CS said last night, there are always others. How many women would arrive at work to find out their hooking up days were over?

Madison's head spun. She'd been through this for countless hours, chasing the same thoughts and fears around her head all night. The tears came again now. At least they were quiet. She was too exhausted to break down again.

CS emerged from her apartment behind the stables, just a flash of movement in the distance, but one that Madison was able to focus on to stop her racing mind. She watched CS look up in her direction, then make her way up the hill.

Uninvited, CS made her way onto the deck. The nearest lounger to Madison was so close that CS's knee brushed hers when she sat. A tiny flicker of warmth entered Madison's world, but it only served to remind her how cold she was. She shivered, but otherwise remained motionless.

"How are you doing?" CS's voice was gentle and quiet.

Madison took a long time to answer, as much because her throat was dry and cracked as the need to consider the question. "I don't know how to answer that question."

"Did you sleep at all?"

Madison shook her head, but the movement snapped her moorings loose and she thought she might float away. She closed her eyes again, listening to the silence CS allowed to stretch between them, and feeling better for it.

Her mind wandered to Kacey's accusations last night. Her insistence that Madison was a slut, and that it made her actions acceptable. To the night she met Kacey. She decided she had to tell it.

She kept her eyes shut hard as she spoke so she wouldn't have to see CS's reaction. "We met at a club in Boulder. I can't remember the name. It was loud and I was there with friends who drank hard and danced hard. I loved the way blacklights sparkled in good tequila."

CS stirred and leaned in closer.

Madison cleared her throat. "I noticed Kacey noticing me. We were both the hot center of our respective groups, and her friends kept inching closer to mine. By the end of the night, I knew she would follow me anywhere, and she did. I didn't even have to ask. Just walked over, took Kacey by the hand and led her to the door. I never even asked her name."

Madison didn't know how to stop talking now that she'd started. She finished in a rush, "I went out again the next night and she was there. I took her home again. We danced to the same tune every night for a week before Kacey finally asked my name. Two days ago, I thought it was a love story for a new generation. Untraditional but no less romantic. Now it sounds like a cautionary tale."

Madison's voice petered out but her mind kept spinning. Their story should have ended long ago. It ended exactly as it should have. Now the memory of their one-night stand that accidentally turned into a relationship felt tainted as it probably always should have. She thought she would feel better with CS knowing the story. Instead, she felt embarrassed and dirty.

"So you think you deserve that sort of treatment from her?" CS asked, her voice cold as the morning.

"I think she was right," Madison finished weakly. "She was right about me."

"No. She wasn't."

There was barely a breath of pause between her words and CS's. The confidence of her denial made Madison finally look up. To her surprise, CS's eyes matched her words. There was no judgment there.

She accepted the denial because she was too tired not to. "If you say so."

"I do." CS's eyes went hard as frozen granite. "Anything that you did with her, that's between the two of you. Everything you did, she did too."

Madison hadn't thought of it that way, but somehow the knowledge that they were both sluts didn't make her feel much better. She nodded and CS seemed to understand that she meant that as an end to the conversation. Madison's throat burned and weariness washed over her again. If only she could make herself go inside and lie in bed, she could sleep for days. She couldn't do that, though. Couldn't go lie in that bed with the sheets that smelled like Kacey.

"Did anything happen when you came back here last night?" CS asked.

"No. Kacey was already gone. She didn't leave a note or anything. Just…vanished."

Madison felt her features twist at the memory.

"I can get her back here if that's what you want." Madison opened her eyes to see CS staring at her own hands, clenched in her lap. "I shouldn't have just kicked her out without talking to you. Asking what you wanted."

"I wouldn't have known what answer to give." The pain in CS's eyes when she looked up made Madison's heart break all over again. She hurried on, "The job is yours to give away."

"If you want to try and make it work with Kacey…"

"I don't."

"If you did, she can come back. I won't stop her."

"That's not what I want. Besides, it doesn't matter. She's gone."

"Okay." CS said with a resignation that sounded less than permanent.

Madison tried to push herself up, but only made it as far as her elbow. "I suppose that means I need to leave too."

"No. Absolutely not."

"The cottage was part of your deal with Kacey…"

"You're going to stay." CS softened her tone. "If you want to. My accountant informs me that having an artist in residence is a significant tax deduction. Please stay."

She couldn't tell if this was a bad joke from CS, but she didn't have much choice in the matter. Beyond the fact that she had nowhere to go, she couldn't lift her arms right now, much less pack up her house.

"I'll stay until I decide what I want to do."

"My contract with Kacey was for a year, the cottage is yours at least that long."

"CS, that isn't fair to you. You can make so much money on this…"

CS stood abruptly, cutting off Madison's words with the movement. "You need sleep."

Madison's face paled at the thought of those sheets again. "I can't."

"You have to."

"No, I mean…I don't think I can stand up."

"Oh. Let me help?"

Madison nodded, using all her strength. CS leaned down and hooked an arm around her back. She set Madison's feet on the ground and helped her stand. The motions were so practiced, so clinical. She wondered whether CS had to help her sick father stand in his last days.

"My god," CS whispered. "You're frozen."

Madison pressed close to her, feeling her heat like a furnace. She began to shiver uncontrollably and her knees were weak. She wrapped her arms around CS's neck, drawing her warmth as close as she could.

"I was out here all night. I forgot to bring a blanket."

It was slow going up the stairs, CS having to help her more than Madison liked. CS took her to the bathroom and set her down on the closed toilet while she turned on the shower and adjusted the temperature. Steam billowed from it within moments, the moisture already working its way into Madison's skin.

"Promise me you'll get warm and get some sleep?"

CS knelt in front of her, worry still etched in the tiny lines beginning to show on her tanned face.

"I don't think I have much choice at this point." The steaming shower beckoned to her and her eyelids hung heavily on her face. "I'm asleep on my feet."

"Take a shower first. You'll feel better." For a heartbeat she rested her hand on Madison's knee. "Send for me if you need anything, okay?"

Once Madison agreed, she slipped out of the bathroom, pulling the door shut behind her. It took Madison an age to stand and peel out of her clothes, but CS was right, the moment the warm spray hit her skin, she felt enormously better. She hadn't made the water too hot, in deference to Madison's extreme cold, and Madison had to turn up the heat in intervals. She allowed the water to carry away last night.

As soon as Madison turned off the water and wrapped herself in the thick, terrycloth robe she loved so much an odd noise filled the house. She stepped into the bedroom to see fresh sheets on the bed. The sound was the washing machine churning away in the mudroom. Madison knew from the empty feel of the cottage that CS was gone, but she had stripped all trace of Kacey from the bed before she left and even started the wash so Madison wouldn't have to clean the smell off them herself.

Dropping the robe to the floor and slipping blissfully between the layers of crisp, clean cotton, Madison wondered if she had said something about Kacey and the sheets out loud. She couldn't remember having done so, but how else would CS have known? The thought died in her brain the moment her head hit the pillow and she fell dreamlessly asleep.

CHAPTER TWENTY-TWO

Madison didn't get out of bed the next day. Tears seeped so deeply into her pillow that she threw it to the ground but when she reached for the other, she couldn't stop thinking of it as Kacey's. She didn't slip it under her head but wrapped both arms and both legs around it, crushing it close as she sobbed.

The tears dried with the inevitable memories of Kacey in the barrel room. Her wail of anguish mutated into a roar of fury and she flung the pillow across the room. Twisting the sheets between her hands, she screamed until her throat ached as much as her heart. For the rest of the day she vacillated between anger and sadness.

She slept at some point, and in the morning a swollen bladder and aching back forced her to stand. The sight in the mirror sent her back to bed, this time burying herself beneath sheets and blankets to keep from searching for her phone. All day she fought the urge to call Kacey, to beg her to come back and apologize for whatever inadequacy had sent her into another woman's arms. On the third day she hated herself for even considering a reconciliation. On the fourth day she made herself shower.

The shower made her hungry but food made her ill. The moment her bagel touched her hollow stomach, Madison heard the waitress's moans and threw up everything. She sat on her bedroom floor and flipped through the photos on her phone that documented her life with Kacey. Most of them were grainy or out of focus, taken in the dim light of bars. She'd thought often of printing some of them. Making an album to commemorate their relationship as it grew. The idea now made her laugh until she cried.

Someone knocked on her door during the fifth day, but they didn't come in. Her phone battery had died and she'd decided not to plug it in, lest she cave in and send a text or an email in her emotionally damaged state. She didn't remember anything else from the fifth day.

It wasn't until the sixth day that Madison woke up angry and stayed that way. When she pictured Kacey cheating, she didn't wonder what she'd done wrong, she wondered why she'd been so shocked. The thought took her to the bathroom to brush her teeth. As she turned on the shower she remembered the terrible things Kacey had said to her that night. This time the words didn't sting but reminded her of other terrible things Kacey had said to her. The way she had belittled her art and dismissed her feelings. The way Madison's needs always came second to Kacey's.

While her coffee brewed, Madison spent less time wondering what life would look like without Kacey and more time wondering why she had wasted so many years twisting her life into Kacey's. She walked into her studio, stewing over the way Kacey had regarded giving her this space a waste. Only watery sunlight showed through the windows today. The clouds obscured any hope at warmth, bathing her wheel and kiln in a gray, lifeless glow.

No urge to create pulled at her. No desire to work. Storm clouds made her turn her back immediately. Sadness was creeping back and she wanted to keep it at bay as long as she could.

When she returned to the kitchen, she plugged in her phone without turning it on. She forced herself to eat breakfast. She took her coffee to the couch and waited for the clouds to break and bring light back into her life. They never did and her good mood only lasted until her stomach rumbled again at midafternoon. She ignored it and by evening she was crying again, but at least she had made it downstairs. It was a victory she would accept.

The next three days were spent on the couch, each one with fewer tears than the last. Some days she was awake with the sun and saw CS emerge from her apartment over the stables and start the work of the vineyard. Some days she did not see another living thing in the winter-cloaked vineyard. She barely qualified as one herself. Eating became more regular, even if showering didn't.

On the tenth day after Kacey left, Madison sat on her couch, hugging her knee to her chest and staring out into another gloomy day. Every day had been gloomy. No rain, but the clouds had blocked the sun and turned Madison's life into an eternal twilight. Today, like every other, she sat here unmotivated, self-pitying.

A flash of color crossed her vision and she thought for one hopeful moment that the sun had finally emerged from behind the clouds. It was Boots, wearing a shirt in a chipper shade of green and carrying a bag of groceries. He waved at her and she found herself waving back, even smiling.

She dragged herself off the couch in time to notice her stained, pungent sweats before Boots burst through the door.

"Hey there, stranger," he called on his way to the refrigerator.

"Hey, Boots."

His smile only faltered for a moment when he turned to look at her, but he quickly turned back to his task. She dropped onto a barstool and he tossed her a granola bar from the box he was stashing in the cabinet. She toyed with the wrapper but didn't open it. He ate his in two bites, his cheeks bulging like a cartoon chipmunk as he chewed, watching her.

Swallowing noisily, he said, "I couldn't help noticing that Kacey's gone."

"Yeah."

"You wanna talk about it?"

"No."

"You want me to go?"

She thought about it for a moment, and determined that, in addition to being heartbroken, she might also be lonely. "No."

His grin was worth the uncomfortable conversation. It lit the room in lieu of the sun and actually made her feel a little better. Grabbing the jar of beans and rattling them in her direction he asked, "Want me to make coffee?"

"God no," she said, pushing off the counter to her feet. "You make terrible coffee."

He feigned outrage for the time it took her to walk around the counter, then relinquished the task to her, dropping onto a stool. While she performed the ritual of grinding beans and measuring water, the ache started to leave her shoulders and back. The weight on her chest lessened with each movement. The sun peeked out from a gap in the clouds as she poured milk into his cup.

"Violet threw another shoe yesterday," he said, grabbing his mug and breathing in the aroma with obvious enjoyment. He had certainly converted to the idea of afternoon coffee.

"Is she okay?"

"Oh yeah. She's just doing it for attention." He laughed and then continued, "Have I told you about that stubborn horse when she first arrived?"

"Nope," Madison said, settling onto a stool a few seats away from Boots so he wouldn't be able to smell her unwashed hair.

"We got her a year ago and put her on the visitor carriage."

Madison tried to reconcile the image of the headstrong, spoiled horse as part of a team and couldn't quite make it work.

"She was awful," Boots confirmed. "Kept trying to duck out of her collar and shake off the traces. Nearly overturned a carriage once trying to pull out of line."

"Did she hurt anyone?"

"Just my pride. The passengers all gave me the side-eye for the rest of the day. So did Violet, actually."

"I'm surprised you and CS put up with that."

"I wanted to get rid of her, but CS wouldn't hear of it. I told her Violet wasn't broken and a wild horse is always a risk. CS wanted to give her time."

Madison stopped mid-sip, realizing where this story was heading. "And she got better?"

"Hell no, she got worse. After a while she stopped trying to pull out of the line and just started withering. She stopped eating. The other horses would nip at her and she stopped defending herself. Buttercup once took a chunk out her flank and Violet didn't so much as cry. Some days I couldn't get her to move. She'd just stand there in her tack and wouldn't pull."

"That doesn't sound like Violet."

"Sure doesn't. After that I was worried that she'd die. She'd lost so much weight and she was miserable. We had to take her off the team for her own safety."

"A skinny Violet, who'd have thought that was possible?"

"CS noticed she did better when she wasn't hooked in with the others. Started to eat again. So CS started riding her every day to get her strength back and soon she was showing off and looking like a new horse. She wasn't thriving yoked to the rest of the team, but on her own she was as happy as I'd ever seen a horse."

He just smiled at her when he finished his story and Madison shook her head. "I get it."

"Do you?"

"That was supposed to be a metaphor or something, right? About how I stayed with Kacey for too long and lost myself and now I have the chance to thrive on my own."

Boots laughed again and this time it made Madison smile. He stood up, drained his coffee cup and patted her on the shoulder. "Nope. That was a story about a horse. Thanks for the coffee, Denver."

He left in such a hurry it seemed as if he hadn't been there at all. She realized that she was holding her coffee cup in midair, preparing for a sip that she had no interest in taking. She set the cup down as a burst of sunlight cut through the kitchen window.

It made her think of a vase she'd been planning to make back when her life made sense and she didn't wear the same old sweatpants every day. A series of vases in burnt umber—the color of the harvest-red dust-covered windows.

She headed for her studio, a design slowly coming to life in her mind. She went back for the granola bar, unwrapping it as she settled down at her wheel.

CHAPTER TWENTY-THREE

"In case you were wondering, I priced hitmen in Oregon and their rates are surprisingly reasonable."

"Jada…"

"Seriously. They have whole menus of options. If you want her to suffer it costs more."

"Jada, I don't want to have Kacey killed."

"They can just wound her if you like, but where's the fun in that?"

"I don't want her wounded either."

"I'll pay for it."

"No."

"You could have them steal her car."

"She doesn't own a car."

"There has to be something we can do to ruin her life."

"I don't want to ruin her life. That wouldn't make me feel better."

"It would make me feel loads better," Jada huffed, adding in a grumble, "the little tramp."

Madison couldn't help but chuckle at the old-fashioned word. It felt good to laugh with Jada on the phone. Normal. Still, listening to her friend bash Kacey wasn't helping her heal. She held the phone a little away from her ear as Jada went again into a long tear about the inequities of her ex. Jada was trying to be helpful, to show solidarity, but Madison didn't want that, even if her name-calling was getting more creative with every passing word.

The truth was, Madison was ready to get into her post-Kacey life. Or at least she wanted to be ready. Her queasiness was steadily being replaced by optimism and she didn't want to regress. It had taken her too much effort to get to this place of shaky normalcy. Ignoring Jada's angry rant was the only way she knew to keep a grip on herself.

Jada wound down quickly, either running out of steam or correctly interpreting the lack of response from Madison. She took a deep breath and asked, "How are you doing, Maddie?"

"Okay."

"Really?"

"Really. I actually managed to eat three meals yesterday without throwing up from crying so hard."

"And it only took you three weeks."

"Progress."

"I wish I could be there with you."

"I know." Madison kicked her bare feet up on the coffee table and wriggled her toes. "I really am okay though."

"Have you heard from her?"

"No. No contact." Her feet were dirty. She should take a shower today. She couldn't remember taking one yesterday and she knew she hadn't the day before. "I'm not sure if I'm happy about that or devastated."

"Let's go with happy," Jada said, injecting her stubborn optimism into the words.

"If you say so."

After a heartbeat of hesitation, Jada said, "Perhaps this is a good time for me to make a proposal. Promise to hear me out?"

"I'm listening."

"Come back to Denver."

Jada's words were like a bucket of ice. Return home. Admit defeat. Go back to where you belong with a crappy day job and scraping to make rent. "No."

"There's nothing for you there anymore, Maddie. You went there with Kacey and she's gone now. Come home. Get away from that place and start over."

Jada had released the words in a rush and they buzzed in Madison's ears. There was something for her here. She thought of her studio and the pots she'd made this morning curing on their shelves, but she also thought of a gnarled tree on a windy hill, a blue bandana that smelled of clean cotton and mint and a clearing in the woods full of liquid light.

"I can't afford to move again, Jada. It cost us everything we'd saved to send our stuff here and I'm not selling enough pottery in the store to ship it all back."

"Then this is a good time to tell you that I have a solo show set up for you." She paused, but Madison couldn't reply, her shock holding her tongue. "I'm sorry to just blurt it out like that. I'm so excited for you. Fly out for the show and we can get your stuff shipped with the profits."

"I can't afford a plane ticket either," Madison said, though it wasn't exactly true. She probably had enough to swing it, but something was telling her to stay in Oregon. Something that spoke in a deep, resonant voice that she hadn't heard in far too long.

A shout in the background of the call distracted Jada. She shouted something back— something about takeout. She must be home with her husband. The age-old discussion about what was for dinner. Madison took herself to the kitchen while they discussed it, her stomach groaning unhappily. She'd been better about food yesterday, but her refrigerator was emptying quickly and she hadn't wanted lunch.

She found the jar of olives and tub of cream cheese just as unappetizing as she had earlier. Her cabinets were similarly bare. She hadn't had much food in the house before her life fell apart, and Boot's delivery didn't improve matters. Tonight was finally the night she would have to venture out. Before everything fell apart, she'd gone to the main building to have family meal once in a while, and she knew she was always welcome. Her stomach writhed just a little at the thought of facing people now, but she knew she had little choice. There wasn't even a pizza place in town that would deliver on horseback.

"Sorry, Maddie, but I have to go. Apparently my idiot husband can't manage dinner."

"Don't be so hard on him, Samuel's wonderful."

"He may be gorgeous, but he's still an idiot. Love you. Please think about coming out for the show?"

"I will. I promise."

There was no more putting it off—she'd have to go up to the main building for dinner. As she headed up the stairs, it seemed as if now was as good a time as any. She made quick work of her shower, but picking out clothes was more of a challenge. She wasn't quite sure what the dress code was for an "I know that you all know I was cheated on, humiliated and heartbroken, but let's all pretend I'm going to live through this" dinner. A light, knee-length skirt and cardigan seemed to fit the bill, though they weren't entirely right for the winter season. The world would just have to accept it.

It was later than she thought when she finally made her way up the hill. The night was pleasantly still, without a hint of breeze to chill her bare legs, and the moonlight shone silvery on the vines. She had the path to herself, the chatter of night insects serenading her as she walked. She wanted the whole world to be like this, quiet and empty, but she'd seen the cart pass by her cottage too often today to expect any solitude. The lobby and tasting room would be swamped as always.

As she neared the winery, a couple materialized out of the darkness ahead of her. They must have wandered onto the road from a side path. The one leading to Cottage Five was nearby. It was one of the most popular on the estate, booked up until next summer last she heard.

Madison slowed her pace, not wanting to disturb them. They looked to be in their late-twenties, a man and woman who had eyes only for each other. He leaned close, whispering into her ear through the long strands of her curly hair. She laughed and leaned against him, wrapping an arm around his waist.

Slightly envious, Madison wondered what their story was. What made her feel so comfortable with him and him so affectionate with her? No doubt their story did not involve anonymous sex that would end in a fiery confrontation in a wine cellar.

Whatever this couple's story, she knew Kacey had been right about theirs. Madison hadn't been embarrassed by her behavior with Kacey, but maybe she should have been. After all, a relationship that started with a random hookup wasn't exactly destined to greatness in the mode of Romeo and Juliet or Elizabeth and Darcy. She should never have expected forever with Kacey.

She came to an abrupt halt in the center of the path. The couple moved on, still oblivious of her presence, and were swallowed by the night. The main building was just ahead, she could hear the roar of conversation from the twin patios of the tasting room and *ambrosia*. She thought about turning back, but her hunger stopped her. She had to see it through.

Sliding in the front door, she kept close to the wall to avoid the bright lights and noise as much as possible. The hotel restaurant was around the corner from the two main attractions, and if she was quick, she could escape this chaos and find a small table in the corner. She might just get out of here in one piece if she was careful.

"Denver!"

Boots waved exuberantly and rushed over to her. So much for a quiet night. There was no such thing when Boots was smiling and bouncing on the balls of his feet like that. He cut through the crowd and was at her side just as she managed to hoist a smile onto her face.

"There you are, Denver! Nice to see you out of the house."

"Hi, Boots."

"You're going to join us for family meal, right?"

"Yeah, I sorta ran out of food."

"Sorry about that. Grocery delivery is tomorrow."

Now that she was here, she really didn't want to face anyone else. She eyed *ambrosia* with something between longing and dread. "I can just grab a table alone at…"

"Don't be silly, Denver." He gave her a look that stopped any possible argument and wrapped an arm around her shoulders. "You're joining us."

She followed him into the now only half-full tasting room and let him sit her down at an empty corner of the bar. When he was called away to help the staff, she was finally able to breathe easy. The room was emptying of strangers and filling up with familiar faces. Even though she didn't know many of their names, the staff was consistent enough to be recognizable. Madison felt their eyes on her and wondered if she was imagining their accusatory stares. She did everything in her power to avoid eye contact with anyone. A cute redhead behind the bar with long bangs over one eye set a glass of white wine down in front of her. When Madison protested, the woman insisted, explaining that the staff could always get a free glass of wine. She moved off before Madison could explain she wasn't exactly staff.

It was the feeling of eyes on her that made her finally sip the wine. It was more something to do with her hands than an interest in the drink itself, but she felt more comfortable the moment she tasted it. She looked around again over the rim of her glass. She didn't feel the stares as much anymore. Maybe she'd just been cooped up too long.

The last of the guests filed out and the room, now occupied by only employees, seemed to take a deep breath. Conversations got louder, shoulders slumped and smiles widened. Madison liked the relaxation of mood. She felt like fewer people noticed her now. Fewer eyes landed on her. Just when she thought she might get through this night feeling like a normal human, the door opened again to a pair of waitresses carrying platters of food.

She recognized both of them from *ambrosia*. One worked the bar and the other the floor. More than once they'd chatted with Madison as she had dinner at the bar while Kacey worked. Neither of them spoke to her now, but they both gave her long, searching looks. Madison was certain this time that they were hostile. Both women were young and show-stopping gorgeous. Now that Madison thought of it, the vast majority of the waitresses at *ambrosia* looked like this. Young, blond, and hot. Just like the one Madison caught her with. Kacey's type.

They deposited the food on the far end of the bar and whipped right back out of the room. Madison gave them a few minutes to leave before she drained her glass and headed to the door. Humiliation had soured the wine and her appetite fled. If she was quick, she could get out of this stifling room and back out into the night before anyone noticed. Before she started crying again.

Her fingertips brushed the handle of the door just as it was yanked away. Looking up through the open door, she found herself inches away from CS, who was skidding to a halt to avoid walking into her. They blinked dumbly at each other. Madison's stomach righted itself for a moment before it began squirming again, but for very different reasons.

"Madison." CS's surprise turned to concern at the look on Madison's face. "You were leaving."

"I...yeah. I don't think I can..."

She stopped talking the moment her eyes began to prickle. She didn't want to cry right now. Not in front of all these people. Not standing here smelling CS's clean, fresh scent and feeling the warmth of her presence. CS reached out, laying her broad, strong palm on Madison's bicep. The contact sent a shiver through every inch of Madison's body.

"Stay. Sit with me. Please?"

Madison still didn't trust her voice, but all thought of tears evaporated at the pleading note in CS's voice. She nodded and turned to go back into the room. CS's hand slipped down from her arm to the small of her back, resting there with the gentle strength Madison had come to associate so inexorably with CS.

Her feet moved, but she didn't feel the ground beneath them. All she could feel was the heat of CS's hand against her back. Squeezing her eyes shut, she could locate with microscopic precision every cell in contact with CS's hand. The way her skin came alive. The way jolts of electricity shot through her body. She felt the danger of that awareness and ignored it. Right now, tonight, she let herself believe that CS was squiring her to dinner and she wrapped herself in the joy of that. She'd had precious little joy in her life recently. She would cherish this moment.

CHAPTER TWENTY-FOUR

Madison drank more than she ate. At first it was because of her nervousness, but then it was because of the food. She'd only come to family meal a handful of times, usually when she just wanted to get out of the house. Early on the food was cooked by the restaurant hotel, but a month ago Kacey started taking over a few meals a week. She never said why, but Madison assumed it had a lot to do with vanity. Trying to get into the good graces of the staff, winning their admiration through their stomachs.

The upshot was that Madison could tell when the food was cooked by *ambrosia* and when it was cooked by the hotel restaurant. This was cooked by *ambrosia*. This was a menu designed by Kacey, and the thought of that turned Madison's mind to booze. She pushed food around her plate but very little made it to her mouth. Even cooked by someone else, this was Kacey's food and Madison wanted nothing to do with it.

CS felt her discomfort and leaned close. "The sous chefs are cooking the normal menu until our new chef arrives."

Madison smiled at her over her wineglass. How was it this woman knew what she was thinking? Considering that CS was sitting so close to her their elbows rubbed each time either of them moved, perhaps it wasn't that surprising that she noticed Madison's lack of appetite.

"So you already have someone new coming?"

CS scanned the table around them before she answered. Everyone was engaged in conversation, the room practically roared with voices. "I've hired Carter. From *Top Chef.* The one who was responsible for Kacey being eliminated."

Madison choked on her wine. "You're kidding?"

Madison's glass was empty and CS reached to the center of the table for the bottle, not bothering to set her fork down as she poured. "I had to negotiate very hard to get him here." She smiled wickedly and finished, "It was worth it."

Madison laughed so loudly she nearly spilled her wine. A few eyes turned to her, but they all had a sparkle of interest to share her glee rather than the perceived judgment she saw earlier. She lifted her fingers to her lips to cover her laughter, but that only served to keep all the giggles inside, shaking her body and her full glass with each new wave. CS was laughing, too, a genuine smile painted thickly across her face. She reached out and took Madison's hand down, exposing her toothy grin.

"I'm glad you approve of my pettiness. Don't cover your smile. It's good to see."

CS was so warm. So full of life. So captivating. Madison felt nothing else apart from CS's fingers on hers. The room around them melted away. Her ears plugged out the sounds of conversation and laughter. All her pain and shame fled in the power of that deep blue stare. When CS would have released her hand, Madison held on, slipping her fingers between CS's and rubbing one thumb across the woman's hard knuckle.

There were tears in her eyes, but Madison knew they wouldn't fall. They had everything to do with the current of electricity from their clasped hands and nothing to do with sadness. She gave CS's fingers a light squeeze and mouthed the words "Thank you."

CS blushed and looked for her wineglass, shrugging her shoulders in a flippant sort of way that was somehow not dismissive. Releasing Madison's hand finally, she sipped her wine.

"Carter made it to the finale. It's an upgrade."

Madison filled the hollowness of the loss of CS's touch with another long sip of wine. Her head swayed pleasantly, like the gentle lapping of waves on an anchored boat, from the company as much as the alcohol.

"So you finally watched the show?" Madison was shocked to hear the teasing note in her own voice.

"Yeah, I…A friend convinced me to watch last season online." She twirled her fork. Madison's eyes were drawn to the graceful dance of her fingers. "Just so I knew who I had in my restaurant."

"I still can't believe you didn't watch it before we got here."

CS set her fork down, hesitated, then reached for her glass. Madison felt her tension as CS stared into its contents. "She shouldn't have gotten that far. She wouldn't have if…she didn't get so much sympathy from everyone." She looked up into Madison's eyes and the rotation of the earth wrenched to a halt again. "Sympathy she didn't deserve."

It took a moment for Madison to drag herself far enough out of that stare to realize what CS meant. She'd watched the season, so she knew about the call. Kacey was on the verge of elimination when Madison called with the news about Robert. It wasn't during their scheduled call time, but the producers allowed Kacey to answer, even though they were in the middle of prep for the elimination challenge. At the time, Madison had been grateful for the deviation. Grateful that she had Kacey there to talk to if not to hold. To be fair, Kacey was wonderful that night. Talking Madison down from her hysteria, reminding her that she was loved. That she wasn't alone. She had been gentle and kind.

Madison hadn't realized the pressure Kacey was under in that moment. She also hadn't realized how much of the conversation was on camera. How much Kacey told everyone else when she got back to the kitchen. Or how much she told the camera during the confessional interview. She'd cried talking about Madison's pain that night, but she had shared quite a lot more than Madison would have wanted, had she known it would be made public.

It had been awful watching it on replay. Awful to relive the pain, but no less for the feeling of betrayal. Kacey was always extremely open with her own life, so it shouldn't have surprised her that she would be open with their conversation, but Madison was not quite so forthcoming with strangers. Millions of people watched this show, and now all of them knew her grief. It was hard not to feel like Kacey had stripped her naked and put her on display.

What no one else knew, not even Jada, was that Kacey had missed their next scheduled phone call. Madison had called, still broken from her loss, and heard an unanswered phone. Kacey never answered. They didn't speak again for ages. Not until the sympathy ran out and she'd been eliminated.

Madison drained her half-full wineglass in one swallow and pushed her plate away. "Why don't we go for a walk?"

"Oh." CS stood abruptly, knocking over some cutlery in her haste. "Sure."

The night was considerably cooler now. Madison and CS walked silently down the path, each lost in their own thoughts.

A sadness crept through Madison at the thought that she did not belong here any longer. Jada had been right—she would have to go eventually. This place would always be associated with Kacey, but, oddly, few of Madison's memories included her. Peaceful walks with CS at her side, her undemanding presence. Their comfort together.

As they neared Madison's cottage a strange energy grew between them. Madison shot a look at CS, wondering if she felt it too. Other than a barely perceptible tightening of her jaw, nothing marred CS's serenity, her gaze fixed on the moonlit trellises, the foliage dying back after the harvest. Their fingertips brushed as their arms swayed and CS did not pull back from the contact. When they entered the pool of light at the edge of

Madison's deck, she took the chance and caught CS's hand as it swung past.

Her attention finally snagged, CS looked over. The reflected light shimmered in her eyes, making them glow as she smiled down at Madison. She did not take her hand away.

"Thank you," Madison started, but couldn't decide how she wanted to complete the sentence. For walking me home? For taking me inside when I was frozen and heartbroken? For making me feel at home here? For the way my heart skips when you look at me like that?

"You're welcome," CS whispered in reply.

She was standing close, but Madison wanted to be closer. She took a step forward, bending her neck back to maintain their eye contact. CS's hand was so warm in hers. It wouldn't take anything at all for Madison to close that distance. To press forward and let their lips touch.

CS took a step back, letting Madison's hand drop and swing in the night air. She took another step back and smiled. "Good night, Madison. Thank you for having dinner with me."

She turned and disappeared into the night.

CHAPTER TWENTY-FIVE

Ever since she started ceramics, Madison had loved the hollow, scratching sound of stacking fresh pots in the kiln to be fired. She couldn't help herself from scraping them along the shelves, just to hear it. Once one shelf was full, she set the four spacers and seated the next shelf. It sat perfectly, just an inch or so above the first layer, closing the low bowls she'd made a few days ago into the depths of the oven. They were the first things she'd made since Kacey left and she had never been prouder of anything she'd done, not because of their perfection, but because of the struggle it took to bring them to life.

Madison was still getting used to the weather patterns here in western Oregon. The nearly constant winter rains meant plenty of moisture in the air. She'd have to account for that when timing her firing. She was nearly certain they were ready, but there was a science to ceramics as well as an art and that lead to uncertainty.

She ran a finger gingerly along the tall vase that was part of her top layer. It felt right, and she had a strange sense that this was going to work. Call it intuition. The pots she was in today, still considered greenware because they hadn't been fired yet, needed to be at the bone-dry stage of the curing process so that they would cook rather than steam on this first round in the kiln. After this she would paint and glaze them before giving them the final fire that would make them safe for use. And add them to her portfolio.

The bisque firing was Madison's favorite step. This was where heat on an almost unbelievable scale turned simple clay into ceramic. It started slowly. She'd warmed her kiln through the day, bringing the heat up slowly. Then the pots were loaded, placed like puzzle pieces so they covered as much of the surface as possible without touching. The superheated air, getting up to over seventeen hundred degrees Fahrenheit in the final stage, needed to flow freely around the pieces so they dried evenly.

The process was delicate, prone to disaster, but also the moment when the most beautiful pieces of art were forged into permanence. Over the course of several hours, the temperature rose in a closely marked schedule. The pot fully dehydrated, then the chemical nature of it changed. The molecules locked. The pot sintered, its disparate bits of clay coalescing into the material known as ceramic. A hearty material, stronger than the clay that bore it, but porous enough to be glazed or painted. Strong enough not to break, and open enough to be made more beautiful.

It was dangerous, though, to risk the pots by firing them this way. Exposure to the extreme heat rooted out every imperfection, no matter how small. Water would steam inside the clay and they would break. Break wasn't exactly the right word. They would shatter. Explode. The pieces shot across the crowded space inside the oven, and inevitably destroyed the pieces near them. Madison had lost some of her favorite pots to this quirk of chemistry. Not by mishandling the piece itself, but because the pieces around them ruptured and took her favorite with them. Collateral damage.

That wouldn't happen this time, she told herself as she set a timing cone in the lid and turned the switch. The motor hummed into life. She watched it for a moment, willing it to be a good batch.

Madison's cell phone blared into life with an electronic cacophony. She trotted out into the kitchen to retrieve it, answering just before it went to voice mail.

She eyed the rain pounding against the living room windows. "Hello?"

"Hey yourself." Jada's liquid voice was smug and silky tonight, a sure sign that she either had good news or was deep into her first martini.

"Almost missed you. I was just starting the kiln."

"At this hour? It must be…" There was a rustling as Jada tried to check her watch. "My god is that the time? Why am I calling you so late?"

"It's an hour earlier here."

"That's right, I forgot." Madison heard a cabinet open in the background and the tinkle of glass on granite. "Heaven love that man, he left me a shaker of martinis in the fridge. If he wasn't snoring so damn loud I'd go kiss him."

"He's a keeper."

"He's a slob and a child, but I love him, god help me. Anyway, enough about my husband. You know what happened tonight?"

Madison's stomach tied itself into knots, but she forced herself to be patient. "My opening."

"Your opening."

The line went quiet for a long time. Long enough for Madison to waver back and forth between abject fear and unbridled happiness approximately seventeen times. She finally blurted out, "Well?"

Jada left a heartbeat of silence, just to drag out the drama, before nearly shouting, "It was incredible!"

"Oh god!"

"You know I'm trying to be a detached professional here, Maddie, but I just can't." She paused for a second to sip her drink. "It was a huge success. You saw the photos I sent?"

Several hours ago, when the gallery was about to open, Jada had emailed her a few shots of her show. Madison had taken a few landscapes of the vineyard and had them blown up to black and white banners, hung behind the pedestals holding her pots. Her art was the only color in the stark white room. The effect was breathtaking, even seeing stills of it rather than being there, and Madison cried with delight at its perfection.

Jada was an expert at staging, drawing out every ounce of melodrama from a piece to entice her buyers, and her prowess was on full display with this show. The tall vase with the relief work she'd spent so much time on during the harvest was the centerpiece. Madison gasped when she saw the staging.

"Your best work yet, Jada."

"*Your* best work. It deserved nothing less from me." Another pause to sip her drink, but also, knowing Jada, for dramatic effect. "Everyone loved it. You should have heard this gallery during the show, it was buzzing. Literally buzzing."

"So they liked it?"

"Liked it? I had two clients nearly in a fistfight over the relief vase. It sold for a disgusting amount of money. Of course, you'll receive a check for slightly less disgusting amount within thirty days."

"What about the blue amphora? Did it sell?"

"For a fine amount. To an anonymous bidder though, it'll probably end up in some CEO's outer office in New York."

"That's fine," she said with the sort of happy disappointment of a parent whose child was moving away for college. "As long as someone wanted it."

"They wanted everything, Maddie. You sold out."

"What do you mean? I sold out at the opening?"

"That's what I mean."

"That doesn't happen."

"It does if you have a fantastic dealer showing your work. In fact, I had people begging for more. One of my best clients bought two vases and asked about your next show."

Panic started to set in. "But I don't have anything more. Nothing ready yet. I've been throwing, but it's been really rainy. I've been ignoring the shop here on the vineyard and throwing gallery pieces, but nothing's ready."

"Calm down, Maddie. Make yourself a cup of tea and listen to me." Madison heard Jada pour herself another drink and appreciated the break. "You don't need to do anything yet. We're going to wait on another show for you for a long while."

"We are?"

"We are. The more people crave something they can't have, the more they want it. I'm going to leave a few of your catalogs around the gallery with big sold stickers on them. By the time we have another show for you, these people will be drooling at your feet."

Madison couldn't sit still any longer, she popped off the couch and padded barefoot across the living room to the windows. The rain was falling in slow sheets, occasionally gusting against the glass with a puff of wind. She pressed her face to the cool surface and let the chill run through her. Her cheeks burned with her smile.

"Maddie? You still there?"

"I'm here. I'm just…"

She couldn't come up with the words, and she didn't need to. With another quick congratulation and a gentle reminder that she should move back to Denver with the proceeds, Jada hung up. Madison dropped the phone to the rug and pressed the rest of her body against the glass, spreading her arms and her legs out for as much coverage as she could manage. The cold seeped into her limbs. She could feel the rain and the wind through the glass as though it were on her skin. Her smile was too wide to ever go away.

CHAPTER TWENTY-SIX

When the doorbell rang, it broke Madison's focus for the first time in hours. She looked up from her wheel, blinking into the shimmering early daylight over the hills in the distance. The sky was clear of clouds for the first time in ages. She pressed down on the pedal and bent her head over the wheel again.

When the doorbell sounded a second time she growled in frustration. Taking her foot off the pedal, she looked over her shoulder. A sharp snap of pain shot through her neck and shoulders. She stood and her body screamed in protest. She couldn't quite remember what time she'd come in here last night, but she hadn't left since. She stumbled out of the room, her body adjusting to movement slowly as she made her way to the front door.

When she got the door open Boots was stepping down off the porch, and turned at the sound of her arrival. Fortunately, she looked down before she rushed to follow him. A massive basket, brimming with all manner of things and covered in a layer of cellophane, sat on the mat.

"Good morning!" Boots said in a cheery voice from the lawn. "Sorry to wake you, but you have a delivery."

Madison knelt to pick up the basket, but it weighed a ton. She grunted as she lifted it, cutting a jokingly mad look at Boots as he laughed at her struggle.

"Late night, Denver?"

She settled the basket on the bench by the door and slipped on a pair of flip-flops to go outside. "That depends on your definition. I haven't been to bed yet."

He scowled. "Not brooding over Kacey I hope?"

"No way." She brandished her dirty hands. "Working."

She followed him into the yard, noticing the vineyard was even more bare than normal. The explanation lay in Boots' cart, piled high with vine cuttings. Gnarled and twisted, and looking more like roots than branches.

He followed her gaze and explained, "We're pruning back the vines. Cutting out the dead growth so next year's can come in stronger. Been at it since first light."

Madison picked up a piece of vine. It was surprisingly light and covered with a papery bark and tiny side branches, all snapped off close to the main branch.

"What are you doing with it all?"

"Taking it to compost on the far end of the property. We have a chipper set up. I just stopped on my way out there to make your delivery."

The cutting in her hand had so much character, so much life, it made her infinitely sad to think it would soon be wood shavings on a compost heap. This was the artery that brought life to the grapes that made the best wine she'd ever tasted. The foundation of CS's special blend that she longed to drink again. It deserved a better resting place.

Boots was climbing back into the cart when she grabbed his arm. "Can I have some?"

"You want the cuttings?"

"Not all of them." She eyed the groaning cart, giving herself time to talk herself out of it, but the madness had taken her and she was determined. "Just a couple of loads. I'll help."

He shrugged and hopped down. "Where do you want 'em?"

They decided on a spot on the other side of the porch, tucked away out of sight behind the chimney and almost under the kitchen window. Madison said it was to keep them out of the way until she decided what to do with them, but it was also so people wouldn't see. She didn't want to have to explain that she couldn't explain why she wanted them. She hated playing the "because I'm an artist" card.

He left with a friendly wave. Madison picked up a piece at random, fingering the twisted curves. The wood spoke to her and she didn't want to ignore that voice inside her. Eventually, it would tell her what to do with them.

Back inside, she carried the basket over to the coffee table, kicking off her flip-flops and crawling onto the couch to open her gift. Setting aside the card with her name scratched on the outside in a spiky, untidy handwriting, she loosened the ribbon holding the cellophane in place.

A bottle of champagne, the label written entirely in French and looking like it cost more than every bottle she'd ever bought in her life, was the centerpiece. Around the wine were jars and boxes of gourmet snacks, several fine cheeses and meats and a bright yellow gerbera daisy in a pretty blue pot. Madison took each item out and examined it, marveling at the good taste of her mystery benefactor. Jada, kind as she was, wasn't particularly thoughtful in this way, so it couldn't be from her.

Madison clutched a bottle of green olives stuffed with garlic, her favorite snack in the world, to her chest as she pulled the last item out of the basket. It was a small box, not much larger than a ring box, wrapped neatly in plain blue paper. When she tore it away and lifted the lid, she saw a simple, teardrop-shaped crystal on a thin wire. She lifted it from the box and gasped.

The crystal twisted on its wire, turning to find its center. It caught the light pouring in through the wall of windows. The light shattered inside the teardrop and sent a thousand tendrils of refracted light. Sparkling light in all colors of the rainbow dotted the room. She stared at the dots of light on the wall, at the beams made visible by the dust motes floating in the air or at the glowing teardrop, still swaying gently as it dangled from her fingers. The sight was so beautiful it brought tears to her eyes.

She finally picked up the card, now desperate to know who sent the basket. Her favorite olives and the beautiful flower were one thing, but the teardrop prism was one of the most beautiful, thoughtful gifts she'd ever received. A simple object revealed an understanding of her love of light. There were very few people in her life who knew about it.

The card was plain, white cardstock. She was so shocked by what was written there that she read it out loud to the empty room.

"Congrats on the show. CS."

CHAPTER TWENTY-SEVEN

The winter cold snap barely lasted through December and by January the weather was mild as spring. It wasn't usual for this part of the country, but Madison wasn't complaining. She rarely worked well in the cold and gloom of winter, and this winter was worse than any she'd ever experienced. Her solitude left her working in fits and starts, barely keeping up with the diminished demand from the winery shop. It wasn't just her mood that thwarted her. The damp slowed her work. Pots that dried in a matter of days during the summer and autumn took a week or more after Christmas. Her shelves filled slowly and emptied even more slowly.

Boots made a bright spot of her winter. With less for him to do around the estate, he had taken to dropping by the cottage for coffee and a chat in the afternoon, keeping Madison from slipping too far back into her depression. Madison's initial assessment that they would end up being good friends, was borne out in those days. She was surprised to see him so often—most of the winery staff worked only seasonally and the place had practically emptied by January. The restaurant staff remained intact, since reservations were as coveted as ever, but Boots and CS appeared to be the only ones working the dormant fields.

Those winter afternoons were fun, sitting in front of a roaring fire and sharing tidbits about each other's lives. Madison told the story of Robert early on, only to discover that Boots knew the basics from watching *Top Chef*. Madison bristled again at the invasion of her privacy, but knew it was as much her own fault for calling when she knew all Kacey's communications were recorded. The mileage the network got from her pain was a sticky subject, and fortunately Boots was perceptive enough to make sure they didn't dwell on her grief.

He shared his own story with candor, which endeared him to her even more. His parents were undocumented immigrants, sneaking north across the border before he was born. Things went smoothly enough for him and his little sister, both born in Arizona, until the recent change in political fortune. Few American Presidents had been welcoming to Mexican immigrants, but this was the first to put them in cages. His father was deported after nearly thirty years in the country and his mother followed him willingly. She loved her children, but they were adults now and she would not be parted from her husband.

During the winter's only snowfall, Madison learned of the struggles his parents had trying to rebuild a life with nothing in a country they hadn't seen in decades. They had no family in Mexico anymore and barely remembered a life there. His sister joined them after graduating from college, but there was little to no chance Boots would see them for a long time. They couldn't even visit him because of the deportation and he worried what it would mean to cross the border these days. There was every chance that an emboldened bigot in Border Control could stop him from coming home just because of the color of his skin.

For as bleak a picture as he painted, there was no self-pity. It was one of the things Madison liked most about Boots. He had an unbreakable optimism, a rosy-cheeked joy in the way he looked at the world. Madison found herself happier in general when Boots was around.

Still, by the time the snow melted, even Boots' company was becoming monotonous. In the new year, Madison began to see CS stalking through the fields more often, and the itch in her feet nearly drove her mad. She wanted to be out in the vines again, even with the cold. She wanted to walk and talk with CS.

All of those desires came to a head one day when Boots stopped by earlier than usual to invite Madison out of the cottage. He and CS were going to ride through the vineyard to inspect the winterization and they wanted Madison to join them. He explained how she could ride Oscar, the calmest of the horses, but Madison didn't hear any of it. She didn't worry that she'd only had two or three riding lessons and the last one was weeks ago. She didn't worry that she would have no idea what they were discussing about the grapes. She didn't worry about Jada's voice in her head warning her to be careful when it came to CS. She ignored it all and ran to get her coat and sturdier shoes, practically pushing Boots out of the house.

CS met them at the stable door, the reins of three horses in her hand. She was attentive and kind to Madison, asking her to be honest about her comfort level and reminding her of the basics of mounting and riding before they set off.

"I'll look out for you. Keep close to me," CS said once they were all in the saddle.

Madison didn't need telling twice. Glorious sunlight washed over her face, warming her soul if not her skin. The day was still chilly, but the air was fresh and carried the unmistakable scent of life hibernating under the earth. Oscar was indeed gentle, with a slow, even step. He was dapple gray with a rump like a Dalmatian puppy and a beautiful silver mane.

The rows were too close to ride three abreast, so they staggered their line, allowing them to be close enough to talk without shouting and still ride comfortably between the vines. CS led the group, with Madison behind and Boots in the rear. Boots kept up a running commentary on the state of the vines.

"They're looking good, aren't they, CS? We've had a great winter. This year will be one of the best harvests."

"Don't jinx it, Boots."

He rolled his eyes when Madison looked back at him, swaying gracefully in his saddle. "She's so superstitious."

"How can you tell it'll be a good harvest?" Madison asked, looking at the bare vines.

"He can't," CS announced, her focus entirely on the vines. She sat comfortably in the saddle, her legs wrapped around Violet's flanks as though they were two parts of a whole. "He's trying to show off."

"Don't listen to her, Denver. I can read a dormant vine like the back of my hand. After all, I am apprenticed to the best winemaker in all of Oregon."

"That's not saying much. Besides, you are my horticultural apprentice, not my winemaking apprentice. Big difference."

The bickering was so adorable, Madison hated to break it up, but the energy of the sunshine was infectious and she couldn't keep quiet. "What did you do to protect the vines?"

If her goal was to get a chance to speak, Madison chose the wrong approach. Boots immediately launched into an explanation of the growth cycle of grapes, explaining the pruning process to encourage new, vigorous growth. She understood that at least since she still had a pile of dead cane behind her house. Unfortunately, he completely lost her after that. Something about bleeding water from the pruning wounds.

She came to understand, while he prattled on and she retained nothing, that Boots was excited by the business of growing of grapes. She hadn't realized his importance at the winery, hadn't known he was an apprentice, hadn't appreciated his enthusiasm. That enthusiasm was not the same as CS's, however. When she spoke about wine to Madison, it was the pouring out of a passion. Like a love story between grape and earth. She loved what she did. Madison craved the eloquence of CS's explanations, not the textbook descriptions from Boots.

As Boots talked, Madison grew restless. She could tell by the rigid set of CS's shoulders as they rode that she was itching to take over, but she never did. She showed a respect for Boots, understanding how his interest differed from her own.

The drone of Boots' voice and the swaying pace of the horse lulled Madison into a waking doze. CS stopped to take a closer look at a series of vines, letting the other two pull ahead. After a dozen paces, Madison turned to look back, wanting to make sure CS didn't leave her alone with Boots for too long.

As she turned, an unnatural movement caught Madison's eye. She looked down at the same time Oscar did, and their reactions were remarkably similar. A snake as thick as a tree branch, its body olive-brown with dark blotches ringed in white, slithered like a snapped whip around the base of the nearest vine. Its mouth grinned wickedly on its spade-shaped head. It raised its white-striped tail and shook it, the sound like dried beans rattling around in a paper cup. Madison's heart turned to ice. Had she been on the ground, she would have jumped, which is exactly what Oscar did.

With a shake of his massive head and a cry like a frightened baby, Oscar reared onto his back legs violently. Instinct alone kept Madison in the saddle. One foot slipped from the stirrup and she felt herself falling, so she threw her body at Oscar's neck and held fast. She caught her own wrists in her hands and locked her fingers in place, the skin pinching painfully. She smashed her eyelids together, pressing her face into the silky strands of the horse's mane so she could no longer see the snake.

Oscar screamed in her ear, drowning out the human sounds around her. Oscar bolted. His front legs slammed into the ground, forcing the stiff leather saddle into Madison's chest and the air out of her lungs. Hooves pounding on dry earth consumed her senses. Dirt clogged her nostrils and clung to her throat. Her heart raced faster than Oscar galloped.

Just as panic overtook her, the horse jerked to an unexpected stop. Madison's arms were at the limit of their strength and she slipped in the saddle, leaning drunkenly off the side where her foot hung free of the stirrup. She could feel the sweat drenching his neck. She started to fall and accepted her fate, waiting to feel a bone-jarring impact with the rocky soil. The impact, when it came, was much softer than she imagined. And warmer.

"I've got you."

Arms wrapped around her waist, easing her down.

"It's okay. You're safe."

Madison forced her arms to move, wrapping them around the body holding her up. Square shoulders and the softness of cotton. Madison opened her eyes as CS lowered her to sit on the ground, their arms entwined. The first thing she saw was Oscar. His eyes were wild and rolling and he yanked hard at the reins wrapped firmly around CS's hand. Seeing him reminded Madison of where she was, and she tried to scramble to her feet, her eyes rolling like the horse's, scanning the ground around her for the snake.

"Whoa. It's okay." CS held her firmly but gently in place. "You're safe."

"There's a snake!"

"You're not near the snake anymore." CS jerked her head over her shoulder, indicating how far they'd come. "You're safe."

Madison clawed at CS's arms wrapped around her, but she saw instantly that CS was right. They were a long way from where they'd started, Boots was barely visible, climbing off his horse, at the top of the rise behind CS. Her breathing slowed as she remembered the pound of Oscar's hooves. CS must have read Oscar's mind and spurred her horse on to follow the moment he bolted.

They'd nearly reached the end of the row and the steep drop of a ditch on the other side. No doubt Oscar would have bucked her off jumping it and torn through the trellises on the other side. Madison would have broken much more in that fall—probably her neck.

Boots gave a shout in the distance and Madison jumped at the sound. CS's arm tightened around her. She could feel the winemaker's breath on her neck, quick and shallow.

"It's okay," she said, breathing the words into Madison's hair.

Madison forced herself to nod, but her fear had not dissipated. She doubted it would for a long time.

"Do you think you could stand?"

She nodded again and scrambled to get her feet beneath her. With a gentle press of muscles into her lower back, CS pulled her to her feet, setting her right so easily she may have weighed nothing at all. Madison's knees weren't up to the task of locking at the moment, and CS held on to her, keeping that band of steely muscle tight around Madison's waist.

"Better?"

"Not really."

"Worse?"

Madison shook herself, trying to convince herself that the approaching clop of hooves didn't make her want to curl into a ball in the dirt.

"You okay, Denver?"

Madison nodded again, her eyes searching him for a patch of blood on leg or arm that would account for his shout.

Boots turned his attention to CS. "Oregon rattler. Big one, too. I made enough noise for him to take off. He'll be at the property line by now."

CS unwound one of the reins from her hand and passed it up to him. "Take Oscar back to the stables and check him out."

"What about Denver?"

"I'll bring her back. It's okay. Just go."

Madison turned back to the group. She smiled up at Boots, but he wasn't fooled. No doubt he could see the strain in her face. She wanted to reach out to Oscar, to stroke his neck and reassure him, but his eyes still reflected the wild fear she felt.

Just as her breathing shallowed and she wondered idly if she was hyperventilating, Boots trotted off and she was left alone with CS and Violet. The more familiar horse was completely unfazed by the whole incident. She nuzzled at CS's shoulder as she had that day by the tree. The third time she pushed at CS, she nearly knocked the woman into Madison.

"Okay, fine!" CS growled, digging a cube of sugar from her pocket. "Spoiled horse."

Watching Violet munch away at the sugar with what could only be described as a triumphant grin on her lips, Madison started to chuckle, then laugh. It wasn't long before the laugh became hysterical and tears started running down her cheeks. She knew in a detached sort of way that she was cracking up. The stress and fear broke over her and the laughter through tears turned into straight tears. CS's arm was still around her waist, and she buried her face into her strong shoulder as her body shook.

"It's okay."

Madison managed to get out through the tears and hiccups, "I know."

"You're safe."

She felt safe. She felt safe with the snake and spooked horse gone. She felt safe with her feet firmly on the ground. She felt safe in the circle of CS's arms.

The tears passed quickly. Her knees solidified and she took a step back, out of CS's arms, to pull a handkerchief out of her back pocket. It was CS's bandana. The one she'd given Madison the day they met under the tree. She'd intended to give it back today, but hadn't gotten to it. Using it now to scrub her face, it occurred to her how often she'd cried in front of CS. The thought brought a flush of embarrassment to her face and she determined to toughen up in the future.

After a long moment, CS asked hesitantly, "Better?"

"Sure."

"Then swing up. Let's get you home."

CS held Violet tight against her side and indicated the stirrup by her knee.

"Absolutely not."

"You don't want to go home?"

"I want to walk home. No offense, Violet, but there is no way I'm getting on that horse."

CS stood straighter and took a step closer, her face deadly serious. "You have to."

"I can't." Madison took a step back, her knees wobbling. "I can't, CS."

"If you don't get up there and ride now, you never will."

"Fine by me."

"Not by me." She reached out, putting a warm hand on Madison's shoulder. "You can do this. Do you trust me?"

She'd expected the question, but that didn't make it any less unfair. It was a coercive question. The sort of thing people ask in movies to convince and cajole. She couldn't turn down the ride now, no matter how great her fear. It wasn't fair, but that didn't change her answer.

"Yes."

CS moved back to Violet's side, making herself an anchor for Madison. "Left foot in the stirrup and swing over with the right."

"I know how to mount a horse."

Madison slipped her foot in the stirrup and hesitated. She knew she wasn't supposed to. CS told her on the first lesson that it was a capital mistake to stand with one foot in the stirrup for too long. It made her vulnerable to injury if the horse was skittish and started to move. Still, she was afraid and CS was there holding Violet in place so she couldn't get hurt. She closed her eyes when she pushed up. Her right knee banged painfully into the rear of the saddle, but she corrected it quickly and was seated. With a wriggle of her right foot, she had both feet in place and felt a little more secure.

Madison looked down into CS's eyes. For one, heart-stopping moment she thought CS was going to climb up into the saddle with her. Blood roared in her ears and she nearly tipped forward. Instead of mounting, she leaned over and adjusted the stirrups to Madison's slightly shorter height. She slipped to the other side and adjusted the one at her right foot, one hand on Madison's ankle.

"Comfortable?"

When Madison nodded, she made a clicking noise with her tongue and started to walk. Violet kept closely to CS's pace, a slow, gentle walk that made Madison sway even more than normal. CS kept the lead short, walking at Madison's side with only enough slack for Violet to keep her eyes ahead.

The first few steps were a nightmare. Had she been alone, she would have screamed in fright and maybe even started crying again. Just in case, she kept a painfully tight grip on the bandana in her fist. The other hand held the pommel as though it were her only life line, though it wouldn't do her much good if Violet were to take off like Oscar had.

Once they turned onto the path, finding smoother, flatter ground, Madison relaxed. She looked down at CS, walking so close that her shoulder occasionally brushed against Madison's knee. Now that she had her wits about her again, she was able to examine the moment when she swung into the saddle. Looking back, it was almost as unsettling as the runaway horse. Perhaps more so, since the implications were far deeper.

She'd wanted CS to climb up into the saddle with her. Wanted them sharing the cramped seat. The plodding movement of the horse making them sway in rhythm together. Their thighs squeezed against each other. CS's hands wrapped around Madison, pulling her close. The press of her body into Madison's back, the swell of her soft flesh evident in the contact with her shoulder blades. Their hips rocking together as Violet picked her way down the path. CS's mouth close to her ear. The whisper of her chocolate-smooth voice. The warmth of her body enveloping Madison.

"Quite a day."

CS's voice jerked her out of the fantasy so abruptly, Madison tipped sideways on the smooth leather. Reaching up from the ground with one strong hand, CS held her hip, setting her back into her seat. Madison blinked hard to force her mind away from the press of CS's fingertips on her waist. She bit her lip to keep from groaning.

"I'm sorry. I shouldn't have made you ride," CS said, doubt seeping through every word.

"Oh no, I'm fine." She moderated her tone, allowing CS to think she was jumpy about the horse, not the daydream. "Violet's very gentle."

Madison focused on the feel of CS's hand on her hips. They were coming up to her cottage now, the lights she'd left on in her rush to leave making it glow like a jewel in the lateness of the afternoon. The sun would be down soon. Another day closing out on the winery, though they were finally getting longer.

CS slowed Violet to a stop and reached up for Madison, who swung her leg over, trying desperately not to feel the way their bodies slid against each other. CS's belt buckle caught the hem of Madison's shirt, pulling it up slightly to expose a patch of skin just above the band of her jeans. When the cold metal of the buckle pressed against the exposed flesh, no amount of biting her lip could keep Madison's body from responding. She hoped CS didn't feel the shiver that passed through her from the tips of her toes to her sweaty scalp, but that was only wishful thinking. Their bodies touched in a dozen places and CS had to feel the electricity.

"Will you be okay?" CS asked, her eyebrows pinching together. "Can I start a fire for you? Make you some tea?"

The prospect was alluring, to have CS come into her cottage and take care of her, but she would feel the aches of her adventure soon and she'd rather CS not see her crumble any more than she already had.

"No, thank you. I'll be fine."

"Call me if you need anything, okay?"

Madison swallowed hard, her legs starting to shake again. All she could manage was a nod. CS watched her walk inside before she led Violet off to the stables. Madison watched her go, her hand gripped tight around the stone of her fireplace.

CHAPTER TWENTY-EIGHT

Madison's artistic inspiration faded faster than her bruises. Doubt crept back in and thoughts of her failed relationship broke her creative mood. When her hands were idle other worries picked at her. The most prevalent was the way CS had held her close after her snake adventure. Madison thought a connection had been growing between them, but then CS had turned and walked away. The constant motion in her mind kept her far from her wheel. Instead she loaded her kiln with the last of her pots and hoped that something would spur her before these pieces were done.

In the end she did what she'd done each of the last three afternoons—pulled out a piece of discarded grapevine and turned it in her hands, willing an idea to come to her. She wasn't much of a visual artist. Ceramics aside, Madison didn't excel in the sort of vision required to turn raw materials into works of art. If it wasn't clay, her mind went blank. When she looked at a blank canvas, all she saw was a blank canvas.

These vines were different. There was something there. Something calling to her from the twisted shapes. Something she just couldn't quite see yet. She brought a chunk no bigger than her fist in the rough shape of a question mark inside and laid it on her coffee table in plain sight so the vine could speak to her when it was ready.

The knuckle of dead wood didn't tell her any more today than it ever had. She jogged up the stairs for her tennis shoes and a thicker sweater. When she checked in the mirror, she was relieved to see that both looked quite good with her gray skinny jeans. Her foot barely touched the hardwood of the living room when the kiln buzzer, muffled slightly by the distance, finally sounded.

With the kiln clicking as it cooled in the late afternoon air, Madison slid open the windows in the sunroom and stepped out the back door into the chilly late afternoon.

The cool air felt wonderful on her overheated skin. It hadn't occurred to her until now how warm the cottage got when the kiln was running. She should have turned the heat down before starting it up, especially since she wasn't paying the electricity bill. The solar panels discreetly positioned on the roof notwithstanding, a kiln was a power guzzler and she should be more mindful. Mundane thoughts of monthly bills carried her across the vineyard in a daze.

It wasn't only restlessness that called her out here. Madison hoped that being among the pruned vines would inspire her. Her best work had come from her walks through the grounds, and the pressure of her success at the Welch Gallery coming so soon on the heels of her life's upheaval seemed to suck the air out of her studio. She needed to be out here, in the fresh, cold air and the silence.

The silence, however, extended to her mind today. She walked through the rows, letting her fingers trail occasionally along the cut vines. The light was diffuse and gray, the winter sun muted by high, insubstantial clouds.

"What am I doing here?" Madison said out loud to the wispy clouds.

The wind cut through her wool sweater and blew loose strands of hair into her eyes. She came to the end of a row and emerged onto one of the cart paths. Looking around to get her bearings, she saw she'd made her way to the back side of the vineyard.

She was about to turn and head down the path to her right, giving her a quicker, more direct path home, when a figure emerged from the rows closer to the main building. It only took a single glance to identify CS's quick, sure gait. She stopped at the edge of the ditch to finish writing in her pocket notebook and Madison was seized with the desire to slip back into the row behind her and hide.

Madison found herself craving the winemaker's company. That craving, more than the foul weather, had kept her inside the last few days. Now there was the matter of the gift basket, the thought of which made her uncomfortably happy, and how CS had cradled her as she tumbled from Oscar's back.

CS finished scribbling and looked around. She stopped when she saw Madison and nodded. Madison waved and thought she saw, though she was several yards off and it was hard to be sure, CS smile in acknowledgment.

Madison should have turned and headed back to her cottage. The cold was under her clothes now, working its way into her skin and soon would be bone-deep. She should go home, start a fire in the living room fireplace and get back to the paperback she'd been struggling through. Or maybe sit at her wheel until the muse found her or the kiln cooled enough to be unloaded. She should do anything other than turn to her left and head up the slight incline of the path toward CS.

"Thank you for the gift," Madison said quietly after arriving at CS's shoulder. "I love the crystal prism. I've hung it in my studio."

"It seemed like something you would like."

That wasn't quite the response Madison hoped for, but it was at least in keeping with CS's personality. Short on emotion and straight to the point. She should have asked her how she knew about the show. Or how she knew it went well. Maybe even how she remembered Madison was fascinated by light and so would probably like a prism. All of those questions went unasked because she feared they would go unanswered.

"No ill effects from your gallop with Oscar?" CS asked stiltedly.

"I was sore for a day, but I'm fine now," Madison lied. She'd been sore for two days and only a long, hot bath this morning kept it from being three days.

They walked together in silence, a habit that had become increasingly comfortable for Madison. Despite the fact that they talked so little and CS rarely shared anything about herself she felt like she knew this woman well. She was comfortable in her company. They had the same rhythm when they walked, both scanned the horizon too intently to bother with conversation. Madison noticed how CS shortened her stride to keep to Madison's unhurried pace. They both seemed to have a destination, though Madison's was dictated more by whim and CS's probably more by familiarity.

"Can I ask you a personal question?" Madison ventured.

"No."

"Oh." She was taken aback and felt her face burn red hot in the cold air. "Sorry."

"That was supposed to be a joke." CS slowed and looked over at Madison, who saw she had a rosy glow to her cheeks as well. It looked distinctly out of place there. "I don't joke well. What's your question?"

"I...uh..." She plowed ahead with her question. "What does CS stand for?"

CS laughed. Actually laughed, although she barely opened her mouth and the sound was so throaty and low it could have been a growl rather than a laugh. "That's one secret I was hoping to take to the grave."

Madison smiled, all thought of the cold and her embarrassment melted in the warmth of CS's unexpected candor. "Now I have to know."

"My mom was a singer before she met my dad. Not a good one, I'm sorry to say, but she loved music and there was nothing that would stop her from singing, even a lack of talent. She liked disco. She was a backup singer for some pretty terrible C-list bands in the height of Disco Fever." She looked at the toes of her boots and finally said, "My name is Cher Sonny Freeburn."

"You're kidding."

"Now you know why I go by CS."

Madison couldn't catch the laughter before it trumpeted out of her. She slapped a hand across her mouth, but it didn't work. She had to stop and bend over, her hands on her knees. To her great relief, she heard CS laughing too.

"Oh god, I'm so sorry." She looked up through tear-filled eyes and said between hiccupping laughter, "Yeah, now I know why you go by CS."

"What can I say? My mom liked them. If I'd been a boy, I'd have been SC, so it could have been worse."

Madison straightened carefully wiping the last tear from under her eye. "I don't mean to be rude, but I'm not sure that's worse."

CS's smile was crooked, hooking up over one squared-off incisor, and her eye sparkled with humor. "No, it isn't is it?"

They started walking again, chuckling occasionally and taking a gentle pace. The path split, one way curving around to meet the main road, the other keeping straight toward the rear of the main building. They slowed, neither seeming to want the inevitable parting. CS stuffed her hands deep into her pockets. The sleeves of her denim button-up were rolled up to the elbow and the blond hair on her forearms stood up from the cold.

"Look, I'd appreciate it if you didn't tell anyone about my name." She ran a hand through her hair. It feathered out softly around her fingers. "Especially Boots. I don't know if he'd let me live it down."

"He doesn't know?"

"No one knows."

"Why did you tell me?"

CS stared right into her eyes and Madison had the sense again that she could get lost there if she let herself. A part of her pulled toward that possibility.

CS shrugged and said evenly, "You asked."

"Oh."

Madison looked away, over her shoulder toward the path home. She thought of the empty fireplace and her empty studio and the empty living room. It felt colder there than it did out here and she groped for a reason to stay. CS started to turn toward the building and Madison's eyes fell, landing on the last few sprigs of lavender clinging to life under the pruned vines.

"Why do you have the mint and lavender planted here?" Madison blurted before she could stop herself.

CS turned back without hesitation. "Mint is a natural insect repellent and lavender keeps deer away from the grapes."

"Really?"

"Not really. They're supposed to, but I still have a problem with both. They do add to the flavor of the wine though."

"You can taste them in the wine just because they're growing here?"

"Sure," she said, scowling at Madison. "What, you can't taste it? Or at least smell it?"

"I've never tried your wine. Other than the special blend…" She let her words fade away so she didn't have to mention the barrel room.

CS came to an abrupt stop, her boots skidding on the rocky soil. "What?"

Madison turned back to her, feeling her cheeks burn at the return of the woman's cold stare. "It's nothing personal."

"You live here. Don't you like wine?"

"I love wine. Yours is just a little above my price point."

Before leaving Colorado, Madison had taken advantage of one of her few drinking nights to try Minerva Hills wine, so she went to her local wine store to pick up a bottle. According to the store owner, the pinot noir had just been awarded ninety-seven points from *Wine Advocate* and a gold medal in a pair of competitions. It was on sale for three hundred dollars a bottle. That was two hundred eighty dollars more than she'd ever spent on wine. She'd thanked him for his time and left empty-handed.

CS's face was stone. Her lips barely moved when she said, in a flat, no-nonsense voice, "Follow me."

CHAPTER TWENTY-NINE

They entered the lobby through the back door and went straight to the tasting room, which CS unlocked with a ring of keys attached to her belt loop by a wallet chain. A couple of people who'd been lazily wandering around the lobby attempted to enter with them. CS stopped to explain through the barely open door that the tasting room was closed on Mondays, and directed them to a handful of other options that did not include interrupting Madison's private tasting.

Every time she'd seen the Minerva Hills tasting room, it was packed elbow-to-elbow. Today, with the room empty, she had the opportunity to look at the place. What she saw was stunning. A rustic yet polished charm, eminently suited to the refined agricultural setting of a vineyard.

The floor was an aged, artfully pockmarked hardwood a shade lighter than the cherry ceiling beams. If Madison didn't know the building was less than two years old, she would have thought a century's worth of boots had trod across these panels. Tall bistro tables dotted the room, each one of polished wood with flourishes of wrought iron. An antique, mismatched hurricane lamp and a small glass vase holding sprigs of lavender graced every table.

There was an equally welcoming modern touch. The wall art was abstract white canvas and slashes of bright paint, their brushstrokes the main attraction. Chrome crosshatch shelving behind the bar stretched from countertop to high ceiling, bottlenecks poking out to reveal their foil caps. With its pale wooden slats and chrome flashing, the bar top perfectly mimicked a wine barrel and its hoops in a modern, minimalist way.

The patio offered a spectacular view over the rear of the vineyard, its sloping hills and the single, gnarled tree marooned in the center.

"Incredible," Madison breathed. It seemed that every passing day showed her one more reason to think that she had, quite accidentally, stumbled into paradise. Heaven on earth here in the Oregon mountains.

CS had made her way behind the bar, snatching a series of bottles from the cooler and shelves and setting out a pair of glasses in front of each. Madison walked slowly to the bar, watching the winemaker's swift but calculated movements and the determined look. She slipped onto the barstool in front of the line of bottles.

"I know why this room is always full now."

CS gave an inquisitive grunt while, with a tiny knife at the end of a folded corkscrew, she set about cutting the foil from one of the bottles.

"Apart from the living room of our cottage, this may be the most beautiful room I've ever been in. I love the décor. It's perfect."

"Thank you." She popped the cork out of the first bottle and set it on the bar before grabbing the second bottle and setting to work opening it. "I designed it myself. I'm afraid I bullied my architect a lot during the planning, but I knew what I wanted."

"You designed this?"

CS nodded, starting on the third bottle, red wine rather than white like the first two. "The restaurant, too, but this room is more important."

Looking around with a more critical eye, Madison could see all the signs that proved CS favored this room over *ambrosia*. Something almost reverent in the slope of the ceiling or the selection of the furnishings. She may not have noticed it without the admission, but now that she knew, it was glaringly obvious. She wondered if Kacey had noticed. The thought had come unbidden and turned her stomach sour.

CS had started pouring samples into the paired glasses in front of each. She stopped, setting the bottle down on the bar with a loud thunk and shooting a quick glance at Madison. If she hadn't known better, she'd think CS's cheeks showed a flush of pink. "I'm sorry. I shouldn't have mentioned..."

"It's okay."

She sighed, spinning the bottle on the countertop and speaking to the label in front of her. "Are you..."

"I'm fine. Really." She was, wasn't she? She hadn't felt like this thinking about Kacey in days. Not since she'd been back to her wheel. She didn't want to feel like this about her ever again.

"Okay then, you've delayed long enough. Are you ready?"

Madison smiled at the challenge, sweeping her eyes across the display in front of her. CS must still give tastings despite her many responsibilities. Madison was impressed with the fluidity of her movements.

"Ready as I'll ever be, just..." It was Madison's turn to blush and she hid it far less effectively than CS. "I'm not really a connoisseur or anything."

"That's okay," CS said. She had the ease of a practiced artist as she slid one of the glasses in front of Madison and picked up its twin by the bottom of the stem. "I am."

The first wine was a chardonnay. Madison had never been a fan, finding it too heavy, thick on her tongue like cream, and buttery in an unpleasant way. This was nothing like that.

"This is really good."

The surprise must've shown in her voice. CS sipped from her glass, but kept an appraising eye on Madison. "You don't usually like chardonnay, do you?"

"Not really."

When she explained the heaviness and butter, CS nodded knowingly. "It isn't the grapes you don't like. It's oak. Specifically American oak."

"Are you questioning my patriotism?"

CS laughed at her rather lame joke a little faster this time, allowing Madison a chance to relax as she explained, "California chardonnays are aged in barrels made of American oak. I use milder French oak barrels. It helps me avoid the heavy-mouth feel of the California bottles."

The explanation made sense, but CS's elegant commentary soon went over Madison's head. That was the moment that CS moved on.

Madison discovered she was quite good at reading her audience. Knowing just how far to take an explanation and how to correct her tasting technique without appearing condescending. When she demonstrated how to swirl the wine and the proper way to smell it, Madison followed along excitedly. She was also pleased to see that CS didn't hold with the odd way of tasting a wine that Madison had seen from a painter she'd met in grad school, who would take a mouthful of wine and make a show of slurping air through his lips, making the most unpleasant gargling noises.

"That's all he was doing too. Making a show." CS tipped her glass back, swallowing the rest of her chardonnay and moving their glasses to the back counter. "It's true that you can taste the wine better that way, but a good wine can be tasted by, you know, drinking it. Plus you don't look like a jackass."

Madison's nose was deep in her second glass, so she snorted her laughter, trying hard to avoid spilling the wine. "He did look like a jackass."

"Wine isn't meant to be studied like that in the glass. Sure, you can taste it better on the first sip by sloshing it around in your mouth, but what about the second sip? What about the second glass? Wine is an experience. The flavor comes as much from the experience as from the bottle."

"What do you mean?"

CS held out the second glass, looking into the translucent contents. Only the slightest yellow glowed in the late sun through the window. "Take our pinot gris for instance. It's light, refreshing in a way that you can't really get from chardonnay. This one is earthy with an herbal bouquet. Can you smell that?"

"I'm not sure, what does it smell like?"

CS reached over slowly, grabbing a vase of lavender from the center of the bar. She smacked her hand on the thigh of her jeans, picking up a smear of vineyard dirt on her palm before snatching the stalk of lavender and crushing it in her hand. She turned back to Madison and offered her open palm full of bruised greenery, reddish-brown dirt and tiny, pulverized flowers.

After a moment's hesitation, Madison bent her nose to CS's hand, closing her eyes as the warmth of her skin and the mingled fragrances washed over her. The moment she closed her eyes, images poured in. Her first walk through the vineyard with the mist trailing into the distance. Running into her grandmother's room and pulling open a dresser drawer, sun-dried cotton skirts and little purple sachets that smelled like home and warmth. Unconsciously, Madison reached out and wrapped a hand around CS's, holding it close to keep the memories there.

A quiet cough from across the bar brought Madison back. She opened her eyes and saw CS's palm, strong and dusty, and her own, thinner, more delicate fingers cupping it. She released CS and straightened, looking down at her glass to avoid her eye.

"Now smell the wine again," CS said in silky whisper.

Madison swallowed hard and smelled again. She caught the scent now. The fruit of the wine was there, but underneath it was her grandmother's farm in Iowa where she grew rows and rows of corn, knitted endless afghans and counted her rosary while watching *The Price is Right*. She could almost hear the clicking of the big wheel and her grandmother's nails against the well-worn beads.

She looked up to see CS watching her and blushed. "Sorry. Got lost in thought."

"Don't apologize, that's exactly what I mean about wine. It's an experience."

Madison sipped the wine, and she could taste lavender and the Iowa sunset. "Incredible."

"If you hadn't thought of that memory, would the wine have tasted different?"

Madison scowled, pushing the memory away as she tasted again. Her grandmother was gone, but so was the life of the wine. It was tasty, but it wasn't the same wine she'd tasted a moment ago. Flowery and fresh, but fluttering about the surface rather than plunging deep into her soul like it had before.

"Definitely." CS dumped the flowers into a trashcan and wiped her hand on a towel.

"It's delicious. What was this again?" Madison asked.

"Pinot gris." CS drained her glass and set it aside. "We don't make a lot of it. The grape is similar to pinot noir, which is what we're famous for, but it isn't a big seller."

"That's too bad. I like it."

"California still dictates what Americans drink, and they make chardonnay."

CS reached next for the bottle, a pinot noir. The previous wines, small pours as they were, was already starting to make Madison's head spin.

While CS cut the foil from this bottle, Madison slowly sipped her pinot gris, wanting it to last. CS's shoulders were relaxed now and Madison saw again the passionate artist who'd come to life during their winery tour.

"So how did a nice girl like you get into a dirty business like winemaking?"

She hadn't meant to say the words out loud really, but Madison was slumping low in her stool now, her mind and body relaxed to a degree they hadn't been in ages. She was enjoying herself and she wanted to know more about her companion. Still, she wondered if the question sounded as flirtatious to CS as it did in her own ears. A growing part of her hoped it did.

CS dug the corkscrew into the bottle, a slow smile spreading across her face. She looked up at Madison as she worked the cork.

"Raiding the liquor cabinet when I was a stupid kid. My parents were away at the opera or something. I was a moody teenager and I decided I wanted to get drunk while they were out."

"I remember a night or two like that."

"Every kid does, right? I came from money and I was a little spoiled. Anyway, the only thing I could find was my dad's wine stash, so I picked a bottle and sat down with a juice glass."

"That's why you're so good at opening bottles. You started young."

"I wasn't so good at it then. Cut my finger wide open on the corkscrew, didn't take the foil off first. I barely got the cork out."

"So your first time drunk was a bottle of wine and you were hooked for life?"

"It's a better story than that." She set the bottle aside, leaning both palms on the bar, forcing out the muscles of shoulders and chest and looking like a looming colossus. "The bottle I picked...I didn't know any better, you see. I just grabbed the first thing I saw. Turns out it was a Chateau Lafitte Rothschild. My dad grounded me for a month when he found me."

There was an expectancy to those words that Madison could feel but not understand. "Why? Is that a good wine?"

CS chuckled, shaking her head. "Sorry, I forgot you're new to the wine world. I told my ex that story and she nearly fainted."

Something buzzed pleasantly in Madison's wine-soaked brain, making her grin wickedly. "So it's a very good wine."

"It was probably worth about four thousand dollars."

Madison choked on the last of her pinot. "Four...thousand?"

"It's a Bordeaux. One of the top five vineyards in the world known as first growths."

"Who would pay four thousand dollars for a bottle of wine?"

"I have six bottles in my cellar." When Madison shook her head, CS just shrugged. "It's the goal. What I want to make. I'm just trying to perfect one bottle of wine before I die."

Madison thought of the liquid light captured on her eyelash. "I can understand that."

CS leaned forward, resting her elbows on the bar, a genuine smile on her face. "I didn't even get drunk that night."

"Don't tell me four-thousand-dollar wine is nonalcoholic."

"Definitely not. I barely drank any of it. The minute I popped the cork on that bottle, the smell of it filled the room.

I'm not exaggerating—it filled the room. At first I thought it was suffocating, but then I could smell so much."

"What did it smell like?"

CS closed her eyes, the smile arching her lips. Madison squeezed her hands tightly together to keep herself from reaching out and tracing the line. The power of that urge shocked her and she shook her head to try and drag herself out of the feeling.

"It was musty, that was the first part. Some people call it a barnyard smell, but that isn't quite right. It smelled like an historic house. Hundred-year-old wood in the walls and boxwoods in the front yard. And the fruit was intense. Red cherry. The sort that soaks in rum or handmade preserves. Old fruit. Prunes and maybe some apricot. It's hard to put it all into words. When a smell overwhelms you like that."

Madison understood the feeling from her summertime journey to the clearing. "So you just sat there and smelled it?"

"I sipped a glass while I smelled it. I wanted to remember everything, but it started to fade. That's when my dad came home."

"I'm guessing he went through the roof."

"Mom did more than anything. He looked mad, but he didn't yell."

"Don't tell me he hit you."

"Nope. He got a glass from the cabinet and sat down at the table with me. We drank the bottle together, talking about how it tasted."

"No way."

"Yep. I told him I wanted to make a wine like that one day." She pushed herself off the counter and grabbed the bottle. "That's a story for another day. We have one more to taste."

Madison giggled, sliding the empty glass on the counter toward her. She was definitely buzzed now, teetering close to drunk. "This one looks nice. I love the color."

CS popped the cork, set the corkscrew down and poured an ounce or so into Madison's glass. Long before she finished pouring, the smell of the wine filtered through the air. It was close to the wine they had tasted from the barrel all those weeks ago, but not nearly close enough. CS opened her mouth to describe the wine, but Madison held up her hand for silence before CS could utter a syllable. It wasn't polite, but the humming in Madison's head begged for silence while it analyzed the wine.

Lifting the glass to her nose, Madison closed her eyes. The first thing she detected was the lavender, its floral notes and pungency. Mixed with the earthiness and the dark berry scents, the mint was nearly lost. She had an inkling it was there if she searched for it, but the experience of just smelling this wine was too pleasant to force. She felt like she was in a museum, looking at an old master painting and studying it minutely. She wished she'd had the explanation of how to smell wine before she tasted CS's blend so she could have appreciated it like this.

Madison's face burned with the stretch of her smile, and she opened her eyes laughing. While her eyes were closed, the rest of the world seemed to have slipped away, and all she could see now was the vibrant blue shine of CS's eyes. There was a contentment Madison had not seen before, the appreciation of an artist sharing their passion.

Madison allowed herself, for a tiny moment, to get lost in those eyes. To stare back into them with the same naked honesty they reflected. To see the woman behind them and let herself be seen in return. She felt like she was falling into those eyes, tumbling toward something beautiful and strange but something intensely dangerous. She knew she should blink. Should sit back. Should do something to break the spell, but she didn't want to. Not yet. Not when she'd just discovered this quiet woman had a loud soul.

The door banged open behind her, startling Madison. She turned to see a group surging through the tasting room door—an older man with a wide smile and wavy salt-and-pepper hair flowing to his shoulders. She turned back to CS, only to find her gone, busying herself behind the bar with glasses and bottles.

"What's this?" the man with the salt-and-pepper hair said in a booming, musical voice. "You've started without us!"

CHAPTER THIRTY

The man was Andrew Drack, but everyone just called him Drack except Boots, who called him Joker.

"And who might you be, my dear?"

"Madison Jones."

She held out her hand to shake, but with a deft little move, he turned her wrist and kissed it with soft lips. "A pleasure."

"Don't let Drack scare you off," CS said, coming around the bar with seven or eight wineglasses in one hand and a pair of the bottles they'd just opened in the other. "He's a nice guy when you get to know him."

"Nonsense." He stepped closer, smiling down at Madison, a feat he managed by standing on his tiptoes and trying to glower. "I'm a complete asshole when you get to know me."

"I can tell," Madison said with a smile.

He threw his head back and laughed at the ceiling. "Oh, I like this one. Can we keep her?"

CS came back over, her hands free, and explained to Madison, "Monday nights a group of the local winemakers get together here."

"We're essentially a gaggle of old women, drinking wine and gossiping about everything." Drack wrapped his arm around CS's shoulders. "Except this one. She usually broods in a corner, watching us all and thinking about her barrels."

CS didn't argue, her face stonily impassive again.

"Usually she relaxes if we can get enough wine into her, isn't that right CS?"

"No."

"Well," Madison said, climbing off her stool and backing toward the door. "I'll get out of your way. Thank you for the tasting, CS. I'll…"

"You'll sit back down and join us," Drack said, hooking his arm around her elbow so quickly she didn't have a chance to dodge. "Or better yet, sit at the table next to me so I can regale you with my charm and wit."

"Oh no, I don't want to intrude."

"Stay."

The simple command brought Madison's attention back to CS. By the time she looked, the woman's face was impassive again, but after so many chances to see the personality hidden beneath her hard exterior, Madison could no longer see her as surly. Now she just saw a woman who didn't say anything unless she had something worthwhile to say.

She replied without considering. "Okay."

"You see what we do here," Drack explained, leading Madison to a large table on the patio with every seat occupied and a dozen bottles standing in the center. "Is talk about our wineries and our processes. You'll find that part boring, but you'll indulge us because, while we talk, we try each other's wines."

He introduced her to everyone at the table, telling her their name and the name of their winery. There were nine or ten of them there, and Madison knew by the first introduction that she wouldn't remember any of their names. Their faces swam past, forgettable and tan. She vaguely noticed one woman, a skinny brunette who was obviously gay and obviously checking her out, and a married couple in their fifties who held hands as though they were providing each other oxygen.

Drack deposited her in the seat next to his and told her she was not allowed to move unless it was to fetch them both more wine. He was precisely the same jubilant, bubbly man who walked through the door with a flourish even as his neck went from tan to pink to red as he drank deeply from glass after glass.

The group chatted like the old friends they obviously were, with three or four conversations going on at once and laughter a constant accompaniment. Drack had been right about Madison being bored by the winery talk, but there was ample distraction in the wine. They passed around one bottle after another, pouring themselves a tasting portion before passing it to the next person. No explanation and no formal tasting routine required, just friends sharing wine.

The volume on the patio rose with each new bottle. Everyone's smiles grew wider and their gestures more exuberant. There was a passion in all these people. A shared love that kept them both in the clouds and firmly on the ground.

Drack poured for Madison and it wasn't long before she had to request he ease off a little. He had a heavy hand and she would have to be carried home if she let him have his way. Subtly, Madison went through the brief ritual of smelling and tasting that CS taught her. She was slightly embarrassed to discover CS's wine was in another league from the other offerings. When Minerva Hills' pinot noir came around, she didn't stop Drack from his heavy pour.

"So you like the pinot, do you? It's by far her best, but that's only because she doesn't make a Meritage."

"A what?"

"Meritage." Drack tipped his wineglass to his lips, holding it by pinching his thumb and first knuckle on the base. "A fancy word for a winemaker's blend. No single grape dominates and the blend changes from year to year."

"I didn't know that's what it's called. I don't know much about wine."

"CS doesn't make one, though we've been nagging her for years. I don't suppose you can blame her. CS's pinot noir is the best wine made in the United States."

Madison looked across the table to CS sitting in the shadows with the brunette. The description Drack gave sounded very much like the wine she'd barrel-tasted with CS weeks ago. Did she have a wine that not even her friends knew about? If they didn't know, why had she shared it with Madison? While she wondered at the incongruity, CS turned her vivid blue eyes on Madison for a heartbeat before turning back to her conversation. Even that brief gaze was enough to make Madison's wine-soaked head spin.

"She doesn't like to admit it," Drack said in a conspiratorial whisper, "but she's much better than the rest of us."

"I just like the lavender that comes through," Madison offered by way of apology.

"It is a neat trick, isn't it?" Drack nudged her. "I wish it were as simple as planting what you want under the vines and having it come out in the wine."

"Isn't that how it gets there?"

"Well yes, but there are a million other little things in winemaking that enhance the quality. CS does better than all of us at each and every one of them."

Conversation had moved on without Drack, but he flowed back into it without missing a beat. While he chatted, Madison watched CS. She let her eyes linger over broad shoulders and long, powerful arms. CS sat quietly in her corner, letting others take the lead in the rare conversation that included her, and sharing a small smile with everyone. She didn't look over at Madison again, but Madison couldn't seem to look away. Hiding her interest behind her wineglass, she thought she was being subtle until the brunette dropped into the seat next to her.

"What are you doing, exactly?" she asked as she reached past Madison for the nearest bottle.

"I'm sorry?"

"You're practically drooling," she said, her eyes narrowing. "I hope your artwork is more subtle. CS said you are a potter?"

"I am," Madison answered, but she was floundering in the multitude of accusations. "And I'm not. Drooling, I mean. I was just…"

"Staring. I understand. It's hard not to." The brunette cut a look over at CS that was half-affectionate, half-hungry. "But stop."

"Why exactly do you think you have the right to tell me what to do?"

"You have no idea who I am, do you?" She rolled her eyes at Madison's vacant expression. "Laura." When that still didn't earn a response, anger started to creep into the woman's face. "I used to own half of this little goldmine."

"You owned half? I thought CS opened…" When the penny dropped along with Madison's jaw, Laura smiled like the Cheshire cat. "You and CS were a couple."

She nodded in response and drank deeply before responding, "For a very long time. Much longer than you and your sexy little chef have been together. Why haven't you run home to her yet? The restaurant's closed tonight, isn't it?"

Lead settled into Madison's stomach and she set down her glass, the wine still floating inside looking more like poison than oblivion. "Kacey's gone."

"Gone?"

"Almost a month ago now. Hadn't you heard?"

The way Laura dressed, every crease and every jewel perfectly in place, made Madison assume she'd revel in her heartbreak. There would always be women who liked to see other women suffer. Apparently Laura was not one of those women, but the way her eyes narrowed didn't express empathy either.

She leaned close to Madison and hissed, "You can't find what you lost here." Laura stood and looked down at Madison with contempt. "Go home."

With that she spun on her heel and crossed the room, back to the seat next to CS. She pulled her chair closer and let her fingertips brush against CS's bare forearm, leaning in close, smiling and batting her eyelashes at CS. To Madison's surprise, CS immediately relaxed and their conversation flowed easily. Madison forced her attention away from them and back to Drack, and she did not refuse when he offered more wine.

She dropped back into the conversation easily as wine slipped past her lips. Occasionally, Drack would lean toward Madison, his eyes on whoever was speaking, and quietly explain one of the finer points of the conversation to her. To her surprise, it didn't take long for her to understand some of what they said. It was almost as intoxicating as the wine, this feeling of community and shared goals. If she got the chance, Madison might even feel at home here.

Eventually she allowed herself to look back over at CS, who had removed herself from the conversation with Laura. It was nice, seeing CS around her peers. The way they all talked to each other as equals, but not in that haughty way of some professionals that left outsiders feeling like just that—outsiders.

Time flew by faster than Madison expected, and before she knew it, the sun was long set and night had draped over the patio. When the group moved to the freshly lit fire pit she used the interlude to make her excuses. CS offered to walk her home, and she accepted with a pleasant stirring in her belly. The last glass of wine left her feeling both warm and daring. She wanted to walk through the vines, to avoid the path and dance among the grapes in the moonlight. More than anything else, however, she wanted to take that walk with CS.

Madison slipped out of her sandals and clutched them in one hand, CS neither encouraging nor condemning her flight of fancy. It felt like heaven to wriggle her toes in the cool night air. She could hear the echo of conversation from the patio drifting through the night, the laughter and drone of voices like the chatter of insects in the night.

After a few minutes strolling downhill, the world went still and dark. She and CS were in the interim, the place between the building at the top of the hill and her cottage at the bottom where the whole world went still and belonged to them alone. The moon was new, providing the world no hint of reflected sun, leaving the stars alone to guide their travels. She felt again that peace of being alone with CS. She slipped her arm around CS's as they walked. It was intimate but she was not frightened.

They arrived at Madison's cottage, a single light glowing inside, and by silent consent went together to the deck. Madison sat down on one of the long loungers and watched as CS stacked some wood in the outdoor fireplace. Once the fire started to crackle pleasantly, she sat down on the next lounger. CS crossed her long legs in front of her, leaning back against the chair with a contented sigh and watching the flames. She turned her head to smile at Madison, who held her look as the firelight flickered over both of them.

Madison didn't know what her future held. Didn't know how long she'd stay here at Minerva Hills. What she did know, what she'd always known but refused to think about, was how drawn she was to this place. She'd been happier here than she had ever been. She'd done better work here than she'd ever done before. That happiness, that inspiration, hadn't come from Kacey. The memories she cherished from this place were those she recalled while she walked home tonight. They were shared memories—shared with CS. Every single one of them. From the sunlight through the leaves in the clearing to the laughter in the moonlight tonight. CS was at the center of everything that made her feel happy and alive. It was true before Kacey left and it was true now. The best thing about this revelation was that now she was free to pursue that happiness. Free to pursue the woman sitting next to her.

She barely felt her feet beneath her as she crossed the few steps that separated them. She didn't think as she moved, but let her body make the decisions her mind wasn't quite ready for. CS watched her, the ghostly glow of her eyes a beacon for Madison while she held her breath. She didn't say a word as Madison threw one leg over hers and settled onto her knees, straddling CS's waist.

She didn't say anything out loud, but her eyes spoke volumes. A mildly curious glow that shifted ever so slightly, nudging into a flame and then sparking white-hot even as the fire behind Madison gave a loud pop and sizzled. Madison lowered her weight into place slowly, sinew by sinew. Her heart thrummed in her ears, blocking out the whole world.

When she settled into place, straddling CS's lap and looking into her eyes, the fire engulfed the deck and the cottage and then the earth and sky. It burned inside her from the places where their bodies touched, multiplying exponentially when CS's hands found their way onto her hips, then to her back, pressing into the thin fabric of her shirt. She reached out with both hands, cupping CS's face to anchor herself as their bodies ignited.

Madison leaned forward, tipping her body with infinite slowness. It overwhelmed her. Swallowed her whole. The tips of their noses brushed as she tilted her head and let her eyes flutter shut.

The kiss was like nothing Madison had ever experienced. CS's lips were soft but firm. Searching but not insistent. She squeezed her eyes tightly shut and breathed in the scent of this woman. This woman who was as quietly strong with her lips as she was with her manner. Madison didn't feel the kiss on her lips—she felt it in her whole body. Felt the way it made her blood flash and her skin tingle. Felt the way it made her bones ache for more.

She wanted to fall into the kiss and let it capture her for all time. Wanted the press of CS's fingertips on the small of her back to hold her in a moment that lasted forever. A moment full of her gentle lips and her sure tongue. A moment full of nothing but Madison and CS.

With a snap like the world ending in ice, the weight was gone from Madison's back. CS's hands were on her shoulders, applying light pressure. CS pulled her lips away and Madison teetered on the edge of madness.

"Madison."

She leaned back in, refusing to open her eyes and curling her fingers around CS's cheeks. She tried to press their lips back together, but CS moved them aside.

"Madison."

"Shhh," she said, releasing CS's face and pawing at the buttons on her shirt with trembling fingers. "Don't say anything. We don't have to talk."

CS lay her hands on top of Madison's, stilling her movements. She didn't grip, just trusted the weight of her touch to stop Madison. The gentleness worked. Madison sat back, ceding every inch between their bodies reluctantly. She opened her eyes to see regret mixed with the earlier lust in CS's gaze. She turned away so she didn't have to see it.

"We do need to talk."

"You don't want me." The words stung as they crossed her lips.

"Look at me."

She waited, the level tone both stern and sweet, and Madison did look at her. Looked into those eyes and felt her heart break at the beauty of them, so close yet so far away. She slid back along the chair, finding a spot at the end where she could sit without touching. CS stood, moving in front of Madison and kneeling at her feet.

"I'm sorry. I'm not going to be your revenge."

The words cut deeply into Madison, echoing in her empty chest. She turned away, ashamed of the heat on her cheeks and the sour taste of her regret. CS, in her style, waited for Madison to speak. Her presence was still undemanding, but Madison hated her for it in that moment. She needed more from CS right now. Some sort of response that was not clinical and level. Madison wanted her to shout and insult her or to kiss and make love to her. She couldn't handle in between right now. Couldn't take cold logic on a night like this, with peace all around her and a burning need in her body. It was apparently all CS could give.

Madison ran to the front door, slipping behind it before the sob ripped through her chest and she peeled apart from her embarrassment. CS did not follow.

CHAPTER THIRTY-ONE

Perhaps staying up all night because of sexual humiliation was Madison's new normal. It had started with her throwing fistfuls of clothes into a suitcase, determined to leave Minerva Hills and never look back. Her frenzied packing had only lasted long enough for her to remember she had nowhere to go and no way to get there. Trapped in her cottage, she had thrown herself into bed. Memories of her sloppy pass at CS kept her tossing and turning all night, one moment cold with loneliness, the next hot with embarrassment. She never closed her eyes for more than a few moments. Every time she did, flashes of the night crossed through her mind, both exciting and mortifying her, all of it illuminated by flickering firelight.

Well before the sun rose, Madison dragged herself out of bed, exhausted but giving up once and for all on the prospect of sleep. Torrents of hot water woke her and cleared her mind. The smell of shampoo and soap scrubbed away the edge of her raw nerves. She took her time about dressing since the sky was still dark. Then she lingered over her hair and makeup, wanting to look good but not desperate. Natural. It was a surprisingly difficult balance to achieve.

Once she finally felt presentable, she hurried out the front door, leaving it unlocked as usual and started off down the hill toward the stables. If she didn't go now, didn't force her body to move without thinking, she would talk herself out of this trip. She didn't want that. Didn't want to lose her nerve and ignore what happened last night. She had to talk to CS, to apologize or explain or something to make sure that scene last night was not the last they shared. She had to make CS understand.

Not that she totally understood herself. Sure, she had known for a long time that she was attracted to CS. Drawn to her in a visceral way that would eventually work its way to the surface. What she had not expected was how her attraction had nothing to do with lust and everything to do with the memories they shared. Happy, sad and even frightening memories. It was trust and affection that led her to kiss CS, not revenge. Madison had to find the right words to explain that before it was too late.

As she walked, she let her mind wander back to the way last night felt. Not how if felt after CS rejected her, gentle as it was—that hurt too much to think of right now. No, she let her mind go back to the way CS's body felt. The muscles that Madison admired for the last months were just as solid as she imagined, but with a hint of the feminine tenderness she craved. The feel of her strong hands on Madison's back, holding her tight. The blazing heat of CS's tongue sliding past her smooth lips to claim Madison's mouth. A shiver started at the tip of Madison's toes and made its way to her scalp. She knew, if nothing else, that CS had enjoyed the kiss when it started. If she could explain that it had nothing to do with Kacey, maybe CS would be as interested as she was.

The sun peeked over the treetops as Madison arrived in front of the stables. As usual, the barn doors were closed for the night and she could hear the soft sounds of horses growing restless in their stalls.

She was nearly to the apartment door when it opened. Her heart leapt into her throat, waiting to see CS's square shoulders and well-set jaw. The happy bubble that had built in her burst, flooding her with all the painful shame she thought she'd set aside. It wasn't CS who walked through her apartment door first thing in the morning—it was Laura. Her hair bounced with freshness, her pouty, ruby-red lips set in a straight line.

Laura caught sight of Madison and held her gaze. The smugness from last night was absent, but the implication was even clearer today. It was far too early in the morning for this to be a social call. She must have spent the night. No wonder CS had turned Madison down. She already had the woman she wanted available at a moment's notice. An ex who was obviously eager to come back.

Madison turned to go. She couldn't stand Laura seeing her cry. She wanted to keep what dignity she had left. Laura, unfortunately, was quicker than she looked. She whipped around in front of Madison, blocking her path. There was something unreadable in her eyes. Something tinged with possessiveness and the raw edge of anger.

"CS is in the shower."

More evidence Madison didn't need. She nodded and tried to slip past Laura, but she was too quick for her again. She sidestepped back into Madison's path.

She squinted at Madison, looking hard into her face, scanning for information. "What are you doing here? Why are you hovering around CS? What do you want from her?"

"I just want to talk," she answered in a numb monotone, wondering if that was the real reason she was here.

Madison waited for Laura to sneer or laugh. To bring up the embarrassing scene that played out on her deck last night, but she didn't. She didn't look angry or hateful, just wary. "I thought I made it clear last night, but apparently you need me to spell it out. CS deserves more than being your rebound. She deserves more than a freeloading, flake of an artist."

"I'm not free…"

"CS has a good heart, but it's too big for her own good. Don't go to her looking for a quick fix, okay? There are a dozen other people you can find for that."

There was no wink to accompany the warning. No sign that she was referencing the mistake Madison had already made. It was clear to her now, as it should have been all along, that CS had kept last night to herself. Laura hadn't known about Kacey and she didn't know about the kiss. It was exactly the sort of thing CS would do, but Madison still hadn't expected it. Her heart ached at how thoughtful CS could be. If only Madison hadn't ruined everything by jumping her last night.

"Maybe you should go home."

"I'm trying to. You're in my way."

Laura stopped short of saying that she meant go home to Denver, but her raised eyebrow and scowl were enough to get the message across. Madison stood still, even when Laura stepped out of her path, crossing her arms, obviously intending to hold her ground. Even though she knew she should go, Madison found herself hesitating, not to spite Laura but because now, more than ever, she craved CS. Craved her company and her understanding. Craved the chance to apologize for last night and thank her for her discretion. If she was honest, what she craved more than anything else was just the chance to look at CS.

Laura growled, "Well?"

Laura's impatience finally sent Madison on her way. She set her feet in the right direction and let them carry her, but left her mind firmly in the stable apartment. It was over now, her chance to set things right. She knew she wouldn't seek CS out again, knew herself too well to even hint at the prospect. She'd lost her nerve.

By the time she found herself at her front door, her mind was just as tormented as it had been when she went to bed last night. Her body begged her heart to be brave, begged her to go back to the stable, push past Laura and find a way to convince CS. Her heart said another kiss would do it. Her head said another kiss would shatter everything irreparably. She wandered around the house, warring with herself.

For the first time since Kacey left, she found herself restless. Grief and pain had occupied her time before, but now she needed something else to occupy it. She stood still long enough to hear the silence of the cottage. Apart from the gentle hum of the refrigerator, the place was still. It was also stale. The air tasted like decay. For a moment she saw her future life, closed up here in this cottage, subsisting on the kindness of strangers but slowly withering away until there was nothing but a shell left. A Faulkner spinster, brokenhearted and alone.

Her eyes fell on the knuckle of twisted vine and she turned away from it in disgust. Her eyes landed instead on the massive stone chimney, crawling up the wall of glass. It was mostly bare, the stark gray stone slipping into the stark gray sky through the windows. Above the top of the fireplace was an aged wooden mantel, floating out from the stone. Above that was a square of canvas, the entire surface painted in streaky reds from fresh blood to black cherry.

Madison hated that painting. It was the one discordant note in the vineyard's symphony to abstract art. It was bland, despite the riot of color, evoking nothing more than an annoying break in gray where none was needed. Kacey had loved it. The brazenness of it no doubt calling to her shallow aesthetic.

The thought of Kacey turned Madison's restlessness into rage. It was her fault. All of this. CS had rejected Madison because of Kacey. Because she thought Madison still loved Kacey, even with all she'd done. And the worst part was that a small part of Madison recognized that she was right. She had loved Kacey and part of her always would. The part of her that loved being squired around by a sexy celebrity. The part of her that loved ceding control of the little things to a stronger personality.

Why had she lost herself in Kacey? Why had she allowed herself to be dragged across the country like a piece of luggage only to be left behind without so much as a backward glance? Why hadn't she met CS years ago? What could have been if not for Kacey hollowing her out?

Madison ran across the living room and grabbed the metal coffee table. It was cumbersome and heavy, but she dragged it across the rug and hardwood floor. When the legs banged against the stone hearth she hopped onto its surface and stretched onto her toes. Her fingers just managed to scrape the bottom of the canvas, but that was all she needed. With one mighty shove the canvas lifted off its nail, tipped and tumbled down, the corner of the coffee table pressing into the painted fabric enough to dent it but not tear.

She was on it in an instant, leaping off the table and tearing at the canvas with clawed fingers. The top of the frame cracked under her assault, staples snapping, and the fabric wilting like a deflated balloon. With it weakened, Madison tore at the canvas. It screeched as it tore down one side, but the painting remained stubbornly whole. She snatched up the first thing that came to hand, the piece of dead, dried grapevine, and plunged it into the heart of the canvas. The fabric ripped, flecks of paint sailing through the air along with Madison's roar of victory.

The painting was in tatters before she finally stopped stabbing at it, her breath coming in sporadic, raspy gasps. Leaning back on her heels, Madison registered a sharp pain in her hand and looked down. The sharp edge of a clipped branch had dug into Madison's palm. A smear of her blood soaked into the bark. Madison sat on her heels and stared at the wound, then at the vine. She turned it in her hand, examining its twists and flat edges.

A moment later Madison jumped to her feet and slammed through the front door, skipping down the deck and skidding to a halt around the back of her cottage, staring down at the pile of cuttings, each a different but similar shape to the blood-soaked piece in her hand. She grabbed another from the pile at random, laying it over the one in her hand. She turned it and tried again when the two didn't fit how she liked. After another few attempts, she grabbed a third and then a fourth piece, turning to lay them in the dewy grass so she didn't lose the shape.

When she found it, she didn't leave it together on the grass. She picked up her four pieces and then another handful from the pile, more sharp pieces pricking her fingers and arms as she ran them back inside. She kicked aside the ruined canvas and spread them out on the rug. It took her five trips back to the pile before she had the rough shape laid out, then another five to fill in the gaps. Before grabbing any more, she ran to her studio and rummaged inside a box of supplies until she found a spool of wire.

She went to the utility closet next, pushing aside broom, mop, and winter boots until she found the battery-powered drill, still in its plastic case. Touching it reminded her of the day she'd bought it.

So we're power tool lesbians now?

Madison pushed Kacey's voice out her head. The teasing had sounded playful that day. Now it sounded like criticism.

The first battery died before the bones of the sculpture were secured. Madison spent an hour twisting pieces of wire through the holes while she waited for it to recharge. After that she kept the backup battery charging so she could swap them out when the other ran out of juice. The sun set and rose again before she ran out of wire. The stash of vines under her kitchen window ran out, but that was okay. She had enough.

She thought of Kacey sometimes as she drilled tiny holes in the desiccated vines. She thought of CS when she twisted wire around itself. She thought of their differences. She had to suck blood from another puncture caused by a sharp twig. The woman she had been with Kacey would have reminded herself on the second day that she was no sculptor. The woman she was now that Kacey was gone didn't listen to the doubts rattling around inside her head. She was stronger now. She was a sculptor if she said she was a sculptor and tomorrow she would be a potter again.

The rug was stained and shredded beyond repair by the time she picked up a piece of trimmed wire and realized that she did not need it. She tested the strength of her creation and found, to her amazement, that it held its shape. Had this been her medium she might have achieved the result without nearly so much weight, but the anchors in the stone would hold. The trouble was dragging the piece up the ladder she'd fetched from outside.

When she had pulled it halfway up, she thought she might not have the strength to get it in place. Her arms trembled with the effort, and so she yelled as she hauled it up another step. Stopping for air on that new shelf, she looked down on the remains of the painting and imagined what Kacey would say. She would laugh. She would call Madison crazy and tell her she couldn't possibly get the vines into place, and if she did they would be weird and ugly there against the stone. Better to give up now.

Madison hauled the sculpture up the next step with Kacey's laughter echoing in her ears. One more step to go and then she would only have to haul it onto the mantel and then up the distance to the nails waiting for the triple-woven loops of wire she'd made.

She made it up the next step by reliving the moment that Kacey walked away from her without looking back. Without calling or texting or saying goodbye. That image had made her weep for days. Now it gave her the strength to lift the wreath of vines up the step and onto the mantel.

The mantel groaned under its weight, but held. If she held it here too long, though, the whole thing would tumble down. To her despair, Madison realized she had nothing left of Kacey to help her over this last hurdle. Everything that she'd left behind, everything that stung and burned was gone now and Madison had only herself. She realized, as she puffed out her breath and heaved, that she was all she needed.

The first loop caught and held on its hook. Madison let out a sigh and quickly secured the others. She nearly tumbled down the ladder, her exhaustion sweeping over her. When she made it to the couch and looked up at what she had created, she wept with the beauty of it. She slept hard for a few hours and woke to the setting sun blazing through the windows.

When she woke, she stumbled to the coffeepot. The mechanics of grinding beans and filling the reservoir soothed her. The fragrant steam and hissing of the machine pulled her back into herself, trying to remember how much clay she had. She'd worked hard that one day, right before Boots brought her the vines, but hadn't managed any more.

Despite the batch she'd fired before her wine tasting, the

shelves were still heavy with dry pots. A few quick mental calculations told Madison she could fire them today and have them done before nightfall. Madison set to work unloading the kiln. A shape was forming in her mind. A tall, thin vase, opening at the top like a flower. A calla lily. She kicked off her shoes while pulling off a chunk of clay. She grabbed a bit more for good measure. Too much would make the lip difficult to sculpt. It would take patience.

Hours later, the coffeepot beeped angrily as the auto shutoff engaged. Madison didn't hear the shrill alarm, and the untouched pot grew cold in the empty kitchen.

CHAPTER THIRTY-TWO

Sunlight glimmered off fresh glaze, sending a sparkling glow all over the studio. The pots, fresh from the kiln and their finishing fire, might as well have been in a different universe for all the notice Madison gave them. The tall vase was there, glimmering not white like a calla lily but bright, robin's-egg blue. Other vases stood near it along with a few bowls wide as her shoulders. Every table was crammed with finished work waiting to go upstairs.

Madison's attention was fixed completely on the pot in front of her, stuck to the wheel with a few bits of scrap clay to keep it in place while she worked. She pressed a stem of dried lavender into the clay. She had waited impatiently for this piece to dry just enough to keep its shape but wet enough to take the impression. It was essential to have the same depth of impressions all the way around, and that meant she had to be both quick and precise. She lived for moments like these.

The doorbell rang, but she ignored it the same way she had ignored everything else. She took another sprig, spreading the flowers as she applied gentle, even pressure. The lavender spread across the clay surface like veins. The effect was brilliant, exactly what Madison wanted. She smeared a few lines of clay across her shirt, wiping her fingertips clean before reaching into the box at her feet for more flowers.

The second ring was more insistent than the first, a loud ding followed by a split second of silence before another. Madison gently pried apart the stem in her hands, the gentle crackle of desiccated herbage far more pleasant than the doorbell. It spread open easily, much more so than the first few she tried. There was a steep learning curve to this, as attested by the pile of discarded flowers surrounding her bare toes.

An insistent knocking marked the third attempt, and Madison wished her visitor would either take the hint and go away or come inside. She didn't quite jump at the banging, but she did twitch, nearly knocking the lavender out of position. She was pressing the last flower into place when she heard the door open and close. About time, she thought, then went back to her work.

"What're you doing?"

"Dancing the tango," Madison replied.

Boots' booming laugh made Madison smile, but she didn't look up. She heard the rustle of what sounded like a paper bag.

"Sorry to barge in. No one's seen you in a long time."

"No need to apologize, come in whenever." She finished with her current piece of lavender and spun the wheel slowly to check her progress. Just a couple more stems should do it. "I've been working."

"I can see that." Boots' boots clicked on the tile floor as he crossed to the tables of finished work. "You been sleeping at all?"

"Not much."

"Eating?"

"I think so."

He chuckled, coming back closer to her but being thoughtful enough to stay out of her light. "CS told me to go get some groceries and bring 'em to you."

Hearing the winemaker's name made Madison's stomach squirm pleasantly, a common occurrence these days. She felt like a teenager, letting her mind wander to her crush several times a day just to feel her heart swoop.

"Was she worried that I forgot to feed myself or that there was a rotting corpse in one of her cottages?"

"Hard to say, but she'd worry more about the smell of your corpse getting into the grapes than the carpet."

They laughed together and it felt good, like old times during the autumn when Madison's life wasn't upside down.

Madison selected a branch of lavender, discarding it and reaching for another.

"What's that all about?" he asked, shifting the bag in his arms again. "The lavender?"

"I'm pressing it into the pot to get the impression in the clay. When I pull them out, the shapes will still be there."

"Like a design?"

"Exactly."

"How long will you let them stay there?"

"Not sure. Depends on how quickly the clay dries. Maybe a few hours."

"All that work and it's only going to be there a few hours?"

"The impressions will last forever. A ghost in the clay. Like a fossilized footprint."

"Cool." The flippant tone he used made it clear he didn't really care, but he was at least polite enough to pretend. "Want to take a break to put away your groceries?"

"No thanks. You can do it."

There was almost enough of a teenager in him to balk, but he opted for a shake of the head. "You're starting to remind me of CS, Denver."

He left the room, heading for the kitchen just in time. The tingle that spread through her body at the thought made her hands really shake this time, and she had to stop for a few deep breaths or else she'd ruin the pot. She hadn't spoken to CS yet. Still hadn't apologized for the sloppy pass or explained her feelings. She had barely left the studio, even sleeping in the guest room some nights. She couldn't remember the last time she showered, but it still felt odd to go so long without talking to CS.

"I was going to leave them for you, but there's a pot of coffee there that looks like it's been sitting for a week or two. I thought it was safer to put everything away. I don't want 'em rotting on the counter."

"You're sweet."

Boots sounded like he wanted an excuse to stay and chat. "It's the first time I've been off the estate in days. Can't have all that effort go to waste."

Madison saw her opening and went for it, trying hard to keep her voice steady and casual. "What have you and CS been up to? She keeping you out in the vines all this time?" Perhaps today was the day she should shower and get out of the house.

"She's a slave driver, that one. We get bud break in March, so we've been inspecting the vines day and night."

"Is it March already?" Madison asked, truly shocked to discover time had moved without her notice.

"For more than a week now," he said with a laugh.

She set another stem in place. "Really?"

"You're kidding, right Denver?"

"I get lost in my work sometimes." She'd thought it had been two weeks since her wine tasting with CS, but apparently it had been three.

"I can tell. You should get out there and see it. New growth is beautiful."

"Thanks." She smiled over at him, peeling her eyes away from her pot for the first time. "I think I will."

CHAPTER THIRTY-THREE

It was like stepping into a dream, walking among the vines again. One of those strange, ethereal places where the dreamer walks in a place that is intimately familiar to them, but the entire landscape is changed. The beauty of the place overwhelmed her, fresh with splashes of yellow-green where there had only been brown. The smile etched onto her face was unshakable. She felt as she hadn't felt in ages.

She felt like herself, but more than herself. As though the trials she'd faced and the art she'd created from it brought her to a better version of herself than she had ever been. It felt good. Freeing. Maybe she'd been inside too long, and the world had changed in her absence. Maybe the vineyard hadn't changed at all, maybe it was only her that was different. Either way, her steps were light and her heart was even lighter.

Thinking of the work left in her studio, she felt even more content. A dam of inspiration had broken. Everything she was making now made her feel like she was finally working toward her dream. Like one day soon she would sit down at the wheel and re-create solid light with her fingertips. The thought made her high and she was almost afraid to stop throwing.

Madison stopped, a clump of green leaves catching her eye. She had wandered into the rows of chardonnay. No grapes hung on the vines yet, but they would be here soon. She brushed her fingertips against the new leaves. Days and weeks and months before they could amount to anything substantial.

The potential energy of this place was infectious. It seeped into her. The vineyard fed her soul, her soul fed her work. They all fed each other, the people, the grapes, the lavender, and the mint.

Madison reached down into the soil. There had been a rare rainfall recently and the ground was still soft with the dampness. She pressed her fingers into it. The lavender was just shooting, delicate stems fresh with burgeoning life. The mint, however, was far hardier. It had already spread its leaves to the sun, leaves twining in among the vines as though holding hands with the grapes.

She was walking through a dream, and so it was inevitable that CS was standing at the end of the row, her eyes on Madison. Her form stiffened when Madison turned to her, the serenity of her expression shifting to discomfort. Madison half expected CS to bolt like a startled deer. She was pleased to the point of giddiness when CS held her ground, even smiling sheepishly as Madison approached.

"Good afternoon," CS said, her voice croaking ever so slightly. "Nice to see you out and about. It's…been a while."

Now it was Madison's turn to be sheepish. She crammed her hands into the back pockets of her jeans and kept her eyes on ground. She blurted out the words before they'd fully formed in her mind. "I owe you an apology."

"It's fine. You can stay inside all you want."

"No, I mean…" Madison tried to ignore the heat on her cheeks, but it colored her words as much as her skin. "I mean I'm sorry for…coming at you like that the other night."

CS answered a little too quickly, "That's fine too."

"No, it isn't. I didn't know you had…something else going on."

CS's eyebrows pushed together, a pair of wrinkles as thin as spiderwebs creasing the skin between them. "Something else going on?"

"Laura." Try as she might, the name still came out with a hint of accusation. "I came to apologize to you the morning after. It was early. Very early. She came out of your apartment and said you were in the shower."

The implication wasn't lost on CS any more than it had been lost on Madison that morning. She opened her mouth to respond, but Madison hurried on.

"It actually wasn't the first time we'd talked. The night before she...warned me off."

"And I'm sure she used the same abundance of tact that she used when she dumped me after a decade together."

Madison's pulse thrummed in her ears. She wished very much that she had a chair or at least a wall to lean against. Some way to ground herself but still keep up the appearance that this was a casual conversation.

"She dumped you?"

"A couple of years ago. We're still friends, but there's nothing else." She looked hard at Madison. "Nothing else."

"I guess I just don't understand why you'd still be friends if she broke your heart."

"Because she didn't break my heart. We both knew we'd never work. Too many things stacked against us. Both too stubborn. We were just...marching in place for a while together because we didn't want to be alone."

Stillness returned to the vineyard while they both digested the words. CS kept a wary eye on Madison. For her part, Madison didn't know what she felt. It seemed to be good news, considering the way her pulse quickened every time CS was around her, but it was also confusing. Then there was the lingering reality that CS had turned her down that night.

"To be clear," CS said, her voice halting. "I didn't spend that night with Laura. She showed up the next morning because she was concerned when I'd left early. In retrospect, she may have been fishing."

Madison thought of the angry look in Laura's eyes, the repeated warning. "I think you're right."

CS said in a quiet voice, avoiding Madison's gaze with practiced nonchalance. "She was pretty annoyed when she didn't get anything."

Madison felt her body lurching forward and stopped herself just in time. She wanted to—ached—to ask CS to explain. To hear her say out loud that she didn't tell Laura about the kiss. She wouldn't do it, though, wouldn't ask why. She wanted a very specific answer to that question and it would hurt too badly not to get it. Better not to ask. For now.

CS wiped at nonexistent dirt on her jeans. "I should be getting back to work."

Madison let out her breath slowly, relieved to have escaped. "Me too. I have pots to throw."

"I…hope to see more of you. Around the vineyard, I mean."

"Definitely."

CS smiled and turned, marching off down the path away from Madison and toward the far end of the vineyard. As soon as she was out of sight, Madison started up the path back home. The air was thin and cool on her face. She broke into a jog and let her feet fly with the same lightness of her heart.

CHAPTER THIRTY-FOUR

Her growling stomach finally pulled Madison away from her studio and into the kitchen. She'd been eating much more regularly these days. Her hipbones, poking at the waistband of her jeans just a few days ago, had slid away under her normal amount of flesh. Still, she'd skipped breakfast to prepare for the arrival of more movers.

Yanking open the refrigerator door, Madison saw that Boots had delivered groceries again. She hadn't heard him come in and wasn't even sure when he'd made the delivery, but she had food and that was all that mattered. A block of cheddar cheese, a jar of pickles, and a package of sliced turkey made it to the counter along with a bottle of seltzer water. She snagged the box of graham crackers for dessert and hopped up on the kitchen counter, biting off a hunk of cheese and fishing a pickle spear out of the jar.

Madison looked around her house. She hadn't taken stock in a long time. The first thing she noticed was a smear of dried clay on the counter in front of the coffeemaker. The handle of the carafe was gray, too, and still half-full of coffee she didn't remember making. Looking around the kitchen, she saw smudges of clay on the sink, a few cabinets, several places on the refrigerator door and on all the dirty dishes piled in the sink. She looked down to see a greasy oil-slick of gray floating in the pickle juice.

Her hands were covered in clay, from wrist to fingertips. She'd meant to wash them in the mudroom sink before coming out here, but she must've forgotten.

Her cell phone rang and she had to weave through vases and carefully stacked bowls on her way through the living room. Her work, destined for another show in Denver, filled every available inch of space.

She dove onto the couch, leaping over a matched pair of milky-jade amphora, their surfaces laced with the delicate pattern of mint leaves. She snatched up the phone as she rolled onto her back, waggling her toes at the soaring ceiling.

"Hey, Maddie. Didn't think you'd ever make it to the phone."

"Sorry." She smiled at Jada's teasing. "Someone made me stack up all my finest work between me and my phone."

"That's ridiculous. Don't you know you're supposed to be attached to your phone at all times? I don't go five minutes without checking mine."

"I'm nowhere near as popular as you are."

"That'll change after you sell out your second show." The shift in her manner was palpable, and her voice went from teasing friend to worried parent. "Are you sure you aren't ready to move here? You have a few weeks until the opening. There's still time to change your mind."

"I still can't afford it."

"I'm worried about you out there all alone. Are you okay, Maddie?"

"To be honest, Jada, I'm not sure."

The question had been loaded, but also off the mark. Madison was still overwhelmingly sad sometimes about Kacey, not least of which because it seemed she had dropped Madison and her old life without looking back. She hadn't called, hadn't emailed, hadn't even tried to pick up the rest of her things. Madison was also relieved, and that was the part she was hesitant to admit. Relieved that she didn't have to hide how happy it made her to catch a glimpse of CS walking through the vines.

She would watch until CS moved out of her line of sight, then she would relive the night they kissed, feeling CS's lips on hers and those hands on her back. Worse were the days when CS would see her, smile and wave or, even better and infinitely worse, come and talk to Madison. They'd become more comfortable with each other since the apology and the Laura explanation, but there had been so much left unsaid. It hovered between them every time they spoke, pulling Madison toward CS yet also pushing her away.

She was falling in love with CS, but it was so much easier to say she didn't know how she was feeling.

"Well, take care of yourself, that's all I can say. You deserve to be happy, Madison. I don't want to see you pine over that shrill little worthless cunt for the rest of your life."

Madison laughed, genuinely this time and made the easiest promise of her life. "I won't."

"Good. On to business." It was incredible how Jada shifted from one thought to another, throwing herself completely into each. "I just got a call from the shipping company."

"Please don't tell me something went wrong."

"Nothing went wrong, but they're pissed. Apparently someone at the gate is telling them they can't drive the truck onto the property. They're angry because they have to haul all of their equipment in and all your work out on…Oh, what did he call it? Right, 'a fucking horse cart like it's a damn hayride.'"

Madison laughed, burrowing into the soft cushions of the couch. "Everyone gets mad about that."

"I made sure to remind them that they are moving priceless pieces of artwork and if they break anything I will personally break every bone in their bodies. On a more positive note, everything will be stored in my gallery until the show, so we don't have to move it again after this."

The usual fear of moving time wormed into Madison's gut, leaving her stomach a pit of wriggling snakes. "They'll be careful? You promise?"

"I promise. Just stay out of their way."

"I always do. Thanks, Jada. I'll keep an eye out for them."

They hung up and Madison stared at the wall, trying to ignore the worry that had been needling her all day. She'd started moving her work down from the loft and out of the studio before sunrise. She agonized over the placement of everything, gulping with dread every time she took her hands off a pot. Now she decided that lying perfectly still on the couch would help with the panic. It worked for the split second before she heard the groaning of the cart and the clopping of horse hooves on packed earth.

Boots didn't knock, just came in, a trio of scowling men trailing behind. He called out when he got inside, and Madison returned the greeting.

"These guys are eager to get going, Denver. Is it okay if we start?"

"Go ahead."

"You don't want to leave? I know how worried you get."

"We're professionals, ma'am." One of the shipping guys said, dropping a human-sized roll of bubble wrap next to his feet. "You don't have to worry about your art."

"I know. Thank you. It isn't you guys, it's me."

She turned her back, letting them get started. Boots gave instructions in his upbeat, joking way. The guys gave him clipped, one-word replies. Madison tried not to cringe at the thought of him insulting the movers and them taking it out on her work.

With her back to the door, she could look through the wall of windows. She saw CS walking nonchalantly up the hill, one hand in her pocket, watching the activity at Madison's cottage. She shot a quick smile through the glass, and Madison returned it, watching her cross the yard to the front door. She gave herself a moment to let her heart rate return to normal.

CS stopped by the door to chat with Boots. Madison slipped into the kitchen to wash the clay off her hands and face. She scrubbed herself clean, feeling infinitely more presentable after running clean fingers through her hair.

"Not to rush you, guys, but there's a storm on the way," CS said to the men in Madison's living room. "I had Boots call for a tarp to cover the cart just in case."

The shippers' tempers had cooled and they were almost polite when they thanked her. Madison felt the moment coming, but still reveled in the way CS turned her full attention on her. The moment did not disappoint. Madison's whole body responded to the depth of those blue eyes. She felt electricity arcing between them. Felt it in the way she couldn't quite keep still. In the way CS shoved her hands further into her pockets, pressing her shoulders up almost to her ears. Her tongue grew so heavy that she wouldn't have been able to speak if she had anything coherent to say.

As usual, Boots broke the moment. He threw an arm around Madison's shoulders, arriving out of nowhere beside her.

"Nice guys, huh, Denver?" He grinned and then went on, shaking her just a little, "Makes you wanna hang around all day and watch them toss stuff into the cart."

"Toss!"

Madison lurched toward the door, but Boots held her in place. "I'm just messin' with ya, Denver. They're fine."

"Oh." She settled back onto her feet, letting her eyes flicker back to CS. "Okay."

"What's going on with them anyway?" CS asked. "Where are they taking your work?"

"Jada's arranging a new show for me. Probably in six weeks or so, but she wants the pieces on hand while she figures out the timing."

"The Welch Gallery again?"

"Yes. Jada's hoping it'll be as successful as last time."

"I'm sure it will be."

Boots, hating to be left out of a conversation, piped up, "What's that over the fireplace?"

CS turned to look. Madison watched her react to the piece, hoping she would approve. It was hard to read at first, but the way she started across the living room, floating through the obstacles like she was in a trance, made it clear how much she liked it.

Madison looked at it with them, her eyes traveling over its swooping curves. The pieces of vine were rough with knots and gnarled edges. Some spots were jagged, some were smooth. A few of the branches had dark stains of crushed grapes ground into their crevices. They were all beautifully weathered from their unprotected winter.

CS walked toward it, gracefully dodging the pottery at her feet. Once she was beneath the sculpture, she turned back to Madison. "You made this?"

She nodded. "Boots gave me some of the cuttings last fall. I just didn't know what to do with them until now."

"It's cool, Denver. What is it?"

"What do you see?"

"I dunno. What am I supposed to see?"

"Oh no," Madison said with a smile. They crossed the living room, joining CS in front of the hearth. "That would be cheating. What you see when you look at a piece of art says a lot about you. And what you think of the artist."

He shrugged and nudged CS with his elbow. "What do you see, CS?"

She was quiet for a long minute, her brows pushed together, her eyes constantly moving. "A crown of thorns."

Boots stroked his chin in a mockery of thoughtfulness. "Interesting observation, don't you think, Denver?"

"Hmmm." She played along, enjoying the relaxed feel of Boots' banter. "Passion, sacrifice, pain."

CS turned her head ever so slightly, shifting her gaze slowly to meet Madison's. She spoke in that low rumble that set Madison's blood on fire and stopped her lungs. "Perfection."

Boots, oblivious as always, immediately asked, "Is that the answer? Is that what you see?"

Madison finally relented. "I like that, but it isn't what I see."

"What do you see?"

She kept her eyes locked on CS, swimming through the crystal-clear depths and loving the feeling of drowning. "A bird's nest. Rebirth, freedom, home."

CS blinked and it broke the spell. Madison came back to herself, looking around the room and feeling the anxiety that came with the bubble wrap and the strangers. Mild discomfort made her squirm. She needed to get out of the house. Breathe the fresh air and forget about all the movers.

"I need a walk," she blurted out, catching the others by surprise. "Can I go for a walk?"

Boots barked a laugh. "You can do whatever you want, Denver. I can supervise here and make sure to lock up when they're done."

"Don't lock up. I don't even know if I have a key anymore. Just close the door when it's over. Thanks."

"Are you okay?" CS asked, concern etching her face.

"She's fine. Denver doesn't like moving day, do you Denver?"

"No. I don't. I hate it."

She was backing away from the sofa, trying not to look at the way the men had moved the pieces all around. They were going to drive them halfway across the country and she couldn't even bring herself to trust them in the entryway. She hastened to the bench by the door, sitting to slip her feet into her shoes.

"Care for some company?" CS was in front of her, looking down at Madison as she struggled with the shoes. "I need to inspect this section of the estate anyway."

Hope bubbled inside Madison, changing the shape of her nervous energy. "That would be wonderful."

CHAPTER THIRTY-FIVE

Walking in comfortable silence with CS, Madison could appreciate the full bounty of spring for the first time. She'd been sequestered at her wheel for days, seeing the emerging green through her studio windows.

The clouds overhead, ominous as they were with their swollen gray bellies, served to cover some of the heat, but it was still warmer than usual. Madison hadn't expected to leave the house so abruptly, but the lack of preparation turned out to be a bonus. She had been working in the barely-there cutoff jean shorts and oversized, slip-shoulder T-shirt she preferred for hot days, and the outfit was perfect for the sultry day. CS's jeans and short-sleeved button-up looked comparatively stifling. Still, her sleeves were very short, straining against the bulge of her biceps and accentuating the muscles of her forearms.

CS stopped and checked a bunch of small, underdeveloped grapes, and something in the cursory way she studied them made Madison think her heart wasn't really in the task. Her eyes wandered to the horizon and to the gathering clouds more than to the vines. They took a more leisurely pace than normal too. Altogether to Madison, it felt more like a casual stroll than an inspection of the fields, which suited her just fine. She loved the way their time together had become friendly. She wanted more than friendly—she freely admitted that to herself now, but she would start with friendly. The problem, of course, was that friendly did not include the desire to reach out and stroke the long, lean muscles of CS's arm the way she yearned to. The way the muscles rippled under her skin was enticing. CS looked over then, catching her staring.

A breeze kicked up out of nowhere, making the skin of Madison's arm pimple with the sudden chill. She saw the delicate hairs on CS's arm sway in the wind. She wondered if CS's skin was reacting to the cold the same as hers was. She wondered what it would feel like under her fingertips. She couldn't fight the impulse any longer, she had no choice. She had to touch CS in some way. The pull of her was so strong, Madison knew she would never be able to breathe again if she didn't touch CS.

Her hand was beginning to move, reaching out for CS's, when the other woman abruptly stopped. She turned to Madison and asked, "Why aren't you supervising your art being picked up? You need to be there, don't you?"

"I can't be there."

"Why?"

Madison scuffed the dirt with the toe of her shoe. "I have to be where I can't see them and they can't see me. I hate this part. So many things can go wrong that I have no control over. What if they drop something and shatter it into a million pieces? Everything I am, I pour into those pieces. To lose them like that? I just…can't be there."

CS's shoulders relaxed and she laughed a breathy sort of exhalation. "I know exactly what you mean. Bottling days are the hardest days of my life. Everything's on a knife's edge. I'm kind of hard to deal with those days."

The wind picked up, whipping at Madison's loose shirt and sweeping the bangs across CS's forehead. Thunder clapped loud and sharp in the distance, but neither of them noticed. They only noticed each other. Neither of them even blinked as clouds blotted out the sun and the air grew thick with the scent of rain.

"We're the same, aren't we?" Madison asked in a voice only just louder than the whistling wind. "Artists who have to learn how to flourish all on our own. It didn't come easy. I guess I didn't realize how alike we were."

"We always have been." CS took a step closer. "You just never noticed before."

They were so close now, sharing the warmth of each other's skin. Heat radiated off the pair of them so intensely it could set the whole world on fire. There was energy in the air between them. Then there was no air between them. Their lips met. Crashed together. It was an earth-shattering, desperate kiss. A hungry kiss consuming all the oxygen around them.

Madison allowed herself to burn, to catch flame in the press of CS's body against hers. CS's lips against hers. CS's tongue against hers. She wanted to burn. To be consumed. Every second that passed with their bodies this close was an eternity in which stars exploded apart and re-formed only to shatter again.

The storm broke in the air around them. Sheets of water so heavy they were like hail pounding against them. They broke apart reluctantly, the separation of their bodies marked by a jagged streak of lightning flashing across the sky, exploding in an ear-splitting thunderclap the moment it disappeared. CS grabbed Madison's hand and turned, sprinting for the tree line and safety, huge, painful raindrops pelting them the entire way.

Both of them were soaked through by the time they made it to the cover of the trees. CS led Madison far enough in that the canopy saved them from the worst of the downpour and the gray daylight disappeared behind a maze of dripping trunks. Looking around, Madison saw nothing but trees on all sides of her. The steady drip of water fell from the leaves onto the ground around them, but they were as dry and warm as they could expect in a storm like this one.

Madison and CS both panted, but not from the running. Even while scanning their surroundings, their eyes kept finding their way back to each other. Each time their eyes met, a bolt of something resembling electricity shot through Madison's body. CS was looking at Madison as though she wanted to devour her. Or maybe that was the reflection of Madison's own need that she could see in CS's eyes.

A few raindrops falling through the thick canopy landed on Madison, doing nothing to cool the burn of her skin. The thick, blue cotton of her T-shirt was heavy and nearly black with the water soaked into it. It clung coldly to her skin, hugging her curves as tightly as a bra would have done if she'd thought to wear one.

She stared at CS, looking at her as she seemed to be trying hard not to stare at Madison's breasts, outlined in every detail. Madison saw the struggle etched across her face, but her eyes kept coming back to Madison.

"The stables are close," CS said, turning her body away. "We can make it if you want."

Frustration bubbled in Madison. It made her bold. She marched up to CS, her feet quiet on the damp leaves. CS tried to turn again, but Madison snatched her hands, holding them tight in her own.

"I don't want that. I want to stay here. With you."

She felt the warmth of CS's hands in her own. The gentle strength. She raised them to her face, laying a soft kiss in the center of each palm. CS turned her eyes on Madison again and this time they weren't stone or ice. They burned with a fire so blue it was white-hot.

"I don't want you for revenge," Madison said, conviction hardening her voice.

She moved CS's hands again, this time placing them over her own rain-soaked shirt and cold breasts. As they cupped her, infusing that gentle warmth in her sensitive skin, Madison fought not to roll her head back and moan. She forced herself to keep her gaze locked on CS's and fought hard to keep her voice steady.

"I just want you."

The world held still and silent. The rain stopped falling on her shoulders. The leaves stopped rustling in the storm. The wind forgot to blow. It was as though the whole world held its breath as Madison held hers. Part of her expected CS to stop things here. They'd been close before, close to giving in to their shared desire, but CS had stopped them. Chosen caution. Madison prayed with all her might that she would be reckless this time.

Everything in the world went perfectly still for a heartbeat before CS shattered. She moved so quickly, trapping Madison's gasp of surprise with her mouth.

For all the suddenness of it, the kiss was surprisingly gentle. Their lips settled against each other. For all its passion, the kiss was slow. Respectful. Even through the fog of need, Madison could tell CS was holding back, waiting to know that Madison was sure.

Madison's body ached for more, the feel of CS's hands on her breasts wasn't enough. She needed to be devoured by this woman so full of passion. She could feel the tension in CS's body, coming off her in waves of heat. She seemed to be ready to explode and Madison would make that happen.

She grabbed CS by the collar, pulling their bodies closer. Some of the tension released, CS's hand moved on her, sending shockwaves from her eager nipples through every inch of her skin. They stumbled backward together until a broad tree trunk blocked their path. The surface of it was exactly what Madison needed, something to hold on to while CS touched her.

Madison broke the kiss, needing now, once and for all, to get all of CS. All of her attention, all of her passion, all she had to offer. She cupped CS's face, forcing those desire-darkened eyes to settle on her face before she begged, "Please don't hold back. I need you."

Her movements were a blur, rushed with overwhelming desire. In one decisive movement she ripped the shirt off Madison and replaced her hand with her mouth on Madison's breast. The moment CS's lips wrapped around her nipple, the need she'd bottle up for weeks exploded from her in a scream.

CS pressed her back against the tree, the rough bark biting into her bare skin. It was ecstasy, the feel of it tethering her to the world while her body fought to fly free. She ran her fingers through the short, wet strands of CS's hair. CS tore at her shorts as though she wanted to shred them off her. She managed to yank them off, pulling her underwear with them and leaving Madison terrifyingly, exquisitely naked in the forest.

Asking her to let go had consequences Madison had not anticipated. Freed from her doubt, CS was like a feral beast, seemingly intent on possessing Madison's body as much as pleasuring it. Madison loved every second. To see such a composed, structured woman crumple into this primal state was more intoxicating than any drug.

CS released her breast, leaving Madison whimpering at the loss, but she didn't let their bodies separate for long. With bared teeth and a look of hunger that made Madison's mind go blank, CS studied her body, inch by exposed inch. Rather than wilting under the examination, Madison felt more desirable than she ever had. She leaned back against the tree, wanting the scrape of bark on her back again, a little bite of pain to temper the pleasure.

She launched herself onto CS, wrapping her legs around the damp denim that encircled her waist. CS grabbed on, holding them together. She pressed Madison back against the tree trunk, her lips traveling the width and breadth of Madison's face and neck, leaving little rosettes of flame behind wherever they touched.

With the tree for leverage, CS was able to free one hand, slipping it between their rain-slicked bodies. Every touch was a tiny miracle of pleasure. She kept her eyes locked on CS's face, using her eyes and the tips of her fingers to trace every line, every muscle, every wrinkle and scar. Despite the exquisite bolts shooting through her, she kept her eyes wide open, wanting to sear this moment into her memory. She wanted to see CS. To watch her move. To watch her breathe in Madison. To watch the way her lips turned up ever so slightly at the corners with each moan that escaped Madison's lips.

CS's skill made it hard to focus. Madison's body shook as it climbed, carried to new heights in deft hands. The yearning in CS's eyes was nearly as powerful as her touch. A strong wind blew through the trees, shaking the leaves above them just as Madison shook apart. She threw her head back and screamed her release to the heavens.

She opened her eyes as her scream died away. The muted glow of the storm-dark afternoon now was bright. The canopy had parted enough to let in a single ray of sunlight. A thousand raindrops fell from the sky above, each and every one of them capturing the light inside them. Each and every one of them a drop of light made solid as it fell on Madison's body, entwined with CS.

CHAPTER THIRTY-SIX

The storm passed at some point in the steaming afternoon, but neither Madison nor CS noticed. When they emerged from the trees, hands entwined and Madison's head resting on CS's shoulder, they didn't notice it was growing dark. They only noticed each other. The way their fingers fit together. The way they matched each other's stride perfectly.

Madison slid her hand across CS's shirt, now untucked from her jeans, feeling the flat plane of muscle beneath. She had not felt this at peace in so long, she wanted to revel in it now. Wrap herself in the glow of CS and the setting sun. They slowed their pace by silent, mutual consent the closer they came to the stables. Madison pulled CS closer, making their steps falter for a moment.

CS stopped first. She pulled Madison against her, no longer to her side but into the circle of her strong arms. Madison burrowed her face in CS's neck, breathing in the scent of her skin and dried rain. In the reluctance to let her go, Madison could feel how much CS wanted her, and it warmed her like the summer sun.

"Do you…want to come inside?"

Muffled by Madison's hair as her words were, the note of worry came through. The gentleness and the hesitance with the thinnest slice of fear. Such vulnerability in such a capable, intense woman sent Madison's head spinning. She dragged her face away from CS's neck just enough to look into her eyes and let herself swim again in their blue depths. She wrapped her arms around CS's neck, holding her body close and pulling her mouth down into a kiss as soft as she could manage. A kiss that would communicate the depth of her desire and the tenderness of her emotion all in one, brief meeting of lips.

"I want to," she said, their faces still so close her lips brushed against CS's as she spoke. "More than anything. But I really should get back home and check on things."

"Of course."

"You could come with me." She let her hands wander, finding the tails of CS's shirt and sliding past them. "I'm sure everyone's gone by now."

"Mmmm."

"We could light a fire. Lie down on the rug…"

"Tempting as that sounds," CS said, the disappointment in her voice reinforcing the words. "I can't. It's Monday. My friends will be here any minute and I should shower first."

Madison hooked her finger in the waistband of CS's jeans, not wanting to let go yet. "Probably."

"I would blow them off, but Drack is bringing a special bottle tonight. He's really excited."

"Am I invited to the party?"

CS smiled so widely she looked like a kid. She even blushed a little. It made Madison want to push her through the door to her apartment and lock it behind, not letting her out for days, or possibly years.

"You have to come. If Drack gets to bring something special, so do I." She blushed even harder, kicking her booted heel into the dirt sheepishly. "That was really cheesy. Forget I said it?"

Madison leaned in, laying a kiss on her bottom lip. "It was sweet. So, no, I won't forget it."

Madison arrived late to the gathering. She had showered quickly enough, but couldn't find the incentive to dress. Instead, she lay in her robe on the bed, her eyes closed, letting her mind wander back to the afternoon. The happy bubble inside her only grew as she lay there, and her hair was completely dry by the time she pried herself off the comforter. She tried not to try too hard in her choice of clothes, but CS made her feel beautiful and she wanted to make herself worthy of being shown off.

CS caught her at the tasting room door, but limited her physical affection to a brief touch on the small of Madison's back. Neither of them could manage more than a few seconds without looking over at the other. It was as if they shared a delicious secret too valuable for the world to see.

After her first glass, Madison was treated to a taste of Drack's special bottle. It was his own Meritage and very good. Still nothing compared to even the humblest Minerva Hills bottle, but Madison was able to praise his work with complete sincerity. Under her approval he preened like a peacock and flitted around the room, pouring tastes for everyone and getting steadily drunk off his own wine and his own success.

Madison took her second glass to a table near the patio far enough removed that she could safely watch CS. She had been talking to Henry and Lisa since they arrived. Madison watched the way the married couple maintained a casual contact with each other all night. When Lisa spoke, Henry couldn't keep his eyes off her. It was charming, sweet in the way of couples who are so very at ease with each other. CS's eyes darted to hers so often Madison almost felt a part of the group.

"Why do I have the feeling you didn't take my advice?"

Laura appeared from nowhere across the table, slipping uninvited into an empty chair. She crossed her legs in that graceful way she had. Like a snake or a dancer, maybe a little of both. Her voice was light, a good-natured smile playing across her lips, but Madison knew her well enough by now to be cautious.

"Was that advice? It sounded like a warning."

She'd been looking at CS, but the snap of Madison's words made her focus on her tablemate. She gave a flippant, casual flick of her wrist. "Relax, Madison. I don't bite."

"Could've fooled me."

"You caught me at a bad moment the last time we spoke." She sipped her wine, a chardonnay Henry and Lisa had brought, and judged it with a dismissive shrug. "I shouldn't have implied more of a relationship than we share."

"Exactly what sort of relationship do you think you share with CS?"

Laura smiled then, staring into her wine and Madison wished her words hadn't come out so sharply. There was sadness in Laura's smile. Maybe even loneliness. "You don't have to worry about me, Madison. We're just friends."

Laura's wistful look made Madison see that loneliness in a new light. Laura wasn't jealous. She was alone and now her friend wasn't. Of all the ways Madison thought this conversation would go, she never imagined she'd end up feeling sorry for Laura.

"Can I ask…Why didn't you two make it as a couple?"

"Because we were young and dedicated to work." Laura sipped her wine again, obviously playing for time. "We never worked the same vineyard. Our personalities would never have allowed it. We worked fields close to each other so we could live together, but we separated for work every morning."

Madison considered interrupting the story. She didn't like to think of CS waking up beside Laura every morning, or worse, going to bed next to her every night. Not now. Not when she could still feel CS's body writhing under her touch.

"Did you know that everything from that spot," she indicated a general line stretching from the fire pit on the patio off into the distance, "to the west used to be my vineyard? The whole back end of Minerva Hills was mine. CS bought it from me when we split up."

"It's good land. That's where all the pinot noir is. Why'd you sell it?"

"I needed to be farther away. To start over." She drained her glass. "I'll be honest enough to admit that I couldn't deal with the fact my girlfriend made better wine than me."

Madison knew how much the admission cost her and all the defensiveness leaked out of her. "You're all artists here. The wine you make is incredible."

Laura laughed her usual, mirthless laugh. "CS is an artist. Most of the rest of them are amateurs. I'm just obsessive and competitive."

Drack came over with an open bottle, tried to engage Laura in conversation while he refilled their glasses but gave up quickly in the face of her polite, if dismissive, answers.

Madison hoped the interruption would change the course of the conversation, but she wasn't so lucky.

"In the end it was my insecurities that made me leave CS," she admitted, drinking steadily. Madison had caught CS's eye again and they were battling not to grin at each other across the room. "We didn't really love each other in that all-consuming way. Not like this."

Madison blushed when Laura accompanied her last words with a little flick of her wrist indicating the way they were staring at each other.

"I'm sorry."

She meant it, but when she looked at Laura, she didn't see the sad, broken woman she expected. She saw a woman who knew her own limitations and how they had caused her pain, but she didn't feel sorry for herself.

"You will be." Laura's face hardened, and her eyes locked on Madison, holding her in place with an almost hypnotic intensity. She spoke with deliberate care, caressing each word. "If you ever hurt her the way I did, I will personally ensure that you die in a fire."

"Wow. That's...specific."

"Don't think I won't do it."

"I don't."

"You better be absolutely fucking sure you're all in or you need to get out now."

Madison had never actually felt fear of another human until this moment. She thought she had, but no one had ever looked at her the way Laura looked at her right now. Like she could cut an artery and watch Madison bleed out on the flagstones at her feet without a drop of remorse.

"CS will pour everything she has into you, so you better be ready to take it. If you aren't, go back to your cottage, pack up your shit right now and get out."

Laura's words echoed in Madison's ears as she walked home, hand in hand with CS through the empty night. It was a threat and a warning, but it was also a plea. She was worried about someone she cared about, and Madison could understand that. What she hadn't anticipated was how she now shared those concerns.

CS kept so much of herself hidden, played her whole life close to the vest. Madison had never been like that. She had always been wild, kept everything on the surface. Even as her life had calmed since Robert died, she was more impulsive than CS could ever be. She found herself comparing her relationship with Kacey to Laura's with CS and she was not at all comforted with the similarities.

She and CS both had a tendency to shut out the world in favor of their work. It seemed clear that, for CS at least, that included her romantic passions. Madison wasn't at all sure she was the same way. Kacey had pursued her until she relented. No matter how invested she was in the relationship three years on, perhaps she hadn't really thrown herself into their shared life. Now Kacey was only a few months gone and here Madison was sleeping with someone else.

What if Laura's concerns were justified? What if she did hurt CS? She didn't intend to, but her intentions and her actions didn't always line up. There was a chance—a good chance given her history—that it was in Madison's nature to push people away. If she was honest with herself, part of the wedge that came between her and Kacey was her distance. She was desperate not to do that with CS, but did she know any other way to live?

"What were you and Laura talking about for so long?"

CS's voice was light, but Madison couldn't help wondering if CS had read her mind. "Nothing really."

"That doesn't sound like Laura." CS laughed. Genuinely, beautifully laughed into the night, reminding Madison of the way that husky sound turned her inside out with every syllable. "She's not one to waste words."

Madison pushed herself closer to CS, needing as much contact as possible just now. "She certainly isn't."

"Look, if it's a problem having her around…"

"It isn't." CS didn't look like she was taking Madison's word for it just yet, but she wasn't prepared to voice her real fears. "Really. I don't have a problem with your past with Laura."

"I just want you to know that it is the past."

Madison tried to force down the fear bubbling inside her. One afternoon of sex in the woods and CS was already willing to disrupt her life. If that didn't lend proof to Laura's assessment, nothing did.

CS cleared her throat. "I never got the chance to ask if your work got off okay."

"Everything went fine." Madison leaped at the change of subject. "The storm delayed them, but Boots says he kept the guys from drinking all my beer. He left a note."

"I think it's wonderful that you live on a winery that makes top shelf wine but you have a fridge full of cheap beer."

"It's not cheap beer. It's brewed with pure Rocky Mountain spring water."

"Cheap, bad beer."

"I'm a starving artist, I can't afford your wine."

"You may have access to a discount."

She said the words with a wide grin, but they made Madison's stomach curdle. The teasing banter felt too comfortable, too soon. When a sharp snap of wind blew her bangs into her eyes, Madison gladly took the opportunity to drop CS's hand and push them back into place. CS came to a stop outside Madison's cottage. She'd forgotten to leave a light on and the building was in shadow.

CS kicked at a large rock, bent and picked it up, hurling it off into the distance and watching it a little longer than was necessary. Madison saw her vulnerability creep back as it had when they arrived at the stables as the sun set. Fear wrapped in desire, seeming to make her both weaker and stronger all at once.

CS spoke first, the thin patina of calm spread over her doubt clearer than ever. "I'm fine with just going home if that's what you want."

How could Madison have found a woman like this? A woman who thought of nothing else but Madison's comfort and happiness. A woman who constantly put her own needs aside for Madison, even before they were lovers. A woman who was patient and kind. She was everything Madison had ever wanted and nothing she deserved.

It occurred to her then, with the darkness all around them and the moon refusing to light even the smallest sliver of the world, that she stood to hurt CS far more by pushing her away. Her only option, and her body was proving the truth of it even as she formed the thought, was to throw herself all in. To give in to her need and her desire. To admit how much she wanted CS and how much she wanted to be wanted by CS. Her past was undeniable, but CS was her present and CS was just as undeniable.

Madison reached out and took her hand, using it to pull her close. When their bodies were connected in a million delicious places, she pressed CS's hand into her own back, needing the sensation of being held so close.

"That's not what I want."

"What do you want?"

"You."

CS leaned close to kiss her, but Madison stepped away, still leading her by the hand. She took CS into the house, locking the door behind them but not bothering to turn on any lights.

CHAPTER THIRTY-SEVEN

Late morning sunlight pounded at Madison's closed eyelids for hours before finally succeeding in waking her up. She came into consciousness slowly, languidly. Her body refused to move and her mind tended to agree with the sentiment. She vaguely remembered blinking at the sound of her front door closing, but wasn't sure if that was real or part of her dream. Either way, it had been a century ago and she had drifted off to sleep again after.

Sadly, she now saw the pillow beside her was empty, as was the mattress. She rolled over onto her back, tiny aches shouting from all of her muscles. Without a clock in her bedroom, she didn't know what time it was, but Madison had no doubt it was late. Closer to afternoon than morning. It wasn't surprising that CS was gone, but Madison would have much preferred to wake up to her touch.

Looking over again, she saw a branch of lavender on CS's pillow, tucked into the still-visible indentation from her sleeping head. That thought alone made Madison smile. CS had slept in her bed. She reached over and plucked the lavender from the pillow, pressing the flowers to her nose and closing her eyes to take in the fresh fragrance. Images from last night flashed across her closed eyelids. A wide smile crept across her face as she remembered each and every sensuous moment.

They had made love in the dark without the urgency of the woods but with the same passion. Well after midnight they had fallen, exhausted, into deep sleep, Madison holding CS close in a cage of her arms and legs, feeling complete.

The phone cut through Madison's memories, dragging her unwillingly back to the present. She discarded the sheet, but held the lavender tightly while she searched for her robe. The ringing stopped, but immediately started again. It had to be Jada. Only she would be so insistent.

"Hey Jada. Sorry, I was working."

"Liar." Madison could hear the tap of Jada's keyboard in the silence that followed her greeting.

"Well, I should be working. Doesn't that count?"

"No, it doesn't. But I'm not calling to chastise you. There's amazing buzz around your next show. I decided to make it a ticketed event."

"That's good news, right?"

"It's spectacular news. That is if your work makes it here safely. I never got a call from you to tell me they arrived and that it all went well."

"Sorry. I got distracted. Yes, everything went off without a hitch."

"So the moving company worked out?"

"Of course. Tell me this isn't the first time you used them?"

Madison didn't hear her answer, if she gave one. Sitting on the counter next to the phone was a sheet of paper with a short note. She read it and the whole world went silent.

Dinner?
–CS

Eight simple letters, but they were enough to set off a riot inside Madison's body. The smile that had faded when real life intruded returned. Her mind wandered to all sorts of things, starting with a pleasant chat over a plate of spaghetti and ending with Madison flat on her back on the dining room table. She let the thoughts coalesce until she heard a shout in her ear.

"Hello? Hello! Did your phone drop the call?"

"No, sorry." Madison put the note down, setting the lavender on top of it and turning before her thoughts wandered again. "I'm here. Just…"

"Distracted. Right. I don't suppose that distraction is a muscular, tan, butch winemaker who walked out of every one of my wet dreams, is it?"

Madison couldn't help but giggle. Not only for her giddiness when she thought about CS but for the muffled shuffling on the other end of the phone and the distant but clearly disgruntled sound of Jada's husband in the background. She traced the pen lines with her fingertip while Jada gently reassured him of her devotion. CS wrote with a heavy hand, the single word and signature cutting deep into the soft paper. In this, as with everything it seemed, CS was strong and assured.

"Sorry, dear," Jada said, her voice dropping and the sound of a door clicking gently shut proving she'd smoothed things over. "You know how men are."

"Not really," Madison admitted. "He's not mad, is he?"

"Nothing a little flirting can't fix. Besides, he says I'm far too vanilla for CS. Is he right? Just how wild is she? I crave details."

"She's not wild." Her doubts from last night came creeping back, threatening to spoil her good mood. She opted to shift focus. "Besides, you're married to a trans guy half your age, clearly you're the more adventurous of the two of us."

"Oh please, being trans doesn't make Samuel wild. His idea of an adventurous night is ordering a Stout. Although I will admit the hormones make him extremely…vigorous, even for his age."

"That's more than I needed to know."

"You brought it up." The sound of nails clicking on teeth came through the phone, a sure sign that Jada was scheming. "I must admit I just assumed CS was on the wild side since you are."

"I'm not wild, I'm just…" She tried to find words to explain the way she felt these days. Like she'd just woken up from a three-year bout of amnesia. She didn't recognize the person she'd been with Kacey. That person didn't feel like her anymore. "Open to suggestion."

"And what precisely is CS suggesting?"

"Dinner."

"A date, huh?" Madison heard the door open on Jada's end of the phone and could tell by the smile in her voice that Samuel had just entered the room. "A date sounds perfect."

It did sound perfect. The only problem was finding the right outfit, surprisingly difficult for Madison as she'd never been much interested in fashion and had a limited wardrobe. She settled on a thin sundress that was light enough to be pleasant in the heat and hugged her curves just enough to show she wasn't wearing anything underneath. She wanted CS drooling over her.

She strolled down to the stables earlier than necessary. She hadn't been out riding in a while now, and she thought she'd drop in on the horses first. Boots was hauling the barn door shut, but let her in.

"You look nice," he said, his hands on his hips and sweat rolling down his forehead. "Something special going on tonight?"

"Just dinner."

After a confused look at his surroundings, the penny finally dropped for Boots. He grinned even wider and shot a glance over his shoulder toward the second-floor windows of CS's apartment.

"No wonder she's in such a good mood. I haven't seen her stop work this early since her dad was here. Thought she'd hurt herself and was too proud to admit it. She's getting old, ya know."

"I'm totally gonna tell her you said that."

"No way you guys are talking about me tonight." He gave her a wink and headed off. "Have a lovely evening."

The cool shadows of the stable felt glorious on her skin. Madison couldn't seem to get cool enough these days. The heat of summer hadn't arrived, but still her skin rippled with warmth every moment, like she was running a low-grade fever she couldn't kick. The dim light and earthy animal smell of the stable was pleasant enough to take her mind off the evening to come. There was a serenity here, with the soft snorts of the horses and hay dust floating in the air.

Violet stuck her head out of her stall and Madison immediately went to her. She nudged Madison with her big, velvety nose, wriggling beneath her arm. Running her fingers down the broad expanse of Violet's nose, Madison marveled at how powerful the animal was. Her body, now stripped of saddle and blanket, surged with muscles. Her coat gleamed in the lamplight. She blinked her huge eyes lazily as Madison stroked the soft hair disappearing into the flesh of her nostrils.

"You smell wonderful, Violet. Did you just get a bath? I can tell you've been brushed."

She shook her head gently, casually flipping her mane. Madison laughed at her playfulness, laying her cheek against Violet's face. They sighed in unison, Violet's breath stirring the fabric of Madison's dress.

"You're a pretty girl, aren't you?" She laughed when Violet gave a soft, answering nicker. She stroked over Violet's cheek, wishing she had thought to bring a sugar cube. "You are. Such a beautiful lady."

"You sure know how to make a girl jealous."

CS's voice was as low and reverberant as Violet's, but it had Madison wanting to do far more than pet her cheek. Violet shook a little more forcefully, still gentle but definitely wanting to dislodge Madison this time. Madison couldn't blame her—she wouldn't want CS thinking she had eyes for anyone else either.

She had to lean against the stall door when she saw CS. Jada had been teasing when she said CS looked like she'd walked out of every one of her wet dreams. In Madison's case, it was absolutely true. CS leaned against the wall near the open door, wearing clean, crisp clothes, her hair still damp from the shower and a half smile on her face that could melt the ice caps. Madison squeezed both hands into fists just to feel the bite of her own nails into her skin.

CS was quiet for a long time, letting her eyes travel the length of Madison's body and back again. She may as well have licked her lips, and Madison enjoyed the scrutiny. They surveyed each other long enough for Violet to get bored and snort, heading back to her stall window.

The hint of a smile made CS's lips twitch when she asked, "Aren't you going to come over and say hello?"

"I'm not sure my legs are working," Madison replied honestly.

CS pushed herself off the wall and strode over with a swaying, languorous strut.

She placed her palm flat against the stall inches from Madison's ear and leaned in close. That clean cotton and mint scent was there as always, but it was mixed with a musky, burnt vanilla that may have been her shampoo or may have been an hallucination. CS leaned closer, eyes locked on Madison's lips.

"Do you want me to carry you?"

With a groan Madison pulled their bodies together. All she could think of was their first time in the woods, the way CS held her up for what felt like hours. The way her strength seemed boundless. Madison wanted to test that strength. To test her stamina, but right now, she wanted to feel CS's lips.

There was promise in the kiss. A deep, searching exploration that hinted at a long night ahead. Their mouths fit perfectly together. Two puzzle pieces that were meant to interlock. Just when Madison considered wrapping a leg around CS's waist and taking the kiss a step further, another mouth tried to get in on the action.

"Violet, do you mind?"

CS gave the horse a stern look and she backed off, removing her twitching lips from their cheeks. Taking Madison by the hand, CS led them out of the stable and closed the door behind her, Violet's disappointed nickering ringing behind them.

"I hope you don't mind," CS said sheepishly while they climbed the stairs to her apartment. "I thought we'd have dinner here tonight. I cooked."

The apartment was comfortable if a bit spartan. The kitchen was tucked into a corner of the living room. It wasn't the open concept of the cottage, but more a home shoved into a space that had never been meant to be living quarters. Still, the couch was deep and heavily cushioned and the walls were covered with photographs and paintings that made the place feel homey.

"I'm afraid dinner won't be what you're used to," CS said, handing Madison a glass of wine and fingering the rim of her own. "After Kacey."

Madison had just been admiring the chiseled curve of CS's jaw, but the comment pulled her out of her reverie and soured the wine. "I don't want to talk about anyone else tonight. Especially not Kacey."

"I guess I was just wondering if you've heard anything from her."

"No, and I don't want to."

CS chanced a glance away from her wineglass in Madison's direction. "So…you and I?"

"What about us?"

"Is there an us, or is this just a casual thing?"

This thing between them was new and fun and Madison enjoyed that, but CS was right. They needed to talk about it. To define it. More than anything else, CS deserved the reassurance. It was neither kind nor productive to keep her waiting.

Madison set her wineglass down on the table, then put CS's down beside her own. CS didn't object when Madison slid her hands into her open, calloused palms. She took a moment to massage CS's knuckles with her thumbs.

"I don't know how you feel, but this is not a casual thing for me. I have feelings for you. I don't know that I'm ready to name them yet, but I want to spend as much time with you as I can and find out."

CS let her lips twitch up ever so slightly, but Madison hurried on before she could speak.

"I was telling you the truth yesterday." Was it really only yesterday? It felt like they'd been precious to each other for so much longer. "I want you. I've wanted you for a long time. I'm not exactly proud to admit it, but I wanted you long before Kacey left."

The conflict was clear in CS's voice, like she didn't want to risk breaking this moment with truth. "Wanting me and wanting to be with me are different things."

"I know. I'm still working through what exactly my heart says. Just because I had feelings for you doesn't mean that I'm not hurt or sad about what Kacey did. It makes it worse, actually, because I'm just as much to blame as she is."

"Absolutely not." CS's hands stiffened around Madison's and her eyes flashed with real anger. "Don't you compare yourself to her. You didn't act on anything—she did. You didn't do anything wrong."

Madison squeezed back, feeling CS's hands relax. She didn't believe she was innocent, but she didn't want to talk about that.

"That's not important now. I want to talk about us." She took a long breath and forced herself to give voice to her fear. The fear that Laura was wrong about CS's feelings. "I want to talk about you. I know this wasn't something you were looking for."

"What do you mean?"

"This was something I pushed for. If you want something casual, I get that."

"You think I don't want a relationship because I stopped you after our first kiss, don't you?"

"I just…I thought you were flirting with me so many times before, but I was wrong. I just don't want to misread anything."

Madison wasn't sure how to interpret the long silence that followed. CS was a thoughtful person—silence was common for her—but this wasn't the time to be taciturn. If she was honest, Madison wanted CS to tell her she was wrong. Profess her undying love. She needed reassurance too.

"Follow me," she said at last, releasing Madison's hands and heading for the back of the apartment.

She followed CS, hope speeding her steps and fear dragging them back. She really just wanted to sit down and have a quiet dinner. That would be far easier than this conversation, but this was a pivotal moment for them. One that would define at least their immediate futures, and being with CS made her feel strong. She could handle anything CS said.

Her bedroom was even barer than the rest of the apartment. A neatly made, surprisingly small double bed nearly filled the room. A thin rug covered most of the hardwood floor and a single, large print of Wyeth's *Christina's World* hung on the wall over her headboard. Apart from these modest touches, the room could have belonged to anyone. At least that's what Madison thought until CS indicated the far corner of the room.

A stunning pedestal end table carved from cherry wood was sighted so that the occupant of the bed would have the perfect view of the single item on its surface. An amphora. Her amphora. The one that had sold to an anonymous buyer during her show at the Welch Gallery. The one she wept at losing. Her favorite piece she'd ever made.

Madison's feet barely touched the floor as she crossed the room. She stroked the glaze with the delicacy it deserved. With a light touch not all that different from the way CS touched her.

"This sold. Months ago. Long before…"

CS was behind her, her fingers reaching out to touch the vase with the same trembling reverence. "I thought at the time…I just saw it and I had to have it."

"This went for a ridiculously high price."

CS shrugged. "I got into a bidding war."

"Why would you do that?"

"I had to have it. There's so much of you in this piece. I had to have something of you." CS's eyes were fixed on the ground. "When I thought I could never have you. This was the next best thing."

Madison never found out what CS had made for dinner. She didn't leave the bedroom again until well after sunrise.

CHAPTER THIRTY-EIGHT

Violet's self-important snort announced her arrival just as Madison set a stone on the last corner of the blanket. It was windier than her last trip to the lone tree at the top of the hill, but the gnarled trunk provided enough protection from the weather.

"What's this?" CS asked as she climbed down from the saddle and held out Madison's note.

"An invitation," Madison explained, reaching up to kiss CS on the cheek. "To lunch."

She'd left the note on the kitchen counter the night before, knowing she wouldn't wake up in time to deliver it in person, and she spent the entire morning preparing the spread. Grabbing CS's hand, she led her to the blanket and told her to sit. It still amazed Madison that all CS required was a simple request and she would let Madison take the lead. Neither her ego nor her machismo rebelled the way Kacey's always had. Once CS was settled, Madison grabbed the canvas bag beside their picnic basket, slipping a few apple slices on top of the grain before attaching the feedbag around Violet's muzzle.

"I saw that," CS said, leaning back against the tree with a groan of pleasure. Her neck and shoulders popped as she slipped her hands behind her head. "You're spoiling her."

"She's already spoiled, and anyway this is the only way to keep her away from our basket."

The wind died down to a breeze and the sun warmed their shoulders as they ate their way through the food. Chicken salad with toasted almonds and raisins was CS's favorite, but Madison was partial to her fruit salad, bursting with berries from local farms and some of the best pears she'd ever eaten. Chef Roger, who had recently been experimenting with sourdough in his restaurant, contributed some dinner rolls and a few of his favorite cheeses. No one interrupted their lunch, not even Violet who munched at her feed and ignored the humans on the other side of the tree.

"I could fall asleep right here," CS said with a contented smile, closing her eyes as a ray of sunlight played across her face.

"Oh no you don't," Madison said, scrambling to her feet. "Take off your shirt."

That got CS's eyes open in a hurry. "Uh…Madison I don't think…"

"That's not what I mean." She laughed and pushed CS away from the tree, sliding in behind her. "Leave your undershirt on. I can see the knots in your shoulders from here."

CS moved with deliberation, looking around the property with every loosened button. It was the busy season and the hotel was booked solid, but while guests wandered the perimeters of the building and grounds, no one ventured this far into the vines.

Tossing her shirt over the same limb where her dusty cowboy hat hung, CS gave one final look around before settling back onto the ground between Madison's outstretched legs. Madison took a moment to watch the play of lean muscle through the thick cotton of her tank top before pulling her close.

She squeezed one of the bunched muscles near CS's neck with all her might. "I'm getting rid of these knots before you go back to work."

Her only response was a groan. CS leaned back into her hands as Madison kneaded and squeezed tortured muscles. "Anything you want, just don't stop."

"I've heard you say that before," Madison said with a chuckle. A red glow crept up CS's neck, which only made her laugh again. "What's got you so tense anyway? Something wrong with the winery?"

"Not at all, we're doing better than we ever have."

"So what's with this?" Madison asked as she ground the heel of her hand into a stubborn muscle on her right shoulder.

CS hissed but leaned into the massage again. "I have to make a decision about the pinot gris. I've been considering switching it over from oak barrels to stainless steel tanks. If I go stainless I need to order them now to have them in time for harvest."

"You think stainless will be better?"

"Yeah, I do. It'll be easier and safer for the staff with fewer small barrels to move. And I think the wine will do well in stainless. Last year's vintage was too heavy, almost like a chardonnay. Not my best work."

"Sounds like you've already decided."

Madison worked her way across to the left shoulder, this one even more tense than the right.

"But oak is traditional and there are certainly benefits to it. Maybe if I move the pinot gris vines to another spot. It's time to rotate in a couple years and if I move them and decide they need oak again I'll have spent a ton of money on tanks I can't use."

"Do you always plan your life out years in advance?"

"Always," she replied, leaning forward so Madison could massage her neck along her spine. "Running a vineyard is eighty percent good planning and twenty percent scrambling to fix your bad planning."

Madison gave one last hard squeeze that had CS groaning all over again before wrapping her arms around her chest and pulling her in. She held CS like that for a long time, resting her cheek on the newly relaxed muscles before leaning back against the tree with CS lying on her chest. The sun sparkled through the leaves, blinding her, so she shut her eyes and let herself soak in the peaceful glow.

"How about you?" CS murmured with a voice wrapped in contentment. "Did you throw anything this morning?"

"Not today. I'm in the planning phase."

She'd been toying with an idea for a few weeks. A new design and she wasn't at all sure she could pull it off. If she was up to the challenge, it would be her masterpiece.

"So we're both planners."

Madison laughed, her mirth not sufficient to move the solid mass of her girlfriend pressed against her. "I suppose we are. I'm thinking of ordering a different type of clay. Something a bit more delicate."

"Won't that make it harder to work with?"

"Yes, but it will also make a vase with thinner walls. It'll be lighter so I can make it taller. It'll be tricky, but I think it'll be worth it."

"I can't wait to see it."

"You're sweet, but this can't possibly be interesting to you."

CS turned her head, trying to look at Madison but not willing to move outside the circle of her arms. "Of course it's interesting. I love your work."

"Yeah, but clay composition isn't the most entertaining subject."

"Almost as entertaining as stainless steel fermenting tanks?"

"Almost."

CS turned her face back to the sun and the ends of her hair, now reaching her collar, tickled Madison's cheek. She reached up and brushed her fingers through it, noticing for the first time stray strands of flashing silver in amongst the sandy blond. Madison leaned in, resting her lips against the shell of CS's ear and whispered, "You need a haircut."

Feeling CS shiver became the new highlight of her day, surpassing even the blush she'd won earlier. Before her mind or her lips could wander, CS pushed herself to her feet.

"I'm sorry, babe, but I have to get back to work." She knelt down in front of Madison, her wide smile outshining the sun. "See you tonight?"

"Of course. Come to my place. I'll be working late."

CHAPTER THIRTY-NINE

"Stellar. Incredible. Huge."

Madison lay on one of the deck loungers while Jada listed adjectives. She'd laid the lounger flat and watched the clouds scamper across the sky, the same breeze that propelled them whipping her hair around and whistling between her toes.

The summer sun toasted her skin so she felt beads of sweat despite the wind. The vines around her were heavy with foliage and ripening grapes. The cycle of life at Minerva Hills was rolling on, finding its peak again. It meant long hours outside for CS, freeing up long hours inside for Madison.

"Everyone loved everything," Jada said. "The sneak peek was a hit. Now it's time to schedule the show."

"That's great news, Jada."

"Not so fast." Her tone changed with the snap of her teeth. "They loved what they saw, but what they really wanted to see wasn't there."

"What do you mean?"

"*You*, foolish woman. They wanted to see you. They wanted to know why this hot new artist wouldn't be around for her own show. Your bio still has you listed as living in Denver."

"Why didn't you change it?"

"I was waiting for you to decide about coming back."

Madison sat up, the heat making her head spin. "I told you I'd think about it."

"You clearly haven't been doing any thinking recently, Madison."

Annoyance stabbed at Madison, the sharp snap of accusation in her voice. "That's not fair. You encouraged me when I told you about CS."

"I encouraged you to get laid, darling. It was supposed to clear your head. Obviously it didn't work."

Madison wasn't sure why the simple statement offended her so much. "My head is perfectly clear."

Jada adopted the soothing, motherly tone she used with her more difficult artists. "I'm just saying you should think about becoming more accessible."

"What does that have to do with me living in Oregon?"

"Being accessible doesn't just mean showing up at your openings. It means you have a studio rich buyers can visit. Living in a cabin out in the woods doesn't work when your pieces are all the rage. If you were in Napa, that'd be one thing, but the mountains of Oregon may as well be the moon."

It wasn't an unreasonable suggestion, but Madison had no interest in logic at the moment.

"I'll think about it."

"Don't think about it too long, Maddie. That's how people go from 'the next big thing' to 'she had so much potential.'"

She hung up without another word. Jada lived for drama. The suggestion wasn't surprising, even if it was aggravating. Jada was right and Madison knew it. She was an expert in this sort of thing. She had turned many artists from unknown to successful with little more than a savvy plan and determination. The only ones who failed were those who failed to take her advice.

Madison looked around. She listened to the lack of sound. She breathed in the fresh air. This place was a dream. Living here was like being on permanent vacation. She sighed, annoying herself with the cliché, and knew that she had to end the vacation if she expected to keep her job. She didn't want to think about what she would lose if she left Minerva Hills, so she decided to pour herself into work.

But everything was off. The clay wasn't cooperating. She couldn't center it properly. Each time she got height, it would collapse. Everything was spinning unevenly. On the seventh failed attempt to make a simple stemmed cup, Madison screamed from the very center of her gut. The sound tore through her throat, ripping it to shreds after so long in silence. The pain felt good, so she stopped her wheel and screamed again.

She closed her eyes and pictured leaving the vineyard. She screamed at the image of CS's imagined features, twisted in betrayal. This time it wasn't angry, it was a strangled cry of pain. Next, she pictured staying, but losing any chance at a meaningful career. Sitting in her home studio, spinning out bud vases to sell for a few bucks in her girlfriend's shop. A failed artist. A kept woman.

Her third scream forced her to her feet. It was the feral roar of a caged animal. She grabbed a fistful of crumpled clay and threw it with all her might. It exploded against the wall, leaving a blood splatter of gray on the windows.

"Fuck." Madison said the word quietly, defeated. She tried again with ever increasing anger and volume. "Fuck. Fuck. Fuck!"

Raging didn't make her feel any better. Cleaning up the mess only stoked her anger. The moment she finished rinsing and wringing out the cleaning rag, there came a knock at the front door. Her annoyance at the interruption was slightly tempered by her relief to be out of the studio.

CS's eyebrows knitted the moment Madison opened the door. "What's wrong?"

"Nothing. Why'd you knock?"

"So you would know I wanted you to open the door." She followed Madison into the cottage and across the living room to the kitchen. "Something's wrong."

"I said nothing's wrong. You own this place, you can just walk in."

CS waited while Madison stared out the window over the sink, twisting Robert's necklace between her fingers.

"Okay, I think I'm going to go back out and try this again."

She actually started walking away before Madison stopped her. "Wait. I'm sorry. I just…You don't have to knock."

"I'm pretty sure that's not why you're upset, but I'll keep it in mind." She came close to Madison, but didn't reach out for her, just stood close enough for Madison to know she was there. "Did Kacey call? Is it about Robert? Please tell me what's going on."

Madison let her head fall between her raised shoulders. "Jada called."

"Did something happen with the show?"

"The sneak peek went well. She's scheduling the show itself for next week."

"That's good news, right?"

"It went too well."

She couldn't look at CS while she outlined Jada's call. Instead, she explained to the garbage disposal how the continued success of her career almost certainly required she leave Minerva Hills. How Jada wanted her back in Denver. How staying here might doom her to obscurity and missed potential.

CS was an artist. She understood. Still, Madison didn't have to look at her to feel how she deflated. She understood because the prospect of this happening had always loomed over them. Madison just hadn't realized it until now. CS had. Even Laura had. She'd told Madison not to do the same thing to CS that she'd done, and yet here Madison was, contemplating exactly that.

Given the circumstances, CS sounded surprisingly level when she asked, "Do you think Jada's right?"

"It would certainly be better for my career if I could attend my own openings. As far as moving so my studio is accessible to potential clients..." She turned at last, crossing her arms over her chest and leaning against the sink. "Rich people like to feel important, like they have access to the personal side of the artist."

"I know exactly what you mean." CS flicked her hand in the air, gesturing to the cottage and, in essence, her whole life. "It's why I built this amusement park and let strangers into my space, even though I don't want them here."

All the fight left her, making Madison feel empty. She walked forward, her arms still crossed, and leaned her forehead against CS's shoulder.

"Do you think you made the right decision?" Madison asked, her voice muffled by dusty fabric. "Doing the whole open access thing here?"

CS wrapped her arms around Madison, holding her close. She kissed the top of Madison's head and spoke in a voice so bittersweet Madison feared her knees might give way.

"It worked out pretty well for me."

Madison wanted to believe she was talking about the rave reviews and the high price tag on Minerva Hills wine, but the way CS held her like a precious jewel was impossible to ignore.

"Take me to bed?"

* * *

Cold blue moonlight spilled across Madison, who was spilled across CS. Her head rested on CS's shoulder, rising and falling with each low, steady breath, her arm across CS's chest, just above the shallowly defined muscles of her abdomen. Madison could feel CS's contentment. She felt it in the one hand settled on Madison's bare hip and the rhythm of her other hand stroking Madison's hair.

There hadn't been many perfect moments in her life, Madison thought as she drifted heavily toward sleep, but this one certainly qualified. She'd lain awake in bed more nights than she could count. Catching Kacey in the barrel room was only the latest cause of sleeplessness. Before that there had been Robert's death and her parents' indifference. More breakups than she wanted to think about and personal doubt on a scale only someone with an artistic temperament could fully appreciate. But Madison had never lain awake like this. Awake because she didn't want this perfect night to end.

She was watching CS's chest flutter with each heartbeat, when CS spoke. Her eyes nearly shut, Madison struggled to keep her grip on consciousness long enough to hear the words.

"You should go."

"Hmm?"

"You should move back to Denver. Or to LA or New York. Wherever you want." Madison felt more alert, but she still had to struggle to comprehend CS's words. "Jada's right. You can't make a career for yourself here. Not the kind you want."

With a monumental effort, Madison forced her lips and tongue into forming words. "I can't. I won't do that to you. I won't chose my career over my heart."

CS laughed, breathy and quiet enough to keep from disturbing Madison. "You need to stop talking to Laura. I'm an adult, I can deal."

"I don't want this to end."

"Some things are meant to end."

"Not this. Not us. How can you say that?"

"I may be a winemaker, Madison, but I'm also a farmer. Some plants grow forever. Perennials that propagate themselves and outlive us all. They're amazing plants."

She stroked Madison's hair and held her close. Madison was losing her battle with sleep.

"Sometimes, though..." She pressed her lips against Madison's scalp. "Sometimes the most precious plants are annuals. They grow for one season, put out the most beautiful flowers and the sweetest fruit, but they don't last."

Madison couldn't respond, couldn't argue. She fell asleep to the sound of CS's breathing and the feel of her heartbeat.

She woke up alone. It was a common enough occurrence, considering how early CS liked to start, but it was jarring this morning. CS's words still echoed in her ears, explaining their relationship with the life cycle of plants. It felt to Madison like she had only just finished uttering the last syllable, even though she was long gone. The conversation had an otherworldly quality in her memory. Maybe she'd dreamt the whole thing.

Even after her shower and a breakfast of black coffee, her fog didn't lift. She still felt out of place, disjointed and confused. She retreated to her sanctuary and it did not disappoint today. Just crossing the threshold into her studio made her feel better. All the frustrations of the previous day went away and sitting down at the wheel felt like coming home.

She started off slowly, throwing a few of the simple designs that were so popular in the winery shop. She knew the inventory there was getting low, and she could fill up her shelves without expending the focus required for her gallery pieces.

That's how it started, anyway, but, as she continued to work, she found herself filled with the joy of these simple pots. The shapes sprung from her fingers with such practiced ease that she normally allowed her mind to wander and muscle memory to take over. Today she let herself enjoy the mechanics of creating art. It reminded her of when she first fell in love with pottery. The clean lines. Watching the shapeless, wet mass grow up and out seemingly by magic. Her slightest touch, precise and steady, coaxing shapes out of nothingness.

After a half-dozen simple pots lined her shelves, she reached into her footlocker for a larger chunk. It was too dry, and she had to spend a few moments working water back into the clay. The texture of it reminded her of something, though she couldn't quite put her finger on what it was. It wasn't until she had the mound centered on her wheel and was about to start throwing that she realized what the image was, tickling the back of her brain.

Madison stopped the wheel and hurried to the sink to wash her hands. She dried her hands on her T-shirt rather than wasting time looking for a towel. Once in the living room, she had to drag the coffee table across the floor to get the height she needed. Even standing on the surface on the tips of her toes, she barely could reach the bottom of her old vine sculpture, but it was enough. She ran her fingers across the pieces of vine, memorizing the touch. The age of the wood. The gnarled surface. Flecks of bark came off in a shower of dust. The last piece of the puzzle settled into place. The last part of the masterpiece she'd been planning.

She went back to her studio and started to throw. The texture would have to wait. She could spend the next day or so of drying time to figure out what appliqué she could use to create the grain. What she was after now was the shape. It would be a challenge, of course, but she lived for an artistic challenge.

She was well and truly lost in her work when she heard the front door open. It was about time CS started coming in rather than knocking, like Madison had so often asked she do. Madison's stomach growled and it was getting on to lunchtime now.

Boots didn't miss the way her face and shoulders fell at the sight of him.

"Not happy to see me, Denver?"

"I'm always happy to see you."

"Oh sure. You're just frowning because your face is upside down." He caught the towel she threw at him and laughed. "Let me guess, you were hoping I was someone else. Someone with soulful eyes and a surly disposition? Someone named after a disco queen, perchance?"

Madison couldn't help but smile. Of course Boots knew CS's secret. He knew everything, including how she felt about CS. The blush was probably avoidable, but she didn't try. "Maybe."

Boots let out a theatrical sigh and leaned against the kitchen counter, looking wistfully at the ceiling. "One day a famous artist will smile about me like that."

"I don't know about famous."

"Whatever. Word is you're taking the art world by storm. Even heard a rumor you were leaving us for glamorous digs provided by the Welch Gallery."

The smile was gone in a flash. "What did you say?"

"Denver doesn't deserve you. We'll be seeing you in all the magazines soon bragging about how we knew you when."

"Who told you I'm leaving?"

"CS, of course. She's putting on a brave face, but..."

"She told you I'm leaving?"

"Just gave me a heads-up that you'll probably need help packing." He finally seemed to realize something was going on. "She was just looking out for you."

"She was trying to make decisions for me." Madison didn't bother to moderate her tone or hide her anger. "It's not up to her to say anything. Especially before I've decided."

"I don't think she's trying to make your decisions. She's just...preparing."

"I can prepare to move myself. *If* I decide to move at all."

"That's not what I meant, Denver."

"What the hell do you mean then?"

"Whoa, buddy, bring it down."

"I will not! I can't believe she would try to control me like that."

"That's not what's going on. I'm sure of it."

"Then what's going on, Boots?"

He pulled out a barstool with a scream of metal on wood. "You know that look a person gets when they've been told they've got cancer but they're forcing themselves to be okay with it? They know the end is coming sooner or later, but they're trying to make the best of the time they have left. That's the look CS's got right now."

Madison didn't have personal experience, but she understood what Boots was trying to say. She slumped against the counter beside him and finally stopped avoiding what she'd been feeling all day.

"I don't wanna go."

"But you know you have to, right?"

She nodded, letting the tears fill her eyes and clog her voice. "I feel like shit."

Boots rubbed his hand across her back. "Sometimes life makes us feel like shit."

CHAPTER FORTY

Madison didn't confront CS about talking to Boots. She saw the look he'd told her about and decided on the spot that she was going to follow CS's lead on this one. After all, she was the one who'd screwed up. She was the one who didn't listen to Laura. Besides, following CS's lead had always served her well in the past, Madison had more than enough reason to trust her judgment now.

It sort of worked too. The next few days were bittersweet, but, as always with CS, the sweet far outweighed the bitter. Madison even occasionally managed to forget how much her heart hurt. She knew it wouldn't last forever, especially since Jada was actively pursuing a new studio for her in Denver. She went with it for now, distracting herself with the twisted vase.

The project had taken on a life of its own. She wasn't really sure what she was trying to accomplish with it, but what she had at the moment was like nothing she'd ever made before. She generally liked making her gallery pieces in the old-world shapes. Amphora, bottle vases, urns, and cylinder vases, but with a contemporary form straddling the line between ancient Greece and modern chic.

This was something totally different and the change both frightened and excited her. It was meant to be more of a bottle vase, with a wide belly tapering to a thin neck. What she ended up with was a wide body and a double opening. Maybe it was the view out her windows that changed everything. The rain had ended abruptly with the arrival of summer, and the vineyard was dry and dusty, little sand devils picking up in the rare breezes, the stony ground bleached to nearly white by the unforgiving sun.

While an undergrad, Madison had done a summer exchange program at Diné College on the Navajo reservation in Arizona. She'd learned more in those three months than she had in the three years she'd been at school, and she loved every minute of it. But she hadn't used any of the Navajo techniques. There was enough cultural appropriation in the American west without Madison being a part of it. Still, she'd always dreamed of making use of what she'd learned then.

Working with the Navajo unity vase form, she'd attached the handles and was now working on the carving. This was what gave it the twisted, vine-like appearance. Without adding too much bulk of extra clay, she'd been able to give the impression of what she saw in the field last fall. After the harvest but before the pruning, the vines were stripped of ornamentation and exposed to the elements. The way they grew, twisted around each other and up the lattice, was the shape Madison had re-created. Once it was glazed, the depth and contrast would be the final element. The vase would become two branches of the same vine, twisting around each other before branching off to create the twin spouts.

Madison had just taken the vase off the wheel when she heard a knock at the front door. She shook her head with a smile, but hurried to answer it. It would be a miracle if she could get CS to stop knocking and just come in. No matter how many ways she asked, she always received a polite refusal. CS just shrugged and said she didn't want to interrupt Madison's life, and, if she was busy, CS could just leave and come back later. It was probably just teasing, but Madison always dropped everything when she heard the knock.

The one positive aspect of having to answer the door was the chance to pull CS into a lingering kiss in the threshold. CS wasn't much for public affection, so even though there was never anyone around to see, she always squirmed when Madison kissed her here. Today she squirmed even more.

"Don't, I'm filthy."

"Not yet, but I intend to get that out of you soon."

Even better than her squirming was her blushing. Spots of red ran up her neck from underneath her collar and Madison knew from experience that her chest flushed red too.

"You're relentless."

"Only when it comes to you."

"I…um…" CS looked over her shoulder, avoiding Madison's eye and indicating Violet, tied to the porch railing in the shade on the far side of the house. "I just came by to see if you wanted to have dinner with me. I was on this side of the vineyard."

This was what their relationship was becoming, tap dancing around how deep their feelings were to make the inevitable parting easier. Any careless word could bring a cloud over their time together. Considering they hadn't spent an evening or night apart since their afternoon in the woods, the excuse was even more disingenuous. CS wanted to come inside, and Madison wanted exactly the same thing.

"Why not lunch?"

"I shouldn't. I have work."

Madison didn't bother to counter the weak argument, just grabbed CS's hand and dragged her inside.

"Just give me a minute to put my pot on the shelf and I'll make us something."

CS followed, of course. "Do you even have food here?"

"Probably." She pushed aside the curtain from her drying shelf as she passed. "Someone keeps buying it for me and putting it in my fridge."

The carving she'd just done on the vase was fresh enough and the clay still wet enough to make moving it difficult, so she was being even more careful than usual with it.

"That's incredible," CS said from over her shoulder. "May I?"

Madison stepped away, letting CS get a look. "It isn't nearly finished."

"It's already incredible," she said, kneeling down next to the wheel to get a better look. "I've never seen a shape like this."

"It's a Native American design called a unity vase."

She didn't tell CS the cultural significance the vase had to the Navajo. How the unity vase was also called a wedding vase. How a couple traditionally drank, one from each spout, at their marriage ceremony to symbolize their shared love and lives or the fact that it was purposefully shaped like the human heart, another vessel with two chambers working as one. Madison hadn't allowed herself to examine the implications or even considered her own motives. She didn't think these days, she just acted.

Instead of explaining the vase, she stuck with explaining the carving. Before she even told CS her vision of the vines growing up the trellis, she'd already spotted the theme. Of course she had. If anyone knew the way grapevines grew, it was CS. More importantly, if anyone knew the way Madison's artistic mind worked, it was CS.

That was the real miracle of this whole thing, whatever it had been and whatever it was. More than anyone else in her life, CS understood and appreciated Madison's art. The night CS showed her the amphora she'd bought, the two of them lay in bed for hours talking about it. Going over every little detail of the piece like they were in a museum. Only it was Madison's piece they were talking about. The same way they'd talked about CS's wine while tasting and wandering through the vineyard together.

Maybe this was something other artists had with the people in their lives, but it was brand new to Madison. Even Jada, while she appreciated the aesthetic of the work, always had a mercantile eye. She was, after all, an art dealer. She wasn't looking at a piece for its intrinsic value as much as its monetary value. Robert had always been proud of her work, but he wasn't versed in art. He liked it because she made it, just like the macaroni art she brought home from kindergarten. Kacey, who could go on for thirty minutes about the choice of arugula over frisée, rarely saw her work as anything more than objects either in her way or standing between the two of them going out for drinks.

CS was different. CS looked at her work. Really looked at it.

"Do you think…" Madison tried to form the question without thinking about her reasons for asking. "Can I have a few of Violet's tail hairs?"

CS stood, turning away from the vase finally and squaring her vivid blue stare on Madison. It made Madison's whole body tingle.

"Sure. Why?"

"There's a Navajo decorative technique I wanted to try." Madison picked up the vase. "Burning horsehair into the pot leaves behind a carbon tracing of the hair. Like black chalk lines. It's really pretty."

"I'll collect some tonight when I groom her."

Madison slid the curtain into place, closing the vase back onto the drying shelf and out of sight. She'd made a unity vase reminiscent of Minerva Hills even as Jada was working to remove her from this place. She was going to burn CS's horse's hair into a wedding vase. There were so many dangers here she couldn't begin to name them, but she convinced herself that she'd shut them away behind the curtain.

"I'm sorry I interrupted your work." CS's voice was soft and low, the one she used when she was hesitant to ask for what she wanted. "We've both been busy and I just…needed to see you."

She was right, of course. They hadn't seen each other much. Just each evening when they met for dinner and each night when they went to bed next to each other. Madison hadn't gone out to walk the vines since she'd started work on this piece. She'd forced herself to stay in and work to have it done before she left. If she left.

Madison looked at the film of pale golden dust covering CS from the toe of her boots to her sun-bleached hair. She wasn't particularly hungry.

"You are way too dirty to sit down in my house. Even at the lunch table."

"I could take a quick shower."

That was exactly the response Madison had sought. She took CS's hand as she walked past.

"I have a better idea."

Madison set the faucet on the soaking tub as high as it could go. The tub was massive, larger than some swimming pools, and with tiled steps leading up to it. It took a long time to fill, but that just gave her more time to undress CS. She started slowly, slipping her wide leather belt through one loop at a time. She treated herself to a long, slow kiss once the belt hit the floor, running her fingers through the coarse hair CS had trimmed close to her skull.

She went to the buttons on CS's shirt next, slipping each one free with a little pop. She kept her eyes locked on her task, eager for the moment when any hint of new flesh was revealed. Tugging the tail of CS's shirt free from her jeans revealed the band of her underwear. CS wore boy shorts with legs long enough to highlight her well-muscled thighs. Madison imagined those thighs while she traced the brand name with her fingertip. CS shivered, the flat muscles of her abdomen contracting while Madison spelled Tomboy X on the fabric above them.

Sliding CS's shirt off, and with trembling hands, Madison caressed the bunched shoulder and chest muscles. She wanted to remember this skin. Burn it into her memory in case her chances were limited. CS leaned forward, trying to catch Madison in another kiss, but she dodged, still focused on CS's shoulders. She laid a kiss on the ball of her shoulder, then another and another, working her way back toward her neck. She licked the skin there, tasting the salt of her sweat and sending earthquakes of desire through her own body. This skin. Wrapped over those muscles, wrapped over her bones and sinews and all the soft things inside. Soft skin wrapped around incredible strength.

CS lifted her arms over her head to help Madison pull off her sports bra. All of her clothes were damp with sweat and caked with dirt, but Madison didn't care. The sweat and dirt were as much a part of CS as the skin and bone.

She knelt in front of CS to untie her boots, earning a soft groan from above her. CS kicked them off hurriedly, but Madison didn't stand. Still on her knees, she went about the slow process of unbuttoning and unzipping CS's pants.

When CS surged forward, trying to wrap Madison in her arms, Madison put a firm hand against her chest, holding her back. She stepped far enough away so that the entire show would be visible before slowly stripping her own clothes off. CS was licking her lips by the time Madison was done, her eyes frantically dancing all over Madison's body.

Madison turned the water off, letting the last few, echoing drips hit the surface before taking CS's hand and leading her into the tub. They stood, face-to-face in water lapping at their calves. Now that they were here, CS seemed uncharacteristically unsure of herself. It was up to Madison to press their bodies together, to draw CS into a lingering, promising kiss.

Following Madison's gentle persuasion, CS sat in the tub and Madison straddled her hips. Their lips never parted as their hands explored, finding again all the soft swells and sharp angles that constituted each other's form. CS regained her confidence, directing the movement of Madison's hips and slowing her when her eagerness took over.

All doubt and worry melted the moment Madison touched CS's skin. That was always CS's effect on her. To make her feel perfectly at ease with a simple caress, a well-placed kiss. Sitting here, feeling the pleasure of CS's touch and her calm, Madison wondered why she had ever thought she could or should leave this place.

This was home.

CS was home.

The shrill ringing of her cell phone echoed from the floor of the bathroom, bouncing off the tile and water. Neither woman so much as blinked at the noise. The rising emotion in Madison and the thrill of CS's attention was all she needed. CS became single-minded when they made love. She heard and saw nothing but Madison. The simplicity of that—the gift of this incredible woman's full attention—made her redouble her efforts.

Soon CS's screams filled the bathroom, drowning out the second round of clattering beeps from the phone. Madison followed not far behind, her back arching and her wet hands squeaking as they fought for purchase on the rim of the bathtub. She slumped into CS's arms, her joints rubbery and her muscles slow to release. CS held her tightly, silent as their heart rates slowed back to normal. Madison laid her hand on CS's chest, wanting to feel the way she made this calm woman's body take flight.

"Someone really wants to talk to you."

"Hmm?" Madison grunted, but her phone chirped a barrage of sounds in answer to the question. A whistle indicating missed calls, a bell for voice mail and a honking horn for new text messages.

"Want me to get it for you?"

"No," Madison answered firmly. "I don't care. I'm exactly where I want to be right now."

"Me too."

Madison felt the truth of those two words in every inch of CS's skin. In the way she held Madison with a warm possessiveness that made Madison feel like she was the only woman in the world. That's how CS made her feel. Like she was unique and precious.

Madison peeled herself away from CS and settled back on her heels. She traced the lines of CS's face, first with her eyes, then with her fingertip, dripping with cold bathwater. This face, with its square jaw and high cheekbones. She craved every inch of it. Loved the way little lines sprang out from the corners of her eyes and creased the space between her eyebrows. Smile lines showing a life well-lived.

Though so much of the world saw wrinkles as ugliness, Madison saw the fine lines of age on CS and recognized the beauty of them. She wanted to see them every day. To learn which were highlighted when she laughed, which when she cried. She wanted to watch those lines deepen and catch new ones at the moment of creation.

"I love you."

Madison hadn't intended to say the words, but she meant them. She knew at the very center of her being that she meant them in a way she had never meant them before. She loved CS in a way she had never loved anyone before.

"I love you too."

A simple statement of fact. A concise explanation. A few words said without flourish or excess in a way that was so entirely like CS. Yet, as Madison came to recognize early on in their friendship-turned-romance, when CS spoke a few simple words, they meant more than when others spoke for hours.

She leaned forward, back into the arms of the woman she loved, and let her lips settle into the only place Madison ever wanted them to be again.

CHAPTER FORTY-ONE

The horse hair burned into the pot perfectly, leaving the carbon ash behind as well as stains of smoke like clouds around streaks of lightning. Madison cried when she saw how well it had come out. She hadn't actually believed it would work until she pulled the glowing pot out of the kiln with flameproof tongs and draped the first of the hair.

That was yesterday, two days after she finished carving the vines and a day after she burnished the surface smooth. She was rushing the process, she knew. Risking the pot with her impatience. Any number of things could go wrong if she wasn't careful, but she was determined now.

Their afternoon in the tub had convinced Madison she and CS belonged together. She wasn't leaving and she could do anything, even fire a pot when it was hovering on the edge of dry.

Now she was glazing it, carefully applying a coat that was milky white but not so opaque as to cover the horsehair markings. The kiln was already warming, ready for the final fire that would make this piece of ceramic last for eternity.

She was lowering the lid into place when she heard a knock at the front door. Setting the timer, she skipped out of the room. CS was now the only person at the vineyard who knocked on her door, and it was more of a game.

"Perfect timing," she shouted as she whipped the door open. "I just put my pot in to fire. If you're really lucky, I'll let you fuck me on the kitchen counter."

"No thanks. Samuel took me on all fours last night and I'm still sore as hell."

"Jada!"

Madison launched herself into Jada's arms. She hadn't realized until seeing her now how much she'd missed her best friend. Phone calls were all well and good, but there was nothing like a hug from Jada.

"Sorry about that," Madison said with a laugh, closing the door behind them. "I thought you were CS."

"I gathered."

Jada was laughing along, but her demeanor was all business.

"Uh-oh. I know that look."

"Get me a cup of coffee, Madison. We need to talk."

"It's a couple hours old," Madison said as she filled a matching pair of mugs. "I would have made fresh if I knew you were coming."

Jada eyed the barstools warily. "On second thought, let's have that coffee on the deck. Now that I know the counter's not safe."

The day was milder than most of the summer had been. It was almost cooler outside than it was in the cottage with the kiln firing away. They sat on loungers facing out over the lush vines and sipped their coffee in silence for a moment. Madison knew the peace wouldn't last long, so she tried to start the conversation in as nonthreatening a way as possible.

"What brings you to Oregon?"

"I'm headed to Seattle for an exhibition. I left a day early to come talk some sense into you."

"Here we go."

"This could be your exhibition I'm preparing. Did you look at my client's offer?"

"No."

"Why not?"

"Because I'm not leaving, Jada. I can't."

"Do you have any idea what you're turning your back on? There aren't many patrons willing to sponsor an artist in this day and age, Madison. When you get an offer like this, you take it."

"I want to make my own work, not be at some rich guy's beck and call."

"You will not be at his beck and call. You will be an artist with your own living space and attached studio."

"That he gets to show off to his friends."

"That he invites to parties where he entertains other very wealthy, well-connected collectors who like to buy art. Everyone wins, no one more so than you. He's one of my best buyers and I trust his motives. A very good man. He's offering it just to you because he loves your work."

"He loves the work I'm doing here. I don't have to live in his mistress's old bungalow to get his attention."

"Why are you doing this?" Jada set her coffee down with a clatter. "Why are you sabotaging your life? I know you're heartbroken over Kacey, but you need to start making better decisions now."

"I'm not heartbroken. I'm happier than I've ever been. It's a relief to have Kacey out of my life. I was in love with CS long before she left. I'll admit I thought I was broken for a long time."

"And then?"

Madison shrugged and let her lips curl up at the thought of CS smiling in the fields or, better, smiling in her bed. "And then there was her."

"She's hot, I'll give you that, but this is…"

"It has nothing to do with her being hot, Jada."

"What is it then?"

"Look around you! Look at me!" She marched over to the end of the deck, indicating her whole life with a sweep of her arm. "I'm making the best work of my life. I feel more inspired than I ever thought possible. That's because I'm here. In this vineyard."

"With CS."

"Yes, with CS. I couldn't do this without her and I won't hurt her, or me, by leaving."

"Darling, I say this because I couldn't love you more if you were my own daughter." Jada went over to Madison and took both her hands, holding on tight. "You moved to Minerva Hills for Kacey. Now you're staying for CS. When are you going to do something for yourself?"

She'd been so happy for so long, it shocked her how close her tears were to the surface. Like they'd been waiting at the corners of her eyes for something to go terribly wrong. Jada wasn't wrong exactly. Madison knew that. She knew that she would already be arranging for clay deliveries in Denver if it weren't for CS. She'd be selling her pieces to corporate offices and movie stars and she'd be drinking champagne at rooftop bars. She wouldn't wake up to the sound of silence and the smell of horses.

Madison crumpled onto the end of her chair, her face in her hands to soften her sobs. "I don't know what to do."

Jada started rubbing her back, like a mother with a fussy toddler. "I know."

"I assume this is about me."

Half of Madison wanted to throw herself into CS's arms the moment she heard her voice. The other half wanted to curl up into a ball of tears and make both of them go away. She settled for remaining where she was and crying harder.

"I'm sorry, CS." Jada stopped rubbing Madison's back, so she looked up to watch her friend walk confidently and square her shoulders in front of her girlfriend. "I like you, but I care about Madison too much to let her throw her dreams away."

CS nodded, her smile sad and ironic as she put as much distance between the two of them as she could without leaving the deck. She leaned against the railing, looking out over her own dream as she answered, "For what it's worth, I agree with you."

Madison couldn't have been more shocked. CS's words cut into her like a hot knife. She'd thought CS had shared her moment of revelation in the tub, but clearly she hadn't. The same woman who had told Madison she loved her was trying to send her away. Casting her off like vine cuttings at the end of the season. The betrayal of it stung. The fact that CS couldn't or wouldn't look at her stung even more.

"The thing is, it's not up to me and it's not up to you." CS turned back to stare hard at Jada. "Madison is the only one who can decide what to do, and we'll both have to live with her decision and love her for it."

CS finally turned to Madison. She was like a warrior. An Amazon standing alone against an army. She didn't waver at the thought of losing everything she loved, forcing herself to smile while everything fell apart around her. If she could be so strong, so selfless in a moment like this, why couldn't Madison? She should see their relationship like CS did, like an annual reaching the end of its season with its flowers still at their peak. She could embrace the beauty of that if she tried. It would hurt, but she could do it.

"It's Monday," CS said, the morning sun a halo behind her. "I've got a lot to do before my guests arrive tonight."

Madison saw the bottle then. The simple, light green glass with no label and the cork wedged in halfway. She stood up when CS held the bottle out, taking it in her hands and realizing what it was the moment she touched it. CS's special blend. The barrels set aside for her masterpiece in a dark corner of the barrel room. A corner where everything started and everything ended.

Before stepping down off the porch, CS said, "It's ready."

Jada was talking, but all Madison could do was nod along. She didn't register the offer to set up the lease and arrange for movers to come. She registered the fact that CS had brought this bottle to her. She hadn't taken it to the grave in the woods to share with her father, she'd brought it here, to Madison. She hadn't brought glasses. Was it because she knew they wouldn't be drinking it together?

Jada was still talking when Madison went inside. Her friend followed as she deposited the wine in a cabinet over the stove, not wanting to share it and not ready to drink it. She floated toward her studio, trailing Jada behind like her personal storm cloud.

Somehow she knew what she would find when she opened the kiln. She could tell herself that she had rushed everything, tried to do too much with this pot too fast. The crack probably formed during the bisque fire, but just didn't grow to something catastrophic until the stress of the glaze. No matter what the science of the thing, fate split the vase, Madison knew that more certainly than she knew anything.

She didn't pick up the pieces of the pot. Didn't touch the smooth edges of the crack running from one of the spouts down to the base and opening a yawning ravine through the center of the vessel. She just closed the top of the kiln gently and finally gave Jada her full attention.

In less than an hour, Jada was on the phone with her client friend about his apartment. Madison had managed to pack a few clothes in a bag, but she felt like a puppet on a string. Sure, leaving was the right thing to do, but that didn't make it easy. She didn't know how long she'd been sitting on the end of her bed when Boots appeared in the doorway.

"Heard you needed some help packing up after all."

Madison didn't reply, just pulled her knees up to her chest and hugged them hard. Boots sat down beside her, the mattress sagged under the new weight and Madison lost her balance, tipping toward him. She didn't catch herself, just let her head fall against his shoulder. He put an arm around her and Madison felt a sharp, deep ache of grief for Robert. Right now she missed having a big brother more than anything in the world.

"We're all gonna miss you around here. CS most of all. You gotta do you though."

Apropos to nothing, Madison asked, "Boots, why didn't you give CS a nickname?"

"What you see is what you get with CS. She doesn't need a nickname. Nothing describes her better than her own name."

Madison started to cry again. She didn't want to. It felt like all she did was cry these days, but, much like the days when she was grieving for Robert, she couldn't come up with a good reason to feel hope.

Boots was kind enough to stay with her until her tears stopped. He even handed her a tissue from the box on the dresser when she was done, but he didn't sit back down after. When she looked up, it was to see him backing toward the door, his hands in his pockets and a look of extreme discomfort on his face.

"You take care of yourself, Madison."

"I'm Madison again, huh? What happened to Denver?"

He looked over his shoulder to answer in one of his rare serious moments. "Denver's where you're from, but it's not who you are. Not anymore."

CHAPTER FORTY-TWO

CS spent most of the night behind the bar. The other winemakers were broken up into their usual groups. Henry and Lisa were chatting with some of the younger crowd, supportive and attentive as always. The "parents" of the group. Laura stood very close to the newest member, a woman as butch as CS but a good decade younger. She'd come to Minerva Hills when she started her winery, and it had been immediately clear to CS the new woman would be a good fit for her ex. Based on the way Laura leaned close, caught by every word she said, CS was right. Apparently they were both destined to fall for younger women. Hopefully Laura's new romance would go better than CS's.

There she was again, back in the gloomy mood that sent her behind the bar in the first place. Whenever she thought she would be okay, she thought of Madison again and lost interest in socializing. It didn't matter that she'd encouraged Madison to go. It didn't matter that she'd known from the start it would end like this one day. It didn't matter that she knew it was the right thing for Madison's career. The pain of this loss was harder to bear than anything she'd known. Emptiness seeped into her bones.

Drack laughed and smacked Laura hard on the back, earning a scowl but also, CS could barely believe her eyes, a blush. The moment he was gone, she turned her attention back to the new girl with a look that CS vaguely remembered from many years ago. Now she'd have to go and learn the new girl's name.

Drack was making his way in her direction, and CS took it as a cue to leave. She hustled toward the door, avoiding the eyes on her. Her reputation for surliness was enough to explain her early departure from her own party. Just as she reached the door, Boots walked through it, his expression telling CS all she needed to know. She considered walking past him, too, without a word, but she needed to hear that it was over.

"Stiletto just left."

"I take it you mean Mrs. Welch?"

He nodded, staring at his boots. She asked the question, but she didn't trust herself with too many words. "Madison?"

"Yeah."

There it was, stated in CS's own style—a few words loaded with regret. He didn't wait for her reply. What could she have said anyway? He briefly laid one broad palm on her shoulder, then slipped past her into the party. She wanted to walk through the door, escape into the night and make it home before the weight of her solitude overcame her, but she wasn't quite fast enough.

"I thought you'd picked a smart one this time," Laura said, her perfume arriving a step or two before her words. "But it's clear you still have a thing for stupid, selfish women."

CS managed a smile, but the reflection of it in the glass door was bitter and hard. "I have a thing for women who don't let me get in the way of their dreams."

"Like I said." Laura slipped an arm around CS's elbow. "Stupid women. Let me walk you home."

She didn't wait for CS to agree, just steered her forward through the deserted lobby and into the night. They were past the rows of chardonnay, close to the pinot noir when Laura spoke again, "You know, CS, the strong and silent thing is hot and all, but it only goes so far."

The light shining over the stable door came into view, beckoning to her bed and the chance to forget this day.

Laura continued, "If you're not careful you'll spend so much time fighting for everyone else's happiness that you'll forget to fight for your own."

"Yeah, well, old habits." CS stopped by her door, trying to come up with a polite way to ask Laura to leave.

Laura leaned over and kissed her cheek, chuckling softly at the way CS's body tensed at her touch. She turned and walked into the night, saying over her shoulder, "Time to kick those old habits."

* * *

When the moving company arrived a week later, CS made herself busy in the vines. Boots found her testing the soil pH on the farthest reaches of the vineyard.

"The movers are at Cottage One," he said, allowing her the pretense that she didn't know. "They need you over there to sign the paperwork."

"Can't you take care of it?"

"Nope."

She scowled up at him. "I'm your boss, Boots."

He snatched the meter out of her hand, replacing it with Violet's reins. "You sure are."

She took the scenic route out of spite. She didn't want to watch men cart away the contents of her daydreams. They could put the final touches on her broken heart all on their own and wait for her to come around and sign the paperwork. It wasn't a long enough trip, though, and they were carrying out the last of the boxes when she arrived.

"We'll be out of your way soon," the mover said, handing her a clipboard. While she signed it she noticed the box he held was labeled with Kacey's name and an address in Los Angeles. Apparently she'd finally contacted Madison for her things.

Considering that she'd furnished the cottage herself, it shouldn't have shocked CS how full it still looked. If she hadn't seen the boxes, she wouldn't have guessed this place was uninhabited. She wandered around the living room, remembering dinners and late-night kisses on the couch. She dug her hands into her pockets, trying to forget the feel of Madison's lips. The room still smelled like her—the sharp tang of minerals from her clay and the rich caramel of her shampoo.

The vine sculpture hung over the fireplace, its brittle arms twisting around themselves. Just like the first time she'd seen it, CS marveled at its simplicity. She remembered the conversation they'd had about it just before they ran off into the woods during a thunderstorm.

CS heard footsteps behind her and cleared her throat, hoping it would help clear her mind before she talked to the movers again. "I'm surprised she didn't ask you guys to take the crown-of-thorns sculpture."

"It was never a crown of thorns to me." Madison's voice rang out clear and sweet. "It was always a bird's nest."

CS turned to make sure she was really there and not just a dream. She'd had more than one moment in the last week when she thought she'd spotted a flash of Madison down a deserted row. Their eyes met and the whole world fell away. The cart pulling away outside and the sun shining through the windows blurred into nothing. All she could see was Madison, the light in her eyes and her wide smile. She looked lighter; happier in some way that CS had never quite seen in her. She was happy and that made CS unbearably sad.

"Hello, Madison," she said and, when she felt like she had to say more, she brought up the most obvious change. "You got a haircut."

She reached up and touched her hair. It was certainly different. Instead of the flowing red locks that reached just below her shoulders, her hair was curled and styled in a loose pixie cut. The shorter style accentuated the length of her face and the width of her eyes, two of CS's favorite features on her favorite face.

"Yeah, well, there are a few more stylists in Denver than at Minerva Hills."

CS let her forced smile fade away. "You look good."

Madison took a step forward and there was a confidence to her movements. "I feel good."

It was the purposeful stride as much as the words that formed the lump in CS's throat. "Then you made the right decision."

"Yes. I did."

She stopped at arm's length from CS and held out her hand. As much as she wished Madison wanted to take her hand, CS knew it wasn't true. She tore her eyes from Madison's and looked down at the plain silver key Madison held out to her. CS took it, the metal still warm from Madison's skin.

"I didn't think you had a key to this place."

"I don't. That's a key to my new Denver studio."

CS laughed to cover her groan. She held the key back out to Madison. "I don't get to Colorado much."

"Neither will I. The bedroom's tiny and the studio isn't half as nice as the one I used to have," she said, turning her back on the key and walking into the kitchen. "If you keep the key it'll keep me from hiding it whenever I have to go back."

CS stood there, her arm outstretched to no one. "I don't understand."

Madison rummaged around in a cabinet. "Jada's right. I have to be more accessible sometimes. Her client is actually a nice guy and he throws a hell of a party. I've sold a dozen amphora this week. Paid for this trip and the one next spring."

When Madison set two wineglasses on the counter and opened another cabinet, CS finally let her arm drop. "Next spring. Meaning…"

"Meaning I have to go occasionally but I'm not going to live there."

She straightened, holding the bottle of CS's special blend. The cork was still securely in place. The wine in it untouched since she'd delivered it to Madison last week.

"You're not living there?"

Madison set down the bottle, turning her attention fully to CS with a distinctly business-like air. "And I'm not living over a stable. The horses are wonderful, but they're loud and I don't want my clothes to smell like a barn."

"Okay," CS managed to choke the word out through her constricted throat.

"I want to stay in this cottage. I like my studio and it has a better view."

CS made her way into the kitchen. "I like your bathroom better anyway."

Madison finally looked at her and CS reached out her hand to rest on the counter. She hoped it looked casual and not like she needed the furniture to support her wobbly knees.

"I'm getting a car. There's a place in Portland that sells better clay than the stuff I get delivered." She took a deep breath. CS heard the air whistle past her perfect lips. "And I need to start going to openings. Visit galleries. Make rich friends."

"An SUV might be better if you're going to be picking up clay. There's a dealership over in Newberg."

Madison focused again on the bottle, going to work on the cork. "You have to start waking me up before you leave. I hate waking up alone."

"I'm up too early for..."

Madison silenced her with a palm in the air. After CS was quiet, Madison poked her in the chest to emphasize each word. "Every. Single. Morning."

Mostly it was the thought that Madison expected to wake up next to her every single morning that made her head spin and her throat close again. She managed a nod, but her mind slipped into thoughts of Madison's body pressed against her, still and perfectly peaceful in sleep.

Madison's poking finger relaxed after securing agreement. She spread out her hand, pressing the palm flat against CS's chest. She stared at her fingers there, examining the way her hand looked against the fabric of CS's shirt.

CS found her voice at last. "So...you're staying?"

The cork released with a subdued pop. Madison poured out two good-sized glasses, twisting the bottle as she finished pouring the way CS had shown her. She handed one of the glasses to CS.

"I'm staying."

Madison swirled the glass, watching the liquid's shifting color within and waiting for the legs to dance all the way down the globe before lifting the glass to her nose. CS, for her part, struggled to collect enough oxygen from air that seemed exponentially thicker than it had been a few seconds ago. Madison smiled and opened her eyes slowly, tilting the glass to her lips.

CS's voice was a hoarse whisper. "Why?"

Madison pushed up onto her toes and kissed CS. She could taste her masterpiece blend on Madison's lips and tongue. Oranges, black cherries, and old books, but now with a hint of lavender right on the end.

"Because everything I want is here."

Bella Books, Inc.

Women. Books. Even Better Together.

P.O. Box 10543
Tallahassee, FL 32302

Phone: 800-729-4992
www.bellabooks.com